WHAT
WE
FORGOT
TO
BURY

OTHER TITLES BY MARIN MONTGOMERY

WHAT
WE
FORGOT
TO
BURY

MARIN MONTGOMERY

THOMAS & MERCER

Published by Thomas & Mercer, Seattle
www.apub.com

Amazon, the Amazon logo, and Thomas & Mercer are trademarks of Amazon.com, Inc., or its affiliates.

ISBN-13: 9781542017640
ISBN-10: 1542017645

Cover design by Anna Laytham

Printed in the United States of America

For the women who have borne the physical,
psychological, and mental heartbreak of a miscarriage

PROLOGUE
Elle

Ten years prior

I'm sitting in the kitchen, playing cards with my grandma's neighbor Murray. He loves to teach me how to play poker and gin rummy, instead of the usual children's games like go fish or Uno.

He's an interesting character—his mustache and hair never quite match, his balding head always a few shades darker. He loves to show me his false teeth, the way he can wiggle them around.

Engrossed, I'm watching him remove what he calls a bridge, revealing a large gap in his top row of teeth. With sleight of hand, he replaces them just like a magician would.

The phone rings, snapping me out of my trance. Always wanting to answer and rarely being allowed at seven years old, I see a golden opportunity, since neither of my parents are around.

I rush to answer it before Murray can protest. "Hello!" I yell into the phone. "Laughlin residence."

A long pause follows.

This doesn't deter me. "May I ask who's speaking?"

A male voice, no nonsense, shrills from the other end. "Can I please speak to Katrina Laughlin?"

"Just a second." I drop the phone, now dangling by the cord off the wall, as I holler, "Mom! Mama, someone's on the line."

My mom's passed out, her hand drooping off the sofa, as if she planned to pick the cigarette back up that's stubbed out in a copper tin next to her on the floor.

"Wake up." I shake her shoulders as she groans.

"Baby, stop," she reprimands me. "Let Mama sleep in peace."

"You have a phone call."

"I can't right now. Take a message." She mumbles, "Or, better yet, have Grandma or Murray take one."

"K." I pretend not to hear the last part as I run back to the kitchen, sliding across the linoleum in my socks. "She's busy. Can I take your number down?"

"No, this is very important. Might there be another adult in the house I can speak with?"

"My father doesn't live with us anymore," I say matter of factly.

Another long pause. "Is there anyone else in the house?" I shrug at Murray, who's now standing over my shoulder. Bored with adult interaction, I shove the phone into his hand.

He addresses the person on the other end, and then he listens. His face contorts, but not in its usual comical way. This time his lips twist into a grimace, and his eyes seem to retreat farther into his head. "We'll call you right back." Ending the conversation, he sets the phone back into the cradle, too carefully.

"Sweetheart, would you mind picking up the cards and putting them away?" He motions to the table. "I'd like it if you would run to the gas station, grab us a Coke to share, and pick us up some snacks."

After thrusting a five-dollar bill into my hand, he rushes me out the door, not even telling me to watch out for strangers or look both ways before I cross the street. His only request? "Make sure you knock when you come back."

2

Striding down the sidewalk, I finger the crisp paper in my pocket, reminding me I'm rich.

A squad car drives by, then disappears around the corner.

I don't know what prompts me to turn around, but I do, running all the way back to the house, tripping over my shoelaces, the money forgotten.

My father's car is now parked in the drive, the rusted-out exhaust system and dirty license plate half covered by dust.

"Daddy!" I shout.

His jaw twitches when he spots me. At first, I think he's acting like Mom on one of her binges, but there's something off, a wild expression tainted with fear in his dark eyes.

"Lovebug."

"Daddy, what're you doing here?"

"I came to talk to Mom and Grandma."

"Did you come to get me?" I squeal. "Can we go to the park?"

"Not now, 'Bug. I've got important matters to discuss." He reaches out to grab my hand, his large palm swallowing my small one. "Come here, baby girl."

Sirens start wailing as my father drags me into the house behind him. He slams and locks the door behind us. Murray's already perched at the door, his hand on the knob as we enter.

Daddy suddenly drops my hand, rushing to where Grandma is seated on the couch, next to my dozing mom.

Startled, Grandma stands up, visibly surprised to see my father, then my tiny figure behind him.

He motions to her, and she joins him in the kitchen, but I can't make out their muffled words. The blare of squad cars overcomes all the noises in the house, from the television to the radio, until tires skid to a halt in the driveway.

Grandma's eyes drift to the small kitchen window over the sink. Looking over her shoulder at me, she snaps, "Elle, go to your room."

I don't listen. I'm rooted to the green shag carpet in the living room as I stare at the adults.

"Daddy?"

He strides over to me and gives me a tight hug and a sloppy kiss, the kind I usually hate, but at this moment it feels right. The smell of his Old Spice deodorant lingers against my cheek. "Listen to Grandma, 'Bug."

The doorbell shrieks, followed by sharp pounding. Deep voices announce a dreaded word in this part of town, "Police," and Daddy leans against the counter, still whispering to Grandma.

My mom, her blue eyes emotionless, hasn't moved from the couch by the time they reach for my daddy with the metal rings.

"I knew he'd kill someone, someday," she mutters before rolling over to her other side, her back to him.

To all of us.

And just like that, he's arrested, my screams and sobs unable to elicit a response as two men—one bald, one young—handcuff him and push him into their waiting car.

Horrified, I watch as his flannel shirt and construction boots fade from sight.

CHAPTER 1
Elle

Present day

I blink my eyes instinctively at what looms ahead beneath an enormous blue sky that offers nothing but prairie grass and asphalt. It's always a surprise, yet never a shock, after passing the long stretch of open road and winding around a sharp curve, to see the massive brick fortress up ahead that houses the male inmates.

Closing my eyes, I imagine the men bare chested, pounding their hands against the concrete walls, slicing their fingers on the razor wire fencing that spans the perimeter, trying to find a way out.

This has to be the definition of hell.

The majority of prisoners deserve to be locked up and kept like the goldfish you win at a county fair, half-dead and googly eyed inside a clear plastic bag. Instead of swimming, they're merely floating in the bag of lukewarm water, their fate sealed by the time you get home, when you're forced to flush their lifeless, bloated bodies down the toilet.

But not him.

He doesn't deserve to be kept here with the real dangers to society.

Clenching my hands against my sides, I squeeze them hard to keep from reaching for the door handle. It's probably a lucky coincidence that the right side is broken. Ejecting myself from the car doesn't seem smart, but my other option is to go through the various obstacles of fencing, prison guards, and searches, through various rooms and hallways, until I get to sit uncomfortably and face him. And this time, I'm scared out of my mind. Fearful in a way I don't think is possible. If he can't help . . .

My foster mom, Diane, glances over at me, her brown eyes magnified by the bifocal glasses she wears only for driving. I am surprised that she offered to take me this time. Usually she fights me tooth and nail on any type of privilege. *Though visiting your father in prison is hardly a picnic,* I think sourly. My monthly visits are on the calendar, but for some reason she forgets every time, and her list of excuses is long and pointless. I either don't go or I ask my boyfriend, Justin, to take me, since he has a car.

"You okay?" She turns down the oldies station she prefers to listen to, the static cutting through the Beatles as they croon about yesterday. I don't long for the day before so much as I wish for my childhood, when it was one of my parents I'd be sitting next to in the vehicle, not this strange woman whom I can't relate to.

I can't speak without my voice breaking, so I nod my head. I don't know if she even notices, and her own unease is clear by the way her shoulders stiffen as she spots the nondescript sign that announces Huberton Correctional Institution. Swiftly, she moves her hands to finger the rosary beads hanging from the rearview mirror, then resumes her tight grip on the steering wheel in one fluid gesture.

What sad shit has the luck of having a prison named after them, I wonder.

I can't imagine a politician asking for their legacy to include a destitute building in the middle of vacant farmland named after them. I almost chuckle out loud, considering the reaction a trust fund kid would have if that were their inheritance. Picturing the wealthiest pupil in my twelfth-grade class, Connor Knowles, I envision the conversation between him and his grandfather: *Look, Connor, I'd like to honor you with not money, not a vintage Corvette, not real estate, but your name stamped on the outside of a chain-link fence where men go to die.* I bite my lip as redheaded Connor Knowles's face appears, freckled and outraged, his nostrils flared at the injustice of this as he has a full-on meltdown, just as he did when someone spilled a beer on his expensive polo at a kegger last summer.

As soon as we approach the spiked metal of the guard gate and the surly-looking men with no-nonsense attitudes, the radio's switched off and we both clam up, intimidated by their guns and stern composure.

As we drive in silence through the open rusted gates, a huge green sign motioning us in the direction of visitors' parking stands tall. Diane's old Buick heaves into a spot, and she thrusts the car with more emphasis than is needed into an empty space.

"I need a cigarette," she states matter of factly, her hands reaching for a half-empty pack of Camel Lights in the console. After thrusting her door open, she fumbles with her lighter as she murmurs, "This place is so depressing. Do you mind if I wait in the car?"

Glancing at her, I unbuckle my seat belt, then turn to reach into the back seat, not only for my small purse but also to scope out what Diane plans to do while I'm visiting my dad. I clasp the faux-leather strap of my satchel and sweep the floor mats, looking for what I know I will find.

A small metal flask is shoved underneath the passenger seat.

"Diane," I say sternly.

Her head swivels toward me, and I have the evidence in hand. She shrugs, her dirty secret no longer a secret with me. After all, I live with her. There's not much she can hide.

"Only one," she says, the cigarette dangling between her lips.

I consider my options and decide to use this to my advantage. "Only if you let me drive home."

"You don't have a license."

"I do have a license," I say pointedly. "I just don't have a car. At least let me drive until we reach the interstate." That would give me about twenty miles of empty roads, allowing me to get behind the wheel and have some much-needed practice.

"You want me to let you drive from a *prison*, where there're more law enforcement than people?"

"Hardly." I stare her down at this obvious embellishment. "Or you could drink and drive, putting us in danger."

"Okay, fine." Diane reaches for the flask. "But if you are reckless, I'm gettin' back behind the wheel."

I giggle, the idea of Diane preaching about proper driving as funny as inheriting a prison. If it weren't for me, she'd have lost her license years ago, since drinking is the one constant in her life. That and gambling.

"What's so funny?" The wrinkles above her upper lip scrunch as she glares at me, aging her. Diane's in her early fifties but looks seventy. Smoking hasn't done her any favors, and neither has the bottle.

"Nothing," I moan.

"Just go inside and get it over with." She steps out of the faded beige LeSabre and comes around to my side, pulling on the handle, the only way to open the passenger door. We lock eyes as she flutters her hand out like I'm some sort of queen getting the royal treatment. Awkwardly she brushes a hand across my shoulder for support.

Taking a final breath, I push myself out of the seat, stepping onto the concrete. Instantly, I shiver, both from the chilly weather and from the nervous anticipation—of not only walking into the prison but also this overdue conversation with him.

The guard gate looms ahead, and I take slow steps, peering over my shoulder at Diane, who is now half her size and perched on the trunk of her car, as if knowing I'd need one final reassuring wave or I'd make a run for it.

There're four levels of men here, minimum to maximum security, each housed in a different wing. I shuffle to the minimum security tower, palms sweating like I just greased them with baby oil. Wiping them on my pants, I wait to inform the guard I'm here to see inmate 107650. Since names don't matter anymore, you're just one more bastard among the prison population. My announcement is the same as everyone else's, and the bored corrections officer barely makes eye contact, scanning my ID and pushing a visitor's badge underneath the glass partition.

I wait to be patted down, a woman guard instructing me to hold my hands out to the side and scanning my body with a metal detector, her gloved fingers poking and prodding me.

The dress code here is strict. Visitors are not allowed to wear blue denim like a lot of the inmates do, or green and tan, since that's the workers' uniform. No strappy sandals or flip-flops, no revealing clothes, minimal jewelry, and the list goes on and on.

My purse isn't allowed in, so I leave it at the front, signing my name and a waiver.

A stampede of us make our way toward the visiting area. If you didn't know where you were, you would mistake it for a school cafeteria, with plastic chairs and scratched tables, light-blue paint, and a mural of people holding hands along one wall, vending machines against the other.

If you stand near the opposite end, you'll notice that the artists of the mural are inmates and the art is focused on diversity and human kindness. It's not until you observe a few wooden podiums that line the front of the room, each equipped with a microphone, that you feel the tension in the air. Each one is positioned with a guard, seated on a high stool, trained to look for contraband and suspicious behavior. If they see someone breaking a rule, they announce it on the microphone, which is your only warning.

The first time I came here, my former social worker, Loretta, joined me, and the whole process terrified me for life. The armed guards barking loud orders, the never-ending rules like being able to hug or kiss only at the beginning or end of a visit. When the guard screamed at me for trying to get closer, I lost it, tears streaming down my face.

Most sessions are family members tearfully sobbing as the inmate looks on, helpless to do more than awkwardly pat their hands. After the first depressing visit, it took a long time before I returned again. The detached coldness of the prison haunted me. I would feign sickness or school events, dreading the whole system. Now, waiting on the hard plastic at a scarred table, I twist uncomfortably as I sit.

Nervous and fidgeting, I stare at the door, my legs tapping loudly on the tile. Sometimes it takes only a few minutes for a guard to lead him in, but sometimes it's an hour.

Before he glimpses me, I watch him, head down, hunched, shuffling his feet, eyes trained on the floor. As soon as he passes the threshold, his eyes, the same blue as mine, dart around the room until he spots me.

Then he becomes human.

His shoulders straighten and his footsteps can't speed up, but they stop dragging as he waits for the guard, who is settling in at the podium to watch the room, to give him permission to move forward and away from him.

Dressed in dark-blue pants and a gray cotton tee, he looks from the front like a maintenance man at any jobsite. When he turns around, the back of his shirt has his inmate number emblazoned across it, the only giveaway he's a prisoner.

Wobbly, I stand, my eyes searching his face, his eyes a couple shades lighter than mine. Steadily, the light returns to his pupils, not as bright as they used to be, but a glimmer of hope's still powering them. He has aged but in a tired way—not weathered from too much sun, but timeworn. He never talks about what happens here. I try not to imagine what he goes through on a daily basis, and he never offers it up.

"Elle." He gives me a quick kiss on the cheek and a longer hug, and his tall, lanky frame holds me tightly for a few seconds. I can feel him sniff the scent of my hair, and he murmurs in my ear his childhood nickname for me again, "Lovebug." His own smell is a toss-up between cigarettes and hickory. I know he's been taking classes in the shop, learning another trade. He says he wants to try carpentry when he's out—a perfect fit with his skills.

"Sit down." He motions to the table I just stood from. I switch seats, since each prisoner must face the front so the guards can see them.

"Dad." I say it in a way that causes his ears to perk up, but not in a good way.

"What is it?" He leans forward, his arms resting on the table, since his hands must be visible at all times. His skin is pale from a lack of sunlight, and dark circles have formed permanent pouches under his eyes.

"How much longer?"

"My appeal wasn't granted."

"S-so . . . ," I stammer. "This is it?"

"At least for a few more years."

"Dad, I can't . . ." I shove my knuckle in my mouth.

I hate crying in front of him. There's nothing he can do, no comfort he can give, even sitting across the table from me.

"'Bug." His eyes beg me to stop as he quickly reaches forward to swipe at my cheek before anyone notices. "You know I want nothing more than to get out to you."

"Will it be different this time?"

"Of course." He hangs his head ashamedly. "I've been sober for almost a decade. I know I screwed up your childhood."

I hold my arm out in front of me. "Do you remember this, Daddy?" He watches as I turn my wrist over, revealing the harsh red discoloration.

"It looks like some type of burn or scar."

"Do you know how I got this?"

He shakes his head. "Was it a fall on your bicycle?"

"Nope."

"You burn yourself on the oven making mac and cheese?"

11

"Not quite."

He shrugs. "I give up."

"Remember how you always carried your wallet and a pocketknife with you, always in the back pocket of your Wranglers or Levis?" He nods. "One day you left it in the truck, and I was playing with it. I used it to give a haircut to one of my dolls. Ah, yes, my Baby Bridget doll."

"And you accidentally cut yourself?" he finishes for me.

"Close." I shudder, my finger tracing the scar. "You were upset because the doll had a pile of blonde hair lying on your seat when you came out of the store. Mad I used your knife and mad I destroyed my doll, you said you would show me what playing with sharp objects did to real people, in real life."

I hold it up closer to his face so he can inspect it.

"I was six."

He shuts his eyes for a moment, then opens them, both blurry.

"I failed you as a parent, but I'm still your father."

"Do you understand why it's hard to believe you didn't hurt her?"

"Elizabeth . . ." He tries to gently push me back into my seat, but I'm done for the day, emotionally drained.

"No, I can't," I cry.

"This is why I want to be free, so I can show you I've changed, reined in my temper, and obviously quit the bottle. Drinking did me no favors. I want a new beginning for us, Lovebug. You have to help me so I can help us." He lowers his voice. "But we need new evidence. Fresh evidence. Or better yet, someone to change their mind."

"The evidence doesn't change, does it?"

"No, but it's all perception. Witnesses can change their mind, or their story . . ."

"And then what?"

"I need you to do something." He reaches for my hand, then pulls back as the guard issues a warning directed at him over the loudspeaker. "I need you to—"

Abruptly I hold my hand up, interrupting. The news I have to tell him I want to swallow permanently in my throat. It might change his attitude toward sending me to college and putting a roof over my head. I'm worried I'll lose the courage to say it out loud if I don't at this very second. "I have to tell you something."

"Okay."

"It's . . . it's heavy."

His eyes pry into mine, and I can't help but break contact to stare at the table next to us, where a tearful Hispanic woman is sobbing.

"Elizabeth, whatever it is, I can handle it."

"I'm just glad we're in a roomful of people," I whisper under my breath.

"What did you say?" he asks, wounded. "You're glad about what?"

"Nothing." I see the hurt written on his face as he slumps in his chair.

I open my mouth to tell him the truth when a loud screech disturbs the room. It sounds like a chair's being dragged across the floor, followed by a popping sound. I push myself out of my seat and instantly hit my head against the tabletop as I duck for cover.

Terrified, I dart my eyes around the room, searching for the cause of the interruption, scared someone has a gun or other weapon. Face to face with my dad underneath the table, I hear him whisper, "I hate to even ask this, but she's our only option."

A voice comes on over the loudspeaker, booming instructions, ordering the prisoners to line up against the wall and the visitors to congregate against the other side.

"You want me to find her?" Shocked, I then add, "She won't want to see me."

"We have no other choice. She's the only one who can help."

"Will she want to hurt me?"

"No." He pats my hand. "Me, yes, but not you." He adds, "She blames me. Not you."

"Line up." A burly guard taps his steel-toed boot in the back of my dad's shirt, motioning him to stand. "Visiting hours are over."

After climbing out from underneath the table, I see that the free and the confined have never been more interchangeable. I watch him line up as I join the other group, our faces helpless as we watch our loved ones disappear behind glass and steel.

This isn't the first time something like this has happened. A couple months ago, it was someone bringing in contraband that resulted in visiting hours being terminated. Today it's a skinny white guy held in cuffs as an even skinnier woman holds her hand to her nose, blood trickling down her chin. She's being ushered to the prison hospital by a guard.

Did she cheat? Ask for a divorce? Find out he had another lover?

My dad mouths "I love you" across the room to me as he's handcuffed and led out by the guards to head back to his cell. Our conversation's unfinished, just as our lives have become one interrupted communication after another in the form of sporadic letters and impersonal visits.

There is so much I know about him but so much I don't.

As I walk back to Diane and the waiting car, I realize that I got out of sharing my news with him. Instead of relief, I feel cheated, the same way I did when I found out he was being sentenced to twenty years and would no longer be a constant part of my life.

I remind myself it's no different than it was before.

CHAPTER 2
Charlotte

It's late afternoon, and the last of the Kansas sun disappears at the same time as the final drops in my glass of pinot noir. After I tilt the bottle to pour another, the few remaining drops settle into the bottom of my stemware.

Shaking my head at my ability to drink copious quantities of wine in record time and mourning the loss of another bottle, I toss it into the recycling bin with a bang.

A shrill ring interrupts my present task in the kitchen, and I squeeze the dough harder than intended, darting my eyes to the phone. If I were talking to a millennial, they'd be abhorred at the old-fashioned monstrosity that belongs in a museum but hangs like a prized trophy from the wall. My English-lit pupils at the local community college can't believe I have a landline, and furthermore when I mention forgoing email for handwritten letters, they groan in protest.

Dare I answer?

The thrum in my chest signals that my heart rate's rising, the beats per minute spiking me up toward panic mode. I have a love-hate relationship with the phone, not only because I inevitably have to use it to communicate but also because I dread the voice on the other end.

Deep breaths, take deep breaths, and don't hyperventilate, I remind myself. My therapist advised me to find an object to focus on, and the sliminess of the raw dough beneath my hand is the first thing I notice.

Frozen in place, I don't move to check the caller ID.

After a couple more bursts of energy, the phone shudders to a stop as the voice mail picks up. I exhale at the same time as her singsong tone echoes through the kitchen.

"Charlotte, it's me. It's been a long time, and I need to speak to you. It's urgent. I'm coming to see you since you never return any of my calls, but I'm torn on whether I should pay the college a visit or your house. Let me know which one works."

The line goes dead.

Shutting my eyes, I grip the smooth surface of the counter, hanging on for dear life.

Just erase it.

I roll my eyes. *She'll never come here, she doesn't exist, and she can't hurt you.* I repeat the mantra over and over in a whisper, the words slipping out of my mouth as I enunciate every single one of them.

A loud beep interrupts my practiced speech.

I jump.

The oven. The oven is ready but the cookies aren't.

Turning back to the dough, I twist the pliable mounds into whatever shape I want, which I was unable to do with her. The word *manipulate* comes to mind, and I squish the formed circle into the butcher block with a vengeance.

Sighing at the lumpy pile, I start over, carefully this time.

I'm arranging the batch of cookies on a metal baking sheet when a threatening rattle shakes the french doors. It breaks my concentration, confirming the impending rain predicted in an earlier forecast.

A warning crack of thunder shakes me from the nagging feeling of unease. After pulling the sheer cream curtains aside, I gaze out from the kitchen to the back deck.

The large pine and spruce trees are planted close to one another in the backyard, creating the illusion of a miniature forest. Usually their shade and soundproofing are welcome, blocking out noise from the bustling traffic. Right now, they are ominous shadows reaching their limbs out violently to snag anything in their path.

Shaking my head, I laugh like a hyena at the vision of being strangled by a savage tree trunk. Then, turning my attention to the cookie sheet, I nimbly open the double oven to slide the tray in the rack, attempting to emulate my mother.

The only dilemma: I can never reproduce the comfort I yearn for inside the house, as much as I try. If only she were seated at the oversize kitchen island, sharing a glass of cold milk and conversation.

I'm startled by a flash across the sky that causes the light bulbs to flicker simultaneously. Nervous, I eyeball the oil-rubbed bronze pendant above me. After striding across the polished concrete floor, I hold my breath as I jiggle the french doors, ensuring they are locked up tight.

An emergency-weather kit is stored in the pantry, and I promptly remove the yellow flashlight, the hard plastic comforting in my hand. The batteries might be old, so I test the flashlight to make sure it's in working order. Light floods the room, and, relieved, I settle the items on the counter, just in case.

Tilting my head, I remember that the television's on in the living room, but there's no noise or chatter. *Did I turn it off?*

And is the dead bolt in place on the front door?

I can't remember doing either. Mentally, I retrace my steps as I tap my fingers restlessly on the counter. I could swear I left the television on, the noise typically a welcome distraction.

After making contact with the butcher block that's near the stove, I carefully pull out a long knife, the longest and sharpest one we have. Slowly, I tiptoe toward the opposite side of the house, holding my breath.

A long sigh of relief escapes my lips as I confirm that the heavy front door is closed, my fingers running over the dead bolt and the lock, just to be sure.

You can never be too careful.

I keep the butcher knife near my side for protection.

The television hangs over the fireplace, and the word *mute* blinks in the corner of the screen. I unmute it just as an announcement breaks through the scheduled programming. "The National Weather Service has issued a severe-thunderstorm warning for Sedgwick County. Potential damage can and will be caused by hail, strong winds, and flash flooding. We suggest drivers stay off the road if at all possible. Meteorologists have advised that a potential tornado watch could be issued. Stay tuned for further updates."

Shuddering, I wrap my arms around myself in a soothing gesture, rubbing the prickly goose bumps. Storms are another fear at the top of my expanding and never-ending list. I move toward the blind-covered windows, sliding them open to peek out into the now-darkened sky. Rain clouds have appeared out of nowhere, obscuring the light as if they have been drawn, angry and foreboding, directly over the rays of sunshine. One minute I'm staring into a cerulean sky, and now the world is plunged into blackness under low clouds.

I strike a match and light a few candles, just in case the power does fail.

I am mesmerized as a sliver of lightning sprints across the sky, as if trying to impress its dance partner by sashaying across such a large span in a short amount of time, and the windows jar as another loud boom engulfs the quiet space. Weather's as transformative as life—it can radically change in an instant, yet it's completely out of our control.

Inhaling a deep breath, I will myself not to succumb to the overwhelming sadness that presses against my chest.

With a loud exhalation, I close my eyes the way my therapist taught me, remembering her words. "Don't ignore your discomfort, Charlotte.

Use the negative emotion as a teaching lesson and trace it back to its source before discounting it."

As if memories were that easy to let go of.

Take a puff of air and they will dissipate, I think wryly, especially the unpleasant ones that destroy you and the ones you love.

When I open my eyes, I feel the sharp wooden handle digging into my side. Wincing, I retrace my steps back into the kitchen and glare at my reflection in the metal blade as I slip it back into its rightful place.

If anything can lessen my tension, it's the smell of a timeworn recipe. I sniff the air, the space enveloped with the aroma of fresh cookies. In some ways, it's as if my mother's presence is felt. Inside the modern farmhouse, the glow of lit candles and the smell of cinnamon and vanilla are the antithesis of the looming storm. They signal warmth and a certain snugness.

I was fortuitous enough to inherit a sizable fortune from my family that allowed the purchase of a substantial place near Pleasanton Lake, a quaint part of the city that feels like its own small community on the outskirts of the sprawling metropolis. Walking trails wrap around the man-made lake. The residents who own homes here are encouraged to fish and rent paddleboats or canoes. It's like its own city within a city, if that makes sense. A safe haven without crime.

It's a slice of heaven, and I love it here.

When I'm not afraid.

But I'm petrified of a lot of things, and *thrilled* doesn't accurately describe how I felt when Noah agreed that the commute to the airport would be worth it for his job. Especially since hotel rooms have become his home away from me. Work travel keeps him occupied during the week, and the airport is a mere half hour away—not a bad commute given the suburban sprawl that's taken over the once-vacant farmlands and empty tracts.

The downside?

He's gone more than he's not. It's hard not to feel resentful and, well, alone. I remind myself that it's just difficult being on my own, tasked with shouldering most of the household responsibilities.

Lonely means something different to me, because you can be in a crowded room and still feel completely and utterly isolated.

At times I'm both, the majority of my hours spent near the majestic stone fireplace, reading steamy romance novels, the opposite of what I teach. I read Steel and lecture on Tolstoy. Characters in books become my friends and enemies, their ill-fated romances and forbidden love laden with obstacles I imagine myself a part of.

It's an escape.

A beautiful, glorious escape from the life I've tried to rebuild without either of them holding me back.

He's coming home soon, so stop feeling sorry for yourself, I command.

The timer beeps, signaling that the cookies are done. Deftly moving around the kitchen, I turn off the oven and transfer them onto a cooling rack in the middle of the island.

Another earsplitting crack trembles through the house, and white flashes split the tumultuous nimbus clouds open, followed by the sound of pounding rain hitting the roof.

At first, I don't hear the loud knock until a sharp thwack draws my attention to the front of the house.

Pausing, I turn the faucet off as a loud pounding reverberates through the house.

"What the . . . ," I murmur, wiping my wet hands on a striped dish towel. It must be the umbrella awning in the backyard swaying in the wind, brushing against the house, or that the storm's uncustomarily close.

Assuming it's the storm, I shift the cookies onto a plate with a spatula and slip the baking sheet into the large farmhouse sink to soak.

A shrill sound echoes as the doorbell chimes.

I hum a childhood lullaby that used to comfort me and peer out the small window overlooking the side yard. Glancing over my shoulder, I bite my lower lip in frustration. I then reason with myself, trying hard not to overthink why someone would be at the door this late in the afternoon. Maybe it's the mailman, or a dog was startled by the thunder and got loose, and a neighbor is frantic to find their beloved pet.

But the unsettled feeling is more than that, more than a punch to my gut.

The past never lets me forget that someone could be watching . . . or trying to get me to let my guard down when I'm the most vulnerable.

Repeating my earlier gesture of grabbing the butcher knife, I wrap it in the dish towel and then pause between the kitchen and living room. My eyes automatically move to the basement door to make sure it's closed and padlocked, behavior that is ingrained in me now. Gulping, I glance at my least favorite part of the house, one I avoid unless absolutely necessary.

After counting to ten, I tiptoe once again across the stained oak floorboards, the color picked to perfectly match the mantel over the fireplace. My bare feet barely make a sound as I close the gap between me and the unknown.

The fervent rumble of thunder matches the thudding in my chest.

A couple of stamps and another knock at the front door.

Ordinarily, I appreciate the heavy drapes covering the front picture windows on both sides of the door, since they're meant to keep prying eyes out. But tonight, they prevent me from seeing what or who's outside on the porch.

I touch the dead bolt, as if feeling the metal will alleviate any doubts it's changed positions. Resting my head against the doorframe, I wish like hell that Noah were here to answer.

All I can manage is to yelp, "Hello?" But it's not even loud enough to muffle the dramatic news reporter on the screen announcing that a tornado watch has now been issued.

"I need help," a female voice shrieks. "Please!"

"Who is it?" I stammer, this time with inflection, staying put on my side of the heavy door between us, the knife hidden underneath the damp cotton.

"It's getting bad out," a distraught woman pleads on the other side. "Can you please help me?"

Shutting my eyes, I wonder if it's a stranded motorist. My hand hesitates at my collarbone, where my beloved cross necklace rests. After saying a quick prayer with my hand pressed against the chain, I ask, "Who is it?"

My remembering that the screen door is also locked provides me with a small dose of comfort and some protection. After unlatching the dead bolt, I slowly pull the door open and come face to face with the outside elements. The torrential downpour's strong enough that rain smacks my forehead through the screen.

After flicking on the porch light and illuminating the shadow of this mystery person, I peer through the darkness at the stranger. The unknown female's face is tilted downward, hair covered by a dark hood, hand balled in a fist, poised to knock again.

"I was walking in the neighborhood."

"Are you armed?"

"You mean, like with a weapon?"

"Yes."

"No."

"Where did you come from?"

"The lake." Her voice sounds pitiful. "And I saw lights on at your house." The weak glow provides an outline of a maroon sweatshirt and her hunched-over stature. When the figure straightens, the eyes look upward, and I'm taken aback. They're bright blue, like perfect azure crystals. Instead of seeing the face of a woman, I glimpse a teenager. The skin is smooth and unlined, the features feminine, although her hair's hidden by the fabric covering her head.

"I'm sorry to bother you, but I'm stuck out in the rain." She moves her hands out in front of her as if showing she's unarmed and, therefore, harmless. "It's really bad out."

"Okay . . ." My voice trails off. I don't want to be rude, but I don't know this girl. I'm not particularly keen on offering my home to interlopers. What if it's some type of a setup?

But I can see the girl's drenched. Beads of water run down her face, and traces of mascara smudge her cheeks.

"I go to Pleasanton High," the girl offers, pointing up the street. "I got caught up in the storm on my walk home."

Eyeing the weather one more time, sheets of rain causing the driveway to shimmer like a pond, I slowly unlock the screen door and take a giant step back. "Come on in." I motion, clasping the door tighter than most would, trying to control my labored breathing as my fingers dig like claws into the wood. I won't be surprised if I find scratches in the varnish later.

Last time I tried to help someone, it didn't go over so well. I hope I don't come to regret this decision.

But that was then, and this is now. And I'm not a mean-spirited person, just cautious.

Feeling a tad guilty for leaving her outside when she's doused and uncontrollably shaking, I offer her a weak smile and a wide berth.

I make contact, blurting out, "Just so you know, I have a panic button." She looks confused, as if she's unsure whom the alert would be for—her or me.

Without showing her the knife, I twist the towel tighter around the blade, keeping it at my side, just in case.

CHAPTER 3
Elle

"I'm sorry." I shiver, tentatively stepping over the threshold. I'm not quite sure what I'm apologizing for, but it seems to break some of the tension in the air. The woman standing to the left of me is clearly wary of my presence. I'm unwanted, which I should be used to by now, but if I'd done what she did and had the kind of past she had, I wouldn't want unexpected guests either.

It wasn't hard to find her, even with the different last name she's acquired. Judging by the pictures on the sideboard, it must be her married name instead of an alias, as I had suspected. I guess she figures no one is looking for her, that her dirty secret is safe now.

Except you always hear that's how people get caught—by growing too comfortable and letting their guard down. And as frightened as I am to be standing here, I pinch myself as a reminder to be extra nice and soothing and not let my mouth get the best of me. It's been a long time since we've seen each other, and I don't want to ruin the potential we have.

"Silly of me to walk home today. I had no idea it was going to unleash a shitstorm of rain."

Shit.

Does she hate obscenities? Consider my generation a bunch of degenerates? Her expression is neutral, eyes trained on my face. Something's pressed against her side, like a baby blanket or swatch of fabric. I didn't notice any baby pictures, but maybe she has one?

"It's just I really like walking the trails. It's super calming after crappy exam days at school. Calculus. Who needs it? It was so nice and sunny, and then boom—the storm came out of nowhere." *Great. Now I'm rambling.*

She stands there unmoving for a second, then snaps into action as I stand there dripping on her expensive-looking but hideous rug. Wealth doesn't equal good taste.

"You're drenched," she states.

Duh, Captain Obvious.

When she steps toward me, she's not at all what I expected from the pictures I'd found in an old photo album. I remember her differently, but when you haven't seen someone in years, time seems to stop and you capture them in your memory the way you would a snapshot.

She was a hard woman to find images of. There were no recent photos I could dredge up, and she had no presence on any social media platforms I could find. Even her faculty profile at the college was sparse and had a blank space where her headshot should be.

Her caramel-colored hair reflects off the candlelight bouncing across the room. I automatically count four lit tapers as I carefully scan the expansive living room. Her chocolate-brown eyes are glued to my every move. I thought she'd be taller, but she's only a couple of inches over my smaller-than-average frame.

Really, I expected a monster, but she's just got a good disguise. And she looks so plain and normal that nothing particular stands out about her. Though they say the same about most sociopaths. *Common* is the right adjective to describe her.

I swipe my hood off my head and brush damp hair off my cheeks, but I leave my sweatshirt zipped up like it's a safety blanket that can protect me.

"You walked?" she scoffs. "No bike or scooter you left somewhere?"

"Nope." I motion to my feet. "Just my legs." My jeans are also damp, and the rough fabric clings uncomfortably to my skin.

She holds out an arm as if waiting for me to hand her something. *Maybe she wants me to remove my wet clothing?* I doubt she'd want to touch my secondhand clothing. It might give her the plague.

Then, as if she's read my mind, she drops her one empty hand to her side, taking a step back. I wait as she opens her mouth to say something, but she either can't form the words or can't decide what to say. So instead she closes it and moves around me in a circle, keeping her face focused in on me like a laser beam.

Weird.

"Would you like me to stay here?" I ask politely.

Ignoring my question, she forces a smile. "Let's get you near the fire so you can dry off."

On high alert, I follow her across the hardwood floors, noticing my shoes are tracking wet marks through the living room. "Shit," I say, flustered. "Sorry. I should've taken my sneakers off."

Visibly cringing at the outline of my footprints, she shrugs. "Not a big deal. It'll be okay. Floors are easy to clean."

Still at arm's length, she points to my hoodie. "I'll throw that in the dryer, if that's okay with you?"

I feel my face flush, even with the trickle of water on my cheeks. "Uh, no thanks. I can just sit by the fire, if that's all right."

"I'll go get you a towel." She seems to notice my chattering teeth. "You must be frozen. Have a seat and make yourself comfortable." Considering me for a moment, she adds, "I'll find something for you to wear that's dry."

"Thank you." I hate to ruin the fabric of her plush overstuffed chair with my wet clothing. Instead, I sink down near the fireplace and reach my hands out, the skin cold and covered with gooseflesh. With one last fleeting gaze, she abruptly turns around, heading down a hallway.

My eyes dart around the impressive two-story brick home. A wrought iron staircase is near the entry and winds around the top floor, overlooking the downstairs. The looming entry has an impressive chandelier above it, the crystals probably Swarovski. It's definitely trendy, this decorator farmhouse chic with its flair for grays, navy blues, and bursts of yellow. It's just not my style. Or maybe I'm just so used to our mismatched garage sale finds that my taste is sorely lacking.

Even after disappearing around a corner, I can feel her watchful eyes on me. When she returns in an instant with a fluffy towel in hand, I can still sense her discomfort. I decide to break the ice and introduce myself. Unsure if she'll shake my hand, I do a half wave. "By the way, I'm Elle."

She nods as she pushes the towel into my hand. "Charlotte."

Awkwardly, I rub my face, worried I'll dirty her egyptian cotton. My body's still quivering from the cold, the chill bone deep. Biting her lip, she murmurs, "At least let me get you something warm to change into."

I focus on rubbing my hands together as she exits the room. The smell of burning wood and heat makes me want to fall asleep. Suddenly I'm dead tired, and my eyes flicker open and closed. As the fire licks at the glass screen, I try to ignore my lingering concerns about being up close and personal with her. But the smell wafting from the other room causes my mouth to water. I notice a plate of cookies through the open entryway to the kitchen. Averting my eyes from the gnawing hunger that's a constant in my belly, I pinch my wrist.

Will it always be this way, I wonder, or will I ever know where my next meal is coming from?

A moment later, Charlotte enters my line of vision. Whatever she was carrying before has now been replaced with a men's T-shirt and wool socks. I notice her with the same man in a few framed photographs, and I wonder if this clothing belongs to him. He seems a tad boring, the ubiquitous flannel shirt and puffer vest screaming outdoorsy, but something about him seems fake. I wonder if he's ever been hiking, let alone on the trail behind their house. Probably not. He's too much of a pretty boy. Probably a corporate job with a six-figure income and a BMW in the garage. He must make that if they live in this expensive home. I don't think adjunct teaching brings in the bucks for this type of American dream. The billboard out by the highway advertises that this development starts in the midsixes.

Thrusting the items at me, she offers a small smile. "Here you go, Elle. Did I say it right?"

"Thanks," I say, smiling back. "And, yeah, you did." After untying my gray Converse sneakers, I peel off my thin, threadbare socks, letting the warmth envelop my toes as I wiggle them to regain feeling. I dry my feet off with the towel and then shove them into the heavy men's wool socks.

"Bathroom's down the hall if you want to change your shirt." She motions to a first-floor powder room.

I stand, suddenly embarrassed at how I must look to her, a drowned rat out of a sewer. Her opinion doesn't matter—it never did before—but I don't like people to assume I'm white trash. She steps away from me to let me pass, her hands knotted in a ball, putting ample distance between us once again. With her eyes glued to my back, I walk in the direction she points and then quietly shut the bathroom door behind me.

I shoot a quick text to my boyfriend, Justin, letting him know I'm safe in the lion's den. I told him to expect a text every thirty minutes and even dropped a pin when I got here so he would know my location in case of an emergency.

After unzipping the dark-red sweatshirt, the fabric soaked along with my T-shirt underneath, which is sticking like a Band-Aid to my black bra, I strip off the cheap cotton I'm wearing. The luxurious fabric of the men's V-neck feels expensive against my skin.

As I stare in the mirror, my eyes red rimmed and my skin damp, I have an overwhelming urge to go through her medicine cabinet. Prescription pills serve two purposes—they can take away the pain, and I can always use the extra cash. After clenching and unclenching my fists, I pause with my hand against the ornate glass knobs. She'll wonder at my intentions if I don't hurry back. And you don't want her to unleash her crazy, especially in this mad storm.

Be patient, I remind myself, smoothing my unruly blonde hair before exiting.

I jump, not expecting her to be lurking, arms crossed, in the hallway outside the bathroom as if she's my parole officer waiting for me to drop a dirty urine sample so she can apprehend me.

Feeling relieved now that I didn't snoop through her drawers, I give her a tight smile. "Thanks for the clothes."

She nods. "I didn't mean to scare you, but . . ." Her eyes harden, and I notice the striped fabric back at her side. Face to face, we each wait for the other to make a move. Motioning toward the fireplace, she directs me. "Go have a seat and get warmed up."

I seat myself close to the fireplace, and the television fills the empty space with mindless chatter as she settles into the overstuffed gray cloth couch covered in pillows.

Charlotte speaks first. "Do you live in this development?"

"No, I don't," I say, shaking my head.

"Oh." She looks almost disappointed.

"But I love it over here. Especially your home." I point to the outside. "Besides the lights being on, I stopped here because you have the best mailbox."

"Mailbox?"

"It's my favorite bird."

"The peacock?"

29

"Yeah, I know it's dumb, but I walk by your house a lot, and it's a landmark to me—halfway to the bus stop."

She seems amused by this. "It was a comical present from my mother that grew on me over time." She laughs. "I'm surprised the neighbors haven't complained that it's not in line with our homeowners' association." The mailbox post is shaped like the legs of the bird, and the actual mail drop is the mouth. The feathers are various shades of blue and purple, and the eyes act as a reflector. I've never seen anything like it.

"Well, I think it's cool. And you have such gorgeous digs." Suddenly my mouth twists into a frown. This should've been the type of house I grew up in. With both parents. Stable. Consistent.

Aloof, she says, "Thank you."

Maybe I said too much. Quickly I think of something to say to ease the tension.

What do people in suburbia love?

When you compliment their family or kids. I search her ring finger and notice a diamond band. Time to redirect.

"He's handsome. What's his name?" I point to a photo on the side table of Charlotte and the dark-haired man. Their arms are wrapped tightly around each other, their eyes twinkling, or maybe just glassy from drinking. The picture next to it is clearly ancient. Dressed in matching football jerseys, they are standing in a stadium at what I assume is a college and wearing cheesy grins for the camera.

He's the complete opposite of what I'd pictured.

Is this the man who ruined everything? I wonder.

"Noah." Her voice softens. "That's my Noah."

"You guys look good together." I busy myself with the towel, rubbing it against the back of my neck.

"He's my favorite person in the world." Her face lights up when she says this, and a huge grin takes over. Now I see her best feature. She has perfectly straight teeth, and her smile changes her demeanor in an instant from a nasty wench to a seemingly decent human being.

Except she's not.

After standing, she crosses to the front window and peers out the drapes. The rain hasn't begun to let up. She darts her eyes to me and seems to consider her options. "While you wait—I just baked cookies. Would you like one? And something to drink?"

"Sure."

She strides to the kitchen and hollers, "Milk okay?"

"Great."

A cupboard opens with a thud and shuts the same way. Glasses clink together; then, like a Stepford wife, she reappears with a plate.

Timid, I take the milk and a single cookie when I want to devour the entire batch. "These look delicious. What kind are they?"

"Homemade." She grins. "My mother's favorite—snickerdoodle."

Tilting my head, I'm unsure what type of cookie this is. It sounds more like one of those designer dog breeds mixed with a poodle I see prancing around the neighborhood like miniature ponies.

"Cinnamon sugar."

"That's what smelled so good." Hurriedly chewing a bite, I decide they're the best cookies I have ever tasted. My mouth inhales one before I greedily grab another. Focused on chewing the cookie, I swallow it down with the milk.

Quiet looms between us for a moment, the television emitting the only sound.

"I take it you like her recipe?"

"They're delicious." My stomach grumbles, and we both laugh. "I guess my stomach agrees."

"What part of town do you live in?"

"About fifteen minutes from here." I lick the cinnamon and sugar from my lips as I stare into the flames.

She taps her palms against her legs, as if my time is up. "Do you need a ride to the bus stop?"

"Nah, I just wanted to wait out the storm."

She mumbles something, but the loud wail of sirens engulfs whatever she said. I freeze for a second, at first assuming it's a squad car and forgetting that this isn't my neighborhood.

But our time together is not up, according to the weatherman on television, whose voice has taken on a tone of urgency, and he directs us to seek shelter immediately. A red emergency bulletin flashes across the bottom of the screen, announcing that the tornado watch has been elevated to a warning after a funnel touched down in the vicinity.

Charlotte starts to shake violently, and I glance at her with concern. This sounds like a potential *Wizard of Oz* scenario, and I don't know what she's worried about, when I'm the one stuck with the evil witch. I don't want to be trapped in a basement with this nutjob any more than I want the roof to cave in on the house.

"Are you okay?" I ask.

"I don't like basements." *You and me both*, I think.

"It's okay; it's just a precaution," I say, setting down the plate of crumbs on the side table. "I'm sure there's nothing to worry about. It'll be over before we know it."

"I'm going to get a flashlight." She strides across the room toward the kitchen, and meanwhile I take my own deep breath. Is going down in a basement with Charlotte worse than a potential tornado? Both have the potential to do collateral damage.

After reappearing with a tool kit and a plastic flashlight in hand, she fumbles with a metal lock on what must be the basement door. Turning her head, she looks surprised to see me still frozen in place.

My mouth gapes open. "Why's it locked?" I blurt out before I can stop myself. It's lucky I don't add my next thought, which is creepier yet: *Why is it padlocked?*

"The door?" Tilting her head, she considers this. "Is that weird? I guess it might be. It's just . . . there are too many things that can hurt someone down there." Her hands shake like there's a motor underneath them, while I'm trying not to lose my shit as I consider all the negatives and none of the positives of going downstairs with Charlotte.

The shrill sound gives me a headache as the wailing increases. Rubbing a hand over my face, I make up my mind that there's no way in hell I'm following her downstairs.

My eyes dart toward the front door, and the rising panic is coursing through my veins, screaming at me to run.

CHAPTER 4
Charlotte

I open the door, flip on the light switch, and exhale sharply. As I start my descent, the single light bulb flickers off, then on, then goes out entirely.

Halfway down, I see the outline of cardboard boxes and furniture covered by faded sheets, mimicking ghosts. Both remind me of my own haunted past, and I shiver.

I can't be down here, and I certainly can't bring the girl down here.

Groaning, I turn on my heel and reappear at the top of the steps. With a shove to the door, I slam it behind me, surprised to see she hasn't moved an inch. "It's not safe down there with the lights out. I don't want you to trip and fall."

Elle stands eerily still, her body glowing from the dim light of the still-lit candles, making her resemble one of those figures in a wax museum.

She stutters, "Um, d-do you mind if I just take cover in the bathroom? I didn't see any windows in there."

"Of course. It's probably the best place on the first floor. Even the laundry room has windows in it." As we enter the small space, the only glow comes from the flashlight I prop on the counter. I settle my back against the closed door as Elle tucks herself into the corner by the toilet.

The wind has picked up, and between the scratch of trees scraping the exterior and the blare of the weather alarm, the noise would drown us out if we spoke. So we remain silent.

My nerves are shot as I aim to center myself. Hyperventilation in this small space, even a room in my own house, terrifies me. The tile floor is cool underneath my fingernails as I rub a small circle on it to keep myself grounded. My hands make contact with the striped wallpaper, the grainy texture a stark contrast to the smooth floor. Another exercise my therapist instructed me to do to regain control.

But I am in control, Doctor, I most certainly am! I shriek in my mind.

I also like to home in on the people in my surroundings, in this case the stranger across from me.

Focused on Elle, I watch as she chews a fingernail. "Nervous habit?"

Bewildered, she shoves her hands into the pockets of her hoodie, I notice. "Yeah, I guess." She shrugs. "I forget I'm doing it."

"I used to suck my thumb." I tap my foot anxiously against the tile floor.

"As a toddler? I think everyone did that." Elle reaches into the back pocket of her jeans, fumbling for something. She pulls out a cell phone. "I think I'm going to call a ride."

"In this weather? It's not safe."

She turns on the flashlight feature of her phone by tapping a few buttons, which then bathes the room in more light. Staring at me, she asks, "Aren't you worried about your husband?"

"Noah had to go to Texas." I smack a hand to my forehead. *Idiot.* I rock back and forth against the wall. I shouldn't tell this girl anything personal. She could rob me or tell a group of her friends I'm alone, and they could case my house. That same scenario happened on an episode of *Dateline* recently. It's hard being companionless during the week. Until this instant, it hasn't hit me how much I miss having someone to confide in. The telephone doesn't offer the same sentiments or affection.

"He'll be back later . . . early in the morning, but I'm glad he's missing the storm." I rest my hands on my knees, trying to keep my leg from bouncing. "What about you?"

"Do I travel?"

"No. I meant, do you have a boyfriend?" I stumble over my words. I shouldn't make assumptions. "Or girlfriend?"

Elle opens her mouth, but, evidently noticing the absence of sirens, she puts a hand near her ear. "They stopped." Clapping her hands, she grins. "I'm going to see about catching a bus."

"I doubt they run during a tornado warning." I flatten my fingers against the beige-papered wall to guide myself up to a standing position. "Please let me give you a ride. I don't want you walking to the bus stop in this weather."

"No, absolutely not." Elle slides her hands into her pockets. "You've done enough."

"Do you always take the bus?"

"Typically. That or I walk."

"And your parents are okay with that?"

"My dad works nights, and someone's gotta take care of the kiddos. It's the easiest way for me to get around. If I'm in a bind, I can always ask my boyfriend."

"Who do you know in this area?"

"Oh, in this neighborhood?" She raises her brows. "Nobody. I just like to walk around the lake and enjoy some peace and quiet."

"Is your house really loud?" I don't want to intrude, but I'm curious.

"You mean, do I have younger brothers and sisters?" She laughs. "Yeah, a couple. It's never without drama when you have little siblings. Someone's always fighting—either over bathroom time or the TV channel."

"I'm not letting you walk home. I've got an extra raincoat that should fit you perfectly." I stop at the hall closet and hand her a yellow jacket.

Elle replies, "You're too kind."

"Let me run and grab you a bag of cookies. I also made some peppermint bark the other day. Would you like some?"

Elle cringes. "Can't say I've had flavored bark before."

"Oh my gosh, no." I bring a hand to my throat, chuckling. "It's basically peppermint and chocolate, nothing from a tree."

"Well, if it's as good as the cookies, I'd be stupid not to try it."

"If my mother were here, she'd be thrilled you think so highly of her baking."

"She's got a gift. I wish my mom were more like that—into cooking and stuff." Rolling her eyes, she moans, "She's still trying to get the hang of the microwave. Can your mom teach my mom some basic skills?"

"I wish she could." My lip starts to quiver. "Sorry, I don't mean to get emotional." Inhaling sharply, I apologize. "It's just . . . my mom died a few years ago, and it's always hard when I make something she loved."

Elle shifts from one foot to the other, toying with the zipper on the rain slicker. "I'm sorry to hear that. Losing someone is hard . . ."

"Have you lost anyone close to you?"

"No." She bites her lip. "Fortunately not."

"How old are you?"

"Seventeen."

"You're lucky," I say. "I'd kill to be that young again."

An odd look crosses her face, something between a smirk and a frown. She tilts her head as if to rebut this, but instead, her mouth twists into a thin line. "I am lucky."

CHAPTER 5
Elle

Give me a break, I yelp to myself, almost biting off my entire forefinger to keep from letting loose a string of cusswords. I can't believe she's trying to make me feel sorry for her.

I watch her test the locks on the front door, the windows, and the french doors in the kitchen. *Must be the constant guilt you feel when you carry such a dark secret,* I think.

She has no idea that her worst nightmare is standing in her living room. Not to mention how easy it was for me to pretend I'd been caught in the downpour.

I follow her out to a mudroom that leads to a three-car garage. Inside the cavernous stalls, a charcoal Jeep Grand Cherokee is parked next to a bunch of lawn ornaments and a mower. A couple of boxes are pushed against the wall, and gardening tools are scattered on a shelf, along with household supplies.

The other two stalls are empty.

After opening the passenger door and climbing in, I casually ask, "What time does Noah come home?"

"Uh, I think his flight gets in around nine." She scratches her head. "He never needs a ride, so I just wait for the sound of the front door."

"Does he have to travel a lot?"

Charlotte starts to nod her head, then stops, her eyes trained on the backup camera.

"Do you get to go with him at all? I bet there are some neat places he gets to visit."

"I guess I could . . ." She taps her fingers on the steering wheel. "He doesn't seem to have a lot of downtime, so I would just be on my own."

The color of the sky is eerie, the moon hidden behind the clouds, which are tinged against the darkness with a greenish-gray pallor. I hope the sirens don't make a reappearance tonight.

Charlotte interrupts my scrambled thoughts. "Your name," she says. "Is that short for anything?"

"No, my mom was obsessed with the model Elle Macpherson, even though I look nothing like her." I grin. Her face darkens when I say this.

"The name suits you, except you look like a young Claudia Schiffer."

"Thank you," I murmur, unsure who that is. "What about you—is Charlotte a family name?"

"I was named after Charlotte Brontë."

"I was going to guess *Charlotte's Web*." I don't add that with her web of deceit and lies it's a fitting name. Instead I say, "Author, right? *Little Women*?"

"No." Her disappointment at my unfamiliarity with dead novelists is noticeable on her pinched face. "She was most famous for *Jane Eyre*."

"Do you have any children?" I ask. "I thought I saw you carrying a baby blanket."

"We are, I mean, we will, someday soon, have kids." She points to the radio. "How about some music? Pick whatever you want."

Turning the dial, I find some Top 40 music and stare out the window as the wipers squeak across the windshield and the water splashes under the tires.

"Which direction should I go?"

Pausing, I point to the east. "Take a left up here. Get on the freeway and exit at Elmore."

"Elmore?"

"No," I hurriedly say. "Sorry, I meant Larchwood Avenue." She seems relieved. Elmore's a rough area with a lot of crime and is a heavily drug-trafficked part of town.

"What does your father do for work?"

"Drug dealer," I deadpan. A look of wonder crosses her face. "Kidding," I say. "He's a doctor, an ER doc."

"Good for him for helping people." She visibly relaxes. "You almost got me."

"Which hospital?"

"Covenant."

"And your mom's at home with your siblings?"

"Technically she's my stepmom." I add, "She's a nurse. They met on a shift." Her eyes widen at this implication.

"You mentioned younger siblings. How many?"

"Two. Both younger boys they had together, so a big age gap between me and them." I don't want to talk about my family anymore.

Changing the subject, she muses, "You know, I really admire medical professionals. I couldn't handle the sight of blood and guts."

"Really?" My eyes widen. "I wouldn't expect that."

She gives me a sideways glance. "How come?"

Because you're a sociopath, I want to add. But I can't. Because she doesn't *know* I know all about her and her sordid past, intertwined with mine.

"I just think people can get used to it after a while—you know, desensitize themselves to the sight of unpleasant things. Plus . . ." Lifting the bag of cookies, I raise an eyebrow. "Your patient satisfaction would be high because of these."

She laughs as her shoulders relax against the seat.

"Oh, turn here." I point to the road ahead. "It's the third one on the left."

Her eyes veer down the street toward a dark-blue shingled single-story with a gabled roof and red shutters. "What a cute house. I love Cape Cod–style homes."

"Yeah, my stepmom said the same thing."

She slows the Jeep down and pulls into the driveway. Lights are shining through the dormers on each side of the chimney, beckoning me inside. "Would you like me to tell your mom where you were?" She puts the car in park. "I don't want her to think you were outside during the tornado warning."

"She's not home."

"Oh, but the lights are on . . ."

"They went to my grandma's earlier." I shrug. "She hates being home alone during storms without my dad."

"Should I call her?"

"I sent her a text."

"Okay, I'll wait to make sure you get in safely."

I groan. "You don't need to do that."

"It's fine." She gives me a small smile. "It was nice to meet you, Elle."

"Thanks so much for helping me out, Mrs. . . . ?"

"Oh no, don't you dare put a *Mrs.* in front of my name."

"Okay, Charlotte." I remember I'm still wearing her clothes. "What about your socks and coat?"

"Keep them."

"No. No way."

"Seriously, I have a million pairs, same with coats. And ditto for Noah—he'll never notice a missing shirt. It's not a big deal."

I slide out of the leather seat and close the door carefully behind me, not wanting the metal to make a loud thud. The rain has slowed to a steady trickle, and I sprint to the side entrance, near the garage. I enter through the rickety door, the broken handle never fully closing behind me.

Charlotte seemed nice, *too* nice, but skittish.

Definitely a woman hiding something.

He might actually be telling the truth for once in his life.

And if he's right, I might not have anything to worry about when it comes to his innocence.

I swallow hard.

But if he's right and she's guilty, my own safety could be in jeopardy.

CHAPTER 6
Charlotte

The next morning, I tidy up the living room, dust the frames, and wipe a lint-free cloth over the glass top of the coffee table. My eyes narrow at the sight of a balled-up T-shirt under the sofa chair with a band's name listed, one I've never heard of. The band's foreign to me—pop culture seems to elude me these days. I tend to live in my own world, or so I've been told. Sometimes staying in my own bubble is safer than the alternative.

Confused for a moment that I've found a woman's shirt that doesn't belong to me, I start to panic.

Was Lauren here for some reason?

Did Noah bring that whore to the house?

My hands start to tremble as I crumple it up in my fists, ready to slam-dunk it in the garbage. Or maybe burn it. Instead, I leave it on the couch.

In a frenzy, I pull every reminder of us off the wall and shove every framed photograph into a box, which I toss into a heap in the garage. My anger intensifies by the minute.

How can he keep doing this to you? I ask myself. *Better yet, how can you keep letting him do this to you?* Slipping the silver diamond band angrily into my pocket as a sign of protest, I kick the tire of my Jeep.

Hands on my hips as sweat drips down my brow, I watch in confusion as the garage door miraculously starts to open and the headlights of a BMW 5 Series shine a spotlight on me.

The face behind the wheel seems just as shocked to see me standing in the stall, and the driver immediately slams on his brakes.

I step aside so he can finish parking.

He shoves his car door open as I stammer, "Noah." Dropping my hands to my sides, I say, "I didn't know you'd be home today."

"Don't sound so disappointed." After popping the trunk, he grabs his leather briefcase and rolling suitcase. "Surprise!"

"It's definitely a surprise. But a pleasant one."

"What're you doing in the garage? You hate darkness, and you looked like you were wanting to gut me with a kitchen knife."

His observation isn't far off from the truth, so I ignore it.

"Ah, nothing. Just had to bring some recycling out to the bin." I don't dare glance in the direction of the box of miscellaneous pictures I've just removed from the house.

He gives me a kiss. "As always, it's nice to see your face."

My cheeks hurt as I force a smile. "Likewise."

"Except I can't stay."

"No?"

"No," he sighs, his frustration palpable as he wrinkles his forehead. "I have to head to Jersey. One of my partners needs help with a deal that's gone awry." I try not to let my own emotions show, a combination of neediness and loneliness. He hates when I complain about something that's out of his control. Plus, it's his career, and he loves what he does, as he points out to me, the same way I love when students fall in love with the classics and speak passionately about Austen or Defoe.

I keep my tone neutral as we head into the house, but I can't wait or I'll ruminate on it for hours, pace back and forth in the living room, and break some expensive dishes.

I have to know about the repulsive shirt.

He leaves his suitcase and briefcase by the hall closet, arching his back in a stretch.

"Question for you."

"Hit me, baby."

I plaster a fake smile on my face, settling into the middle of the couch, a spot that sags just a tad, one most people would avoid so they don't hit the dreaded crease. Not me. "Did Lauren happen to come by?"

His naturally tan skin goes red. "Charlotte."

"I found this." I heave the crumpled ball into his hands.

Perplexed, he unfurls it and holds it up. "This is a T-shirt . . . for the Jonas Brothers."

Staring at him, I don't comprehend the smirk on his face.

"The Jonas Brothers, Char. Do you know who the Jonas Brothers are?"

I shrug. "No idea."

He starts to chuckle; then, bursting out in laughter, he falls into the chair. "You have to be kidding me with this shit."

"I don't understand what's so funny." Now it's my turn to blush.

"Char, the Jonas Brothers are a boy band, geared toward tweens. I mean, they've aged and now they're older, but this shirt—this definitely does not belong to Lauren." Noah's demeanor changes from fun to serious with a warning look. "I wish you'd quit bringing her into this or acting like I'd let her in the house. You know it's over. I've told you that many times. Finished. No going back. It's done."

I nod. Because that's all I can do in this moment. Especially when I just made an amateur move and wasted an accusation on something baseless.

"Did you have a housekeeper come and clean, or did someone stop by?" He should know I don't trust people in the house, *but . . . the storm, the girl,* I remind myself.

Elle.

I'm getting senile at thirty-five, I decide.

"I'm going to wrap this deal up hopefully soon." He reaches to brush a strand of hair off my face. "Then I want us to go on a vacation, somewhere tropical, a beach with white sand . . ."

"And unlimited piña coladas," I finish.

His voice softens. "You doing okay? I saw there were tornado sightings last night. I figured that's why you didn't answer when I called to check on you."

"I did have a visitor."

"The one who the T-shirt belongs to?" He gives me a playful punch on the arm.

"No comment," I giggle.

"Who was it?"

"A complete stranger. They knocked just when it started to get bad out."

"In the middle of a storm?"

"Scary, right?"

"Yeah, definitely."

"It was a teenage girl, drenched and in need of shelter. She seemed sweet enough. I gave her a ride home."

"Char, was that really smart?"

"She's harmless. Just a high school student who got stuck. You know how those flash floods and storms can be."

"Yeah, I do." His voice falters. "But I can't protect you when I'm not here." I ignore his last sentiment, since it has no merit. He's rarely home and I don't want to start a fight, but his absence is felt more than his presence.

"She seemed so young and innocent. It made me feel old. I thought about when we first met . . ."

"Freshman year of college. You were arguing with my roommate about his inability to do laundry."

"He seemed to think it was okay to leave it in the wash for hours without even transporting it to the dryer, while the rest of us waited."

"Hey, I supported you until you brought it up to our room and accidentally dumped it on *my* bed, soaking wet." Noah twists my hair in a knot.

"I was trying to teach him a lesson."

"That you did." Noah touches my lower lip. "That's one thing you've always been good at—teaching other people lessons, right or wrong."

Neglecting his last statement, I turn to look him directly in the eyes, the green flecked with brown—one of his best features, in my book.

I begin, "Do you . . ." Then, balling my hands into tight fists, I continue. "Do you regret what happened with us?"

"What do you mean?"

I wring my hands. "That we weren't careful . . ."

"It was one time, and it was over a month ago." Noah gives me a strange look. "Why would I ever regret having sex with you?"

"Because we didn't . . . we weren't safe."

"I'm not worried about it and neither should you. Whatever happens, happens." His phone buzzes in his pocket as he examines his wristwatch. "Unfortunately, I'm going to have to take a shower and go. Care to join?"

"Of course," I say, grinning, and he leads me by the hand to the walk-in shower.

After Noah leaves, I busy myself with the laundry, minus the sheets, since they still have whiffs of his scent attached to them. A combination of expensive cologne and sweat. I stick Elle's tee into the load, chuckling as I reflect on my earlier concerns.

After heading upstairs to where the guest suite, office, and other bedroom are, I pause near the last door on the left. It's closed, just as it should be.

But is it locked?

Brushing my hand over the doorknob, I flinch as if I've been burned. Then, after confirming it's locked, just like the basement door, I retreat to the laundry room to fold the last of the clothes in the dryer. I pull Elle's shirt out and sniff, the smell of spring-breeze fabric softener better than the stale cigarette smoke it previously reeked of.

I wonder if she's a smoker.

As I fold the cotton, still warm from the dryer, a sneaking suspicion tells me that biting her nails isn't the worst of Elle's habits.

I wonder if I should've asked for her number, but that might've been weird, except now I'm holding her displaced shirt in my hand. I feel a responsibility to return it, since I had a favorite concert T-shirt that was my lucky test-day shirt in college. It was actually Noah's Nirvana one, but still, I would break out in hives if I couldn't locate it on exam day.

Wondering if I'll be able to retrace directions back to Elle's house, I decide to attempt it after a visit to the grocery store.

"Larchwood Avenue wasn't it," I murmur to the radio announcer as I drive.

Slowing down on the street, I realize in the daylight that there's more than one Cape Cod–style house, and they all look the same. All I could make out in the rain was that the front door was bright red, with a large wreath, and so were the shutters.

Déjà vu overcomes me as I pull into the drive, yet I feel weird for the intrusion. After putting the Jeep in park and letting the car idle, I walk up the cobblestone path. The yard's well kept, the grass is mowed, and a huge elm tree looms over most of the tidy front. Bushes line the walkway, and though I'm no landscape expert, I've done enough gardening to know the type—burning bushes, named for their crimson-red color. A perfect complement to the house. Eventually the color of the shrubs will change to green.

After stepping onto the welcome mat, I lift my hand to meet the brass knocker perfectly centered in the middle of the welcome wreath. I take a deep breath that catches in my throat, signaling my stress. I've never been a fan of forced social interactions. *But you chose to come here,* I remind myself. *You're making a nice gesture, returning Elle's shirt,* I chastise myself, *and that should make you feel good.*

The knocker makes a sharp thwack against the door, and out of habit I tap my foot. The sound of wailing ricochets through the house, and the noise startles me. When Elle mentioned younger siblings, I didn't expect ones in diapers.

The door swings open, and a haggard woman cradling a baby stands before me. She's of a totally different ethnicity than Elle, but she did mention she had a stepmom. A short, petite Asian woman with a toddler wrapped around her leg stares at me in frustration. "I just got the baby to sleep." Her eyes droop, and it's clear she's struggling with a newborn.

"I'm so sorry to bother you, but—"

"What're you selling?" The woman exhales, blowing a tendril that's escaped from her messy ponytail. She looks to be midthirties and is casually dressed in jeans and a button-down, barefoot with a look-alike child tugging on her thigh.

"Selling? Oh, nothing." I suddenly feel stupid as I hold up the shirt as a peace offering. "I wanted to drop off Elle's tee."

"Elle?"

"Yeah, Elle." After glancing at the numbers on the side of the house, 1812, and peeking at the garage, I confirm the latter is a two-car with a side door that Elle disappeared through last night.

"I'm sorry, who is Elle?"

Now it's my turn to be confused. "I dropped a girl off here last night." Over my shoulder, I gaze up and down the street. "I'm on Larchwood, right?"

"Yeah, this is Larchwood."

"A teenager—blonde, named Elle, doesn't live here?"

"Nope, last time I checked, I named my kids." She sighs. "But can we just say Elle is my mother-in-law's name, and you can take her with?"

Unsure how to answer, I motion to the children. "Your kids are adorable." I'm a big fan of children, especially babies, their tiny hands and feet and cherubic faces exuding such innocence.

Clearly anxious to close the door and slowly starting to shut it in my face, the woman pulls her head back inside, warning me that her time is limited.

"Ouch," the woman moans, because her toddler has now resorted to pinching her skin instead of merely pulling on it.

"Okay, so no Elle. Do you happen to know if she lives on this street and I maybe got the address wrong?"

"No." The woman scrunches her face. "Not that I know of. We've lived here for seven years, and I don't know anyone by that name."

"I watched her walk inside . . ." I'm silenced by a death stare.

"During the storm? We were all here last night, even my husband."

"Darn. I must not have gotten the address correct last night."

"I don't blame you. It was rough, especially the tornado warning. I thought our basement was going to flood."

"It was dark when I brought her," I muse, "so I must've gotten mixed up. The house was the same style."

"Try the next street over. There're a couple look-alikes. Maybe you're one street off. Look for Larchmont."

As I thank the woman for her time, I don't bother arguing that it was definitely *this* street and *this* particular house. I watched a girl swallowed up by the gloom enter the side door. But there's no use in quarreling with a sleep-deprived new mother about a teen who isn't around.

Elle doesn't live here. That's all that matters.

But why would she lie?

And if the homeowners are unfamiliar with her, then where did she go?

I slide back into the driver's side, refolding the T-shirt before laying it on the passenger seat. Maybe Elle was scared of a stranger's taking her home. That makes sense.

Of course, that must be it.

I feel like an idiot. Even though I gave the girl a ride, she probably felt uneasy about taking me to her house.

But if Elle doesn't live here, then where does she live?

I might be stuck with this tee after all, from a band I've never heard of.

CHAPTER 7
Elle

I wake to my alarm blaring country music, my least favorite, meant to entice me to get up.

It doesn't work today.

My eyes are filled with sleep, and I rub them. Stretching my arms, I roll over the lumpy makeshift mattress I shove in the closet while I'm at school.

This place is such a dump. Yet I don't ever want to leave here. It's better than living on the streets. And I'm not an entitled teenager who can be choosy.

Once again, I overslept after hitting the snooze button multiple times. Another red mark on my tardy and absent report at school. It's my senior year, and they don't take kindly to your missing your first class at least once a week. Especially when you are responsible for attending only four classes, and three of them are fluff. Physical education. Art. Study hall.

Sighing, I know Principal Mitchum will jump down my throat. He and his frumpy secretary.

Diane is not home to chide me. She uses the system to get a check, but I couldn't care less. I'm about to age out of the system, and she's already got two more kids staying here. They're brothers, ages ten and eleven, and they share the bunk beds I used until she decided she needed more money for her habits.

I moved to the couch when she brought them home a couple months ago, reminding me that my time is indeed limited. Then I got tired of waking up with severe back pain, so I asked around the complex for an old mattress. I was in luck—a neighbor was ready to discard one.

It works, as long as I keep clean sheets on it. I try not to picture where it's been before me.

It is history.

The history we all have.

Besides indulging in her vices of drinking and smoking, Diane likes to gamble. She can multitask and do all three at the same time, most days, except when she is doing the part-time job she manages to keep as a cashier.

The apartment smells like stale cigarette butts and soiled kitty litter that hasn't been emptied for days, though I can't say I've spotted the cat recently, and I'm pretty sure it doesn't have a name. Diane isn't a housekeeper, a cook, or motherly at all, really. But she's good at pretending when the time calls for it.

There's never any food in the apartment, so I don't bother searching the cupboards. Last week, all I found were empty ramen packets, a couple cans of soup, and a dead rat. I made chicken noodle for the boys, but nothing new has appeared since.

The boys are at school; they take the school bus, since she takes the car to work or the casino. I check for any missed calls—she allows me to have a cell phone only because it benefits her. If she's stuck at the casino on a hot streak, I can help with after-school pickups. It also allows her to demand that I drive her places if she's drunk. Even though it's a prepaid plan and the phone is refurbished, it's better than nothing.

Luckily, Charlotte sent cookies and peppermint bark home with me, and, wearing the yellow rain jacket she gave me last night, I devour both as I wait for the next city bus. She didn't want it back, and the truth is it's insulated and warm and I could really use one.

Especially now.

Plus, it's a small consolation prize for all the trouble she's caused in our lives.

When I reach school, I try to slink by the administrative office. Mrs. Marsh, the receptionist, doubles as a parole officer, and her beady eyes watch every move I make like a hawk. Her nasally voice echoes in the empty corridor. "Elizabeth?"

Dammit.

I consider running for it, but she's already spotted me. I stop in my tracks and then walk backward in a shuffle.

"Really?" She puts her hands on her generous hips, ones Diane would call childbearing hips.

"Yeah?" I play stupid, acting like I'm headed to class.

"You're late." She taps her wristwatch. "Halfway through period two."

"I had to use the bathroom after first period. I'm sure you understand." I raise an eyebrow. "Women troubles."

"Mr. Roberts already called the office. Said you didn't show. That's another mark."

I roll my eyes. "Thanks for the update."

"Always an attitude."

"Mrs. Marsh, Diane is always running late, so I had to catch the bus. What do you expect me to do when she's the *adult* in the household?"

"Then I need to speak with her about making other arrangements."

"Fine."

"Come with me." Her tone brooks no argument.

Reluctantly I follow her into the lion's den. She lifts up the receiver at her desk, ready to dial. "What's her number?"

"You're calling her now?"

"Of course." She frowns at me over heavy spectacles that rest on the bridge of her nose. "Is she too busy to care about you flunking out of high school?"

"She's at work." I sigh. "I figured her number would be on speed dial by now."

"If I can reach her, maybe she'll pay more attention to getting you here on time, when I interrupt her day." Lowering her voice, she allows a touch of humanity to cut through. "Elizabeth, you are smart, with so much potential. I want to see you apply yourself. Go to college. Principal Mitchum said you haven't applied to any schools."

"I can't afford it."

"Scholarships," Marsh suggests, "or student loans."

"Who would give me a scholarship? I'm practically failing. And I don't want to acquire crippling student loan debt; no, thanks."

"I know you can do better."

"It's too late. I'm a lost cause."

"Elizabeth, you're seventeen. You have your whole life ahead of you."

I'm too tired to argue, and nausea replaces the frustration in my chest. I can feel bile rising, and I don't want to be sick in the school office. The stress of my situation keeps becoming more real. It's like I'm standing outside my body looking in, a silent intruder into this conversation.

"What's Justin going to do after high school?" Justin Pence is my boyfriend of a year, and his plans are as disconcerting as mine. Whereas mine are pretty standard—get a job and hope to swing being on my own—he has delusions of grandeur that involve moving cross-country and becoming the next Tony Hawk.

"Still up for debate." I swallow hard.

"Well, he's got his looks to fall back on." She attempts a smile, which makes her look constipated. Justin's insanely handsome, in a California surfer kind of way. He has longish blond hair, green eyes, and a face that is devilishly attractive, reminiscent of male models straight out of a Calvin Klein ad. It doesn't hurt that he is six three and built not from the gym but from hours spent working at a scrap-metal yard.

Just thinking of him leaving me for another life, a *better* life, sucks the air right out of me. He's my rock, and if it weren't for him, I'd be a sunken ship instead of treading water with this clusterfuck I call my life.

Shoving a hand over my mouth, I sit forward in the chair, resting my hands on my knees.

Marsh's beady eyes express concern. "Are you okay?" She pushes a trash can near me. "Are you sick?" Out of the corner of my eye, I see a well-dressed woman pausing in the doorway. I see perfectly coiffed brown hair and assume she must be a goddamn PTA president, so I don't bother making eye contact.

It's also the same point I lose the contents of my sugary breakfast. Admittedly, the cookies were better going down than they were coming up.

"Can I help you?" I hear Marsh say with an air of dignified authority.

"I just found what I'm looking for."

The voice.

It's her voice.

Scared to make eye contact with the source, I shut my eyes, praying she'll disappear. I don't want to see the remnants in the trash can or the woman standing in the school office.

What the hell's Charlotte doing at my high school?

And more importantly, *How did she find me?*

I told her I went to an entirely different high school.

Not only that, I gave her a completely bogus story.

"Are you okay?" A tissue is pushed into my outstretched fingers. After wiping a hand across my mouth and blowing my nose, I nod.

Eyes watering, I boldly meet her dazed expression. She darts her head between Marsh and me like it's on a swivel.

Alarmed, I grip the tattered backpack lying on the floor between my legs tighter in my hands as she whispers, *"Elle."*

Now it's Marsh's turn to be caught off guard. I can't say I don't enjoy the surprise in her dry voice, since she is rather nosy.

This interruption takes the attention off my embarrassing display of public puking.

"You two know each other?" Marsh intones.

Charlotte's face relaxes into a smile, relief palpable on her face. I'm unfamiliar with the emotion because I've never seen Diane show anything but disdain for me.

Grumbling, I look up at Marsh. "This is my aunt."

"Since when do you have an aunt in town?"

"It's Diane's sister. Aunt Charlotte."

"Her?" She turns her nose up. "They don't look anything alike."

"Half." I smirk, adding, "Guess it's clear who got the better gene pool."

"She seems young." Marsh taps a gnarly finger to her lumpy chin.

"Uh . . ." Charlotte's stumped, unable to form a complete sentence. She's not a very good actress. I assumed she'd be better at lying, considering what she's been able to twist into truth, especially on the witness stand.

"Half," I say again. "Diane's at work, so she brought my lunch." I leave out the fact that I've never seen Diane bring home a paycheck from her job, and Charlotte actually has one, from what I've dug up on her.

"I forgot money for lunch." I then turn to Charlotte. "You brought it, right?"

All she can do is nod as Marsh quips, "I hope it's ginger ale and saltines."

Charlotte takes a hesitant step toward me. "Are you okay?"

"No. I feel like I'm coming down with something."

"You better go home." Marsh has seen students use every trick in the book to cut class, but even she has her limits when it comes to dislodging the contents of your stomach in front of her. "Do you want to wait in the car while I speak to her about your attendance?"

Shaking my head, I moan, "No."

"Then I'll say the same thing I've already said to you." Marsh pushes her glasses up her nose, her eyes enlarging behind the gigantic frames. "Please pass along to Diane that if *she*"—Marsh gives a stern nod in my direction—"continues to be late, she won't graduate on time. Better yet, I have a letter for Diane to read and sign."

Charlotte looks between us. Baffled, she says nothing.

"This can't keep happening," Marsh sniffs. "The importance of her being in class and on time is . . ."

"Paramount to her success," Charlotte finishes for her. "Absolutely." Awkwardly, she pats my shoulder. *Not so fast, lady.* My instincts kick in, and I pull out of her grasp.

"One more tardy or absence and you're suspended for a week." Marsh sadly waves a highlighted printout of my attendance record. "This is your last warning, young lady." Relieved that she folded it into a sealed envelope out of the scope of Charlotte's prying eyes, I shakily rise to my feet, depositing it in my backpack.

"What about being ill?" Charlotte looks at my sickly face with concern.

"I can see she's not feeling well. If she's not better tomorrow, I need a phone call before first period." Turning to me, she softens her tone. "Feel better, young lady." Narrowing her eyes, Marsh opens her mouth to say something to Charlotte, then abruptly shuts it.

Before Charlotte can start babbling, I exit the office, her boots clumping behind me.

"What was that?" she whispers as we walk out into the hall.

"Nothing," I mutter. "Just a typical day of school."

She touches my shoulder. "I'm sorry you're sick."

I cringe at her touch.

"Got a minute?"

I don't stop until I reach the locker I share with Justin. Spinning around, I hiss, "What are you doing here?"

"Do you mind telling me what's going on?"

"With the receptionist?" I shrug. "I was tardy today. I have a hard time waking up in the morning, and I'm clearly not feeling like roses today."

"No . . . I didn't mean that. When I tried to find you before this—"

"Find me?" I'm incredulous. "Find me *where*?"

"At the house."

"House?"

"On Larchwood."

I lower my voice. "Oh yeah, my house. You should've called first," I say, knowing full well she doesn't have my contact info.

"Yeah, I know." She stares at me, her eyes unyielding. "But I spoke to the woman who lives at the house, and she doesn't know you."

"So?"

"So, I dropped you off and watched you walk in the side door."

"And?"

"You had me drop you off at a house you don't live at."

"It's a friend's house."

"They don't have kids your age. They have a baby. And a toddler."

"I babysit them."

She stares me down. "What're their names?"

In return, I glare at her.

"This was the third high school I went to this morning. If you hadn't happened to be standing there, I wouldn't have found you."

"Seriously?" I turn crimson. "This is ridiculous. I don't even know you."

"You knocked on my door!"

"Yeah. I needed help. If I'd have known you were going to start investigating me—" I run a hand through my tangled hair. "I don't need a crazy stalker."

Charlotte's face grimaces when I call her crazy. I must've hit a nerve. Gingerly, she holds up a plastic bag. "I washed it."

"What is . . ."

"Your shirt. Figured you'd want it back."

Stubbornly, I say, "You could've kept it, but thank you."

"Why don't you have any Jonas Brothers posters in your locker?"

I give her a strange look. "Because it's my boyfriend's locker. We share."

"Do you always refer to your stepmom by her first name?"

"Just to be clear, it's *none* of your business." I bite my lip. "But thanks for returning my shirt."

Loudly, she says, "I was worried something happened to you. I watched you walk into that garage, and it was like you disappeared into thin air . . ."

A teacher sticks his bald head out, frowning at the two of us. Noticing the present adult, he grumbles incoherently, then slams his door.

"Lower your voice."

"It scared me, and," she whispers, "you're so young and pretty, and it just . . . I overstepped my boundaries coming here today." She sighs, "Look, you're right, it's none of my business." The air slowly expels out of her body, like she's a helium-filled balloon I just popped, and her body goes slack.

"Charlotte . . ."

After thrusting the bag into my hand, she spins on her heel and walks toward the bright-red exit sign. Without glancing over her shoulder, she disappears into the daylight.

CHAPTER 8
Charlotte

I barrel back to the Jeep, an angry tear caught in the corner of my eye. Swiping it in frustration as I'm perched in the driver's seat, I stare out at the cement parking lot and the remaining puddles filled with leftover rainwater.

As a woman, I understand why you would protect your identity from a stranger, and if anyone can relate, it's me. But the nagging feeling of giving Elle shelter and then having her make up a pretend life is peculiar.

Why would a seventeen-year-old be scared of providing insignificant facts? Most teens post every detail about their lives on social media, as if being immersed in the moment isn't enough. They tout almost every waking hour in front of an audience, begging people to comment on the most mundane details of their lives—the pumpkin-spice lattes at Starbucks or the selfie they took in a dangerous locale.

Maybe she doesn't have a good homelife. She did mention that her father married a nurse he worked with. Maybe it was an affair that ended poorly and uprooted her from her mother?

And I guess to her I am practically a stranger. Yet on some level that I can't quite describe, I feel an inkling of a motherly instinct toward her and detect a pain behind her blue eyes that's unvarnished. There's something familiar about her, but I don't know what it is. Maybe, just maybe, we have commonalities.

My cell rings, and I swipe it to answer.

"Charlotte, it's Dr. Everett. I'm checking to see how much longer until you arrive."

Shoot. I forgot my appointment. I glance at the clock on the dash. "Can you give me twenty minutes?"

"Sure. Camille stepped out, so you can come straight back to my office."

"Sounds good." I disconnect, my movements jerky as I head down a side street and make a U-turn. *Get it together, Charlotte.*

When I arrive at the nondescript building reminiscent of a mid-century bungalow, I stride up the walkway to the office of Dr. Meredith Everett. As she prewarned me, Camille is not at her post, so I rap the half-open door sharply.

"Come in."

"Hi, Dr. Everett."

"Hi yourself, Charlotte. Is everything okay?" Her pale-blue eyes greet me with worry. "You seemed rushed on the phone." Her hair's prematurely white, a contrast to her leathery tan skin, yet the lines on her face make her appear distinguished instead of old.

Sinking into the soft, buttery leather couch, I nod. "Unforeseen circumstances."

"I'll be right there." She shuts her laptop, then stands to close the blinds to shutter the sunlight. "This okay?"

"Yes." I lean my head against the back of the couch, automatically closing my eyes.

"I know you don't always like the dark." She switches on the brass lamp that's next to me.

"It's good right now. I have the start of a headache."

"How're your meds?"

"Depends on the day. With my list of phobias, it's amazing I function at all." I keep my eyes shut and hear the rustle of her notepad as she moves to the overstuffed chair and matching ottoman across from me.

"Do you feel they are helping you to function at a less-heightened state?"

"I think so."

"Well, you've had a lot of upheaval in your personal life," she muses. "I'm proud of you for continuing to come to therapy and engage with me, so thank you."

"I should be thanking you," I say. "I think Noah and I are making strides, or at least we were until today."

Her pen floats over the page. "Do you have something to share?"

"I think Noah and I are pregnant."

"What? That's wonderful news." Her voice rises an octave as she tries not to sound too over the top. I can tell she's not the type to let emotions get the best of her, which is part of why I respect her. She's reserved yet forthcoming. "Since you started coming to see me a couple months ago, you've shared your desire to someday have children."

"It's a bit premature." I try not to sound as giddy as I feel inside. "But all the signs are there."

"Did you tell Noah yet?"

"He said whatever happens, happens."

"How does that make you feel?" she presses. "Excited? Vulnerable? Hopeful?"

Suddenly I feel shy and rest my hand against my face. "A combination of all three. Noah travels a lot, and I'm hoping he might cut back if we have a little one on the way, so I don't feel so emotionally detached, like last time."

"But that was a different relationship, was it not?" she gently probes, consulting her notes.

I nod but don't elaborate. I'm not in the mood to dismiss my happy news for something that was gut wrenching. For once, they don't need to share the same space, the emotions of both on opposite ends of the spectrum.

"We can discuss your meds at the end of our session, in terms of what can interfere with your pregnancy and what you can take. It's imperative you keep attending our sessions, especially since your hormones will be jumping all over, and you'll be dealing with fears from the past and phobias that will continue to manifest, based on your history."

"Of course."

"So back to why you were late?"

"I found myself in a predicament."

"In terms of?"

"It brought to my attention how untrusting I am of others. And how others are the same of me." I pause, gathering my thoughts. "I prematurely accused Noah of cheating . . ." I stop briefly. "At least, this time."

"And?" she intones.

"This woman is still a permanent itch that can't be scratched."

"Is this," Dr. Everett asks, scanning her notes, "Lauren you are referencing?"

I sigh. "Yes."

"What makes you bring her up today, and how does she hinder your trust issues with your husband?"

"I thought she might've been at our house."

"Inside?"

"Yes." Overwrought at the thought of her rifling through my drawers or being privy to my most personal effects and Noah's, I feel a sharp stab of anger that shifts me in my seat. "I felt this sinking feeling, like we were starting over at the beginning, and I wondered if I'd be able to go down that dark path again." I shrug. "I felt helpless."

She motions to my ring finger and points out, "But he's your husband." As I gaze at my wedding band, the light from the lamp next to me dances off the diamond baguettes.

"But . . ."

Dr. Everett gently chastises me. "Why is there always a *but*?"

"She took him from me when I needed him the most."

"And that's how you see it?"

"No, it's not how I see it. It's the truth, based on facts, not my opinion."

I watch as she peruses her notes. "And you blame Lauren more for the encounter than Noah?"

"Yes." I pick at an imaginary piece of lint. "She was the aggressor."

"Okay, so let's discuss this transgression. How is Lauren the only one at fault here?" Dr. Everett peers at me, her blue depths searching mine. "How does Noah not have a part in this? I don't want to sound insensitive, since he's your spouse, but I'm trying to piece this together."

"It's a valid question." I give her a small smile. "We were drunk, Noah and I. We had been out on the town, and since Lauren was staying with us, I didn't think it was an issue to tell them to go back to the house while I made sure a friend got home safely. I've known them both since college, and I trusted them together until I walked in on them in bed together."

It's clear by the tears how much this still affects me. I can picture my horrified expression as I walked in the dark bedroom, greeted by a moan I knew belonged to Noah, followed by a strange guttural sound that was out of place and didn't belong in my bed.

Startled, I told myself I was imagining it, that Lauren must've brought another guy back to the house—my refusal to comprehend that either could have violated my trust and loyalty, not to mention the emotional damage they had inflicted on me.

Dr. Everett leans over and hands me a tissue. Déjà vu from earlier, when I passed Elle a tissue. "You still feel Lauren has it out for you?"

"Yes." Blotting my wet cheeks, I continue. "Back then, she pined for Noah, and I ignored all the signs." My fingers dab impatiently at my nose. "Friends told me she wanted him and to watch out, but I assumed she'd never act on any feelings, even if she did have them. Christ, we used to be roommates."

"And now you are afraid history's going to repeat itself, and she's somehow going to end up back in your house and in your bed and lay claim to your husband?"

"Honestly, yes. I don't want her intruding in my life or *our* lives."

"But why is this manifesting itself now, Charlotte?" She muses, "Is it because you see a potential pregnancy as something that would bring her back into your lives?"

"I know how much having kids means to her."

"And she doesn't have any?"

"As far as I know, she can't. Something with her ovaries."

"Okay, so back to my original question." Her pen clicks against the pad. "What does this have to do with you?"

"I'm scared she hasn't let go of him."

Gently she asks, "Or maybe that he hasn't let go of her?"

I recoil, the truth of her words stinging with authenticity.

"What will it take for you to trust your husband again?" Dr. Everett leans forward to drive her point home. "I want to hear you say it out loud, connect the dots, Charlotte."

"I need to know they aren't in communication."

"Anything else?"

"Him to be present more." It's vague, so I add, "Physically and emotionally."

"And with this pregnancy, you're going to need all the reassurance you can get. Is that right?"

"Absolutely." I brush a frustrated hand through my hair. "I need to know our family life is stable and there's no chance of him ruining it again." I continue, "And I know nothing is absolute." My headache threatens to puncture my skull as it stabs at my temples. "But I'm tired of feeling alone in this."

"But guess what, Charlotte? You have coping skills and mechanisms, and from our time together, I've watched you grow in your strength and resolve to put this behind you, which isn't easy. I admire your ability to forgive."

Nodding, I grasp the tissue in my hands hard enough that it starts to rip in half.

"Charlotte, Lauren's not getting in the way of your happiness anymore. You are."

A beep interrupts us, the timer signaling our session is over, and I haltingly rise from the couch.

"We will continue this next week. I'd like you to consider how Lauren impinges on your ability to be happy."

I dig in my wallet and pull out cash, the way I always pay, and fork over $300 for the session. No wonder Dr. Everett is a fan of my dedication to therapy.

"Yes, will do. Thank you, Dr. Everett."

"Let's discuss your medication before you leave."

After she explains what is safe during pregnancy and what has harmful side effects, she gives my arm a light squeeze. "Please call me if you need anything."

CHAPTER 9
Elle

After Charlotte stalks out of the building, I slam my head against the cold metal locker.

Stupid, stupid, stupid, I berate myself. What the hell am I doing? I *need* Charlotte. She's my way out. How am I supposed to get close to her if I push her away?

And in typical Elle fashion, I let my stubborn side rear its ugly head—or as my mother used to call it, my "bull in a china shop" attitude. In less than twenty-four hours, I've messed up what I started out to accomplish.

I need to backtrack, and fast.

When I run out to the parking lot, I see no sign of her charcoal Jeep. I check the teachers' lot and the roundabout where parents drop their kids off. She probably tore out of here like a bat out of hell. *Shit.* I clench my fists. I royally screwed up.

Since this is now an excused absence, I leave Justin a note in his locker telling him to stop by the apartment after school. I curl up in a ball when I get to the apartment, and not even the sounds of my neighbor's barking rottweiler can rouse me.

It's not until I'm awakened later by the sound of the front door and look at the ugly grandfather clock that stands foolishly in the living room that I notice the time.

I croak, amazed at my ability to sleep all day.

Expecting the boys to run inside with their usual whirlwind of energy, I squeeze a smile on my face.

What am I going to be able to make them for a snack?

Tired of living like this, I forcefully slam the cupboards, their peeling wood and broken handles a constant reminder of my situation.

Instead, it's Justin, wearing his typical outfit of ripped Levis and black Vans sneakers, grinning with his lopsided smile. His skateboard's always tucked underneath one arm, and as if it's a newborn, he delicately sets it down by the door.

"Where you been, woman?" He leans in casually, teasing me with his tongue. Usually I love the taste of him, but today the smell of his cigarettes mixed with cologne makes me queasy.

As I turn my face, his lips brush my cheek instead. "I'm not feeling well."

"Oh shit, that's not good. Cold or flu?"

Weakly, I smile. "I threw up in the office today."

"Ouch. That's rough. You seem kind of hot." He rubs a hand over my forehead. "And your forehead does too."

I giggle. He always finds a way to make me laugh, even when he says dumb shit.

"Can I make you anything?"

"Unless you can magically make food appear, the cupboards are bare."

"Your phone working?"

"No." I roll my eyes. "It ran out of minutes today. Think you can get me another prepaid card?"

"I'm just glad you had it during the storm."

"I know."

"Diane's such a lowlife." He mutters, "Yeah, I'll see what I can do." He tugs gently on my messy ponytail. "Why don't you come stay with me?"

"At your brother's?" Then I sigh, "Where would we sleep?"

"Where I sleep." He shrugs. "We could get an air mattress, snuggle up together on the floor, be together all the time." Pulling me in to him, he seems *so sure*. But Justin's situation is no better than mine. He got kicked out of his parents' house a couple months ago after his dad took a swing at him when he went to defend his mom from his father's abuse. Now he mooches off his college-age brother, Brad, who lives with three friends in a house that reeks of marijuana, dirty socks, and expired Chinese food.

His "bedroom" is a rinky-dink secondhand couch that was left on the screened-in back porch by the previous tenants. It has more stains than my tie-dyed art projects from junior high. Some are beer—I can tell by the barley smell—but most are suspect.

The time I've spent there over the last three months has been hell, the space heater never reaching far enough to warm a substantial amount of space. There aren't enough blankets to prevent the frigid air from squeezing into every invisible nook and cranny, even the ones you'd swear were covered. The few times I've stayed over, all of this was made worse by the fact that I would wake up to loud metal music, pot smoke, and the sorest throat ever, the chills running bone deep. Probably why I'm sick now. Even with winter behind us, the thought of staying over there causes me to shudder.

"I'll think about it," I say, not wanting to hurt his feelings.

My focus on how to make amends with Charlotte is at the forefront of my mind, even while we watch an afternoon talk show, which, without cable, is one of our only choices.

I must've fallen asleep, because when I wake up, an old blanket has been laid across my frame, and a bowl of chicken noodle soup is on the dusty coffee table next to me. Justin's brought a couple packs of ramen back for the kids as well.

I smile, his thoughtful gesture appreciated.

The next day I feel fine, but the wave of nausea hits me out of nowhere, and I alternate between throwing up and sleeping. Between my fatigue and my illness, I'm hell bent on reconnecting with Charlotte. It's not a matter of want; it's a matter of need. I have to figure out a way to approach her and apologize for my bad attitude toward her kind gesture.

Without having minutes for my phone, I cannot contact her, and the number I found online is disconnected—probably an old cell number.

Torn, I don't want to email her at work. That would be an invasion of privacy, since she hasn't told me where she teaches. I don't want to freak her out when she's skittish enough.

After going back to the scene of the crime, specifically our introduction, I ring her doorbell to apologize, but she never answers the door. I don't even see the blinds move to uncover her face peering out at me.

After writing a thank-you letter, I leave it in her mailbox, and, frowning at the bright peacock, I silently beg it to give her the message. Then, getting desperate, I consider finding her class schedule and showing up. *But you can't,* I remind myself. *That's crazy behavior and will push her further from you. She will wonder why it matters so much that you find her.*

One night, I'm huddled on my mattress underneath the threadbare Spider-Man comforter I borrowed from the boys and staring at a pile of clean clothes on the couch—I just washed them in our community laundry room with some quarters that Diane brought home from the casino. I don't ask if they're her winnings or the leftover change from what she spent. I don't ask because I don't want to know.

Bright-yellow fabric peers out from the bottom of the pile.

Snapping my fingers, I have it—the golden ticket. Charlotte's raincoat. She told me to just keep it, but I'm going to *have* to return it to her.

But how?

She's been a ghost.

Impatient, I've been strolling around the lake, walking past her house, and I never see any vehicles come or go. I'm worried the neighbors are getting suspicious, since I'm always alone and out of place or futilely knocking on her door. And as much as I try to blend in, I'm not one of them.

Spending another aimless afternoon walking around the lake, I hear two women in an animated discussion about an upcoming trip to the Bahamas one's family is taking. As they walk and jog, I stay behind them, eavesdropping on their conversation.

"What're you going to do with Checkers?" the shorter one, wearing skintight jogging pants, asks. "The last time you boarded him, he came home ten pounds lighter and with kennel cough."

"Well, the Carters told me about an app that pairs you with dog walkers and sitters near your location."

My ears perk up, the conversation securing my undivided attention. "You can find someone local that comes to your house, or vice versa. We're going to try it for this trip, see how it goes."

The women switch topics, this time to boring housewife shit, like whose friend's husband slept with the new Pilates instructor, but inside I'm tingling with excitement.

Inspired, I start to actually run, passing them both as I make my way around the length of the water, a fire lit under my ass. A job I can make money at that provides me a reason to be walking in her neighborhood?

Perfect.

The only issue is my inconsistent phone plan, but I have an idea.

If Diane knows I have a job and plan to contribute to bills, she'll be willing to help. I decide to talk to her later that night.

At first, she looks skeptical.

"People need pet and house sitting that much?" Her glasses move down the bridge of her nose as she wrinkles it.

"Yes," I say. "I can show you the app." Diane lets me download it on her phone, just so she can scroll through the current list of available pet sitters.

"Well, I'll be damned." She gives me a Diane smile, which is more of a sneer. "I'll get you some more minutes on your phone."

Then she gives me a brilliant idea for when I set up my profile—to use the neighbor's mutt and a feral apartment cat as previous experience. I embellish a bit, pretending I once worked at a now-closed pet store. I mention my years of babysitting experience. That has to count for something.

I upload some references and hold my breath.

Using Charlotte's zip code as my own, I get an in-box full of potential clients before long. Because I'm flexible and can stay at their homes, I can do double duty and water plants while watching their houses as well. I reject the ones that are too far away and make up excuses for people who want their pets to come to me.

Over the next couple of weeks, I stop by Charlotte's house and ring the bell. It goes unanswered. I'm almost positive she and Noah are on vacation. The house shows no signs of life, and even the peacock fills up with mail.

One of my jobs involves house and dog sitting a terrier named Benji for a family a few streets over from Charlotte. I stroll past her house daily, sometimes multiple times, as he sniffs his way through the immaculate lawns. I'm careful to clean up after him, not wanting to get bad reviews or complaints from the neighbors.

The assignment is a long one, over two weeks, and one day I'm rushing to catch up as he roams his way through the subdivision. Benji has stopped to mark a shrub when I hear a dull thud, and the squeak of a garage door occupies my attention.

It's Charlotte's stall slowly opening.

I watch her shift into reverse, my legs feeling like rubber.

It's now or never.

I'm tired of wearing or carrying her damned jacket all the time in case I finally spot her. I yank it off.

Launching down the street, Benji yaps at my heels, sure we're playing a game of tag. I pause at the end of her driveway, but she doesn't notice me in her mirrors until I'm standing directly behind her, waving the bright-yellow coat like a flag.

Taking a deep breath, I yell, "Wait!"

The Jeep hesitates as her window slides down. "What in the . . .?"

"Wait, please wait." I hurry to the driver's side. "I still have your jacket." Scared she'll close the window before it's safely in the vehicle, I hold it in the air as a peace offering.

Gaping at me, she considers me for a moment. "It's okay, you can have it. You didn't need to make a trip back here for that old thing."

"But it's not mine, it's yours." We stare at each other in tense silence, her eyes darting down to the twenty-pound yapping dog beside me.

"Keep it."

"I'm really sorry," I say.

Benji barks, and Charlotte peers at him. "Is that yours?"

"No." A blush burns on my cheeks. "I'm dog sitting."

"In my neighborhood?"

"Yeah, I've met a lot of the neighbors from hanging out at the lake. Someone needed a dog sitter last minute, and I volunteered." I grin and add, "It was a lucrative job opportunity."

She nods, her eyes shifting to the rearview mirror, and her hand lifts from the gear shift.

"Look," I rush to add, "I'm sorry for how I acted. You were so kind and thoughtful, and I was an asshole."

Her face tightens. "It's okay, Elle, really. You were right: I am a perfect stranger."

"Yeah, but you're not." I shrug. "You were so nice to me, and I didn't deserve it."

Giving a backward wave, she says, "It's water under the bridge."

"I can't handle you being mad at me."

She brusquely motions toward the street. "Don't worry about it. I'm a nobody." Her eyes glance at the digital clock on her dashboard. "I've got to be going or I'll be late for an appointment."

"Can we talk again?"

"About what?"

"I want to interview you."

Her knuckles go white, and I glimpse trepidation in her eyes. "For what?"

"For one of my classes—home economics."

"They still have that?"

"It's more PC now," I snicker. "They call it 'life skills.'"

"What do you need me for?"

"Those cookies," I say, grabbing my stomach, "are the best I've ever had. I think I gained five pounds from eating them in one sitting. We're supposed to pick a family recipe that means something to us and bring it in for the class to try, with a typed interview of who it belongs to and the significance."

"Why not someone in your family?"

"Because no one cooks. I can't bring in Stove Top Stuffing or mac and cheese and explain the importance."

"I don't think so." Charlotte bites her lip. "It's painful to talk about my mom."

Benji interrupts by letting out a loud yip, then a growl, at a rabbit that catches his eye. Tugging on the leash, he leaves me no choice but to follow—or risk his running off and being dragged along with him.

"Have a good day." Backing out of the drive, she offers, "And good luck with the dog." Rushing to keep up with Benji, I watch her speed off, my attempt at a second chance dissolving into thin air. Then, stomping my foot angrily, I crumple the raincoat up in my fist.

CHAPTER 10
Charlotte

I heat a kettle on the stove top and drum my fingers impatiently on the kitchen island. It's a Friday night, and people my age are out to dinner, or at the movies, or spending time with their families. Noah's nowhere in sight, stuck at the airport due to a flight delay, and I'm cooped up in the house, per the usual.

Worse, I've been squeamish all day—the effects of morning sickness, I presume.

I slam a mug down harder than I intend, the ceramic handle cracking, the extent of my frustration realized. Is it so bad to want a reason to get dressed up, go out on the town, change out of stained sweatpants, and celebrate with Noah?

My eyes are tired from grading student essays, and after posting feedback online, I settle back against the couch, restless. Tapping my laptop keys with no real purpose in mind, I can't believe what I type in the search bar.

Lauren Wilder.

Her face pops up, her dark-brown hair cut into a chic bob, her figure still athletic and taut, her smile still slightly crooked. Her profession is listed as a "labor and delivery nurse." I almost laugh at the irony. I guess if you can't have your own, you might as well deliver them.

Before I can control old habits that haven't died hard, or at all, I anxiously type in another name from the past. Almost as if I expect him to appear out of thin air, my eyes dart around the living room, and I visually inspect whether the dead bolt is secure.

My face turns crimson as I imagine what Dr. Everett would say if she were in the room, along with the disapproving stare she would give me at my time-management choices.

Jonathan Randall.

Article after article pops up on the screen.

"Kansas Man with History of Reckless Behavior Sentenced."

"Man Recently Charged in Vehicular Manslaughter Now Charged with Attempted Murder."

"Domestic Abuser Crosses Over to Murder."

The blood rushes to my head, and instantaneously I'm overcome with a sense of despair that latches on to me. Curling my legs up, I rest my palms against my forehead, my accelerated pulse a sign of an impending panic attack.

The phone rings, and I fumble for it, grateful for the interruption. Earlier, when I was unnerved, I left Noah a voice mail. Assuming it's him, I don't bother looking at the screen. He told me earlier he'd call me before he boarded his flight.

Before I can say a word, a throaty voice purrs through the line. "It's about time we talked, honey." My stomach flutters as if I have just been launched on an upside-down roller coaster. Multiple times.

"Nancy." I curl my fingers. "How'd you get my cell this time? I just had it changed, yet again."

"By now, I would think you'd get smart and stop switching numbers, since I always manage to find it." Then she huffs, "Besides, is this any way to address your own mother?"

"My mother is dead," I say coldly.

"You always did have a flair for the dramatic."

"What do you want, Nancy?"

"For you to stop ignoring me," she grunts. "How long are you going to blame me?"

"You wrote *him* a letter."

"Charlotte, he's been in prison for ten years."

"It's not enough."

"The child needs her father."

"*We* had a child who needed a father." My voice rises. "He almost went free because of you."

"I told the truth." Then she pointedly says, "He's served long enough."

"That's *your* opinion."

"Hasn't therapy taught you anything about forgiveness?"

I don't respond, and an uncomfortable silence ensues.

"You don't have to worry about me anymore, Nancy. Everything is fine. But when we speak, it dredges up the past, and I can't go back anymore. I'm sure you can understand. I'm going to go now, okay?" Without waiting for an answer, I end the call.

I shut my phone off and shove it underneath the cushion next to me.

Curling into a fetal position, I picture a morning almost eleven years ago when I wasn't estranged from my mother. It was the middle of January when I woke up and the power was out. My second call after the electric company was to my boyfriend at the time, Jonathan. It went straight to voice mail, as if the phone was dead or shut off. I tried again. He always charged his phone on the nightstand, but maybe the power had been out for most of the night.

I need warmth and a cup of coffee, so I brush my teeth, lace my snow boots up, and drive to my mother's house a few miles away. The road is icy, because the snowplow hasn't reached our dead-end street yet. Driving under the speed limit in normal conditions would take all of five minutes, but today it takes twenty-five. I am awed by the lack of color, and just a white maze of bleak landscape stretches for miles in the distance. I turn the heat on high and rub my gloved hands together for warmth, eyes laser focused on the patches of glaring ice. The worst is the black kind, invisible to the naked eye but capable of sending you into a tailspin. And that's exactly what my life turns into at that juncture—a tailspin.

When I arrive at my mother's, the front door of her cozy bungalow immediately opens, and the look of concern on her face is replaced by one of pity.

"Oh my God, thank the Lord you're okay." A hand is laid over her heart, her gold cross necklace nestled in the collar of her turtleneck sweater.

"Yeah," I say, stamping my feet on the mat, "we're freezing, since the power's out, but everything's fine."

"I've been trying to reach you for the last hour, ever since I heard the news." A cup of hot coffee lands in my hands, and I gratefully hold it to my chapped lips. "I was about to head to your place, but you know I have a terrible time in this kind of weather."

I sink into the couch—the small living room filled with warmth, the fireplace loaded with logs, the aroma of cinnamon and sugar wafting from the kitchen—and ignore the tension in her voice.

"I hope the power will be back on by this afternoon. I can't get ahold of Jonathan. Weird he's gone so early."

A puzzled look crosses my mother's face. "Oh my God, honey, I thought that's why you came over."

"No, we have no heat." I grip the cup in my hand. "This fire feels amazing."

"I'm sure he'll be calling you soon."

"What do you mean?"

"He was on the news."

I go completely numb. "What're you talking about, Mother?"

"There was an accident."

Paralyzed with fear, worried my boyfriend has been gravely injured, I start uncontrollably shaking. "What're you talking about, what kind of an accident? Speak!" I command her. "What is going on?"

"He's alive, but he injured someone—pretty badly, from what the lady on TV said."

"How?"

"He was drunk, Charlotte."

"Mother, you always say that."

"Charlotte Rose, this isn't my opinion, this is a fact. He was drunk driving and hit a woman."

"When?" The earth starts to sway beneath me. Could Kansas have earthquakes, I wonder, and in the middle of winter? "Is he hurt?"

"Early this morning."

"But the storm, there was a bad storm, it could've happened to anyone."

"Charlotte, he's in jail. He has a broken arm, but she's . . . they aren't sure she's going to make it." My mother reaches for my hand, holding it in a viselike grip. "And Charlotte, the woman he injured, she's nine months pregnant, and they don't know if either her or the baby are going to make it."

Trembling, I pull myself out from under the heavy weight of this memory, inadvertently rubbing a hand over my own stomach, and the weight of bringing a child into this unforgiving world gives me pause. Ruminating on these thoughts, I warn myself not to go down the rabbit hole to my previous life again.

When I sit up and touch my laptop, the screen flickers from dark to light, forcing me to read the headline of an article I dread. "Man Charged with Manslaughter in Unborn Baby's Death."

Unsteady on my feet, I feel a rattling sensation underneath me. In a hampered state, I walk to the kitchen, fumbling at the tap with a glass of water to down some headache medicine with.

A strange throbbing pulsates through my body as if Jonathan's inside my very being, shaking me like a rag doll. When I realize the groaning protest is coming from below the polished concrete, I shift my weight over the sink in apprehension.

It's coming from the basement.

Tentatively, I close the gap between the kitchen and basement door and fumble with the padlock, whose key is attached to my cross necklace. After managing to open the door, I stare down the steep, threatening stairway. The rest of the house is lived in, carefully decorated, and tasteful. But the basement . . . the basement is unfinished, uncultivated, and bare.

Agonizing over what to do, I fling the door shut and frantically lock it.

I need to go down there, but the memories . . .

I stand back from the door as if it will swallow me whole and press my eyes shut, trying not to collapse into a heap.

"I can do it, I can do it, I can do it," I repeat, over and over.

But I'm not ready, and, leaning against the wood, I breathe heavily as I repeat the opposite, over and over.

"I can't do it. I can't do it. I can't do it."

CHAPTER 11
Elle

Tonight's my last night dog sitting Benji before his family gets home from vacation. I think they said the Caribbean, but it makes no difference to me, because an island is surrounded on all sides by water, and from my place in the Midwest, it's just a dot on the map. It's somewhere I'll never visit.

I give Benji one last belly rub and dog biscuit before I close the door and then slide the key into a lockbox out front. Touching my face, I trace the outline of the nasty scratch I got from a monster-car rally the boys and I had last night. One got too rough with his vehicle and rammed it into my cheek, along with his grubby fingernails. I thought the point was to drive on the makeshift track I'd made from construction paper and designed to look like a raceway, but he went off-roading, as he called it. It didn't help that Justin had encouraged them to pick their own paths to the finish line, and therefore, since he was a god to the boys, they decided that there was no set track.

When the race ended, we had a long talk about being respectful of other people's personal space, and I was forced to use a bag of frozen peas as an ice pack.

As I walk down the street, I ignore the bus stop and the fact that there's only one last coach running in this subdivision tonight. For some reason, the route ends earlier in this part of town. Probably to keep out the riffraff like me.

I put my hand in my pocket, closing it around a metal clasp.

It's now or never.

I can't lose my confidence.

Jogging down the street, I feel my heart pound with exertion as I run a couple laps before I make my way up the steps to Charlotte's porch. I pound hysterically on the door, screaming, until I hear timid footsteps.

"Help me, help me, Charlotte, please . . ."

A light flickers on inside as I heave, doubling over to catch my breath.

"It's me, Elle, help me, open up," I cry, slamming my fist against her heavy door. My knuckle cries out in pain. The porch light beams a slight glimmer of illumination.

She cracks the door open an inch, her hands pressed against the screen. "What's going on?" An edge fringes her voice. I can understand why. It's after ten on a Friday night, and it's me again.

"Elle." She rubs a hand over her eyes. "What is it?" She looks past me, as if anticipating bad weather or a gang of thugs. Standing up straight, I yank a red leash out of my pocket.

"Benji, he . . . ran . . . oh my God, he ran . . ." I grab the column on the porch for steadiness, as if it can hold me together.

"Who?"

"The dog," I stammer, "the one I'm watching. His owners come home tomorrow, and he got away from me." I thrust the leash in her face. "He ran off, down by the lake." I gasp in disbelief. "Another dog came up to us, a shepherd mix of some sort, and I had to let poor Benji go . . . he was going to be attacked."

Looking startled, Charlotte asks me to describe the vicious dog. "I wonder if it's the O'Connors' down the street in the white house. They have a German shepherd." She unlocks the screen door and steps out barefoot, pausing on the welcome mat.

"No, I've seen that one before."

"Did he get your face?"

"This?" I rub my hand over my cheek like it's nothing. "Yeah, but who cares? I just want to find Benji. He means the world to those kids."

"Did the other dog chase after him?"

"At first, but a man started calling for him, and he ran back up the hill. I couldn't catch Benji; he was already gone." Trembling, I sniffle, "His owners are going to kill me, and what if something happens to him? He's only a year old . . ."

"Wait a minute." She holds up a hand. "Calm down and take a deep breath."

"I'm sorry to bother you . . . it's late, but . . . I don't have anybody else to help, and you live so close."

"Which way did he run?" She motions me to follow her into the house, back in the direction of the kitchen. "Did he go toward the wooded area or more toward the other cluster of homes?"

"He went toward the woods."

"Do you have any dog treats?"

"Yeah, I have a couple of Milk-Bones, his favorite."

"Okay, let's split up." Charlotte looks for a pair of shoes and shoves her feet into slides.

"You'll really help me? Oh my God, thank you, Charlotte," I sigh. "You're a lifesaver."

"Don't get too excited yet," she warns me. "We have to find him first."

"You think something bad will happen to him?" I run a hand over my eyes. "This is a nightmare. I never should've taken on this responsibility. I suck at this."

"Elle, it'll be fine. The hardest part is coaxing him home, and with treats it shouldn't be hard."

"You're right," I murmur. "He's just gotta be found."

"I'm going to go out the back and head toward the wooded area, okay? I don't want you going in that part, just because it's easy to get lost in the dark. You head toward the other side of the subdivision." She reaches into the emergency kit she had the other night. "Here, take a flashlight, and I'll just use the one on my phone. Hand me a couple of treats, and we should be good."

"What do we do if we find him? How do we communicate?"

"Call or text me. You have your phone, right?"

"Yeah." Shakily, I pull it out. She starts ticking off her number but stops when she looks at my fingers trembling. Evidently taking pity on me, she grabs the phone. "I'm shooting myself a text so you don't have to worry about dialing it wrong."

With that, she runs off in the direction of the looming forest, her phone light barely making a dent in the darkness. She heads down a small path as I sprint the opposite way, shrieking "Benji!" and shining my flashlight through the grass for the missing dog.

I walk around the neighborhood, halfheartedly calling his name. I make sure it's far from the owners' house, because I don't want the neighbors to tell them I misplaced their dog. My five-star rating will tank before my gig has even begun to grow.

Eventually, I make my way back to Benji, and after clipping his leash on him, I take him for one last hurrah around the block. I wait at least twenty minutes before I snap a picture of him to send to Charlotte, and she responds with a smiley face emoji. I let her know I'm going to take him back to his house, and then I'll stop back over. She opens her front door before I can even knock. "I'm so glad you found him—especially since I couldn't. It was touch and go for a while."

"Me too." I shrug. "It's amazing dogs have the instinct to find their way home. He was waiting for me, completely unbothered."

"You can have these back." She hands me the treats. "Are you staying over at their place?"

"Yeah, for one last night." She doesn't ask any follow-up questions or press the ride issue, probably because of how it turned out last time.

"Can I buy you breakfast in the morning to thank you for everything when I leave their place?" I offer.

"No, that's kind of you, but Noah will be home."

She must catch the crestfallen expression on my face and evidently reconsiders. "Are you starved right now after that search and rescue, because I am."

I've ignored the hunger pangs in my stomach, but now that she mentions food, a loud growl interrupts us. "More than I thought."

"Then let's go to one of my favorite diners. It's open twenty-four hours and has all the typical greasy food that tastes amazing." Charlotte grabs her purse. "I need to get out of the house—I'm going stir crazy."

We climb into her Jeep, and a call comes through her Bluetooth as we're driving. Noah's name pops up on the screen.

"Mind if I answer?"

"Of course not," I murmur, staring out the window and pretending not to listen to a conversation for once I'm forced to eavesdrop on.

Charlotte presses a button on her steering wheel. "Hi, Noah."

"Char, is everything all right? I got your message."

"Yeah, the furnace is just acting up, making a strange rattle."

"It's probably the blower. I'll have someone take a look at it this weekend."

"Not you?"

"No, not me." He sighs audibly through the phone. "I'm sorry, Char. The plane's finally here after another delay—this time a maintenance issue—but I've got to head back and take care of some business."

I see her face droop. "What type of business?"

"I have to get all the papers signed. Meeting with the attorneys and everything should be all good on this end. I'll book a flight and hopefully be there by Sunday evening. I didn't wake you, did I?"

Giving a lopsided grin to the speakers, she seems less melancholy. "No, I'm just heading to the Thirty-Sixth Street Diner." The sound of her voice makes her seem younger. Not so buttoned up and serious. "I'm craving their infamous grilled cheese."

"It's only that good because they use a pound of butter." Noah whistles. "But damn, do they do a good job." In the background, a woman shrills something over a loudspeaker. "Oh, preboarding has started. See you soon."

"Safe flight."

"Yeah, get some sleep. Love ya."

With that, Noah's rich baritone disconnects, and the DJ replaces his voice with "Can't Buy Me Love," by the Beatles, a song even I know.

CHAPTER 12
Charlotte

At the diner, I lead Elle to a back table, the place surprisingly packed with an eclectic mix of customers. Teenagers are blowing the paper-straw wrappers at one another, watching as they fly across the booth.

The other group is "after-activities people," as I refer to them: those who went out to a movie or a show and crave comfort food at the end. The third group is senior citizens who walk across from the retirement home, tired of rice pudding and runny cottage cheese.

Elle's face lights up as she scoots into a shiny burgundy booth that has flecks of silver glitter and white piping. "This is totally old school." She examines the menu eagerly, her eyes scanning the extensive list of ice cream flavors.

"I love the banana-cream malt." I grin. "And they have the best fries—they're crispy, not soggy." After our earlier interaction ended with Elle berating me, I'm uncertain on what topics are safe. With my eyes glued to the laminated menu, I'm contemplating the food options, knowing full well I'll order the grilled cheese.

Elle follows my lead and orders a malt, her attention focused on the retro jukebox that cranks out oldies by artists like Buddy Holly and Ritchie Valens. The diner's known for its plethora of malt and shake options and the black-and-white tiled floor and mirrored ceiling.

"Charlotte?" Elle asks. "What does Noah do for work?"

"He works for a real estate investment company and handles properties all over the US, but really even international."

"Wow, sounds important." She folds her hands in her lap. "So he deals with lots of land and paperwork and travel."

"And litigation," I say. "He stays busy, and it's not a nine-to-five job, which is why things come up last minute with travel."

"Does it make you sad when he's not at home?"

"It can, but I know it's for us, and the . . ." I stop, about to offer information I'm not ready to. Instead I say, "Our future."

As I go back to my menu, Elle says my name again.

"Uh-huh?" I keep my gaze level with the menu. The waitress brings our waters and malts. Strawberry for Elle, banana cream for me. We both settled on grilled cheese and tomato soup, splitting a platter of fries between us.

"Charlotte?"

"Yes?" I meet her eyes, her thick lashes fringed with tears.

"I'm sorry." She plays with a bracelet on her thin wrist. "I shouldn't have been so bitchy about you coming to my school. Thanks for bringing my shirt back. And letting me stay at your house during the storm. That was really cool of you."

"You're welcome," I say, holding my breath, unsure of where to go from here. Do I dare ask anything personal, or will it drive a wedge further between us? I decide to let her lead the conversation.

I unwrap my metal spoon from the napkin. I prefer to scoop the malt instead of sucking it through a straw.

After we've had time to devour our desserts, our faces sticky with ice cream, she offers, "It's just . . ." Her face burns red. "I don't like where I live."

"How so?"

"I wish I lived in that Cape Cod house. Or in your subdivision. But I don't."

"Is it because you just like those houses better than yours?"

"Not even." Elle lowers her eyes. "I'm in an apartment over by the Elmore district."

"Okay." I don't know where that is, but she makes it sound dangerous. "Is that bad?"

"It's a rough neighborhood."

"And you're seventeen, is that right?"

"Yeah, though sometimes I feel like seventeen going on forty-seven." She taps her fingers on the shiny tabletop. "How about you?"

"It's impolite to ask a woman her age."

"Then why did you ask me?"

"You're a teenager." I point to my forehead. "Until you have fine lines and wrinkles, it's okay to reveal your age."

Scrunching her nose, she says, "I don't see any on your face."

"I'll take that compliment." I laugh. "I'm midthirties."

"I just don't like talking about me." Elle shrugs. "I never feel like there's anything interesting to mention."

A server interrupts us with the food, the Formica table filling up with plates and soup bowls. My mouth waters as I take a bite of the grilled cheese, and I can't help but murmur, "So good." I can tell Elle feels the same by the way she's inhaling the soup, each spoonful disappearing swiftly into her mouth, the bowl emptying faster than I can find my silverware.

Feeling like I'm propped on a land mine, I decide to risk an explosion. "Do you live with both of your parents?" Lowering my voice, I add, "Or is that asking too personal of a question?"

"No, it's fine." She shakes her head. "My dad died of natural causes, and my mom died in a car accident when I was a small child." Fixing her gaze on her french fries, she adds, "Before people cared as much about seat belt safety."

"How tragic." I tug at the napkin in my lap. "You're so young to have lost both of your parents." Her confession is powerful, and I find myself with blurred vision as I try to control the tears threatening to moisten my cheeks. "I know the feeling," I whisper. "I miss mine every day. It's hard not having them around."

"Yours are gone?" Elle says, then chews a mouthful of food.

"Yes, and let me tell you, it doesn't get easier as you get older." I squirt some ketchup on my fries, thankful to be keeping my hands occupied so she doesn't see them tremble. "You always need your parents. They are the anchor in the madness of life."

"What about Noah?"

"He's an anchor, but it's different . . ."

Shyly, Elle interjects, "No. I mean, do you guys want to be parents? Do you want to have kids someday?"

"We do. But it hasn't happened for us yet." I inhale sharply. "It'll happen when it's meant to."

She takes a gulp of water, avoiding my eyes. "You're a really good person, Charlotte."

"What makes you say that?"

"I can tell. You've helped me multiple times and you didn't know me, and even after I was a total bitch, you still didn't let me down." Giving me a small smile, this time she makes eye contact. "I hope one day I can repay the favor."

"I'm sure you will." I pat her hand. "I'm not worried about it."

"I'll start with our late-night diner food that hit the spot." Elle swipes the bill before I can even glance at it. "Stellar choice."

CHAPTER 13
Elle

We both stand, and Charlotte grabs her leather tote from the back of the booth. It has some designer name on it I can't pronounce. I swear, it's a prerequisite for being a fashion designer, I guess. The harder the pronunciation, the more expensive. The popular girls at school would probably drool over it.

"Laughlin." I hear my last name called.

Shit. I ignore it.

"Laughlin!" More emphasis this time. Definitely more insistence.

Charlotte twists her head in the direction of the female voice yelling loudly. I know she doesn't know my real name, at least she's never let on she does, and I assume she's peering toward the voice because it's obnoxious.

Unable to hide the flush creeping up the back of my neck or run in the opposite direction, since there's no escape through this end of the diner, I do what any innocent person does.

I dart underneath the booth, pretending to look for a lost item.

I catch Charlotte's bewilderment in her tone. "Did you leave something down there? Need help?"

"Dropped the bill. This one's on me."

"Don't be silly."

It's while I'm hunched over, disgusted at the amount of food underneath the booth, that I hear the approaching footsteps and the female voice, up close and personal.

Shit balls.

My Converse sneaker is rested half on the booth, my body twisted at an odd angle underneath.

"Elizabeth Laughlin, what the hell are you doing under the table? You scrounging for food? I knew you were hard up, but come on! You're better than that."

I'd know that whiny voice anywhere.

It's my archnemesis.

Under my breath, I mumble, "I was looking for leftovers to pack for your lunch, since I hear another maid quit."

"You two know each other?" I hear Charlotte say from above me.

If hating each other's guts counts as familiarity, then yes, we are best friends.

I pull myself out of my tangled position, face to face with the world's biggest egomaniac, Courtney Kerr. Wearing a pencil skirt, a silk halter top, and platform suede heels, she twists her signature shade of red lips into a sly smile.

"Hi, I'm Courtney Kerr." She reaches out a bronzed arm to Charlotte, pumping her hand up and down.

Glancing down at Charlotte's hideous yellow-gold watch, she coos, "By the way, I love, love, love your Tiffany. They don't make anything that isn't timeless. My daddy gave me a bracelet, and it's my favorite piece of jewelry . . . so far."

"Thank you." She lovingly touches the black leather band. "I've got a good husband." Turning to me, she asks, "Are you both in the same grade?"

"Yes, we are, and in fact, we've gone to school together most of our lives." Courtney elbows me. "Isn't that right, Elizabeth?"

"Unfortunately, yes."

"Is this your new mom?" Courtney twirls her Fendi wristlet around her bony wrist. "Another foster family didn't want you? By this point it would seem you're the common denominator."

I retort, "Is this where Brandon has started taking you on dates? I mean, I guess I get it. He didn't want to be seen in a public place you'd run into any of his friends, and it's cheap, perfect for a . . ."

She loses her composure, and her face falls flat. "Oh." I clasp a hand over my mouth. "That's right—he dumped you last week. So sorry."

"Speaking of friends, where are yours?" Courtney tosses her long, silky blonde hair over her shoulder. "Oh, that's right, what friends?"

The question stings, but there's truth to it—I really don't have any friends. I would never invite anyone to my slum apartment, and my free time I spend with Justin or alone.

Or babysitting the other fosters Diane has.

Charlotte seems fascinated by this interaction as her eyes dart between us like it's a tennis match and she's contemplating who's going to lob the next ball and who's going to serve it back like a steaming pile of shit.

Ignoring her, I spin on my heel, leaving both Charlotte and Courtney in my wake.

When I get to the counter, I pay the tab, not only annoyed that Charlotte's still standing with Courtney but also peeved at what Courtney might be saying. Neither of them makes a move to come toward the cashier, so I have no choice but to go back to the booth, where they are both chattering like long-lost friends. As I shift uncomfortably from foot to foot, I almost sink through the black-and-white tile when Charlotte insists on giving Courtney a ride.

I shove my hands in my pockets to try to keep from elbowing Charlotte in the ribs.

"Will you just let your mom know I'm dropping you off?" Charlotte gives me a small smile, then Courtney.

"Sure." Courtney shrugs. "Though it's probably easier to first drop off *Eliz-a-beth*, since she lives on the way to *my* side of town."

I seem to be the only one who catches the subtle snub about what side of town she lives on—the wealthy, snooty side.

"If your parents are so rich, why don't you have a car?" I turn to Charlotte. "No, let's *not* drop me off first, Charlotte. I want to make sure you're safe from Courtney. She's kind of a psychopath." I fire back at Courtney, "And what did I miss? Where are we giving Courtney a ride?"

"*We* are not giving Courtney a ride; *I* am." Charlotte pats my shoulder. "Since you are dog sitting in my neighborhood, it makes sense to drop Courtney off first."

As we walk out of the diner, I hiss, "What the hell are you doing, Courtney?"

"Just acquainting myself with another part of your life." She gives me a grin. "Just be glad it's not Justin."

When she says that, I have to hold myself back from landing a punch across her jaw, wanting nothing more than to wipe the self-satisfied smugness off her face.

"Shotgun," she hollers, rushing to the passenger side. I slide into the back seat, buckling my seat belt harder than I need to.

"Thanks for dinner, Elizabeth." Charlotte smiles haughtily into the back seat. In return, I give her narrowed slits in the rearview mirror. Courtney doesn't stop babbling, and I tune out, staring into the darkness, the city slowing down in terms of traffic noise.

Suddenly, bright lights flash behind us and sirens shrill.

My natural inclination is to crawl away and hide from the sound like I did when I was a child, covering my ears against the noise. Touching my wrist, I feel the hardness of my scar. It's a reminder that this time the whirl of red and blue sirens is meant for someone else.

It's funny. I used to think that the police meant "safety" and "trust-worthiness." They catch the bad guys and the crooks, and they proudly wear a badge of honor. It wasn't until my father was locked up that I became less sure about their public acts of service.

I close my eyes against the glare, going back in my mind to that awful day, easily the worst of my life, that ended with sirens, law enforcement, and handcuffs.

"Was I speeding?" Charlotte asks out loud, speaking to no one in particular. I see a look of horror on her face as she glances in her side mirror. The squad car's riding her bumper, impatient for us to stop.

"What did I do?" She swipes a hand across her face. "What could I have possibly done?"

I wish I could tell her that I know what she did, but Courtney still hasn't stopped rambling. Biting my lip, I realize that the metallic taste of blood is better than accidentally screaming at her and giving up all my cards.

Because I know everything.

And what Charlotte seems to forget is that you can bury lies for only so long before the truth surfaces.

Face flushed in embarrassment, she asks, "Was there a traffic sign I missed?"

Courtney shrugs, finagling a piece of gum out of her wristlet.

Muttering, "It's late at night; maybe I only paused at a stop sign," Charlotte slows to a crawl, piloting the Jeep to the side of the road as gravel crunches underneath the tires. She shifts it into park and hits the hazard lights.

"Probably," I add, "because typical Courtney can't shut up until something's shoved in her mouth."

Glaring over her shoulder at me, Courtney starts to reach into the pack of gum. "Did you want a piece?"

"Sure."

Shaking the pack near her ear, she shrugs. "Oh, I'm sorry, guess I chewed my way through all of them. That was rude of me, especially since you really needed the breath freshener. Please tell me you don't kiss Justin with that mouth."

"Girls," Charlotte warns, "can you please be quiet?"

Trying not to smirk at Charlotte's trembling hands on the wheel, I lower my lids against the offending brightness of the headlights behind us.

Now the police intimidate her?

Funny, she didn't use to feel that way. We wouldn't be here if she didn't have a love for the authorities and restraining orders.

Ducking her head, Charlotte rolls down her window.

Footsteps chomp over the rocks as Charlotte greets the officer, a flashlight in his hand. His crew cut's peppered with gray, and a brass badge is attached to his lapel. But in the dimly lit cabin I can't make out his name, especially when he shines the beam directly into the back seat, blinding me.

He doesn't waste his breath on formalities. "Where are you headed tonight?"

"To take these girls home."

"And where are you coming from?"

"We just got something to eat."

"A bar?" he intones.

"No, the Thirty-Sixth Street Diner." Charlotte keeps her hands in her lap but motions upward. "These girls are in high school, sir."

"But you are not."

"No, I am not. And no, I have not been drinking."

Evidently satisfied with her answer, he moves on to his next question. "License, insurance, and registration, ma'am."

"Do I have a taillight out?"

"No." He points to the cargo area. "Mind if I show you something?"

"Is it fine for me to unbuckle my seat belt?"

"Yep, follow me to the back of the vehicle."

"You guys okay?" she whispers to us as she opens her door. We nod as she steps out.

As she follows him, I hit my window button so I can hear better.

His flashlight illuminates her license plate as he aims it at the tiny sticker in the corner. "Your Cherokee registration expired in January . . ."

I hear her say, "I thought the registration was good for two years. We've always done the longer option."

"It's not. It clearly spells out the month and year." A condescending chuckle follows, as if to say *Typical woman*.

He's going to want her papers, so I nudge Courtney, who's texting on her phone.

"Reach for the glove box, and get her papers."

"What papers?"

"Really?" I groan. "You don't know what you have to have in the car with you?"

"I'm sorry, Elizabeth, you've had more face to face with the cops than I have. But don't worry—when Daddy buys me a car for my birthday this summer, I'll be sure to ask for your help." Rolling her eyes, she offers, "In fact, I'll come straight to your trailer and show it to you."

Before I can shove her shoulder, she reaches forward, fumbling with a bunch of disorganized papers.

My eyes trained on the rearview mirror, I continue to watch Charlotte and the cop until I hear an audible gasp from Courtney as she slams the glove box closed.

"What?" I sneer. "What is it?"

"I think I felt something hard; it felt like a gun."

"A gun?" I shake the headrest of her seat. "Are you just going to leave it there?"

"What else would I do?"

I'm about to instruct her to open the glove box again when there's a crush of gravel and the sound of impending voices. Charlotte reenters the vehicle, the officer holding her door. Looking uneasy, she shifts her eyes to where Courtney's hands just were.

Keeping my voice neutral, I ask, "Everything okay?"

"Expired tags."

The officer thrusts his hands on his holster. "Can I see your papers now, please?"

Squirming in her seat, she responds with, "Not a problem."

Innocently enough, I reach around Courtney, who sits with her arms crossed, annoyingly chomping her gum. "Do you need me to open the glove box?"

Before I can turn the latch, Charlotte grips my wrist, hissing, "I got it."

"Okay, okay." I yank my hand back. "No problem."

Her fingers grasp for the middle console, and with a smile plastered tightly to her face, she tries to appear casual.

"Here you go." She hands him her license and registration, then fumbles in her tan leather wallet for her Kansas ID.

He thumbs through her papers before handing them back. "I'm not going to bother writing you a ticket. It'll take longer than it's worth, and you'll have a late fee anyway. Go home and get your registration renewed."

"Understood, Officer Armstrong." Awarding him her best smile, she thanks him. "My husband would be pissed if I got a ticket for this."

I watch as she clasps her hands together so we don't notice they're shaking.

"By tomorrow!" he barks.

Nodding her head, she keeps her smile intact.

To his back, she says, "Thank you again, Officer Armstrong," since he's already headed to his squad car.

After stuffing the papers in the console, she slides her ID back in her wallet and shifts her attention to us. "Phew, that was close." She switches her hazard lights off. "Sorry to snap at you guys." Charlotte gives the rearview mirror one final check, and the officer's blinker flashes as he prepares to move onto the concrete.

"No biggie." Courtney shrugs.

"I just don't keep my papers in the glove box, like most people."

"Why not?" I ask.

"Just a habit, I guess."

"You acted like something was going to pop out and get us." I raise my eyebrows. "Are you hiding drugs in there?"

"Of course not."

I hurriedly interrupt when Courtney motions to the glove box. The easiest way to get Courtney's attention is to shower her with attention.

"So, Courtney, where did you get your heels?"

She starts talking about shoes and her favorite places to shop, while I tune her out. I observe the freeway beneath us, a constant chaos of traffic, mostly semis at this hour, as I nibble away at my polish, an old and very bad habit.

When Courtney's finally forced to take a breath before she suffocates, I ask Charlotte to please turn up the radio. To appease us, she has it on Top 40 hits of today, and Courtney bops her blonde hair along as I silently mouth the words.

Charlotte seems a little less tense, her hands relaxed on the wheel, no longer acting as if they're having a seizure.

The only lapse in silence is when Courtney disturbs the music to give Charlotte directions to her house.

And by house I mean minimansion. It looks like a replica of George Washington's Mount Vernon, complete with a red-shingled roof, portico, and imposing columns. The circular driveway alone is half the size of my apartment complex's parking lot, and an expansive lawn creates the illusion we're on acres of land instead of in the middle of the city.

The only thing missing is a river for Courtney to drown in, but I'm sure she has a heated pool.

After Charlotte puts the Jeep in park, she turns to Courtney. "Would you mind if I come inside with you to speak to one of your parents? I want to tell them I was pulled over with you in the vehicle."

Courtney glances up from her phone. "It's not a big deal. My dad's a lawyer, so it's not like he's going to care."

"At least let me come to the door and apologize."

"Suit yourself." She shrugs. "He'll probably be busy in his office, working. He's always working, which is why he told me he couldn't give me a ride home."

"I could speak to your mom . . ."

Biting her lip, Courtney hesitates. "Uh, she's asleep. Her bedtime is, like, nine."

I crawl out of the back seat and slam my door shut. "I don't care who you talk to, but can we at least make it to the front door?" I pout. "I need to use the bathroom."

Courtney gives me a death glare but shoves her key in the front door. She looks like she wants to object, but Charlotte would overhear.

Under her breath she seethes, "Only if you don't take more than ten steps into the house. I don't want to tell Daddy we have to have the place exterminated."

I salute her as they knock on the door of what must be her dad's office.

The downstairs bathroom is easily the size of my apartment and has a bidet, which throws me off for a second. When I exit, I can see Charlotte shaking his hand.

He's not at all what I expect. I pictured Courtney's dad as some old, decrepit, bald, Daddy Warbucks type.

Instead, he looks like a green-eyed version of Gregory Peck, and not just because he's wearing tortoiseshell glasses or recalls Atticus Finch in *To Kill a Mockingbird*. We recently watched that in our American literature class when we studied Harper Lee.

Courtney's nowhere in sight, and I figure she went to bed.

Good. The less of her, the better.

I decide to avoid the adults and go back outside to the Jeep.

I'm trying to quietly shut the front door when I feel something brush past me.

Courtney.

"I thought you were inside."

"Obviously not," she says scornfully. "I forgot my purse in the Jeep, and I didn't want to leave my Fendi for you to steal." Resting a hand delicately on my shoulder, she adds, "But this doesn't mean I won't steal your boyfriend. Might be a fair trade."

I flick a piece of her hair. "Looks fake, am I right?"

Before she can tell me off, Charlotte appears.

"Courtney, your dad is brilliant. You should've told me he was a lauded criminal defense attorney."

"I wouldn't know." She peers at his now-closed door. "He'd have to be available, and that usually involves an appointment." Looking between the two of us, she rolls her eyes. "Come on, guys, I'm joking. He's the best daddy in the world." She touches my wrist. "It's wonderful to have a daddy, isn't it, Elizabeth?" Faking a gasp, she lowers her voice conspiratorially. "Oh, I'm sorry. That was . . . I better get some sleep." Embracing Charlotte in a warm hug, she thanks her. "I really appreciate the ride home. Thanks for saving me from that annoying guy. You're a sweetheart."

She winks at me over Charlotte's shoulder as I flip her off.

We avoid saying goodbye to each other, and after Charlotte and I exit, the door slams behind us, the lock clicking shut.

"What was that?" I huff, sliding into the passenger seat, which now smells like Courtney's overabundance of perfume.

"What?"

"Why did we give the world's biggest bitch a ride home?"

"She was trying to get away from the guy at the diner—he was being too aggressive with her. Plus, you guys know each other from school. I thought it'd be a nice gesture."

"I don't think anyone is too aggressive for Courtney," I mutter.

"If the roles were reversed, I would hope someone would give you a ride if you needed it. In fact," she says, tapping a finger to her mouth, "I believe I did."

After I fume under my breath, "Such a Good Samaritan," she ignores my comment. Irritated, I want nothing more than to get away from her, away from everyone, and sleep. I can barely keep my lethargic eyes open.

"So which is it?" Charlotte tilts her head to the side. "Is it Elle or *Elizabeth*?"

Indifferent, I say, "Elizabeth is my given name, and Elle is a nickname."

"If Elle is a nickname, why doesn't Courtney use it?"

"Because until recently, I've always gone by Elizabeth. Someone called me *Elle* once, and it kind of stuck with *actual* friends."

We're quiet until Charlotte turns into the gated subdivision, pressing a button on her visor to enter. "Which street are you staying on?"

"Grover." I point down a long cul-de-sac. "Turn on Forrester and then hang a left. Third one to the right." Slowly, Charlotte drives down the empty street, the only glow emitted by streetlamps.

The house I'm pet sitting at is a large two-story with a balcony off the second-floor master bedroom that overlooks the front yard. Though, after being at Courtney's palatial estate, it appears small. Rosebushes line every inch of the walk, and flower beds take up a majority of the lawn.

"Whose house is this?" Charlotte asks, pulling into the driveway.

"The Lamberts'," I say. "Todd and Marjorie."

"I don't know them, but it's not surprising. There have to be at least a couple hundred houses in this development."

"It's one of the biggest subdivisions I've seen." I remind her to renew her tags when she gets home.

"As if I could forget." She puts a hand over her face. "Noah's going to be so annoyed with me." Pointing to the front door, she says, "I'll wait until you get inside to leave. Make sure you lock the door behind you."

"Of course." I start up the sidewalk, pausing when I hear Charlotte say my name.

"And Elle," Charlotte calls after me. "It's always better to have someone owe you a favor, especially when it's an enemy."

Unsure how to respond, and a little perturbed, I pause, nodding back at her.

True to her word, she idles in the drive until I close the door behind me.

But she doesn't immediately leave, and I watch her from the second-floor window, her eyes fixated on the house.

CHAPTER 14
Charlotte

Even after I observe Elle safe and sound in the house, my eyes stay glued to the two-story house, watching a light from a second-floor window twinkle on. Something about Elle's mannerisms is familiar, but I can't put a finger on exactly what it is.

It might be the way she holds herself—prickly yet stoic. There's something familiar about how she picks at her cuticles and bites her fingernails, a bored but timid look in her eyes.

Those eyes speak volumes.

With my hands tense on the wheel, I'm drawn to the sheer curtains in the upstairs window as I fervently try to jog my memory. An emphatic barking jolts me from my rumination, followed by the shrill response of another yap, and reluctantly I back out, concentration lost, heading the short distance to my own home, where I mostly feel trapped.

What an odd turn of events.

A runaway dog.

A classmate of Elle's who calls her by an entirely different name.

Expired tags.

The glove box.

I'm going to have to be more careful. I'm not used to driving with anybody else in my vehicle. We usually take Noah's car if we go somewhere. I should've been more cognizant of the unlocked glove box.

That was a close call.

It would've been impossible to explain to the two girls why I have it. I would've had to explain my past, the restraining order, the tumultuousness of my former relationship.

I reach for the dark-green satchel tucked in the back of the glove box. The thought of it makes me cringe in disgust but comforts me at the same time. As much as I hate having to carry a weapon, it provides a sense of security.

Tonight, feeling vulnerable, I bring it inside the house. I settle the green satchel in the nightstand next to me for safekeeping.

The worst part of Noah's work schedule is sleeping alone, the fear of being harmed oppressive when the daytime phases out and the darkness replaces it.

As I rest my hands on my belly, the fear becomes magnified, since the thought of protecting another human life is becoming undeniable. I'm filled with a combination of excitement and nerves, wondering when and how I should tell Noah about the baby.

I try to conjure up sleep but I can't.

Should I get a test and surprise him with the results or take it when he's present?

Do I need to do something cutesy like I see on Instagram, where people make elaborate announcements with props and clever hashtags?

When I start to toss and turn, I give up and sit cross-legged in bed with my laptop, amassing ideas from Pinterest.

But something else is bothering me . . .

Or someone else, I should say.

Elle. A.k.a. Elizabeth Laughlin.

As much as I'd like to think she's just a teenager who came to me by accident, a nagging feeling has settled in the pit of my stomach, making sleep impossible.

Who is this strange girl who seems invested in my past, present, and future?

My mind clicks through the timeline of Elle like a photographer taking pictures, each frame from a different angle, a unique perspective. It makes me uneasy to think Elle has become fascinated with the development I live in, for no good reason that I can determine, save for the fact that she seems to run from her own upbringing. She likes the lake and the neighbors, sure, but there are many other areas that provide nature and solitude that don't take a long bus ride to get there.

And now she's pet sitting in my neighborhood, out of the blue. She said she was asked, but it can't be convenient.

I prefer to question the motives of people all the time instead of taking them at face value. Call it my trust issues.

At the diner, Courtney was easy to pry information from in the short time when Elle had walked off. She has loose lips—not the girl you want to confide in, that's for sure. She would be fun to play a game of telephone with, though. I giggle to myself and can only imagine what she would conjure up.

But for being a known rival, she knows a surprising amount about Elizabeth Laughlin. I guess it makes sense in the same way I had classmates throughout my childhood who grew up with me not by choice but by proximity. We attended the same schools and inadvertently became, at the very least, acquaintances.

Courtney and Elizabeth have grown up together and attended the same schools, and, according to Courtney, Elizabeth's grades once propelled her into the talented and gifted program and AP classes, before she stopped caring. Or at least it appears that way from her sporadic attendance and tardiness.

The wrought iron bed frame is solid against my back as I rest my head against it to consider both girls. Elle didn't understand I was trying to help her by doing a favor for Courtney. Maybe it backfired, but if the two of them spent some time together, they'd probably find out they had more similarities than differences.

You thought the same about Lauren, and look how that turned out.

Curiosity causes me to forgo sleep for detective work. If Elle can meddle in my life, I can return the favor. I'm not one to let strangers in, yet this girl has become entwined in my life, and *who* is she?

Starting a new search, I use both names, Elle and Elizabeth Laughlin, spelling both multiple ways. It should be made easier since I now have her cell phone number, but for some reason, it's not.

I'm perplexed more by what *doesn't* pop up, which raises a streaming bright-red flag.

Every teenager has some type of social media, and most are active on multiple platforms. It's unheard of that a teen would be able to fly under the radar in this day and age. It's as if the internet has been scrubbed of her. Not even an address appears.

No Facebook. Instagram. TikTok. Twitter.

Nothing's listed on the school website, no extracurricular activities or pictures with her name or face. All I find is an article in a student newspaper from last year where random high schoolers were asked what their aspirations were. Elle mentioned she'd like to be a judge so she could counteract the bad with the good. She said her preferred college or university was "undecided."

Maybe she *does* have something to hide.

And this puts me on high alert, hence the reason I prefer to stay in my bubble.

I reach out to touch the green velvet case again, just to be sure.

Sleep refuses to come, and, paranoid about Elle, or Elizabeth, I realize I must make it my job to find out who she is and what she wants or needs.

Everyone wants something, I muse, but what does Elizabeth Laughlin want that I have?

The furnace rattles, startling me out of my reverie. The vibration's strong enough to echo through the vents.

I let out an agitated sigh.

In the morning, I'll call a repairman to check it. One of the pitfalls of being alone in the house while Noah's gone. He might earn thousands of airline miles, but at the same time we accumulate costly home repairs. He did mention he would fix it when he got home, but time with him is so limited that I don't like fixing what's broken to cut into our time together.

Especially because it's we who are damaged.

We need the majority of the work.

Twisting my necklace, I'm conscious that one aspect of our relationship we've never struggled with is passion.

Noah's good with his hands, and I imagine his fingers, how they run through my hair, the way he ignites unfettered desire in me.

My face burns as I bury it in a pillow, cringing.

I don't want to have to tell our child how they were conceived. I picture our evening of truth or dare that ended with us naked on the hood of his car in the middle of a field. It reminded me of college, going into a cornfield to drink beers and smoke a joint underneath the stars.

I must've fallen asleep to this image, because the next thing I know, I'm jolting upright at the sound of heavy footsteps.

My instincts kick in, and I claw at the side table for the green satchel, my heart thumping with enough adrenaline to jump-start a marathon.

I hear a door slowly open, a soft creak followed by more footfalls.

My eyes are blurry as I scan the muted darkness of the room.

Then I see the outline of him.

Jonathan.

This can't be happening.

Wailing, I reach my arms out like tentacles, grabbing whatever's in their reach.

My arms are pulled to my sides, and his voice cuts through my sobs. "It's just me, Char." Noah grabs my shoulders tenderly, rubbing them in a circular motion. "I wanted to surprise you."

Heaving for air, I give him a well-deserved smack. "What're you doing home?"

I search for the green illuminated digits on the nightstand.

"It's four a.m. I caught a red-eye." He flicks on the lamp next to me, bathing the room in pallid light. "Everything okay? You look like you've seen a ghost."

I can smell liquor on him; his breath reeks of airplane bottles of vodka.

"I did."

"Am I really that pale?" His attempt at a joke falls flat, and he knows it. "Is it him you thought you saw?"

We don't dare utter his name.

"Yes." There's no point in lying. I run a hand through my unkempt hair.

"That was insensitive of me," he slurs. "I didn't want to call you, since I knew you'd be asleep." He pauses. "Hey, I noticed on the sideboard that picture of us was gone." His nose wrinkles in confusion. "Char, where's that pic of us?" Incoherently, he stutters something about imagining it there and it being dark.

"I'm redecorating." I wipe the sleep from my eyes. "So, how did it go?"

"It went well, just like we expected." He pulls at the tie around his neck as if it has him in a chokehold. "I'll be relieved when it's over."

"What's next?"

"I don't know yet. When I know, you'll be the first to know." He climbs into bed, not bothering to remove the comforter, instead lying on top.

He settles me in the crook of his arm. "Why are you thinking about him? You haven't mentioned him in a long time. Is therapy dredging up all these old feelings?"

"Somewhat," I groan. "It doesn't help that Nancy keeps calling."

He whistles. "Your mother loves to feel needed."

"I can't forgive her for reaching out to him." I swallow. "It's like she forgot how much she hated him back then. I'm convinced she's trying to ruin my life. I think she's upset my father left me enough money to buy this house."

"Nah, I don't buy that. She's lonely but not vindictive." He pauses. "I've always wondered this, and if I'm out of line, or you don't want to discuss it, I understand, but why?"

I wait for the rest, but he leaves the question hanging in the air, so I finish it for him. "How could I forgive you and not my own mother?" His question holds so much weight, and it's heavy in my hands, and heart.

I've been waiting to have this conversation for years, but it's never come to fruition. And now that it's presented to me, I wish it would disappear into thin air. Noah and I are in a semigood place now. Why rock the boat?

"Do you have to be drunk to talk about this?"

He doesn't answer, instead responding with, "I left you when you needed me."

"Yes, you did."

"And I'm the reason . . ."

". . . you are not to blame."

Wobbly, he presses a hand against my knee, tracing one of many scars. "I absolutely am. You wouldn't have been alone, or at the mercy of his anger, had I been there to protect you. I . . ."

Shakily, he holds a hand up when I start to interrupt. "No, let me finish. I have to get these words out. It's been driving me insane, driving a wedge between us. What I did to you. It was selfish and irresponsible, and I failed you. I failed to protect you."

My eyes fill with tears, the reality of the past like a burdensome weight I've had to carry alone for so long.

"I'm sorry, Char." He pulls my chin to his face. "I'm so sorry for not stepping up. I have more to tell you, my truth, but I'm not ready yet. But I will be soon."

We don't bother removing what's left of our clothes.

Ravaging each other is our own attempt at redemption and forgiveness.

When I wake up the next morning, Noah's gone, as if I dreamed him. If I hadn't woken up to a sock and his tie in bed, I'd have thought he was a mirage.

But I know he wasn't, because I'm greeted by a morning text that announces his run for coffee and bagels. When it's just me at the house, I don't bother stocking the pantry or fridge.

After his admission of guilt, I feel like we've crossed into new territory, and I'm cautious but optimistic that this is a stepping stone for us. There's so much from our past that we've buried, and while we keep moving forward, what we've interred keeps pulling us back, reminding us how we failed each other.

For some reason, this morning I feel an overwhelming sense of longing to be near the box I've kept hidden in the basement for so long, an attempt at closure.

"I can do it, I can do it, I can do it," I repeat.

It's just the basement.

I unlock the padlock with the key around my neck and then attempt deep-breathing exercises I learned from a meditation seminar. After a conditional pause at the basement door, I turn the handle and inhale. The rest of the house has an aroma like vanilla and sandalwood. The basement, on the other hand, smells musty and dank.

Reluctant, I take one step forward.

My pulse starts to race, my heels immovable on the floorboards, as if I'm superglued to the exact spot I'm standing on.

Paralyzed, I feel my lip start to quiver.

Usually I can pull myself back up to safety and slam the door shut behind me, as if all the excruciating memories are tucked in the basement. But this time, I'm stuck.

I hear the garage door shudder to a close, and then Noah's voice cuts through the silence before I sense him behind me.

A hint of concern laces his question. "What are you doing, Charlotte?"

"I, uh . . . I need to go down."

"Charlotte." Noah pats me on the head like I'm an incorrigible child. "Let me set our breakfast down." I still can't seem to pull myself off the first step, so I wait for his return. The gravity of my fear hasn't affected him yet. He knows about my phobia of basements and small spaces, but he isn't privy to the panic that spiders its way down my body when I do attempt to come downstairs.

His hand comforts me as he gently caresses the back of my neck. "Let me go first, Char." I'm relieved as he moves around me. His purposeful steps retreat as I wordlessly follow, tears streaming down my face in fear and gratitude. When we reach the bottom, Noah cradles me in an embrace, and we both sob, our hands wrapped around each other in remembrance.

"Did you ever tell him about us—you know, before the trial?" he whispers in my ear.

I feel the dampness of his cheek on mine as I whisper back, "No, I couldn't. I knew he was prone to violence. But I guess it didn't matter. It still went that way."

"I didn't want to believe you."

Pushing off of him, I look him directly in the eyes. "You didn't want to believe what?"

"That someone could hurt you like that. That you would be in that type of situation. I was a dumb twenty-five-year-old. I thought those relationships existed only in Lifetime movies and on *Unsolved Mysteries*."

"It's down here," I sob. "Everything from that time. The baby's sonograms . . ."

Noah holds my hand as I peer in the corner, where a wooden box holds the precious remains of what could've been. Along with the crib and other trinkets I've held on to.

My first true loss.

Or, I should say, our first real loss as a couple.

Closing my eyes, I imagine our baby boy, with Noah's hazel eyes and his height, my smile and tinkling laugh. A beautiful boy, a striking combination of both of us.

Edward Noah was going to be his name.

Edward after my father, a name that sounded regal, just like I pictured he would be. My father could be cold and stoic, the very definition of tough love.

But he always put family first, and I admired that quality in him.

That he was dedicated to loyalty was an understatement. As the mayor of the town where I grew up, he stood for what he believed in and would fight like hell for it.

He died suddenly when I was only nineteen, a sophomore in college. Noah and I had known each other for only a year at the time, but it felt like we'd always been connected on a deeper level.

To me, Noah was a saint, my shoulder to cry on.

During the funeral, I felt safe in his arms, and his protective nature steered me through that awful week. He was steadfast through the crowds, at the cemetery, and at the parade to commemorate my father. When I was overwhelmed, he gave me space to cry and laugh and, above all, hurt.

I pick up the wooden blocks that spell out *Edward Noah*. "You know why I chose that name?"

Baffled. "Is this a trick question?"

"No, I mean, I know you know where both came from. But do you know why?"

He settles himself on an empty milk crate, pulling me into his lap. "The week of my father's death, do you remember how you were with me?"

Noah murmurs, "I remember we spent a lot of time at your parents' house, going through the motions. And lots of stuff."

"You protected me like a shield of armor. My feelings changed for you then; they deepened into love."

"And we were just friends at the time."

I reach a hand back to touch his face, the growth of his beard scratchy. "When did your feelings change for me?"

"Mine were all tied up and twisted. I was an idiot in college, confusing lust with love. It takes us boys a long time to grow up."

"*Edward Noah* was a name born out of love. I connected two of the most important men in my world: one leaving this earth, the other signaling a new life . . ."

We both stay silent, because we know this wasn't what was supposed to happen. The only noise is the occasional clamor of the furnace, until finally I open my mouth to speak but close it.

I want nothing more than to instruct Noah to start moving the baby furniture back upstairs. That we've been given a second chance.

But I can't, not just yet.

It's premature, and I have to keep this one close to my heart for a minute.

"I'm going to fix the furnace while we're down here." Noah strokes my hair, my cheek wet against his lips as he gives me one last squeeze.

"Thank you." I give the box a last longing gaze before I turn and head slowly up the stairs. My hand cradles the banister as I create distance between us, but yet, I feel closer to him than I've felt in a long time.

CHAPTER 15
Elle

On Monday, I sit through my last class of the day, nibbling on some corn chips from the vending machine. With my fluctuations between wanting to sleep and constantly having hunger pangs, it's a toss-up, depending on the hour, as to whether I'd rather nap or down a greasy cheeseburger. This makes concentrating on American lit a near impossibility. Reading and analyzing dead authors who are so far removed from the world today is boring as fuck to me.

I run a palm over my pocket, hoping Diane hasn't tried to reach me. One of the boys dunked my phone in the sink last night, using it in a makeshift study to determine how long you can leave a cell submerged in water before it ceases to operate.

Unfortunately, he forgot to "eventually" remove it from the basin, and now it won't power on.

As I scowl at the notebook in front of me, I realize I can kiss dog sitting goodbye for the present time. I'm feeling sorry for myself as I concoct other ideas on how to make money and don't hear my name being called.

I tune out my teacher, who's referencing our latest book assignment, George Orwell's *Animal Farm*; I'd rather concentrate on Charlotte. No offense to Orwell, but she seems more fascinating. The look of terror in her eyes when I reached for her glove box was almost comical. She certainly didn't want the police officer to see she had a gun. It's probably not legal.

But then she stuck Courtney on me, and that was ballsy.

"Elizabeth," Mr. Mueller mildly requests, "do you have an answer?"

Tapping my ballpoint pen against my notebook, I stare at him, openmouthed.

Other kids have their expensive MacBooks open, pretending to study notes while concealing what they're really doing—scrolling funny memes on Instagram and watching muted YouTube videos.

I'm not that lucky.

My paper has more doodles than notes, indicative of the fact that I currently have a D in this class.

I shake my head, embarrassed. I left my dog-eared copy of the book in Charlotte's Jeep on purpose so she'd have to get in touch with me. I can't risk her going silent again, especially now that she knows my real name. She'd be appalled if I failed this class because I didn't have the reading material.

"Let me repeat myself. I asked your thoughts on the song 'Beasts of England.'"

The dazed expression on my face must give my ignorance away. Some dumb jock in the back of the room starts snorting like a pig while another pretends to whinny like a horse. I don't dare turn around and glare at them.

"The farm animals were taught it; I'm asking you why."

Mum's the word, and when Mr. Mueller realizes I'm not offering up an answer, he tugs at his themed tie in annoyance, a habit I'm surprised hasn't strangled him yet with our generation.

Exhaling, he turns his attention to another student, and I turn mine back to Charlotte.

All my suspicions are coming true.

Does she have another identity that she uses?

Maybe there was more to it than just a weapon. Could she be hiding a large stash of bills in the glove box she didn't want us to see? Something from her past?

Hmm . . . I chew on the pen lid. Whatever it is, I need to find out, especially if it will help with my own search.

I could've pushed her hand away, played dumb, and pulled the gun out, busting her to the cop. It would have been so easy. And I would've done it all with a wicked smile.

But I'm not ready to do that *just* yet.

Charlotte has no idea how what she did in her past has affected my entire life for the bad. And worst of all, she wouldn't care even if she did.

Flicking the cap off my desk, I eagerly anticipate the final bell. This is much more interesting than some dumb political novel from the 1940s.

Mr. Mueller tries to motion with a jab of his wrist that he wants a word with me, but I keep my head down, sprinting for the door. Lucky for me, one of the class suck-ups has stepped between him and the exit, trying to hog his attention with their own boring thoughts on Orwell.

I've walked out the double doors of the school building, free at last, when I spot a charcoal Jeep idling near the curb. I'm not expecting a ride, so I head down the sidewalk, where a loud honk is interrupting the chatter of students. Startled, I glance over my shoulder.

The woman behind the wheel is wearing dark sunglasses as she motions me toward her vehicle.

Charlotte.

That was fast.

I stride over to the passenger side, feigning surprise, as she rolls down the window. Being in the system rarely has its perks, but with Charlotte, I can twist her around my pinkie finger just by making her feel guilty. I'm still learning what makes her tick, but she is a fixer and likes to solve problems. It's in her nature and helps her to manage her remorse.

"Hi." She gives me a small wave.

"Hey." I push a strand of hair behind my ear. "Is something wrong?"

"Nope, everything's good, but you forgot your book in the back seat. I figured it was for a reading assignment." She shrugs. "I was going to drop it off with the neighbors you were dog sitting for, but you said you were done with that job."

Smirking, I say, "You didn't think I'd read Orwell on my own?" I tuck the book into the front pouch of my backpack. "Thanks."

"Not with how much you abhor reading." Charlotte glances in her rearview mirror. "I tried to call you . . ."

". . . but my phone's dead," I finish.

"Why don't you charge it?"

"I wish it were that easy. It's not dead like dead, it's dead like *dead*."

"Did I miss a step?" Charlotte laughs. "Did technology change in a blink of an eye?"

"It's broken."

"You didn't drop-kick it at Courtney, did you?"

I give her a death stare. "Be careful what you wish for."

"Guess it's a good thing I'm wearing these shades."

I shift my backpack to the other shoulder. "It fried in water." I explain to her about the boys and their ridiculous experiment.

"Ouch," she moans. "That's an expensive project."

I wince. "And it's not like I can take from their allowance jar."

Charlotte directs her attention toward a tall, lanky high school guy wearing ripped jeans and a skull-covered hoodie. "Is this what the kids dress like now in high school?"

"Uh-huh."

I don't have the heart to tell her that's Justin, my boyfriend.

Looking disgusted but at the same time curious, she watches as he throws a skateboard down, yelling to another similarly dressed classmate with sagging jeans, except this one has arms covered in tattoo sleeves. "Is he even old enough to be inked? The first one's really good looking.

Though I wish he'd pull his pants up, maybe wear a belt . . ." Her voice trails off. "Do you know him?"

"Um . . ." I hesitate, looking wistfully after Justin. "Is Noah in town?"

"He was until this morning." Charlotte gives me a coy smile. "You want to run some errands with me? I could really use your help." Shoving open the passenger side, she chides, "Come on, it'll be fun."

"I guess." I squeeze inside, shutting the door behind me. Justin doesn't seem to notice me driving off with Charlotte, so I don't try to draw his attention.

I smile to myself at his focus, his eyes zoned in on the concrete steps near the auditorium. I've seen that intent stare, and he's determining if he can put the board up there and do a trick called a backside.

"I made a hair appointment, and I need your assistance."

"Oh, really?"

"Do you need to call anyone and tell them where you are?" Charlotte takes her eyes off the road for a split second to point to her cell in the console. "You can use my phone."

"No, I'm covered." I switch the subject. "Any ideas on what you want to do with your hair?"

"What should I do? I'm in a beauty rut."

Pursing my lips, I ask, "Well, what does Noah like? Does he prefer your hair long, or what kind of celebrities does he find attractive?"

"Celebrity wise, he likes blondes." She gives me a wink. "But he's come to the other side, the dark side."

I giggle, watching out the window as we drive toward the wealthy side of town. We chat about our weekends as Charlotte pulls into the parking lot of what looks to be a high-end salon, the outside of which doesn't display the price of the discount haircuts I typically get.

"Don't be mad . . . ," she starts to say.

I narrow my eyes. When people start with the phrase "Don't be mad," they anticipate your being just that. "Charlotte?"

"I called earlier to see if they could fit you in."

"What for?"

"A highlight and cut."

My insides spin out of control, like I'm on a Tilt-A-Whirl. "That's really sweet, but, uh . . . I'd rather go to my place."

"You have a stylist?"

"Yeah," I mumble, tugging at my tangled mess. "I just need to run a brush through it."

She says, "I didn't mean to be presumptuous."

"It's okay, but, um, this looks like an expensive place."

"Elle, it's my treat."

I jump out, and, uncomfortable, I bend down, pretending to tie my shoelace. "No, I couldn't. You've done so much for me already."

Charlotte lifts her shades so they're on top of her head. "Don't you want to be pampered?"

"It's not about that." Inhaling a sharp breath, I explain, "I just don't like the feeling I'm indebted to someone, is all."

"You're not." Charlotte gives me a toothy grin. "Think of it as an even exchange. You help act as my hair guru, and in return you get a service as well."

"But they have professionals for that. Why would you want me?" Warning bells go off in my head. Why is Charlotte so adamant about this? A shrill noise redirects Charlotte's attention, and she pulls her cell out.

When she spots the caller, her brows furrow at the screen.

"Are you all right?"

"Yes, it's no one." Rolling her eyes, she presses the mute button and shoves the phone back in her handbag. "Just a wrong number. I'm tired of telemarketers buying lists to annoy us."

Holding the door open, Charlotte lets me walk inside first, and the opulent chandelier and elaborate display cases take up the bulk of the waiting room. Here, a bottle of shampoo costs more than the price of getting haircuts for our entire family.

A dark-haired woman walks up to Charlotte immediately, grabbing her hands and teetering like they're long-lost friends. "Charlotte, hi." They exchange hugs, and Charlotte introduces me to Marina, her hairstylist. After handing both of us glasses of lemon water, she leads us back to the salon chairs.

"Your stylist, Angel, will be with you in just a minute." Marina settles me in a chair with a stack of gossip magazines. She and Charlotte start to chatter, their voices rising an octave when they get excited, usually at the same time.

When Angel arrives, she stands behind me, plumping my hair as she makes eye contact in the mirror. "Hi, Elle, I understand you're due for a highlight and a cut?"

"Actually," I say, pausing until both Marina and Charlotte have disappeared to the shampoo bowls behind the heavy curtain, "I'd just like my hair trimmed, and a deep condition, please."

She winks at me, and, sipping the lemon water, I watch as she transforms me.

It's like I've morphed into someone else.

CHAPTER 16
Charlotte

After we leave the salon, it's later than I expect, the appointment having taken almost three hours. The look on Elle's face is worth it—she's now wearing a satisfied grin. She says, "Who knew a scalp massage could make me feel like a completely different person?"

Brushing a piece of hair caught on Elle's cheek, I exclaim, "You look fantastic—that cut is meant for your face shape."

As I back out of the parking spot, I'm focused on the rearview camera, but it's always at an inconvenient time that I remember what errands I still have to run. "Do you mind if we make one more stop?"

"Anything to take me away from my essay on *The Scarlet Letter*."

"I definitely don't want to pull you away from that," I chuckle, "but this will be quick. I just have to run into the grocery store. Noah ate us out of house and home this weekend."

We ride in companionable silence until we reach the parking lot of the big-box store.

"Do you want to come in?"

"Mind if I stay here?" Elle closes her eyes. "I'm feeling pretty beat. It snuck up on me out of nowhere."

"It's the scalp massage and the blow-dryer." I motion to the ignition. "I'll leave the keys so you can keep it running. Be back in a few."

Languidly, she leans back against the headrest. "I'll probably be asleep when you come back."

"No problem." I run into the store, feeling like an ass for keeping Elle out this late. The purple splotches underneath her eyes are readily apparent, and she looks like she hasn't slept in days. *Is she coming down with mono, the kissing disease?* I had it in high school just from sharing utensils.

My motherly instincts kick in, and I feel sorry for her. I want to broach the subject of her having a foster home but don't dare until I know she feels comfortable confiding in me. She should open up to me instead of my prying into what might be a sensitive topic.

I'm already alarmed by the obscureness surrounding her. Maybe if I show her some decency, she'll start to shed her tough outer layer and open up to me. It appears that what would be normal is not her normal, I remind myself. Which is why I wanted to do something nice for her—let her be a teenager for a minute instead of rushing home to babysit other children or walk dogs.

After grabbing some tea and honey, a carton of milk, and a loaf of bread, I add bananas and cereal to my basket and head to the checkout.

I stop in my tracks and turn to the aisle marked "family planning."

Are you ready, Char? I ask myself.

There's a rush, as if I've had a sudden high. But then there's a swoop, like I'm crash-landing.

It's time. I have to know for certain.

Hands shaking, I grab a couple of boxes of pregnancy tests, which is a bit much, but I don't care. They claim to detect pregnancy hormones earlier than the other brands, and, given the cost, I sure hope this is an accurate advertisement.

After the items are rung up, I realize too late that I left my wallet in the vehicle. A line has formed behind me, and, flustered, I touch both pockets as if confirming my mistake.

Empty.

Biting my lip, I fumble at the bottom of my purse, relieved that a credit card I have on hand for emergencies is stored in the front pocket.

As I walk outside, nervous anticipation courses through my veins at the possibility that Noah and I could soon be parents. I have to stop procrastinating and avoiding the reality, as the small pudgy spot becomes a baby bump.

Trying not to act too giddy, I slow down my steps to a more natural walk.

As I approach the Jeep, I notice that something's wrong. The back passenger door is wide open, and I see the outline of a body sprawled facedown on the seat.

Stifling a scream, I cup my mouth in horror as the body lies there, immobile.

Frozen in place, I watch as it miraculously shifts.

Elle now moves from her stomach to her side, shrieking in terror when she spots me behind her. She turns crimson.

"What are you doing in the back seat?" I'm not upset, just confused. The two plastic sacks have fallen from my grip, and my gaze is fixated on Elle's hands, how her fingers are pried between the seats.

"This isn't what it looks like."

"What does it look like?" I ask. "I returned your book to you. What else did you lose back here?"

"Courtney asked me to check for her library card. Said it fell out of her purse. I thought it might have slipped between your seats."

"Courtney had a small wristlet on. She wasn't in the back seat, and her purse never touched the back seat." My tone frigid, I add, "But what's in your pockets?"

Her face flushes too bright, too guilty. "Nothing."

"Show me, then."

Swallowing hard, she says, "This is so embarrassing."

"What is?" Making no move to walk around to the driver's side, I stand in her line of vision, blocking her path.

"You're going to think less of me."

"Just tell me. What're you looking for?"

Nervously, she licks her lips.

"Are you looking for my wallet?"

"Charlotte . . . no."

"Then what is it?" I demand.

"Nothing. Never mind."

Annoyed, I retrieve the bags and toss them in the back seat. "Why would Courtney's library card be buried in between the cracks of the back seat when she sat in the front, Elle? That's not even a good excuse. You can do better."

"I know."

My nose wrinkles in disgust. "There's a stash of twenties in the middle console. You had to have noticed that earlier." I shrug. "Plus, I left my wallet in here, so I'm sure you've cleaned that out."

Elle shifts from foot to foot, her eyes darting around the parking lot.

"So why not go for that?"

"Because it's stealing."

I tilt my head. "Where's my wallet?"

"In the back seat." Elle points behind the driver's seat. "On the floor."

"Hand it to me." I tap my foot impatiently as she reaches in to grab it. Not fast enough, in my mind, so I snatch it out of her palm. She watches nervously as I unclasp it and peer inside, scanning the contents.

"Get in," I coldly instruct her, walking around to the other side of the Jeep. She follows suit, quietly buckling her seat belt as she hangs her head.

Gawking at her, I murmur, "What?"

"I only wanted your change so I could get something off the dollar menu. This way, I can justify that it's not causing anyone harm or bad karma for myself. Just like at the gas station when you use the penny jar."

"All right" is all I say as I shove my wallet in my purse and dump it in the back seat. "Where am I taking you tonight, since your dog-sitting gig is over?"

Elle stares straight ahead, the dim streetlamp we're parked under illuminating every vehicle in an eerie glow.

"I think it's best we don't see each other again," I say flatly.

"No," Elle whispers, "please, Charlotte. I certainly don't want to steal from you." She swivels her head toward me, tears springing to her eyes.

"I value honesty and trust, and loyalty. The simple fact is I can't trust you."

"I'm sorry." She tries to give my arm a flimsy squeeze. "I'm so ashamed."

My lips are drawn in a straight line, practically invisible, and I exit the parking lot, my fingers punching the touch screen, changing the station to talk radio as we drive in an uncomfortable silence.

Elle says my name out loud, but I don't respond, my eyes frozen in a perma-glare at the traffic ahead. After a couple of minutes of the silent treatment, Elle flicks the radio off in frustration.

"Excuse me." I reach forward. "I was listening to that."

She opens her mouth, the words rushing out. "Courtney and I found the gun in the glove box and now it's not there, so I searched the Jeep to see if it was stashed somewhere else, and I can't find it."

Trying not to look shell-shocked, I'm being hit left and right with bombs that're detonating in every direction. Meeting Elle has turned into a game of *Where's Waldo?* converged with Clue.

"I was searching for your gun," Elle confesses, "and I'm sorry."

Slamming on the brakes, I exit the interstate and turn sharply onto a side street. I drive until I reach a cul-de-sac and then put the vehicle in park.

As it shudders to a halt, I turn to Elle. "What do you mean, you were looking for a gun?"

"During your traffic stop, we found it in the glove box."

Running a hand through my now-limp hair, I exhale sharply. "And?"

"And it's not there now."

"I know, I moved it. It shouldn't be out in the open like that without being locked up." I fold my hands in my lap. "It was my fault for not having it properly put away."

"Is it registered to you?"

"Of course." I give her an odd look. "I have it for protection, Elle, nothing malicious."

"Why?"

Resting my hands on the wheel, I turn to her. "Why do I have a gun? For a lot of reasons, but mainly because I had a relationship that ended in violence."

"And you're worried the person will find you?" Elle chews her lip. "Is it a man?"

"Potentially, and yes."

"Am I in danger?"

My eyebrows rise. "Why would you be?"

"I don't know. Just because I know you."

"Not at all."

"Do they live here?"

"No." I put the Jeep back in drive. "It's not something you need to worry about, Elle. It's an adult problem, and it's been . . . resolved. The weapon is for my own safety, and I've moved it to a secure location where it's locked up. You don't have to worry."

"Okay." She rests her head against the leather, shutting her eyes.

"Are you okay?"

"Yeah."

I let her rest for a couple of minutes until I hear soft snores from her side of the vehicle, signaling she's asleep.

Crap. I don't know where she actually lives, and even though I'm having a hard time trusting her, there's something about her that resonates with me.

She seems familiar.

I just don't know why at the moment.

A joint up ahead is screaming my name, and it seems to be the only place open at this hour.

My bladder's about to burst, and Elle's fast asleep on the passenger side. She must be worn out because she doesn't even stir when I park.

I leave the Jeep running. I order us a meal and use the restroom, and, when I come back outside, my jaw comes unhinged.

Elle is no longer peacefully asleep.

She's gone.

CHAPTER 17
Elle

After making my way down a ravine and up a hill, my shoes muddy with damp soil, I spot a gas station up ahead. I beg the clerk to use the phone for one call, tears streaking my cheeks. Charlotte thinks I'm a lying sack of shit, and I botched gaining her trust.

I've screwed everything up.

Dialing Diane first, I don't get an answer, which isn't unusual. The clerk's staring daggers into the back of my neck as I hurriedly call Justin. "You can't tie up the phone line."

"One sec." I hold up a finger. "Please."

He answers, his voice laced with sleep, and promises he'll be here in twenty minutes. I huddle outside until the clerk takes pity on me and ushers me inside to wait.

An hour later, Justin squeals into the parking lot, the earsplitting muffler of his ancient car poison to my ears. I grit my teeth, hands clenched into fists as I open the rickety door and shove his shit from the passenger side to the back seat. As I toss his skateboard with force into the back, he protests, "Hey, watch it, babe."

"You said twenty."

"I'm sorry, I had to wait for my brother's dumb-ass roommates to move their vehicles. They were parked behind me."

"It's been over an hour."

"I'm sorry." He tries to comfort me by rubbing my knee. "What the hell's going on?"

"Everything."

"Do you want to stay at my place tonight?"

"You know I can't do that. I have to check on the boys. Diane's probably gone; she's unavailable."

"She's always out." Then he complains, "She needs to get used to you not being there."

Glum, I say, "Well, soon she won't have a choice."

He speeds up, his foot tapping the gas pedal. "Seriously, what's she going to do when we move?"

"You mean, move in together?"

"I was thinking in bigger terms."

"Like?"

"West."

"Where out west?" I raise my brows, sucking in a breath. "California?"

He gently tugs on my ear. "The West Coast. The best coast."

"How would we be able to move to Cali? It's not cheap to live there. We can't even afford a place here."

Pointing to the board in the back as if to confirm its legacy, he adds, "Could be huge for my career."

"What if something sidetracked us?"

"Like what?" He turns down his vibrating stereo system. "Your father?"

"Do you want to get married someday? Kids?" I ask.

"I don't know, babe, I'm just trying to get through high school." He maneuvers around a slow-moving truck. "I'm sure, yeah, someday, I will. Not anytime soon, though."

"If we got pregnant, what would you want to do?"

He doesn't say anything, but I notice in the way he tightens his hands on the wheel he is listening, so I continue. "Would you want to keep it and raise it? Or there's adoption, or would you want me to have . . . an abortion?"

"Jesus, Elizabeth, what happened to you tonight? Where's this coming from?" His chiseled face scrunches up as if he smells something putrid. "You call me for a ride, and now you're giving me hypotheticals."

I'm staring down at my hands, twisted into a knot, the same as my stomach.

"Elizabeth." He pulls into the parking lot of my apartment building with a clunk, slamming his car into park. "Look at me."

It's better than looking at my surroundings. I'm relieved it's evening. My crippled apartment building doesn't look as disgusting in the dark, except for the overflowing garbage in the dumpsters and the junk vehicles that're good for nothing but scrap.

Justin clasps my chin in his fingers, softening his tone. "Look at us, babe. You live with a foster mom in a tiny apartment with three, sometimes four, other people. You don't even have your own bedroom. I live in a makeshift frat house where they deal weed." His face twists into a grimace. "Can you imagine? A baby there, crying, while we sleep on the porch and listen to house music?"

Tears sting my eyes as I'm confronted with the truth.

"Don't you want more?" He waves his arm in the air. "We don't have a dime between us. I'm working at a scrap-metal yard; you're not working, since Diane has you acting as her live-in babysitter."

"I started pet . . ."

Shaking his head, he says, "Doesn't matter." He wipes a tear off my cheek. "I really want to get the hell out of here. Go explore somewhere else, be near a beach, and nice weather, and start living. Wish for more than inheriting another scar from my mom's piece-of-shit husband." Tucking back a strand of hair off my cheek that got caught in my tears, he kisses my forehead. "Your hair looks nice, by the way. It suits you."

"Thanks," I murmur.

Unbuckling my seat belt, I climb out as his eyes relay a deep sadness to me. "Elizabeth!" he hollers after me as I turn toward the apartment. Halting my steps before I shift, I almost don't want to know what he's going to say, because deep down I already know.

Slowly I face him, and I see the tears. His face matches mine, pained and hollow.

"If there's one thing I know, it's that I love you. So don't ever question that, okay? But this has me thinking about how serious we've become, and I don't want to hold you back, or vice versa. Skateboarding is my life—you know this—and becoming something."

The thought of forming words is too much, so I nod.

"I think we should take a break, Elizabeth, and just be teenagers."

With that, I turn on my heel, my world spinning out of control.

I don't dare look back as I half sprint to the stairs.

CHAPTER 18
Charlotte

Worn out from the night's turn of events and afraid I overreacted, I feel a stab of guilt. It wasn't my intention to raise my voice at Elle or scare her.

On the flip side, even though I feel a hint of remorse, stealing, whether it's done for good reasons or not, is something I won't tolerate. And trust, in my situation, is paramount. I can't expect Elle to understand my life or why it matters more to me than most.

I trudge up the stairs to the office when I get home, skipping my usual nighttime tea of lavender and chamomile. After exchanging dress clothes for a pair of sweats and one of Noah's V-neck tees, I sink into the desk chair. I boot up my laptop and start to grade papers, but my mind keeps drifting, and I'm forced to reread paragraphs, the words swimming in front of my eyes.

Pandora's box.

I shouldn't open it.

But a woman's gut is all she can trust.

My hands pause over the keyboard, electricity shooting through each digit, my body wired into an anxious, frazzled ball.

I balk before typing in his password.

Noah has no idea I keep such close tabs on him. He would be appalled if he knew; it would sever every bit of trust between us.

I have to know, though.

A hunch tells me I'm right.

I *deserve* to know.

Justifying it because of our future as not just partners but parents, I need to settle the unease in my gut. After accessing his email, I find at least fifty new ones since the last time I checked, all bold text, a signal they're unopened.

Most are junk, but as I scroll down the list, the dreaded name stands out as if it's emblazoned in red and spelled out in ALL CAPS.

It's from *her*.

The screen becomes a blurry mass of words. I shut my eyes, in part to block out the hurt and in part to keep from absorbing the rest of her bullshit. *Will this ever stop?* As I rub my temples in agony, the pounding cues a headache is building.

When will Lauren take a hint?

Furious, I hit the delete button hard and drag the email to the trash, where it belongs, just like her. I permanently erase it from his email, which I wish I could do with her once and for all. If only we could get rid of Lauren this easily, eliminating her from our thought process and lives. Why can't she let us be happy together?

The synopsis is always the same, even though Lauren struggles with her writing. Her thoughts are all over the place, scattered as the misspelled words run rampant.

But it's always the same message, loud and clear.

She wants Noah, and she won't take no for an answer.

Helpless, I move to the window seat, grasping for a pillow as the room spins out of control. I tighten my fingers around the silky fabric, gripping something that's tangible, unlike the never-ending history between Lauren, Noah, and me.

Screaming at the pillow, I punch it repeatedly, one blow after another. After letting out all my raw emotions, I stop yelling, my energy expended from all the lies and bullshit. This wasn't how I envisioned life progressing.

Angry that I even have to keep checking Noah's account, I contemplate how to respond and if I should.

I don't want Noah to be aware I know she's still contacting him.

Should I threaten a restraining order?

Don't waste your emotions on her, I warn myself. *It just breeds negativity.*

Switching gears, I reach for my phone but then automatically set it down.

Elle said her phone was broken, and besides, if she's sleeping I don't want to wake her, wherever she might be.

CHAPTER 19
Elle

We live on the fourth floor, and I'm weary by the time I reach the second set of steps and completely out of breath as I enter our apartment. Diane's passed out on the couch, snoring up a storm, a quilted afghan wrapped around her shoulders. Due to our paper-thin walls, I can hear the television down the hall. After struggling to locate the remote, I find it lodged in an empty bag of chips.

Longingly, I imagine what it would be like to have a mom I could confide in.

Hell, a foster parent even.

Recollections of my own mother are fleeting. She's been out of my life for so long, since I was seven. And the last memories I have of her are not happy ones.

I check on the boys, both asleep in their bunk beds. After switching off the small lamp on the dented dresser, I trip over a Hot Wheels before catching myself.

I mouth every cussword in my vocabulary and shut their door behind me. I'm tempted to hurl the damn toy car out the window, but instead I set it on the counter.

After dragging my mattress into the hallway, I curl up in a ball, shutting my swollen eyes. The tears come easy, and I silently cry before I drift off, the drowsiness pulling me in swiftly.

I wake only when I feel a painful nudge to my arm.

Ignoring the angry gesture, I burrow my head deeper in my shoulder.

"Get up," a gravelly voice demands. "It's time to get up."

Another push, this time more forceful.

Opening one eye, I see Diane's bare foot next to my head.

I moan.

"First off, young lady, it's almost seven thirty. Second, I need you to cash a check for me this evening." I want to cover my ears at the sound of her voice, an evil squawk.

"Why can't you?" I mumble.

"Account's overdrawn."

"Can't you go to a payday place?"

She kicks me with her heel. "Can't you shut up and do as you're told? Geez, you have a roof over your head, and you still act like an entitled brat."

Rolling over, I sigh, "Fine, just stop talking."

There's the tolerable Diane, and then the hungover version. I'm getting her straight-off-a bender-before-she-starts-up-again model.

Translation: cranky and mean.

"What happened to your hair?" She whistles. "That idiot boyfriend of yours cut it in the middle of the night so you can be twins?"

"No, I think one of the boys did. They said you're next." I wait for a smack, not bothering to open my eyes.

"Get the hell up." She wobbles as far down as she can without falling over. "Or you won't be able to make it to school, since you'll have a black eye."

Groaning, "Try it," I rub the sleep from my half-closed lids. Her threats don't scare me. She's frail, and her drunken binges usually mean she can't throw a punch.

Sticking my tongue out, I sit up, tracking a roach as it crawls across the kitchen floor. Yuck. I'll have to get some spray and try to exterminate them. In a slum like this, the landlord is useless.

After locking myself in the bathroom, I take a quick shower, careful not to mess up my hair.

When I emerge, Diane's seated at the flimsy kitchen table that doubles as a desk, a pantry, and a catchall for storage. She has a beer in hand with a shot of tequila settled next to it, a cig hanging from her lips.

"Ah, the breakfast of champions." I lace up my shoes. "Shouldn't you eat something first?"

Flippant, "Did you bring home any groceries?"

"Last time I checked, you were supposed to be the adult."

"You're seventeen, and it's time for you to get a job." She flips ash from her cigarette butt onto what I think is yellowed newspaper but in reality is mail. "The dog thing is a good start, but it won't cut it."

"Shit," I mutter.

It's an envelope, stamped *Mailed from a correctional institution* and addressed to me. I swipe it from underneath her lit cigarette, replacing it with a dirty cup from the sink.

Diane's still droning on. "You turn eighteen soon, and you're out of here unless you start forking over some rent. They don't pay me no money after that."

"What about the boys?"

"What about 'em?"

"Won't they need childcare?"

"Nice try, girl. They can manage on their own. You know I work my ass off for you kids and get little in return from the government." Leaning back in her rickety metal chair, she jabs at the table for emphasis with her cancer stick. "It's a thankless job, being a foster parent."

As I mouth, "Yes, Miss Hannigan," in reference to the drunken, crazy orphanage caretaker from the musical *Annie*, she pins me with a dirty look. "What?" I gasp. "The two of you seem to have a lot in common." Before she can throw something at me, usually breakable but never valuable, I grab my backpack. I slide the envelope in the front pocket, too emotional to open it. Another round of bad news coupled with a broken heart is not what I need right now.

I board the city bus to go to school, and the other passengers look as weary as I feel. Some have headphones on to block out the noise; others examine their phones, read, knit, or harass each other.

Staring out of the smudged window, I think about my father's temper, my first recollection. I'd been spanked and slapped for sure, but this time his violence toward grown women took on a new meaning.

I'm six, and we're semipoor, living in a small rental house on the northeast side of town. I sleep on a green cot with a small kitchen and living room separating the two tiny bedrooms.

Katrina, my mom, isn't addicted to hard drugs yet, but she smokes a lot of pot and works a minimum wage job. My father works construction during the day, but at night, his demons cut loose, and he loves the bottle. Every night the garbage can's loaded with empty glass, and every morning he leaves at the crack of dawn, coming back home after it's dark.

He's already had one drunk-driving arrest, and he was twice the legal limit. They yanked his license, but he's got to get to work somehow.

The worst of their fights are when he's drunk and she's stoned.

This night's no exception.

A fight erupts at the dinner table, where I sit between them like a miniature mediator.

I remember it like I'm witnessing it right now, from the window of the bus, watching it unfold.

My father's pissed because my mother's been spending money foolishly.

"Katrina, we don't have the extra money for that kind of shit." He looks at the dime bag of weed lying on the counter. "You need to knock it off."

She retorts, "We would if you didn't get busted for drinking and driving."

"You gonna keep bringing that up?"

"It's just so dumb." She smirks. "What if you get pulled over with a suspended license? What then? Then we'll really be screwed."

"If you're so smart, why do you keep spending *my* money on drugs?"

"It's not yours."

"Oh, okay, it's *ours*."

"If I had married Billy Thorpe, I'd be living high on the hog."

"Oh, here we go again. Billy this, Billy that. Go find fucking Billy, then."

"I'm just saying—"

"I know what you're *saying*." He gives her a murderous glance. "You want to fuck Billy Thorpe."

"Cut it out." My mom points at me in disgust. "Our daughter's right here."

My father turns his bleary stare on me. "Do you know what *fucking* is, Elizabeth?"

Trembling and afraid of answering wrong, I shake my head, pushing my canned peas around on my plate. I know it's a bad word.

"See, she's fine." He shrugs. Nonchalantly, he asks her to pass the plate of Spam.

I sigh in relief. This time it's going to blow over. We all sit in silence for a moment, waiting . . .

Naive, I ask my mom, "Is that what you do when the guy comes to the house and you make funny noises?" After spearing a now-cold pea, I choke it down.

My mother's face drains of color, and my father's mouth gapes, exposing his silver crown in the way back.

"What?" His chair squeaks in protest as he turns to face me. "What're you talking about, Lovebug? Who is the man that—"

Interrupting fast, my mom flips her hair over her shoulder. "She's not talking about nothing. She's been watching too much of that damned TV." The glimmer of fear that settles behind her eyes is a dead giveaway.

"What man?" he asks again.

I shrug. "Just the nice man that Mommy moans with." I add, "He brings me candy if I'm quiet." I've never seen my father rise so briskly in anger, not even when I get the belt.

After I slide my chair back just in time, he heaves the table with his fist, the force enough to push it halfway across the small kitchen, pinning my mother against the wall. "What the hell is she talking about, Katrina?"

"I don't know." She tries to push the table forward, but my father doesn't budge.

"You ruining my daughter's innocence?"

Her eyes are wild, but she stays silent, focused on me.

Swiftly, my father moves to her side, yanking her chair out with her in it in one smooth move, and she glides across the flowered linoleum.

I'm afraid the wood's going to splinter in his hands as he grips the arms of her chair. "One more time, Katrina." His massive palms move to her chin, where he tightens his hold, moving her head back and forth with his forefingers. "Who is coming over here behind my back?"

"No one," she whispers. She is weeping, and her blue eyes are filled with terror.

Scared in a way I couldn't comprehend then, I let a stream of urine run down my leg.

"Daddy," I yell, "leave Mommy alone!"

I forgot my manners, so I try again, the tension in the room thick. "Please, Daddy, please."

He doesn't turn to look at me, his eyes still locked on hers. "It's okay, Lovebug, you didn't do anything wrong."

"But Mommy . . ."

"Mommy's been bad, and just like you, she has to pay when she messes up." He pinches her chin forcefully. "Isn't that right, Katrina?"

"No . . . this is crazy." She shrieks, "Stop it!"

"Who is the man, Katrina?"

"Please don't do this, please." Tears run down her cheeks, unchecked. "Not in front of her." Brusquely, he swipes them with his calloused palm, dragging a thumb over her ruddy complexion.

"Who is it?"

All she can do is shake her head, over and over, darting her eyes around the room for help that's not going to come. Focused on the telephone, she tilts her head at me to call for help.

"Don't you move, 'Bug," my father says over his shoulder to me.

His hand smacks her hard across the cheek. "I asked a question, Kat."

The maddening pause feels like forever, but it's probably only a couple of seconds. As they stare at each other, she waits him out. He doesn't release his hold on her, instead clenching a fist around her blonde hair. As he yanks it violently, she finally mouths, "Robert."

"Robert, as in Robbie, our landlord?" His jaw goes slack at the same time his hands do, and he drops them to his side. "That why you're able to buy weed and not spend all my money on rent?"

She doesn't respond.

A second later, he pulls back and strikes her with an open fist.

Over and over, he hits her.

I see flashes of red, and it's a combination of his rage and her blood.

Crying, I knock my chair over, tugging with my small hands on his flannel-clad arms. I catch the back of his palm, flying across the kitchen.

I crawl under the table, sobbing, and with my hands over my ears, I scream bloody murder. Ignoring both of our pleas, he reaches forward, clutching her around the neck, squeezing, like he's trying to expel the life out of her. She must realize his evil intentions at the same time, and I watch as her pupils dilate, the blood vessels enlarging in what's left of her battered face.

As he is choking her, I watch her eyes become cloudy, and futilely I hit his back over and over, uselessly trying to keep a raging bull from his target, until finally she slumps over, sliding to the floor. Eyes closed, body lifeless.

I believe she's dead, though in reality she's unconscious.

And it's all my fault.

A bony elbow uproots me from my thoughts, and I turn to confront the person. An elderly woman is smiling at me, not unkindly. "Honey, I've seen you on this bus before, and you always get out here."

"Thank you," I whisper, grabbing my backpack. "You're absolutely right."

After my conversation with Diane, it's become more apparent to me than ever that I have to fix things with Charlotte, even if it means laying myself at her feet.

How bad can it be? I ask myself.

Bad, I think bitterly. *She's the reason your life has turned out this way.*

CHAPTER 20
Charlotte

In the afternoon, I finish one of the only on-campus classes I teach, my eyes burning. Rubbing them, I wonder if this is an early sign of pregnancy. I can barely keep my lids open. As I pull into the garage, a nap sounds like a welcome idea.

That and taking a pregnancy test.

It's time, Char. Stop putting it off.

Shifting my eyes to the corner of the garage, I notice the box, the one containing pictures of Noah and me. *Stop punishing him for Lauren,* I tell myself.

I retrieve it and the wedding band from my jewelry box and then slide it back on my ring finger, where it belongs.

After putting one of the framed pictures back on the wall, this one of Noah in his tuxedo, I step away from it, admiring how dapper he looked getting married.

Eight years ago . . . unbelievable.

I twist the wedding band as I smile at the photo, in which he's showing his toothy grin and lopsided bow tie and acting as if he's holding on to a hefty secret that only he's privy to.

He'll be home soon, I remind myself, and I won't feel so out of sorts. Everything will go back to normal.

The bag from last night beckons me from the kitchen counter. I unwrap the plastic on one of the boxes and come face to face with one of the pregnancy tests. I head into the bathroom with it when the doorbell rings.

It chimes again, and I sigh, resting the unused test on the bathroom counter.

Last week, I ordered a few unisex items from a department store, but it seems awfully fast for the shipment to have arrived, since it was on back order. *Maybe it's a sign you're really pregnant.* I clap eagerly.

I stare at the bathroom door, debating if I should answer the doorbell or take the pregnancy test first. I've waited long enough, and if it's a package, they'll leave it on the doorstep.

Instead, I whisper, "Who is it?" softly enough that not even I can hear, and certainly no one outside could. Plus, the television's providing the usual background noise and comfort.

"It's me, Elle." Another rap on the door, this time harder. "Charlotte, are you home?"

Slowly, I move the heavy drapes from the picture window and stare out at her. People watching, especially when they least expect it, is a favorite pastime of mine.

I watch her demeanor—hair still fairly intact, oversize sweatshirt and leggings, dirty sneakers, and a determined look on her face, her shoulders pulled back instead of in their usual hunched position.

After I unlock the dead bolt and open the door, our eyes meet through the screen.

"Can I talk to you?"

"I know I shouldn't have gotten so upset last night in the parking lot—"

"I deserved it. You don't know me."

"You're right. I don't." I stroke my chin. "You can come in, but I think it's best we remain friendly, but with distance."

Her eyes narrow. "What do you mean?"

Motioning Elle through the screen door, I give her a wide berth. Her presence isn't as imposing as it was the first time I encountered her, but I still need space.

I point to the living room. "Have a seat, make yourself comfortable."

Attempting a joke, she says, "This time, I'll even make sure to take off my shoes."

While she unlaces her sneakers, I take my usual spot in the middle of the couch, while she settles into the side chair.

She doesn't waste any time on niceties. "What do you mean, Charlotte, about distance?"

"Elle . . . ," I begin. "First, I feel ridiculous." I pull at a thread on a pillow, suddenly nervous. "I like you, and I think you're a good kid—"

"But you think since I'm from the wrong side of the tracks, I must be trash?"

"Huh?" Shaking my head, I lean forward, tossing the pillow aside. "Not at all what I was going to say." She stares at me expectantly, her lower lip trembling.

"What I was going to say was that I tend to keep to myself. I have a hard time trusting people, and right or wrong, it affects the number of people I allow into my life and the boundaries I set with them."

"And you think we need boundaries?"

"My therapist thinks boundaries are . . . useful." I gently smack my forehead. "This is the kind of information I shouldn't share with you, because I don't know anything about you. You showed up on my doorstep in the middle of a storm and gave me a fictitious story about your life, and it reads like one of my literary novels."

"Yes, I lied to you," Elle says, her voice coming out strong, "about some aspects of my life. And I'm sure you heard Courtney mention I'm a foster kid—that's true. I live with a woman named Diane and two other kids she fosters."

"Your parents are really both deceased?"

"Yes."

"Your foster mom, is she really a nurse?"

"No, Diane's the opposite kind of person." Elle adds, "The kind they typically treat in the ER."

"Meaning?"

"She's clueless." Evidently feeling the need to clarify, she continues, "Diane isn't a bad person; she's just lost and gets in her own way. She's reckless with her spending and lives for only today. I don't fault her; I mainly feel sorry for her. I know she doesn't mean to punish us by ignoring our basic needs. She's just incapable of taking care of herself, let alone us."

Miffed, I mutter, "Then she shouldn't have you." Elle doesn't disagree, but I can see the frustration on her face. Foster care is a world I know nothing about, and I'm sure she's used to everyone giving their opinion but no one providing an alternative.

"What does she do for work?"

"Retail."

"Is she married? Or is there someone who helps, like a significant other?"

"Depends on the week," Elle says bluntly. "But not currently."

"Who did you live with after your mom and dad died?" I replace the pillow on my lap. "Not like it's any of my business, but I just wondered if you went straight into foster care."

"My grandma, until she passed."

We sit in silence, both lost in our own thoughts until she speaks again. "She passed shortly after my dad. It was too much for her—she had a lot of health problems, and the loss of my parents was a lot for her. I'm lucky she took me in and made it as long as she did."

"Thank you for sharing." I give her a genuine smile. "I mean it. I know it's tough to discuss unpleasant or difficult things."

"Why do you go to therapy?"

I consider Elle's intent for a moment, and whether she's being flippant or sympathetic. I decide on the latter. "Because it helps to discuss trauma in your life. In order to move on from what my therapist calls the 'wreckage of the past,' you have to get comfortable with your demons."

Elle suddenly looks uncomfortable, and I decide we both need a break from the serious discussion we've been having.

"I'm sorry, I haven't been a good host. Would you like a beverage?"

"Um . . . yes, please."

"Tea, pop, water?"

"Water, please."

"Bottled okay?"

"Let me grab it, Charlotte." She rises to stand. "Would you like something?"

"The same. Cold ones are in the fridge." I lean back against the couch, my hands moving to rest tranquilly on my belly.

CHAPTER 21
Elle

I head into the kitchen, noticing a contrast from the other night. This time, it looks cozy and welcoming in the afternoon light, and even with the size, it has a feeling of comfort. It's different from the way it seems in the middle of a tornado watch, when you feel like you're a cast member in a horror flick. Especially when a basement and a deranged woman are involved.

The sun filters through the half-open blinds of the french doors, shining on the polished concrete floor. A small window over the farmhouse sink looks out onto a grassy side yard. I gaze at the wooden privacy fence, painted a shade of cream.

It's like the picket fence we hear about as children.

Marriage. Two kids. A dog. House. And a white picket fence to complete the package. Speaking of which, a pink and blue box on the island catches the corner of my eye.

I pull out two bottles of water and stare at the minimal contents inside. After resting them on the counter, I unscrew one, taking a large swig as I scan the open box in front of me.

Pregnancy tests.

How did she know?

Ashamedly, I stare at the belly I've been trying to disguise under oversize sweatshirts and baggy jeans or sweatpants. Clearly, I didn't do a good enough job of hiding it. If Charlotte noticed, then everyone must be able to tell.

Shaking my head, I realize it doesn't matter. What matters right now is that she got me the tests for a reason.

But when I examine the contents of one of the boxes and count the plastic wands, I see that one is missing.

It dawns on me as Charlotte hollers from the other room, "Find them okay?"

I jump, screeching out a pathetic "Yep."

Charlotte's possibly pregnant?

Holy shit. At this stage, I can't wrap my brain around the announcement. *You need to take a test,* I demand, *and that's the most important thing right now. Confirmation. You can't ignore what's going on any longer.*

Would she notice if there was only one left?

There's another box, unopened and intact, still in the plastic bag.

Before I can change my mind, I shove one in the waistband of my leggings and meet her back in the living room. I give her my biggest grin as I push a water into her hand. "Mind if I use the bathroom?"

She starts to protest as I walk toward the hall bathroom. "Wait, it's, uh, it's broken." She seems flustered, her cheeks coloring. "The handle, it's not flushing properly."

"Oh, um . . ."

"Just go upstairs and use the hall bath up there."

"Sure thing." Carefully I make my way upstairs, holding the banister, since I get out of breath quickly these days. The open railing of the two-story foyer means I'm under a microscope even from below, and she can watch every step I take.

The first door is wide open. I presume it's a bedroom, probably a guest room, since it's perfectly clean but empty save for a queen-size bed, dresser, and side table.

Noise from the television startles me as it drifts upward.

The second door is partially closed, and when I peer in I can tell it's an office, a desk against one wall with a built-in window seat underneath a large window.

A small nameplate on the left of the desk says *Woman's Mess*, and another on the right says *Man's Treasure*. This office is definitely masculine, the wood some type of rich mahogany or oak, with framed pictures of sports figures and old antique cars on the wall.

Another built-in feature, this one a bookshelf, covers the whole length of the other side and is filled with thick books. Hemingway is next to Sylvia Plath. But what catches my eye is in the middle, where a framed picture of Noah and Charlotte dressed in fancy attire is located.

Afraid she'll think I'm snooping, which is exactly what I'm doing, I tiptoe back out to the hall, Charlotte downstairs and nowhere to be seen.

Walking on, I try the third door handle.

It's locked.

Hmm . . .

I shake the knob.

Nothing.

I hear a faucet running downstairs.

Retracing my steps, I discover that the bathroom in the guest room is actually one of those Jack and Jill bathrooms I've read about in magazines, meaning one door is accessible from the hall and one door leads into the bedroom I initially passed. Making sure both doors are locked, I take another sip of my bottled water, pacing the small floor of the bathroom.

Staring in the mirror, I give myself a pep talk.

It's only a test. It's only a test. You can't flunk it.

But it can come back positive, meaning you're pregnant, I remind myself gloomily.

I try not to let the weight of what a positive pregnancy test would mean get to me, especially since I just lost my boyfriend and I'm about to lose my foster care when I turn eighteen.

But you know you are, I chastise myself. It's true. I'm just in deep denial.

My hands shake as I hold the plastic clumsily underneath me on the toilet. I have to hum before I can force myself to go, almost dropping the stick in the water in the process. It has a digital screen and is supposed to be as accurate as the doctor's test.

Shit.

Now what? I ask myself. I roll my eyes at my reflection in the mirror. *Duh, you have to wait for the results.* Clicking my teeth in nervous anticipation, I leave my urine-soaked test on the edge of the counter. If only I had a working phone, I could play a game or look for future pet-sitting opportunities.

Or adoption agencies.

The reality of my breakup hits me again, complicated by the fact that I'm knocked up and alone, and I freak out inside.

Wringing my hands together, and without any desire to sit in the bathroom and wait, I step into the connected bedroom, where I notice a balcony that faces the lake. When I step outside, the cold spring breeze hits me while the sun gently reminds me it will be summer soon.

I stand nervously as I clench the handle of the wrought iron railing.

Lost in thought, I don't even hear Charlotte until she taps on the french door behind me.

Fuck.

"Everything okay?" Charlotte doesn't sneak up close behind me, instead resting her hands on the doorframe, giving me space.

"Yeah, sorry." I try not to act surprised. "I didn't realize you had such a good view of the lake."

"Impressive, huh?" she says. "I like to people watch; there's always bird feeding and joggers. They stock the lake with fish, so it'll be prime fishing soon."

It's unfair that Charlotte can walk along this trail anytime she wants, while my father rots in prison.

"Yeah, it looks different from up here." I then explain, "The lake's never looked huge until now, when I'm above it."

"You ready to come back downstairs?"

I start to follow her out of the room, noticing how careful she is about locking doors behind her. She closes the thin, gauzelike curtains as I start to follow her across the threshold. My face reddens. I need to grab the pregnancy test before she spots it on the counter.

"Let me just grab a tissue and blow my nose. I'll meet you downstairs." I disappear behind the bathroom door, a positive plus sign innocently staring back at me. Beads of sweat form on my brow, and I feel the rising of my paltry breakfast as I sink to my knees in front of the toilet.

After rinsing out my mouth, I finish off the rest of the water. Sticking the completed test in my waistband seems pointless, so I carefully wrap the stick back in the opened plastic, hiding it in the trash can underneath a handful of tissues and inside an empty toothpaste carton.

When I exit the bathroom, I hear Charlotte moving around downstairs.

Weirder yet, I hear the flush of the toilet from the bathroom she told me was broken. As I walk down the stairs, dizzy with sickness and faced with a positive pregnancy test, I watch Charlotte come out of the bathroom, wiping a hand across her mouth.

Is she experiencing morning sickness, I wonder, at the same level I am? "Is everything okay?"

She gives me a weak smile. "Yes, everything's good."

In an accusatory voice, I snap, "I thought the toilet didn't work."

Charlotte seems surprised at my tone. "I just needed to rehook the flapper thing. That plastic thing in the tank." Seeing the blank expression on my face, she shakes her head. "Never mind. I don't know the technical name for it. Noah had to FaceTime me to show me how to do it."

Feeling like a jackass, I want to ask about the next time Noah will be home, except her demeanor has changed in the instant since my heated question. The way she carries herself is now hunched instead of self-assured, her lips tightened into a hard line. "I'm going to go take a nap. Can you see yourself out?"

"Sure, no problem," I say, pulling on my sneakers. "Thanks for speaking to me."

"Yeah, Elle, it was good to see you." Her smile doesn't quite meet her eyes. "Have a good rest of your evening; good luck with everything."

"Charlotte . . ."

She pivots on her heel.

"Are we all square?"

"We are." She pauses to watch me remove the dead bolt and unlock the door, her hands resting on her hips.

I nod, feeling out of sorts, the heaviness of what to do on my mind. I dread the next conversation I need to have, but it has to be faced. It's the right thing to do. He should know.

But the question is when. I have to decide when to tell Justin.

Unsure where to go or what to do, I catch the next bus out of Charlotte's development. The apartment sounds depressing, but telling Justin sounds even worse.

You need him, I remind myself, *and you didn't do this by yourself. Just because you're taking a break doesn't void the fact that he's been your boyfriend for the past year.*

Except this is the opposite of what he asked for, a less serious relationship.

Tough shit. This is his responsibility too.

I chew my already-sad-looking fingernails down as the bus bounces its way to its other stops. I want to catch him before his shift starts at five and have to switch buses three times just to reach the edge of town, where the junkyard sits, and even then I'm still a few miles away, at a truck stop on the outskirts, where the bus line ends.

Relying on a stranger who got off at the same stop, I ask if I can make a call on his cell. Sometimes there is camaraderie with the bus crowd; other times, it's a war zone. It depends on who has taken their meds, who has eaten, who is coming down from a trip, what kind of trip, and the weather. All these factors determine the mood of the passengers.

At first, the man curls his fist around his phone, ready to battle me, under the impression I'm trying to be sneaky and steal it. His mannerisms soften when he sees a tear spring to my eye.

Under his pity-filled gaze, I cross my fingers that Justin's not at the skateboard park, his phone usually tossed in his bag if that's the case.

As if he's expecting a call, he answers immediately, his voice low pitched and sensual. "Hey, sexy," he murmurs seductively.

"Hey, I'm at the gas station near the junkyard."

"Uh, Elizabeth? What number are you calling me from?"

My heart drops when I realize I'm not the one who is supposed to be on the other end. How quickly feelings change. I swallow, barely able to whisper, "Does it matter? I need to talk to you."

"Elizabeth, if it's about the other night . . ." His voice rises to its normal pitch. "I meant what I said. I love you, but we both need space."

I feel like I'm chewing cotton, my throat parched. The words are as powerful as a punch to my gut and just as hurtful, compounded with what I now know is a baby growing inside my womb. "Yeah, I hear you. But this is important. Please."

He has the audacity to hesitate, and in this instant I want to pummel him.

"Please, Justin. I won't make you late for work. Promise."

"Okay, I'll head over now."

I hand the phone back to the man, and he nods at me as if he understands. I wait outside, kicking rocks, and Justin's muffler pierces the air before I even see his old sports car.

After he parks, he reaches over to unlock the broken passenger-side door.

I slide inside, my head down.

He speaks first. "What's up, Elizabeth?" His greeting is so generic and immature I want to scream. Instead, I fidget with my hands in my lap, my cuticles torn and bloody. "Just say it. Whatever it is, it can't be that bad, babe."

"I took a test, since I missed—"

"What class?" Justin interrupts, ignorant to what I'm saying.

Taking a deep breath, I say, "I haven't had a period in a few months, so I took a test today and . . ."

". . . and you're telling me this now?" His eyes widen in disbelief. "You're pregnant?"

"I'm pregnant."

"And you're just telling me this now?"

"Didn't you wonder why I hadn't had a period since after Christmas?"

"I guess I didn't pay attention." Justin shakes his head. "This can't be happening."

"Well, it is."

"You're being manipulative."

"What?" I jerk my head back against the seat. "Seriously? I have no reason to manipulate you."

"You need a place to go, I get it." Justin sighs, "I wanted a break—I thought *we* wanted a break—and you come at me with this."

"I was trying—" I take another breath. "Last night, I was trying to find a way to tell you."

"You knew then, and you didn't tell me?"

"I hadn't taken a test then." I add, "Though the fact you haven't noticed any of the symptoms is a little alarming."

"You just happened to go to the doctor today, and they said with one hundred percent certainty you're pregnant?"

"I haven't been to a doctor yet. This was a test from the store."

Clearly relieved, he says, "So, it's not for sure?"

"Justin . . ." Then I say with a sigh, "It's a digital one. They're about as accurate as the test at the doctor's office."

"How many did you take?"

"Just one."

Stubborn, he snaps, "It could be broken."

"You mean, defective? I guess . . ." I rest a hand on his biceps. "But I doubt it. Haven't you noticed I've been throwing up, tired, and gaining weight?"

"I thought it was stress." Justin bites his lip. "How far along do you think you are?"

"I'd guess fourteen to sixteen weeks, but the doctor will have to confirm that part."

"That far? You're that far along?"

I shrug.

He whispers, "Do you wanna keep it?"

"I don't know . . . this is all a shock."

"Yeah, but you've had time to think about it." He sniffs and says, "No wonder you were asking me all these damn questions last night. Shit, I just didn't see it coming. Like, how will you support it?"

"You mean, how will *both* of us support it, right?" Sarcasm drips from every word.

"Elizabeth, I'm telling you right now, this isn't something I want."

"You act like I planned this, or did this to myself. Last time I checked, you were in the room."

"I wore a condom."

"Sometimes." I brush a tired hand across my forehead. "Justin, that isn't the point right now. I don't want to fight about it. It's done. I'm knocked up."

"Can you ask Diane for money to—"

I cut him off. "Why would I ask her? This isn't her problem."

Justin slams his palm on the console. "I don't have the money right now to take care of it."

"I don't know that I want to have an abortion."

"It's gotta be an option that's at the top of the—"

Interrupting, I fire back, "We discussed *all* the options."

"And I said I didn't think a kid was good for us."

"And I said that wasn't a good enough reason." I shove open the door. "Forget you ever met me. I don't want anything from you."

I slam the door, which shuts with an indignant thud, and take off at a frenzied pace, hands shoved in my pockets, unsure where I'm going to go or how long I'll be able to walk.

Sobs rack my body as Justin speeds along next to me, pleading, "Let me at least drive you home."

"No." I kick gravel at his car. "Leave me alone."

Flipping him off, I take off through someone's field, hobbling over a lowered fence.

It feels like hours have passed as I roam through grass and dirt, every muscle in my body sore, but it's really only been a half hour or so. I pant, thirsty, and in the distance I see an old farmhouse. I go to it, and a big-breasted woman inside takes pity on me. I spend the evening eating dinner with her family of five, having forgotten what family dinners were like.

If I have a family . . . I change my thought process. *When I have a family, we will always eat dinner together,* I solemnly vow. After a dessert of homemade custard pie, her husband and young daughter drive me back into town on their way to pick up supplies at the hardware store.

For once, I don't fib and give a fake address, or have them drop me off in Charlotte's subdivision or at my favorite Cape Cod–style house.

I'm too weary for even that.

Resting my head on the floor at Diane's, I'm plucked into sleep when I lie down on the stained carpet, not even bothering to find a pillow or drag out my mattress.

CHAPTER 22
Charlotte

Feeling reprimanded, I feign a nap to get Elle out of my house. Her accusatory tone was a trigger for me, and it placed me smack dab in my past, with Jonathan.

I'd sent her upstairs to avoid her spotting the pregnancy test and prevent any further comments or questions. Noah deserves to be the first one to hear the news, and he'll be home later this evening.

Plus, Elle doesn't have a right to know about this until we're ready to tell people. After all, she has her own secrets, and I'm entitled to mine.

With an overabundance of caution, I take a second test just to be absolutely positive.

While I wait, I absentmindedly grab the opened box off the counter. I'll just read the directions while I wait to ensure I'm doing everything perfectly right.

As if you haven't done this before, my snarky voice intones.

Except . . . I just took a second test, but there are supposed to be three in the box.

I shake it, but nothing but the white page of instructions falls out.

Mistake at the factory?

No . . . too much of a coincidence.

Elle hasn't been feeling well. She's had fatigue, shadows underneath her eyes, and nausea, and her body's been hidden underneath baggy clothing most of the time.

Yes, but she's a teenager, I remind myself.

But still . . . when I approached Elle earlier, she seemed stunned, as if she had just heard unexpected news. And she did take an awfully long time upstairs.

Did she leave any evidence? I wonder.

I take the stairs two at a time and fling open the bathroom door. Everything looks the same as it did this morning except for the trash can, which is filled up with tissue and a toothpaste carton that is no longer empty. Inside the cardboard, I notice the tip of a pregnancy test sticking out. I ignore the fact that I'm touching someone else's potential good news. As I squint at the small digital screen, I understand now why she's been snappish and scared. You can't mistake a positive plus sign.

Sinking onto the toilet, I instantly feel for her, especially to be in high school and pregnant. That was when I had my first miscarriage, and to be that young and alone—it's not ideal.

My thoughts are interrupted when I hear the tremor of the garage door shaking the house.

"Babe?" I hear Noah yell from downstairs. "You good with the Beemer parked in the right-hand stall? A storm's coming, and I don't want to have to worry about taking it to the car wash again."

"Sure." I stride to the door and peek over the open railing. "Hello to you too," I tease, making my way down the staircase.

"Oh, and I can't forget this." He leans forward to kiss me, his hands caressing both sides of my cheeks. I snuggle into him for a moment, then step back as he gives me a questioning gaze.

"You're glowing, Char. You want to tell me what's making you this happy?"

"You." I grin facetiously.

"I can't wait to hear how." He gives my cheek a gentle tug before he disappears. I watch him through the side door as he pops the trunk and pulls his suitcase out.

Batting my lashes at him, I lower my voice. "Do I get you for the night?"

"Yes, you do."

"Good, because no other answer will do."

He leaves his suitcase by the door, winks, and carries me directly to the bedroom. After we finish making love, I untangle myself from his arms. Shyly, I say, "I'll be right back. I'm going to grab us something to drink."

"Char, will you please bring me a water? You got me thirsty," he chuckles as I emerge from the bathroom in a silky robe. Whistling, he gloats, "And it looks like round two is about to begin."

When I reenter the bedroom, I have two bottles—one of Moët, one of sparkling apple cider—next to two champagne flutes. Raising his brows, Noah slaps the satin sheets I vacated beside him. "Wow, this must be quite an evening. What did I do to deserve bubbly?"

"You'll find out."

I hand him the champagne bottle to uncork, and he pops it with a flourish. He pours both flutes and hands an overflowing one to me.

"I can't." I point to the sparking apple cider. "I'm drinking this."

"Are you not feeling well?" Noah playfully puts a hand on my forehead. "Is this a new resolution? No alcohol during the week?"

I give him a mischievous smile, pulling my positive test from behind my back.

"What's this?" he asks as I hand it to him.

"The reason for my happiness, for *our* happiness. I'd like to propose a toast."

Noah looks startled as I continue. "Here's to happiness and health, and the arrival of our little bundle of joy. I can't wait to start this new chapter in our lives, and I'm confident that this time it will be right, since timing is everything."

"You're pregnant?" Noah looks stunned, his hands tight around the champagne flute.

"I am." I sink down beside him and drape my legs over his body. "Are you okay?"

He closes his eyes for a minute, rubbing a hand over his face. "I'm . . . shocked, Char."

Dejectedly, I moan, "Oh God, I'm sorry, this isn't what you want right now, is it?"

"Char." He sets both our flutes on the side table. "This is just coming at a crazy time. In fact, I came home to tell you about a promotion I got—"

"What?" I shout. "That's wonderful. Now we have two things to celebrate."

"But it's not like that." He touches my arm gently. "Look at me."

I gaze into his hazel eyes, shiny with tears. "They want me to take on a project in Tokyo."

"Okay." I shrug. "An international trip is doable right now."

"It's at least six months."

"What?" My face crumples. "What're you saying?" I move my hands to my ears, trembling at the idea of Noah gone, not just domestically, but abroad.

"You're leaving me?" I sit straight up, slamming my back into the headboard.

"No, it's not set in stone." Noah laces his fingers through mine. "Forgive me, I don't mean to be callous. This is a shock, and if I'm honest, this is a huge bomb you dropped on me. I need a minute."

"If it's about the past, we can't let it dictate us anymore." I then say confidently, "It's not going to happen again."

"I know." He slowly nods his head. "But you can't blame me for being scared. That was traumatic, and I don't want to minimize how it was for you, but it screwed me up, Char."

"I know." I squeeze his hand tight, his palm sweaty to the touch.

He takes the flimsy plastic wand from me and stares hard at the plus sign. "This is a miracle, baby." Taking my arm, he pulls me close against his chest, cradling me in his arms.

I must've fallen asleep in this position, because the next thing I know, I feel an emptiness beside me in the bed, the satin sheets cold to the touch. Noah's body heat is absent.

The water's running in the shower, and I sniff fresh coffee brewing. It doesn't have the same negative effect on my sensory neurons as it did last time. Relieved I can tolerate the smell, I pour Noah a cup and knock on the bathroom door.

He responds by pushing it open, his lower half wrapped in a towel. "Good morning, beautiful." He ruffles my hair as I press the mug into his hands.

"Is it even morning?" I mumble, half-asleep.

"Close enough. Five a.m." He taps my chin. "You should go back to bed. You need your rest, Mama."

"I like the sound of that." I steal a glance in the mirror at my luminous complexion, my skin for once clear and bright. "We must've slept like rocks." I walk like a zombie to the other sink in the master suite. I brush my teeth and then watch Noah's reflection in the glass as he gets dressed, admiring his trim physique and tailored suit.

A man in a suit does it for me, and I tug gently on his striped tie. "Do we have time for round two?"

He laughs. "I wish. I've got a flight to LaGuardia." As he kisses me hard on the lips, I close my eyes, tasting his peppermint mouthwash and his aftershave.

"You didn't even get a chance to unpack."

"I've got some fresh clothes in my trunk. I'll switch it out—not a big deal."

"Okay, but throw the rest in the laundry. I can drop your dry cleaning off when I go there today, after my doctor's appointment."

"You're the best . . . new mommy." He swats my ass playfully. "Wait, you're going to the doctor without me?"

"Just this once." I hold up a finger. "It's for them to confirm it with a blood test."

Noah slides his watch on, clearly annoyed. "I should switch my flight and go with you."

"Can you?" I beg. "I'd like to have you with me."

"Yep." His phone starts to buzz, eliciting a weary look. "Give me a minute. Let me see what I can do." He steps out of the room for a few minutes; disappointment is written on his face when he returns, his mouth drawn into a frown. "I want to go to the next one."

I can tell he's getting tired of being away from home so much, and I need to fix that. Hopefully, our baby will help him realize that we need him on the ground, and not overseas.

"Please." He takes my hands in his. "Can I go with you to the next appointment?"

"That will be an ultrasound, so absolutely."

Before he walks out the door, he hesitates, rotating to ask me a question. "Charlotte?"

"Yes?"

"Who drives the black Mercedes that's here some nights?"

My mouth tightens. "What black Mercedes?"

"It's parked on the street, right outside of the house."

"No idea." His observation makes me nervous. "Should I be worried?"

"No," he mutters. "I thought you might know who owned it."

"I'm surprised I haven't noticed. As you know," I warn him, "I'm more aware of what's going on around me than most people."

CHAPTER 23
Elle

Charlotte's parked near the bus stop after school. Self-conscious, I flinch when I see her wave me over. It's becoming obvious to me by the rumors that I can no longer hide my pregnancy, and frankly I'm not in the mood for adult interaction today, especially when she seems elated to see me.

"Hi, Elle, do you have time for a snack?"

"I can't."

"Oh, bummer, do you have plans?"

"I'm busy now." I bite my lip.

"What about tomorrow?"

I sigh, "Charlotte . . ."

"What?"

"I have a lot going on right now. It's not a good time."

"Can I call you later?"

"Sure, go ahead." I shift my backpack to the other shoulder. "You'll get my voice mail, but feel free to leave a message, and I'll return it *never* because I don't have a fucking phone."

She recoils like I slapped her. "Excuse me?"

"Money doesn't grow on trees for kids like me. I'm not fucking Courtney or an unlucky future child of yours."

"Is that so, young lady?" Tinged with steel, every word drips restrained fury. "Something tells me that you're feeling spiteful, since you stole a pregnancy test and it's the *only* test you've passed lately."

I'm sure my blue eyes spark with outrage as Charlotte glares right back at me. Even though I'm hormonal and temperamental, there's an ounce of respect buried underneath for her bluntness.

"I saw your boxes of pregnancy tests on the counter," I mumble. "Are congrats in order?"

"And I saw yours. So why don't you tell me what the hell's going on?" Charlotte points an irritated finger at me. "Because I don't do this."

"What's 'this'?"

"Put up with a shitty attitude, because life is unfair."

"You came here," I retort.

I take a deep breath, reminding myself not to let my mouth get ahead of me. My goal is not to make an enemy of Charlotte. I need her in my corner, at least for now.

"That's why you're here, isn't it?"

"Why?"

"Because I'm a charity case you feel sorry for."

"Let's make a deal," she remarks. "Let's both stop making assumptions about what the other person is thinking and feeling. It's getting us nowhere."

My mouth goes slack. "Why would you want to help a perfect stranger?"

"Because I feel a kindred spirit with you. You didn't just show up on my doorstep out of nowhere. It must've been predetermined. Call it destiny or fate."

Or totally intentional, I howl in my brain.

I want to scream at her, tell her to *fuck off,* but I can't. His advice and warnings flash in my head like a public service announcement, but until justice can be served up in the form of a steaming platter of shit with her name written all over it, I'm at a loss.

This just got one hundred times more complicated now, if she's pregnant.

My throat goes dry.

How am I going to tell him Charlotte's knocked up?

I clench my fingers around the straps on my backpack. This could work . . . it will be more upsetting than my own admission and will take the disappointment off of me.

This is advantageous.

The bus shudders to a stop at the curb. "I gotta go."

Looking at the people who have begun to board the bus, many transient, some homeless, Charlotte lets her face betray her. "Can I give you a ride?"

"No." I pause. "You were right, you know."

She tilts her head. "About what?"

"That we shouldn't be involved in each other's lives." I scrunch my nose up. "This will be me in a couple months, destitute. Better just stay away. Go back to your side of town."

Crestfallen, she looks like she might cry, her face contorted like she smells something unpleasant. "That's not fair."

"Life isn't fair. I can promise you that."

"I can help you." She pushes open the passenger door. "Stop being so argumentative and get in. At least let me give you a ride."

"Fine, I'll take a ride."

"Which way is home?"

I point in the direction the bus is headed.

"Do you mind if we grab some food first?" Charlotte flashes her blinker. "I know a great deli."

"Whatever." I have to pretend like I'm not starving as my stomach growls at its lack of nutrition.

I stare out the window at the afternoon traffic, the wind picking up this afternoon and taking with it newspapers and Styrofoam cups.

I watch them blow through the streets like they're on a rush to somewhere important.

Charlotte and I order at the counter, then make our way to a booth, this one an old and faded brown pleather. The place is practically empty; it's too late for the lunch crowd and too early for the dinner rush.

"Do they give a senior citizen special at this time?" I wonder out loud.

"I don't know, do delis do happy hour?" Charlotte quips.

After we're seated, we sit in silence for a couple minutes and then concentrate on our sandwiches. I ordered a toasted hoagie that could feed a family of three. I'll have some leftovers, which is a relief. The boys can eat this for dinner.

Breaking the silence, I ask, "So are you?"

Charlotte plays coy. "Am I what?"

"Pregnant? Knocked up? With child?"

"I went to the gynecologist today and can confirm that yes, I am." There is a sparkle in her eye. "I'm almost twelve weeks."

"Shit." I try to match her excitement. "Congratulations, Charlotte."

"Thank you."

"Does Noah know?"

"Yes. I told him last night."

"But he wasn't here with you for your appointment?"

"Unfortunately, no. But next time. The ultrasound one is what counts."

"This is big news. Were you expecting it?"

"It wasn't a surprise." Charlotte raises her eyebrows at me. "But I take it yours was?"

"No, I mean, it was an accident, but I knew deep down; I just haven't been ready to face it." I sip my water and apologize. "I shouldn't have said what I said to you. It's been a shitty day. I'm scared right now." Smirking, "Actually, terrified, if I'm being honest."

"Are you involved with the father?" Charlotte shifts uncomfortably in her seat, probably unsure how or what to ask, and I'm uneasy about how to respond, since we broke up.

"You know the guy you pointed out earlier?"

Her face looks at me blankly, the same way I respond to teachers when I don't know the answer.

"The two boys skateboarding at school?"

"Oh, from the other day?" Recognition crosses her face. "The tatted one?"

"The other one, the tall guy with the good looks?"

"Yes?"

"That's my boyfriend, Justin." I start to tear up. "Or I should say, ex-boyfriend." After reaching for the napkin dispenser, she hands me a stack.

"Everything's a mess." I rest my head in my hands. "We just broke up."

"Because of the pregnancy?"

"Kind of." I then say, "It's complicated."

"He's not hurting you, is he?" Charlotte peers at me like she's trying to see into my soul. I'm creeped out she can seemingly read everything about me with that intense stare.

"No, not physically." Without thinking, I add, "I've had enough of that for one lifetime."

"By whom?" In a hushed voice, she asks, "Diane?"

"No."

"Did something happen to you as a child that put you in foster care before your parents died?"

"No." I run a hand through my matted locks. "It's over and done with."

"Do you want to talk about it?"

"It's just my dad—he had a temper."

She opens her mouth to ask a follow-up question, but I shut her down. "But my boyfriend, er, ex, he's not abusive. That's not why we're having issues."

Charlotte brushes a hand over her face. "I can definitely relate to relationship troubles. In my past, of course."

This is my golden opportunity to get Charlotte to open up. I have to take it, or I might not get another chance. She is vulnerable right now. I can tell by her pensive gaze.

"You don't seem—don't take this the wrong way—I don't know, overly excited about having a baby." I then say casually, "Is it not what you want?"

My question rattles her.

I catch a glimpse of guilt on her face that disappears in an instant.

"Or," I press on, "it's not what Noah wants?"

"No, no, nothing like that." She shakes her head back and forth, as if she can convince not only me but herself. "A long time ago, I had a relationship that was a perfect storm. A combination of passion, volatility, and jealousy."

I say nothing, fearful if I take even a sip of water, it'll make her reconsider telling me.

Charlotte continues softly. "It became too much for both of us. And we were young, God, were we young."

"When was this?"

"Over a decade ago." She then murmurs, "We lost a child."

"You and Noah?"

Her face collapses, and it shatters in such a way I would imagine a building falls, tumbling down into a maze of rubble. A look of absolute devastation is tattooed on her features.

I look down at my hands, suddenly feeling ashamed.

"No."

"Was it an ex-husband?"

"Goodness no," she says, shuddering. "Marriage would've been even worse."

"Did this man hurt your kid?" I've heard my father's side many times, and now I want to hear Charlotte's. They always say there are two sides to every story, and the truth, well, that lies somewhere in the middle.

Charlotte swallows hard, her eyes reliving the horror right in front of me. "It . . . the baby wasn't born yet. I was seven months pregnant."

"So, he didn't hurt you?"

"No. I mean, yes, that's how I lost the baby. We had a terrible argument, and he pushed me . . . I went headfirst down our basement stairs."

"Jesus, Charlotte." I settle back against the booth. "What happened when you fell?"

"I bled out and lost the fetus to a miscarriage. I fractured my wrist and was pretty beaten up and bruised, but that didn't matter. The baby . . ." Now it's my turn to shove some napkins in her hand. "The baby couldn't be saved."

"And the guy, did he get in trouble?"

"No."

"He didn't go to jail?"

"No, he didn't." Her voice sounds weary.

"Did you call the police?"

"Sometimes. We would have these screaming matches that would turn violent. But not this time."

"Shouldn't he be in jail for this?"

Her jaw hardens. "I never wanted to see him again. He took off that night and never resurfaced, thank God. He's around somewhere, another state probably." Charlotte folds her hands around her glass. "That's why I'm so paranoid about my safety. It's like I'm waiting for him to come back and finish me off."

Incredulous, I stare at her, unflinching. She probably assumes it's the impression her story has had on me. Instead, I'm suspicious of why she would lie about my father being imprisoned.

"Does Noah know about him?"

"Yes." Her voice falters. "That's why we're both super cautious about this pregnancy." She takes a napkin and blots her face, eyes bloodshot and smeared with mascara. "I know this is an overwhelming life change for you, Elle." Charlotte gives me a sad smile. "But children are a blessing. Have you talked to Justin about what you want to do?"

I sigh. "I'm not sure I'm going to keep it."

When I hear myself say this, I feel like a horrible person for verbalizing this after Charlotte's own heartbreaking miscarriage. That is, until I remind myself that she's a fantastic liar and this is a tear-jerking story, but that's exactly what it is, a fictitious story. It's nothing but a ploy for her to play the victim.

But my own guilt is a powerful emotion, and as I rest my arms on my expanding stomach, I start to sob. "Justin doesn't want me to have it." Balling my hands, I prepare for her outrage. Her hypocritical, holier-than-thou judgment. It doesn't come.

Instead, her face registers surprise, but not anger. "Oh, Elle, it's a huge decision. I get it. And I know you don't have the most stable homelife, and you and your boyfriend just split." She touches a hand to her cross necklace as if issuing a silent prayer. "Just think about all your options. There are a lot of families that can't have children and would love to adopt. Let it be a last resort instead of your first."

"Deal."

"Have you at least seen the doctor?"

"I haven't made an appointment yet." I blush. "I only have state-run insurance, and I think I'd have to tell Diane. She's got the information."

"Elle," Charlotte says, "you're going to need a lot of help and assistance navigating this."

"I know."

"Why don't you want to tell her?" Charlotte asks. "Is it because you're scared of her reaction?"

I tap my fingers on the scratched tabletop. "I'm worried she'll kick me out of the house."

Charlotte looks horrified, and her water glass splatters as she accidentally elbows it.

"She can't, can she?"

"Not for a couple more months, at least until I turn eighteen."

"Don't worry about that for right now. That's down the road. You have to go to the obstetrician. I'm going to make you an appointment. I'll try and get you into the same clinic that I go to."

"Okay," I agree.

We make small talk, but it eventually dies down, both of us lost in our own potential dilemmas.

I have Charlotte drop me off at the library, a few blocks from the apartment. As I trudge up the stairs, my steps are slow, my energy lagging. A male voice is loudly talking inside, and I assume it's a gentleman caller for Diane.

It's not.

My backpack slides to the floor as I secretly watch Justin play a game with the boys, and before anyone notices I'm home, pieces of my heart splinter and shatter in my chest.

"So this is what a broken heart feels like," I sigh out loud.

Disbelief clouds my face as I blink, wondering if I've finally lost it.

I can't stay concealed for long. In a matter of minutes I've been spotted, and the boys run to give me a hug.

"What're you doing here?" I mouth to Justin over their heads as I tuck them into the crook of each arm.

He doesn't answer, instead telling the boys to brush their teeth and get ready for bed. Amazed that neither one is arguing about their bedtime, I watch them both disappear into the bathroom while I settle on the couch, as far away from Justin as I can.

"So why are you here?" Then I joke, "You decided you missed the good old domestic life I can offer you?" Speaking in an announcer's voice, I say, "It comes with a baby of your own and two additional children, but no additional baggage in the form of luxury goods!"

"Don't sell yourself short, Elizabeth." Justin's green eyes glint with a flash of anger. "You didn't sign up for this life—it was inherited."

"And now that you feel tied down, you're doing what everyone else has done to me in my life," I jeer. "You leave."

"I was harsh about it." He tugs on a strand of his dirty-blond hair. "I didn't handle things right. That's why I'm here. I'm sorry."

Ignoring his apology for now, I ask, "How did everyone find out I was pregnant?"

"What do you mean?" Justin points to my protruding belly. "I'd say you gave it away on your own."

"Normally, I'd agree, except it never was a rumor until after I told you." He looks down at an ugly metal ring he made from a steel pipe at the scrapyard. "So, who did you tell?"

"About the breakup or pregnancy?"

"Both."

"Nobody." Justin's a terrible liar, because his hands always touch his face immediately after he's been untruthful. This time he taps his nose.

"Justin Pence, don't lie to me."

"Clint."

"And Clint dates Courtney's friend Sheena, right?"

"No idea." Another tap to the nose, another lie.

"Okay."

He exhales, clearly relieved I'm going to drop the topic.

Until I point out, "The other night when I called before you went to work, you said, 'Hi, sexy.'"

"Uh-huh."

"Except it wasn't directed at me."

"Yes, it was."

"Justin, you didn't know I would call you. My phone's busted, and I called from a random number." I nudge him with my knee. "What gives with all the lying? You're better than that."

His face reddens. "Okay, I thought Courtney was calling."

"And now you call her 'sexy'?" My blood starts to boil, and I'm sure this is what a chicken in a pressure cooker feels like before it cooks or, in my case, explodes.

"It's not like that. She had concert tickets I wanted."

"Let me make sure I'm getting this straight." I point a finger at him, disgustedly. "You can attend a concert with Courtney Kerr, the demon seed of middle America, while I'm pregnant with your child, not to mention poor?"

Dizziness hits me as I shoot up from the couch. "I think it's time you saw yourself out of my apartment and out of my life. We're fucking done."

"I didn't go to a concert with her, Elizabeth. She just had the tickets. They weren't even for me. They were for my brother." He lowers his palm, motioning me to simmer down. "And just because I don't want a baby my senior year doesn't mean I don't care about you. All of this grown-up shit scares me."

"And it doesn't terrify the hell out of me?" I quiver. "I'm the one about to lose a roof over my head."

"That's part of the reason I came over." Justin leans toward me. "I have an idea."

This is the time I expect him to reach for me, tell me he loves me, and promise to help with any decision I make regarding our child. Basically, to step up and do the right thing.

Instead he stares at me, his green eyes solemn.

"Unless it's robbing a bank, I don't know how you can help," I say, expecting a chuckle. But Justin's face is rock solid, his chiseled features rigid.

"Justin?"

"You said the woman you're trying to get to exonerate your father is wealthy, right?"

"I mean, she lives on Pleasanton Lake." I lean back against the sofa. "She's certainly not poor."

"Does she carry cash? Cards? Wear anything flashy?"

"A wedding band is all I've seen on her finger," I say. Without thinking, I mention a watch that Courtney complimented her on. Then, realizing I'm just encouraging him, I grumble, "What're you suggesting?"

My wordless expression must have come across as dumb.

"Don't play stupid, babe," he excitedly says. "Let's do both at the same time." Grabbing my knee, he shakes it. "Let's rob her, and you can keep working to free your father at the same time."

"It won't work. I just found out she's pregnant."

"You're shitting me? No way." Then he groans, "She's pregnant?"

"Yeah, she just told me," I mutter. "It's too risky to rob her, and I don't want that on my conscience, beating up a pregnant woman."

"We can do it without hurting her." He taps a finger to his chin. "Does she have cameras at her house?"

"I haven't seen any, but I wouldn't put it past her. She doesn't need them; she rarely leaves the house."

"You better start paying attention to your surroundings." Justin points to his eyes and ears. "You need to keep these open, and you need to take notes. What's her last name?"

"Coburn. But I've already searched, and there's nothing on social media sites. Even her faculty page at the community college is sparse."

"Elizabeth, we need this. Don't you want a new phone? And extra cash?" He claps his hands together. "New clothing for *our* baby?"

"That's a cheap shot." I give him a lethal stare. "We both know you don't want the responsibility." He doesn't argue with me over this, since it's reality.

"Don't you want to get payback on the bitch?" Bitterness laces his words. "She's the reason you don't have a father or a mother. Do you really think your mother would've killed herself if it weren't for the negative publicity of the case?"

I can't believe Justin just said it out loud.

Sure, I've thought it.

I've even screamed it before.

But I've never heard someone else say it so poignantly to my face.

"Look at me," I say to Justin.

His words strike a chord in my heart as I lean down so we are at eye level.

"I'm scared out of my mind about having a baby."

"I know. Me too."

With a stroke of his cheek, I murmur, "But don't ever talk to me like that about Katrina again, do you hear me?"

"Yeah," he whispers. "I didn't mean any harm."

"I don't care what you do to Charlotte *fucking* Coburn, but don't ever use my family against me or as a reason to act on my behalf. You got me pregnant, and you're fucking Courtney Kerr—don't think I don't know."

"I am not." I can feel his warm breath on my face. "I would never do that to you."

"Put the boys to bed," I order, "and tell them you won't be seeing them anymore."

"Elizabeth, you can't—"

"Oh, but I can."

I've had to deal with half truths and lies all my life from the adults who were supposed to be responsible for my well-being.

I think of Charlotte's face, how effortless it was for her to sit there and lie to me. Her claim that her infamous fall down the stairs was my father's doing and not her own.

And my father, an alcoholic wife beater and all-around piece of shit, with his empty promises to get the family back together.

But Justin. No, not Justin. I never thought he'd turn into one of them.

He went from being the center of my universe—the only reason to keep climbing out of this black hole—to being the crater, the one big empty depression, that my life has collapsed into.

Unable to look at him, I step backward, turning toward the wall as I face away from him.

He stands and hesitates before I feel a light pat on my shoulder. Then his footsteps disappear into the boys' room.

And, unable to stand any longer, I do what I do best in situations like this. I lie down on the floor, shove a pillow over my face, and tune out the sounds of the television, Justin's animated voice as he acts out a bedtime story, and the guttural sound of a young girl crying.

Justin comes out into the living room and yanks the pillow off my face.

It isn't until he's standing there, aghast, that I realize the noises are coming from me.

CHAPTER 24
Charlotte

Over the weekend, I have a yearning for another home-improvement project. Even though the house is relatively new, I'm obsessed with scouring local flea markets and antiques shops for Tiffany lamps or the perfect dishware. I make my way to a dealer across town and rummage through vintage-book sales to find first editions for a bookshelf in the baby's room.

When I arrive at home, Noah's car is parked in the garage.

Strange. I check my phone for any missed calls or texts. I'm surprised as I step over the threshold into the house, since he always lets me know when he's on his way home.

"What's this?" His voice startles me from above.

I look up toward the chandelier. "What's what?"

"This framed picture of me on the wall."

"I changed some of the photographs out." Then I snicker, "What, you don't like how young you look?"

"It's becoming a blip on the map." He shakes his head. "Char, we need to talk."

"Can you at least greet me with a kiss first?" I tease.

"That's the problem. I've got to get going or I'm going to miss my plane."

"You're not staying?" I try to keep the disappointment out of my voice. "I thought we'd spend some time before—"

"I can't." Noah abruptly motions to his suitcase. "My luggage is all ready to go."

"You didn't even bother unpacking." I point to his Tumi bags. "You need fresh clothes, Noah."

"Be right back." He gives me an irked sigh. When he's annoyed, his hazel eyes shift to green. "I need to grab my charger."

Standing at the doorway, I don't break my concentration on him. His tie's loosened, and his three days of scruff makes him look older and haggard. He's still sexy as hell, but he is closed off.

And when he's closed off from our history, it's a sign that something's bothering him. Or someone.

Gritting my teeth, I wonder if he's communicating with Lauren again.

I cross my arms when he comes downstairs. "How long this time?" I try to sound upbeat, but my voice betrays me. It quivers as I reach out to touch his cheek.

"You really want to know?" He presses his car keys in my hand, holding on to my wrist for a minute. "This is what I want to talk to you about."

"No, I don't want to know."

"The promotion came through." He rubs his hand over his eyes, and I see the angst. "I hate that I won't be there as much for you as I'd like, and I feel like a deadbeat." Sighing, he adds, "Until it closes, I'll have a few days here and there, but when that's finalized, it's a three-to-six-month assignment." He straightens his tie in the hall mirror, mumbling, "At least."

"What?" The color drains from my face. "You've got to be kidding."

"This is a huge conglomerate, a lot of moving pieces. I might end up back in New York during the transition, but that's it." Noah adjusts his leather laptop bag on top of his suitcase.

Gently, he touches my arm. "Before you told me you were pregnant, I was going to ask you to come with, Char . . . and it's such great news, but the timing . . . it's never been our thing. I don't expect you to travel to Japan when you're pregnant."

"You were?" I'm surprised.

He nods. "I just feel like something is going on with you. Like something you're not telling me. I don't want there to be anyone else."

My eyes fill with tears. "Don't you dare make this about me." Then I whisper, "I can feel it."

"Feel what?"

"You pulling away again."

"Don't be ridiculous." He clasps my hand in his. "Please don't pick a fight with me before I go. I hate that."

"Did you tell anyone the news?"

"Which part?" He grins, kissing my hand.

"Why do I put up with you?" I groan.

Noah pulls me in close, holding the nape of my neck against his chest. "I will be there for you, Char. It just won't be as much face-to-face as we'd both like. I'm sorry."

"You love your job, and that's why I admire you."

"I'm tired of being pulled in opposite directions all the time." His phone chirps in response. "It's exhausting."

"They'll let you have some time off soon, right?"

"When this is over."

"That's when it counts." I try to sound strong, independent, but the tears are starting to caress my cheeks. "We'll need you soon."

"I know."

"Let me take you to the airport."

"No, it's okay. I know you have stuff to do today, Char. I've got an Uber coming. It's on the way."

"But it's more time we get to spend . . ."

His phone beeps, as if impatient to get his attention. It's my biggest competition besides her, I think. All of us trying to be number one and hold the position.

"I've got to answer these work emails that never stop piling up." His voice softens as he adds, "It's okay, Char. We can Skype this weekend."

He embraces me, giving me a sturdy hug as a black Lincoln Town Car pulls up. He whispers "Love you" in my ear before I watch him walk out the front door.

The driver pops the trunk, loads Noah's bags into the car, and opens the back door for him. He disappears behind the tinted windows as I stand there, looking after him, my body tense, a hand automatically reaching for my belly. A pained expression crosses my face as I remember a day not unlike this.

It was cloudy, overcast, the same time of year—late spring.

I was scared of the future, just as I am today, except it was a decade ago.

Sinking into the couch, I shut my eyes, the timeline seared into my memory. Instead of being at the start of my pregnancy, as I am now, I am nearing the finish line, about six months along. Noah and I have fallen out of touch for a few months. His broken engagement still isn't enough to bring us together, except for a couple of nights of passion, and I am still living in hell with my ex, Jonathan.

I hold the phone in my grip as if it's a lifeline, which I suppose it is. My heart pounds out of my chest as it rings twice before a male voice answers.

I whisper, "It's *me*."

"*Me* who?"

Relieved he isn't too mad to play our same silly phone game, I bite my lip. "You know, *me*."

"Oh yeah, *you*. I remember *you*. Of course I know." His voice becomes husky. "How are you, stranger?"

"Pregnant."

"What?"

"Yeah, I'm due in a few months."

"Oh my God, congratulations." Noah's voice goes up an octave too high, and he adds, "We're still in the same boat, unable to conceive."

"Thanks." I shut my eyes. "And I'm sorry to hear that. I know how badly you both want children."

"I've missed you."

"I know, me too," I sigh. "How's everything else with the two of you?"

"We actually, Charlotte—" There is a pause. "We eloped."

It's then I feel the earth open up and swallow me whole. Speechless, I sag against the wall in our kitchen, the phone dropping from my hand as if it, too, can't stomach the news.

I hear Noah repeat my name a few times.

As I replace the receiver at my ear, I hear him say, "Charlotte, are you there? Are you okay?"

"I . . . I'm . . . I have no words."

"Shit. I should've told you before we eloped. Not like this."

A loud gurgle escapes my mouth.

"Oh my God, Char, what is it?"

I press my eyes shut as I murmur, "I need your help."

And just like that, the trajectory of my life changed.

But that was then, and this is now.

I have to let the memory slide back into its rightful place in the past.

Uneasy about history repeating itself, I settle into bed for the rest of the afternoon, nausea overcoming me. I manage a small cup of broth and some caffeine-free tea and nibble on some toast points.

Before I can focus on my work emails, I have to know. I go to Noah's office.

In Noah's email account, another email appears, this one already read, sent last night from Lauren. My hands grip the edge of the screen, wanting to toss it across the room.

Did he respond to her?

Holding my breath, I check the sent box and am relieved to see he hasn't answered.

At least not yet.

I'm going to have to be more diligent about checking his email, I decide.

CHAPTER 25
Elle

As soon as I get home from school and launch myself through our fourth-floor apartment door, I'm on my knees hunched over the cracked porcelain toilet bowl. Diane's seated on the couch, smoking like a chimney.

"What the hell's wrong with you?" she hollers from her spot. I didn't bother to shut the bathroom door when I ran in, and the door is ajar as her cigarette smoke permeates the hall. My body trembles as I lose the contents of my lunch into the toilet bowl.

"I think I'm catching a bug," I whisper, dry heaving.

"What?" she yells, the television noise going down just a notch.

Rolling my eyes, I shift back from my knees and settle against the hideous puke-green wall for a moment to catch my breath.

I wipe a hand across my face, and the smell of vomit makes me lurch forward again. I thump my head against the lid. When I finish, I catch out of the corner of my eye the outline of Diane leaning against the doorjamb. She stares at me, her eyes defeated. "Oh, my dear heavens, you're pregnant, aren't you?"

"Huh?" My sweaty face stares up at her, beads of perspiration dripping down my back.

"Don't 'huh' me. You're knocked up!" She jabs the air with her cigarette butt. "I know that face. And that telltale sign."

"You don't know shit." I close my eyes as I hear the faucet turn on. I refuse to look at her and feel something cold pressing against my forehead.

Oh God, has she gone mad?

I open my eyes in surprise at the wetness, and Diane's holding a washcloth against my face. Gently, she says, "You know you can't be bringing no baby into this house . . ."

I nod.

"We don't have the room."

"I know, Diane," I moan. "Believe me, I know."

"I wanted you to have more . . ."

"More than what? This?" Incredulous, I motion around the dumpy apartment. "Any part of town is better than here."

"That isn't so. You have a roof over your head, and you don't live on the streets."

"But I will soon," I say dejectedly.

"Well, maybe we can work something out. You can get a job and pay rent." She juts her bottom lip out. "Is that wannabe model skateboarder the daddy?"

"Justin?" I say. "You mean Justin."

"Yeah, that one." She punches the air with her cigarette butt. "He's a wannabe something." She claps her hands gleefully, forcing me to catch the rough cotton before it drowns in the toilet. "Is he going to help?"

"Diane . . ." I swallow hard. "It's nobody's, because I'm not pregnant. The flu's going around. Half my class is sick."

"Sure, it is," she says, eyeballing me intently, her wrinkled face aged beyond its years by nicotine and alcohol.

"Can I use your bed to sleep? I need some rest."

Tiredness settles in, bone deep, as I struggle to keep my eyes open, even in my current state. I could just lie down in the small closet-size bathroom and sleep for days, or maybe years, like Rip Van Winkle.

"No, not if it's really 'the flu,' as you claim," she says, using air quotes. "I can't get sick. I got an overnight shift tonight." Snatching the washcloth from my hand, she adds, "Get some sleep, because later I need you to watch the boys."

She stalks out of the room and slams the bathroom door behind her, its rickety frame groaning. I reach a hand out for the edge of the countertop and slowly pull myself up. The vanity has seen better days, the rotted oak stained in places. It's like a guessing game, trying to figure out which of the drawers open and which are glued shut. The disgusting aftertaste in my mouth is overpowering, and I scrub my tongue with my toothbrush, gargle with mouthwash, and then repeat the process, trying to erase the taste of vomit and bile.

Still feeling dizzy, I ease myself back down to the faded linoleum. I can hear the television blaring a soap opera from the living room, the volume back up to obnoxiously high. Wrapping my arms around my knees, I curl up in a ball, the raggedy bath mat acting as a buffer between me and the cold floor. Reaching up, I yank a towel hanging from the rack and use it as a blanket. Diane's voice shouts at the TV, or maybe me, through the thin door. I pay her no mind, shutting my eyes in surrender.

I drift off, and the image of Charlotte's face, along with my father's shadow, haunts me. Both of them dance in front of my eyes, their expressions a stark contrast to each other. They keep asking me questions, but no one responds to mine. It's like neither one hears me, my voice on mute, so they talk to me over and over, but it's the same loop. Frustrated, I start to scream, hands pressed to my ears, but they don't notice. Louder and louder I shriek, which makes them talk faster and faster until their words are nothing but jumbled thoughts. Then I suddenly appear in a dark room, with no lights and no furniture, lying on my back on cold concrete. The ceiling starts to move, but it doesn't levitate; instead it closes in on me, slowly shrinking the space above me inch by inch, until I can reach a hand out to touch it. As I press my palm to it, the last inch between us is removed, and my nose now rests against it.

It doesn't stop; the smell of paint and cigarette smoke fills my nostrils as I take my last breath, and the desire to scream echoes from my lips as it clamps down on me.

I jerk awake to one of the boys perched on my chest, his weight the reason for my sense of suffocation. Tugging my hair, he giggles, "Why are you sleeping in the bathroom, silly?"

"Because I'm a silly goose." I tickle his sides. "Okay, get off me so I can get up and make you a snack."

"Do we even have anything to eat?"

His question breaks my heart, and I consider Justin's idea. "Soon we'll have all the food in the world." I tap his nose as I slowly rise, my hands grasping for the towel rack. I'm careful not to yank it from the wall, where rusted screws precariously hold it in place.

"Someone left something outside." He grabs my hand. "Come see."

He tiptoes out the front door like we're on a secret spy mission, holding his finger up like a fake pistol, his eyes darting left and right to check the hallway for the bad guys.

Pointing down, he mouths, "There it is."

A tied plastic bag rests on the faded welcome mat, which until now I've never noticed. I'm unsure of when we even acquired it, and the colors are muddied by time and dirt.

Great. Did Justin bring the few items I left at his place as further confirmation that we're broken up? My eyes start to fill with tears, and I roughly wipe them with the back of my hand.

No, he wouldn't have come here today.

It's the beginning of the week, and he has a full load of classes.

Maybe it was our neighbors, who couldn't be bothered to dispose of their waste, human or animal—one and the same to me. One has a yappy terrier mix that constantly gets into scuffles with a pit bull down the hall, both trying to assert their dominance.

Kind of like Diane, I think.

Gingerly, I touch the plastic bag like it might attack me, thankful there's no awful smell of dog shit.

Must be garbage someone left.

Deciding to take it to the dumpster, I shudder at the thought of more cockroaches and rats than we already have. But because you should always check for buried treasure, or in this case, food, I take a quick peek inside the bag.

A neighbor scrawled a quick note, saying someone in the parking lot was looking for our apartment number. In this complex, our neighbors know better than to snitch, just in case you don't want to be found, so they dropped it at our door.

A small cardboard box is inside.

Uneasy about opening it, I take my time. Inside is another white box, this one sleek.

A phone.

Not my broken phone, but the latest model, and way better than my old one. I don't know what shocks me more—that the package hasn't been stolen or that a new phone is waiting for me on our doorstep. The residents must've thought the same thing I did: that it was either garbage or dog shit. No one's dumb enough to leave cash or gifts outside in this complex.

That was sweet of Justin, I think, holding the package to my chest.

But why wouldn't he bring it up to the fourth floor?

There's a small card inside with a note addressed to me.

"You can't be pregnant without a phone. I added you to my plan, and you were able to keep the same number. XOXO, Charlotte."

My mouth drops, and I almost feel guilty about my conversation with Justin last night.

A few nights later, I'm at the apartment helping the boys with their homework, Diane nowhere in sight. She's probably playing the penny slots, losing her minimum wage earnings.

I make the boys shower before they do their assignments, checking beforehand to make sure there's actually a bar of soap to scrub with. Diane's not one to reinforce hygiene; she's far too lenient to care if they actually get clean in the tub or just piss in it.

They're typical boys and hate the feeling of being spotless or having shampoo lathered in their hair. They'd rather spend the few minutes it takes to shower racing their toy cars or terrorizing the other apartment kids with their toy guns.

My phone starts vibrating on the counter.

It's probably Justin, another harebrained scheme on his mind. We agreed we wouldn't text about Charlotte or anything that could implicate us in case something happens. Tempted to silence it, since the boys are close, I hem and haw until I notice it's not his number on the screen.

Unknown caller.

I never answer these. In the past, Diane's given my number to bill collectors in lieu of hers so they'll stop harassing her.

It stops.

I stare the phone down, daring it to ring a second time, and it flashes the unknown-caller ID again. I stick my tongue out at it and turn back to the boys.

The buzzing starts again.

"What the hell?" I mutter.

Rolling his eyes at me, one of the boys looks up from his math equations. "Answer it, dummy."

"Is it Justin?" the other one asks; the first one then chimes in, and they both chant, "We wanna talk to Justin, we wanna talk to Justin."

After they high-five, they make faces at me.

"Shut it." I point at the blank paper. "Answer these problems."

They exchange exasperated sighs with each other and hunch over the kitchen table. Swiping the answer button, I say "Hello?" more aggressively than I mean to, sure it's a pissed-off representative from the utility company.

"Hi, am I speaking with Elizabeth Laughlin?"

"You sound too formal to be a bill collector, and," I say, glancing at the wall clock, "it's a little late to be calling, don't you think?"

"This isn't an attempt to collect a debt."

"Sure." I bite a fingernail. "Who wants to speak to her?"

"Her, who?"

"Diane."

"This is Officer Mahoney, calling for Elizabeth Laughlin."

There's silence as I process this information. The police have my number. How'd they get it so fast? Frantic, I scan the kitchen. Did Justin really plan to mug Charlotte?

I stammer, "Okay . . ."

I drop to a chair, my legs shaking in fear. Shit, he must've got caught. Am I an accomplice? Did he name me as one of his coconspirators, or whatever they say on television?

"Can you confirm you're Elizabeth Laughlin?"

"Yeah." My palms start to perspire as I wipe them on my knees. "Is everything okay?"

"No, I'm afraid not."

I clench the phone, waiting for him to say *arrest* or *jail* with the name Justin Pence attached to it.

But I remember that Charlotte doesn't teach a class tonight, so it could as easily be Diane. She isn't home, and she was trashed this morning. I can't imagine she's sobered up any. *How am I going to get her home?* I wonder.

If she gets a DUI, we're screwed. Maybe she finally got caught.

Or it could be related to your father.

Taking a deep breath, I ask, "Does Diane need help?"

In the background, Officer Mahoney whispers to someone, a female. "Does she want to talk to me?"

I wince, my nail bed starting to bleed in protest.

"No," he says. "No one named Diane is present with me. The name's Charlotte. Charlotte Coburn."

Did Justin roll over and tell on us? I didn't commit to anything, I fume. My blood stops cold, turning to ice. "What happened?"

"Charlotte asked me to phone you." There's a lull as he waits for me to confirm I know the woman he's talking about. My lower back is now clinging to my shirt, damp with the sweat of trepidation. I wait for him to continue. When the silence lingers on, he speaks. "She's had a bit of an accident . . ."

"Is she okay?"

"She's all right, just shaken with minor injuries, all superficial."

"Did you mean to call Noah?"

"Who?"

"Her husband," I say. "Why did you call me instead of her husband, Noah?"

"He's out of town. She said you were the second-best person to contact."

"Oh." The boys are starting to lose interest in their assignments and are taking the liberty of throwing pencils at each other. Narrowing my eyes at them, I make a throat-slitting gesture and head into their bedroom for privacy. The officer waits for me to bombard him with questions, but I hold my breath, unsure of what I'm supposed to say or do.

"We'd like you to come down to the station."

"What for?" My tone clipped, I say, "I mean, I'm babysitting tonight. Can I help from here? Does Charlotte want to talk to me?"

"Certainly, but we'd prefer you come to the station. She's shaken up, and we can fill you in when you get here." Another hushed side conversation between them ensues before I hear a rustle. Or is this a trick? Their sneaky way of getting me down to the station so they can interrogate me?

Officer Mahoney replies, "Here she is. Charlotte's getting on the line."

At first, only pitiful sobs come through the line. Any words drown in her hiccups. "Charlotte?" I plead multiple times. "Charlotte, please calm down. I can't understand you."

She tries to tell me what happened but seemingly can't force the words out. She is stuttering incoherently, and Officer Mahoney finally interrupts a wail after three failed attempts. "Elizabeth?"

"Yeah?"

"She's having a rough time. Let's let her gather her thoughts and calm down first."

"Okay."

"Do you have a license?"

"Like a driver's license?"

"Yes."

Flustered, I say, "I don't have a car." Even though I took drivers' ed, I have no one to practice with, and Diane trusts me to drive only when she's too drunk. Justin's piece-of-shit Camaro's almost twenty years old and has a new leak every week. Plus, it's a stick shift.

"No problem. I'll send a squad car to your house to take you to the police station."

"What about the boys I'm babysitting?"

"Are you the only adult in the house?"

I roll my eyes. "Yeah."

"When will your parent or guardian be home?"

How do you tell a police officer you *are* the parent and guardian?

There's no point in lying. "I'm not sure. Let me call and ask their mom."

"I'd like you to drive Charlotte back home, if you feel comfortable." He then explains, "My partner drove her car back to the station.

I'd prefer she wasn't behind the wheel right now. We offered, but she insisted we call you. As I understand, she's a few months pregnant, and I don't want her to get worked up more than she already is."

He asks for my address, and it takes two times for me to provide it correctly. "Officer Sparrow will be there in fifteen minutes, car number ten-seventy."

Hurriedly, I call Justin as I herd the boys like cattle into the bathroom to brush their teeth and get their pajamas on.

He doesn't answer.

Our neighbor Sandra, whom I ask to babysit only in dire emergencies, is a floor down. She lives with her boyfriend, who works the overnight shift. I leave Diane a scribbled note and walk them to Sandra's before heading the rest of the way downstairs.

After calling Justin a second time, I get no answer.

Sparrow steps out of the vehicle to greet me, probably familiar with this area. The police are always here, it seems, for vandalism, assault, and domestic violence.

"What happened to Charlotte?" I ask as we pull out of the broken-concrete parking lot.

"Charlotte was mugged." I expect him to say it happened at the college and am stunned when he mentions the "parking lot of the Van Hessen's Grocery Store, the one on Twelfth and Melcher."

"Wait, the one, like, *two* miles from here?" That store is on this side of town, nowhere near her safe and well-lit organic and all-natural markets. What would Charlotte be doing there, especially at this time of night?

Troubled by this piece of information, I tell myself my discomfort is heartburn, but the reality of the events is unsettling. What if Charlotte went to pick up groceries to drop off to me because she knew that money was scarce and there were more mouths to feed than food?

My mouth is dry, like I inhaled a dust storm worth of dirt. "Did you catch the person?"

"No, not yet. She's pretty shaken up, so details have been slim, but hopefully, with you there for moral support, she can provide a better description of her attacker."

"And you're positive she was at the Melcher store?"

Sparrow gives me a side glance. "Yeah, you go there?"

"Sometimes. But it's close to me. It's not close to her."

"You seem like you have street smarts. Just as a precaution, be careful there or in any of those massive parking lots. Stay aware of your surroundings at all times. Put your phone away and watch around you. Park in a well-lit area." Sparrow eyes me. "You look like you know this, though."

I nod in agreement. "Growing up on this side of town, definitely." Finally, I say it out loud. "What was she doing at that store?" I intone, "She lives by much nicer and safer ones."

"Said she was running errands." Sparrow glances over at me. "I think she was trying to bring you some groceries. Said 'a friend in the Meadowlark apartments.' I'm assuming she meant you."

"Now I feel like an asshole," I mutter.

"Rough homelife?" Sparrow asks, not unkindly. He has no idea the depths of the hatred I feel toward myself at this low point in time. Charlotte's kindhearted nature has been swallowed up by my shitty antics.

Quietly, I rub, underneath my sleeve, the jagged scar strategically hidden beneath a leather bracelet I wear sometimes. In this moment, as I trace its rough outline, I feel deserving of it, like I got mine. My father's nasty temper followed him into any relationship, and this was no different, another permanent reminder of his wrath.

Asking myself an honest question, I have to wonder: *What if Charlotte isn't guilty and you're bringing all this on an emotionally vulnerable, pregnant woman?*

Interrupting my thoughts, Sparrow says, "I'm not judging or trying to pry. I grew up around the corner. Product of a crack mom."

Emphatically, he slaps the steering wheel to drive his point across. "We gotta stick to our own, especially with all the clowns out there."

"How'd you get out?"

"I had a mentor at school, a coach who pushed my ass every day. Hated him at times. But I ended up on a b-ball scholarship and in college." He looks upward. "Thank the Lord."

"I don't have the grades for college."

"High school doesn't mean everything. You can apply yourself in college."

"Yeah, I guess." I don't bother to add that I'm knocked up, about to be kicked out of the foster system, and at risk of flunking out of high school. .

Before he asks any more questions, I switch the topic back to Charlotte.

"Is she going to be okay?" I squirm in my seat, thinking of her unborn baby. I told Justin he couldn't do anything that would hurt the child. Regardless of what she's done to break up our family, I don't want that on my conscience.

"Yeah, I think emotionally it'll take some time. It definitely scared the hell out of her. She's not the same stock as you and I, you know?" He grunts. "A total sweetheart, but you can tell her upbringing wasn't the same, lucky her."

I want to tell him about the *Jonathan Randall v. The State of Kansas* trial, but I don't. He can read about Charlotte Coburn another time. He pulls into the station parking lot, where Charlotte's charcoal Jeep is parked in a visitor's space. "Imagine if someone tried to attack you."

I want to add, *They have.*

But, terrified that the police are going to give me the third degree, I am thinking about what will happen when I walk through the doors of the station. As I walk slowly behind Sparrow into the building, I shove my hands into my pockets.

CHAPTER 26
Charlotte

I'm sitting on an uncomfortable folding chair, hands clasped tensely in my lap, when Elle and Officer Sparrow walk into the office, if you can call it that. It's claustrophobic and tiny, two of my biggest triggers.

I hear the voices of Elizabeth and Sparrow behind us.

Officer Mahoney is seated and half rises to greet them as I stare straight ahead. He motions to the empty chair next to mine, which is covered with paper and more paper.

"Elizabeth, hi, thanks for coming." Like his desk, the chair is barely visible underneath a plethora of files and documents. "Sparrow, can you clear that for Elizabeth?"

"No problem." In one swift movement, he sweeps the pile of papers off the chair. Leaning against the wall, Sparrow crosses his arms as Elle tentatively sits, her back rigid against the hard metal, her eyes darting awkwardly around the small office.

I glance tearfully at her, aware my face is splotchy. The bruise is worsening on my left cheek and will probably be purple next time I check a mirror.

"Thanks for coming," I whisper as she peers in surprise at the white muslin wrapped tight around both of my hands.

She examines my hand. "Oh my God, what happened?"

"Did Sparrow fill you in?" Mahoney asks, gazing between both Elle and Sparrow.

"Yes," Elle says.

"The assailant shoved her into some glass." Mahoney grimaces, staring at the crumpled tissue balled up in my fists as my shoulders shake.

"She's lucky she doesn't need stitches," Sparrow adds, "and that she had her keys in hand so the perpetrator didn't steal her vehicle."

"Is this what it was, attempted carjacking?" Elle asks.

Mahoney shrugs. "We're unclear, since the suspect took off without Charlotte's keys, but that's what it's looking like."

As I release a fresh flood of tears, the officers want to recite my story so I can confirm the details.

"Are you sure you're okay hearing this, Elle?" I ask her.

She nods. "I'm here for moral support."

As I fill in any gaps for Mahoney and Sparrow, Elle sits absolutely still, as if she's scared to move. It doesn't help that Mahoney's attempt at a soothing tone comes out gruff. His eyes are trained on his notes. "This happened after nine thirty p.m. at the Van Hessen's Grocery Store, Twelfth and Melcher?"

"Yes."

"You were walking out of the store when someone, an unknown suspect at the present time, grabbed you a few feet from your charcoal Jeep, license plate KTZ013?"

I nod.

"They yanked the hood of your jacket, which is how you first came into contact with the assailant?"

"Yes." I take a deep breath. "They spun me around until I was facing them. A one-eighty. The person had a black or navy ski mask on; I'm almost positive it was black. Black clothing, long-sleeved shirt, black cargo pants, black combat boots, black gloves."

Mahoney continues, "They hit you with an open fist across your left cheek, then demanded you raise your hands, is this right?"

"Uh-huh." I chew on my lower lip, remembering how they shoved me. "When I didn't respond right away, because I was, you know, stunned, they pulled out a gun and instructed me to remove my wedding band and Tiffany watch, along with my cross necklace." I tremble at the thought of my missing jewelry items, their sentimental value more priceless to me than their retail cost.

"I had my phone in my hand, along with my wallet, and they took both."

Sparrow cuts in. "Was it a real gun, and were there any discernible qualities you noticed regarding the make or model?"

"I'm not well versed in weapons. I think it was real, but again, I wouldn't know." My face burns as Elle stares at me, her jaw tight.

"And what next?"

"They asked for the keys to the Jeep. Out of the corner of my eye, I saw an employee walk out to take what I assume was a smoke break, so I started screaming. They proceeded to shove me to the ground."

"And the injuries to your palms are not from the mugging, per se, but from glass on the parking lot ground, correct?" Mahoney pushes a half-filled coffee mug out of his reach. I notice an abundance of mugs and glasses, most half-empty.

"It's from glass, I'd say a bottle, on the ground."

"What did the person look like?" I close my eyes as Elle squeezes another tissue into my lap. Nodding my thanks, I blow my nose.

Muffled, "I say *they* but I think it must've been a man, because of how they were built, taller and stockier than me, but I can't say the gender for sure. They seemed pretty built."

"And were there any lights or anything specific you remember about the area you parked in or were assaulted in?" Sparrow asks.

"I was dragged behind a maroon truck, and no, I wasn't next to a lit-up area. It was dark, which is why I was worried they had . . . other intentions. I yelled I was pregnant, but I don't remember much else." I shake my head at what could've happened, and Sparrow and Mahoney exchange glances above me.

Sparrow pounds the wall. "Damn, not the time to be mugged." I look over my shoulder at him, and he hurriedly adds, "I didn't mean it the way it sounded, ma'am, not that there's ever a good time, ma'am, I just mean . . ."

"I know what you mean." I give him a weak smile.

"Was the person wearing any jewelry of their own? Earrings, necklaces? Speaking of their face, any look at their eyes?"

"No jewelry I could see. Eyes were green, I think. Are we almost done?" I rub a hand over my face. "I'm exhausted and I'd like to try and get some sleep, though I doubt it'll happen tonight. I just want to lie down, if you don't mind."

"Of course," Sparrow says.

Mahoney looks at Elle. "Elizabeth, are you comfortable driving Charlotte home in her vehicle?"

I give her a small smile. "I'm so sorry to involve you in this and be a pain, but I don't feel like driving."

"Understandable." She squirms in her seat. "I can drive."

"Thank you, gentlemen, for your help." They advise me on what to do with insurance for claims regarding my jewelry and tell me they will have a detailed police report after they interview the employee at the store who interrupted the robbery.

Mahoney stands, this time making it to his full height. "Sparrow and I will walk you out."

We follow the officers out of the rear entrance of the police department's redbrick building to the parking lot. Mahoney hands Elle my car keys, instructing her to make sure I ice the nasty shiner on my left cheek.

Sparrow gives me a terse smile and a delicate pat on the shoulder. "We'll be in touch."

I notice Elle's tentative gestures in the vehicle as she slowly adjusts the rearview mirrors and her seat, as if she's nervous about driving.

"Are you okay with this?" I sigh. "I should've asked how you felt about driving someone else's vehicle. I should've just gotten an Uber, but you were close."

Looking apprehensive, she puts the Jeep in reverse. "No, it's fine. It's just not something that's a habit yet."

"You have a license, right?" Then I prod gently, "And know how to drive?"

"Yep." Elle gradually backs up, watching over her shoulder. Apparently unused to a rearview camera, she is startled by the beeping and responds by slamming on the brakes.

"Put it in park for a minute," I say.

After I demonstrate to Elle how the technology works in the Jeep and what the buttons on the dash and steering column mean, her face softens, and a small smile of relief lights up her eyes.

"How often do you get to drive?"

Mulling the question over, Elle responds, "Not often. I don't have access to a car, and this is a larger SUV than I'm used to."

"Would you prefer to take city streets or the freeway?"

"Whatever's fastest."

"Okay, I'll direct you to the quickest route." I use the in-dash navigation system and hit the home button as a detailed map flashes across the screen. "You'll just follow the voice prompts." We ride in silence except for the voice guidance, giving Elle time to adjust to the turn-by-turn directions.

I break the lull. "Does your foster mom ever let you drive?"

"Not usually." Elle keeps her eyes trained on the road. "Are there any stops we need to make?"

"No." I gingerly touch my face. "Just home."

Elle stops at a traffic light and steals a peek at me. "Why were you at the grocery store?"

"What do you mean?" I raise my eyebrows. "I needed to get groceries. Though they are probably still on the ground where I dropped them."

"I mean, why the Twelfth and Melcher one? It's a seedy location."

"I like the Thai place over there. I went for take-out . . ." Elle slowly lets her foot off the gas. "But really, I wanted to get some groceries for you. I know you said it's hard without Diane contributing much."

I'm shoved forward as she hits the brake.

"Oh, Charlotte, you've done so much. You shouldn't worry about me, or the boys, or the baby."

Pointedly, I reply, "You have a little one to worry about." I lean back against the headrest, resting my hands on my stomach in agreement.

"Is the baby . . . are you and the baby okay?"

"I hope so. It was scary, but it happened in a flash. Thank God the employee came outside . . ." I shudder at the thought of what could've happened.

Don't go there, don't go there, don't go there, I silently repeat to myself.

Elle swerves, pulling back just as she's about to sideswipe another vehicle.

"You okay?" I ask, concerned. Her hands are trembling on the wheel.

"Yeah, just not used to driving." She keeps her eyes focused on the windshield. "I better pay closer attention and stop talking."

We sit in silence as she maneuvers us back to the safe side of town, where the streets are wider, the homes double in size, the manicured yards larger and better cared for. Shoddy wood fences become wrought iron, the names of the developments fancier and richer sounding.

Iron Gate.

Wooden Cove.

Bradbury Villas.

And then Pleasanton Lake.

Elle crawls to a stop, reaching her hand out to the keypad as we come to the gate. "What's the code?"

I motion to the visor and point to the clicker. "Just press the black button next to the garage door opener. Have you ever stepped foot inside Pleasanton High School?"

Following my instructions, Elle drives cautiously through the seri-ous-looking metal bars as they stretch out their arms, welcoming us back to Pleasanton Lake.

"What about Pleasanton?" I ask again. "You know, since you *fake* go to school there?"

"We played them once for volleyball."

Surprised, I say, "Oh, you play sports?"

"Not anymore. But I did."

"Anything else besides volleyball?"

"I ran track." Elle haltingly drives down the suburban streets, slow-ing when she sees the reflective colors of the peacock mailbox, signaling my house. It's fully dark and unwelcoming, unlike the lighted gates at the entrance. It's the same as the other night, except for the weather.

"What made you stop?"

"We couldn't afford the cost of extracurricular activities, not to mention the boys needed a babysitter."

"But wasn't it important to you?"

Elle mumbles, "Not all of us get to go home to our huge houses. In fact, I need to get a job, and soon." After pressing the clicker, she pulls into the garage, careful when she groans to a halt to check that the Jeep's in park and not still in drive.

After turning off the ignition, she sets the keys in my lap.

"I didn't mean it like that," Elle says. "It's just that . . . never mind, I'm sorry." She runs a hand through her hair. "I'm just pissed about what happened to you—it's awful, and I'm being a brat. I feel bad that you do so much, and then this shitty stuff happens."

"I just . . ." I falter and add, "I'm just afraid of the world." The white bandages look ghastly underneath the measly garage lights as, forgetting its absence, I move my fingers to touch the small cross that is now missing from around my neck. "And the sad thing is I have every reason to be."

CHAPTER 27
Elle

Reluctantly, I creep inside, pausing in the hallway to kick off my shoes, the soles hitting the creamy alabaster wainscoting in protest. Feeling bad for lashing out at her, I ask what I can do to help. She doesn't answer at first, so I call out again, my eyes drifting up to the massive two-story entrance and then to the living room. In the pitch black, I don't immediately see Charlotte until I spot a hunched outline, seated in the middle of the couch.

Though the house felt comfortable and welcoming the other day, now, with her motionless shadow in the dark, an aura of misery overcomes it. Justin still hasn't returned my calls, and I'm dying to find out what the hell he was thinking.

Would Charlotte ever be able to pick him out of a lineup? He does have one-of-a-kind green eyes, but would the ski mask distract from those or not?

"Would you mind pressing the on switch for the fireplace?" Her dismal voice fills the air. "I'm going to go take some Tylenol."

"No, don't move." I tiptoe to the fireplace. "Where's the bottle?"

Uncommunicative, she points behind her to the powder room. I flick the button for the fire, and the flames roar to life after a minute.

"And the cops said to put ice on your cheek. Any chance you've got an ice pack?"

"Might be an ice pack in the freezer."

I rummage in the glass cabinet for her medicine, along with a hand towel. In the kitchen, I wrap an ice pack from the freezer in the soft cotton and grab a bottle of water. As I hand her the items, I notice she hasn't made a move to turn on any lamps or the overhead chandelier. "Do you want any light?"

A sharp nod of her head answers my question. "Just the fire." Charlotte swallows a couple of capsules and shudders at the cold against her left cheek.

As she mumbles her thanks, I stand in front of her for a second, contemplating what else I can do to help her rest. I'm about to take a step back and mention grabbing a ride home from a friend when she pats the seat cushion next to her. "Will you sit by me?"

Close personal space is not my forte.

Uncomfortable, I freeze, taking a giant step back toward the chair, where I sink down.

A wan smile crosses Charlotte's face. "Or in the chair. Sorry," she says, shrugging. "Sometimes I ignore people's personal space, which is odd, since I don't like being confined to small spaces. I guess I'm feeling alone tonight, and vulnerable."

After thinking about what to say, I offer, "Would you like to call Noah?" I hand her my phone. "You can use it—it's yours. Or I can call him for you."

"He's in New York, so it's even later there. I had the cops leave him a message, which he isn't going to like, but he'd be upset if he didn't hear."

"He must worry about you, being gone so much." Pulling my legs up underneath me, I say, broodingly, "It's gotta be hard having him travel all the time."

"Yes, it is." Her shoulders tense, and I know I've hit a sensitive spot. "It gets to be a lot to handle. I probably should join some clubs. A book club, or cooking or gardening. Anything to keep me occupied."

"Your work seems to keep you busy," I say.

"It does." Charlotte keeps the ice propped to her cheek. "Teaching students is such a gift."

"That's why you're so smart."

"What do you mean?"

"You seem well educated."

"Just with books. My main focus area is literature."

"That's one of my worst."

"Reading?"

"Yeah, I just find it hard to focus."

"It can be, and if you're uninterested in the subject matter, that's the kiss of death." Licking her lips, Charlotte whispers, "Speaking of death, I saw my life flash before my eyes tonight. It was surreal, like I was standing outside of my own body, watching it happen in slow motion."

"Was it the gun that made it seem real?"

"I don't think so. It was the entirety of the chain reaction of events." She stares into the flames. "But it made me question why I brought my own gun back in the house." Under her breath she murmurs, "Damned if I do and damned if I don't."

"Why did you lie . . ." As soon as the word leaves my mouth, I regret it, and her head swivels toward me. Smoothly, I rephrase. "Poor choice of words. What I meant to say is: Why don't you want the cops to know about your gun or your experience with having them?"

"Because then I'd have to talk about my past." She gives me an intense stare. "Imagine if you have to keep reliving the worst periods of your life, because of who you're tied to in your past. That it's not just your pain or secret alone. That anyone can look it up online and know who you are."

"But I thought the person who hurt you disappeared on their own?" I play dumb. "Or did I get that wrong?"

Her puffy cheek looks more pronounced because of her evident distaste for the question. "I didn't want you to find me in an online search."

"How come?" I tilt my head.

"Because you'd have questions and want to talk about it." She sighs. "I don't want to feel forced to keep dredging it up. Does that make sense?"

I wish I could argue with her logic, find fault in it, but I can't. Who would want the general public finding out details and ripping off old Band-Aids when they discover who Charlotte was, as opposed to who she is?

She's a bystander, and though I'm not ready to use the word *innocent* yet, she's caught in the crossfire of her past.

I must've sighed loudly at the fire, because Charlotte looks at me in surprise. I'm no different from Charlotte, I suppose, because I'm also caught in the choices of my father, and even my mother. They call it *family* and *blood* for a reason.

"What are you scared about, when it—"

A ringing interrupts my question, and I'm surprised to see Charlotte stand and disappear into the kitchen. Peering over my shoulder, I watch as she rests her shoulder against the open door of the pantry, speaking in a hushed voice on what looks to be a landline.

I didn't even know these relics existed or that I'd see one in my lifetime. Though I suppose, since her cell phone was stolen, she's smart to have a backup.

I hear her say, "Good point, thank you." And then, "Hold on, please."

As I pretend to read a magazine I found in a woven basket next to the chair, Charlotte reappears by my side. "Noah just gave me a second reminder they could try and use my credit cards. Would you mind grabbing my laptop for me?" She scans the room, as if trying to conjure up where she last left it. "Hmm . . . it's probably upstairs in the office, second door on the left."

"Sure thing."

I walk upstairs. Before going into the office, I twist a knob, checking that the door that wouldn't open before is still locked, and when I get to the office I notice a pair of reading glasses perched on the window seat next to a striped laptop case.

Darting my eyes to the door, I close it halfway so Charlotte won't see me from down below if she decides to check on me.

Pausing first to make sure I still hear her hushed voice, I open the closet door.

I move my eyes upward and notice a couple boxes of various sizes resting on the top shelf.

One in particular stands out to me, since every other bin or box is labeled with its contents.

But this one isn't.

It's nameless.

I have to stand on my tiptoes, and my fingers barely make contact with it, but I'm able to jump up a few times, catching the corner of the box with my hand; I then give it enough of a pull to heave it an inch forward off the shelf. The cardboard edge hangs over the side, and, grunting one last time, I'm able to tug at it enough for it to tumble to the ground.

Unfortunately, my timing's off and I don't catch it, and instead it lands with a clatter on the floor. Holding my breath, I wait for something breakable to add another crash. When nothing but silence follows, I stand for an instant, relieved.

Cursing, I realize I am directly above the master bedroom and that Charlotte's probably on her way up, wondering what the thud was.

Sneaking a peek out the door, I anxiously wait, expecting to see her haggard face.

The box is closed and expertly taped, and there's no opening it without having to retape it shut. I'll need packing tape to close it back up.

Most of the desk drawers are locked, and Scotch tape is all I can find in the desk drawers.

I bring Charlotte's laptop case downstairs and set it on the coffee table. I can hear Charlotte in the kitchen, so I tiptoe out to the garage in search of some packing tape. Relieved, I find a roll balanced precariously on a Tupperware container, like it was left there as an afterthought.

I have an excuse ready if I run into Charlotte as I come back in the house. I'll tell her it's to tape the gaping hole in my sneakers.

Holding my breath, I want to run the entire way up the staircase, but that would cause louder footsteps. I duck into the office, swiftly shut the closet door, and lift the box before carrying it to the bathroom.

After locking the door behind me, I use a pair of scissors to open the box, and, as I cut through the tape, I'm careful not to damage the cardboard.

My stomach is filled with dread as an invisible hand wraps around my neck muscles, tensing my back and shoulders.

Sinking on my knees, I rip off the last piece of tape and delicately peel away the flaps. Inside is a sonogram of a baby, and, checking the date, I see it's from 2010, which lines up with when the accident happened.

Except for one thing . . .

The father listed is not Jonathan Randall. It's Noah Wilder.

In fact, as I thumb through stacks of papers, I discover a few yellowed pages of medical records that indicate that Noah was the actual father, based on a paternity test.

My heart sinks.

Is this what happened when my dad went to prison? Did he find out the baby wasn't his and lose his shit on her?

And why did Charlotte tell me it was Jonathan's and not Noah's?

I sigh, and the truth of this new information makes me believe all the more that my father's guilty. This doesn't help his case, that's for sure. I'm starting to feel hopeless, like there are so many buried memories and half truths and no one seems to know who exactly is at fault anymore, and everyone has a percentage they're responsible for.

The outcome of this is not black and white, open and shut, and that's what's scaring me.

I'm terrified my dad's lying to me, or that he's remembered the chain of events a certain way for so long that the truth is no longer concrete, but blurred. His temper has never been extinguished—it's been on display, and I've seen it up close and personal.

But I remind myself that Charlotte also lied when she told everyone the baby was Jonathan's.

I repackage the box and listen at the door for movement.

It's eerily quiet.

Before I step out with the box, I want to make sure the hallway is clear.

And it's lucky I do, because Charlotte is standing at the bottom of the stairs, her eyes narrowed. "Are you okay?" she asks. "You've been up there for a while."

Shaking as I hold the door, I groan, "I was feeling sick. I'll be right down." I point to the coffee table. "I put your laptop right there."

Her expression changes, as if she thought I was holding her computer hostage.

"Oh, thank you," she says. "Take your time."

I watch her retreat into her master bedroom, and I hurriedly replace the box on the top shelf.

When I creep back downstairs, she's staring vacantly at the television screen.

I expect her to say something when I walk down the stairs, but only the noise on the TV greets me.

"Charlotte?"

There's no movement when I say her name.

I try again. "Charlotte?"

Her shoulders flinch as if I hit her.

I take slow steps toward her, as if she's a shelter rescue who's distrustful of humans. Uneasy, I don't want to sit down. Charlotte seems like a caged animal ready to pounce.

"Can I take the ice and put it back in the freezer for later?"

As she hands it over to me, I offer to make her some soothing tea.

Whatever she's focused on or imagining, she snaps out of it. "Oh, yes, please. You can just microwave some hot water and pour it in a cup. The lavender chamomile is in the cupboard closest to the sink." She pauses and adds, "And Elle, boil enough water so you can have some with me."

I notice that the picture of Noah and her at a football game is back in its original place on the sideboard. I pretend to busy myself at the side table, where I can watch her out of the corner of my eye as I examine the photograph.

"You put it back?" I put it as a question.

"Uh-huh." She's not paying attention, her focus glued to the screen.

I count the keystrokes and watch her tap her fingers on the keyboard, but I can't distinguish what the password might be.

Then, in the kitchen, contemplating Justin, I rest my hands on the counter as the water warms up.

Where would he get a gun?

He's a skateboarder with an appetite for beaches and surfing.

His brother's roommates, I bet. It wouldn't be that difficult to get one, if you asked the right people.

Or could this be a random act of violence?

Justin wouldn't have wanted to take her vehicle, and I still don't know how he would've managed to find her and follow her out of a grocery store.

My hands go to my pocket, itching to call him again, but I don't dare in this house.

Angry at the possibility that Justin might have had a part in a mugging and frustrated at my father for not telling me the baby wasn't his, I accidentally drop one of the mugs out of her perfectly organized cupboard and watch it shatter into hundreds of tiny pieces on the floor.

But did he know?

I hear Charlotte holler from the living room, asking if I'm okay.

I need to go talk to my dad—maybe even Charlotte's mother. Or Noah.

Someone who can tell me what the fuck's going on in this house of secrets. *Does she know who I am?* I wonder.

The thought of her discovering that my dad is none other than the Jonathan Randall she's spent her life running from makes me shudder.

Ignoring her, I find the dustpan. As I kneel, I blink away the tears running down my cheeks. I brush the glass into it and force myself to hum a song. When I finish sweeping up the shards, I dump them into the trash.

Who said breaking shit wasn't cathartic?

"Is everything all right?" Charlotte's head shoots up in concern as I reenter the living room with our tea.

Sheepish, I hand her a mug. "I had an accident."

"Are you okay?"

I blush in response. "Yeah, but I broke one of your coffee cups."

"That's replaceable, not a big deal, but did you get hurt?"

"Nope."

"Is there anything I need to sweep up?"

"Nah, I got it." I shrug. "I found the broom and dustpan."

Charlotte's legs are tucked underneath her, and her gaze is still on the fire. The sole purpose of the television is for the sound, I suppose.

We sip our tea in silence.

Then she says something inaudible, and I have to ask her to repeat what she said, the noise drowning her out. She repeats, "Was Diane okay with you leaving tonight?" Then she turns down the TV.

"I don't know."

"Is she home?" Charlotte peppers me with questions. "Did you tell her why you had to leave?"

"She's got enough problems to worry about, least of all me."

"Oh, I'm sorry, Elle, I'm prying . . ." She touches a hand to her mottled cheek. "Please don't mind me. We can talk about something else."

"I'm just super tired, and I need to go check on the boys."

"Oh no, they aren't home alone, are they?" She seems upset. "It was so selfish of me to call you."

I swallow the last of my tea, unsure how to respond.

"I'm sorry," she says.

"There's nothing to be sorry about." I push a strand of hair off my face. "Don't feel sorry for me. I don't want a pity party."

"I know, but it must be hard to feel like nobody cares about your time."

"It's whatever." I glance at my phone. "I'm exhausted. Do you mind if I head home?"

"No, of course. I'll request an Uber or Lyft." She pauses and then adds, "Oh, wait. I don't have my phone. Crap, can you request one, and I'll give you some cash?"

The phone buzzes again from the kitchen. "Hold on a sec." Charlotte motions to the phone and stands. She heads into the kitchen, and I again hear soft whispers.

There's a lag, and I think they've disconnected until she becomes loud and insistent. Meanwhile, the laptop tempts me from the couch, the lid firmly shut.

After walking to the doorway, I lace my sneakers up, staring at my reflection in the hallway mirror. My cheeks look abnormally rosy, and acne is popping up in angry patches all over my chest. Charlotte's voice carries over. "Okay, yeah, definitely, I will. Good night." She strides back into the living room.

"I was thinking . . ." She approaches me. "Would you mind staying tonight? I've obviously got the room, and I'm on edge. I told Noah about you earlier, and he mentioned I should ask."

Then, giving me a small smile, she continues, "We'd both feel better about it if you stayed here tonight." Her eyes never leave my face, and I feel myself shrinking. "Peace of mind, if you will."

She adds, "I should ask—are you even okay staying here?" Charlotte looks like a sad puppy, eyes hopeful that someone will make her a permanent part of their life. As much as I don't want to be in her presence, her digs are way nicer than mine.

At the apartment, I'd be sleeping on the floor on the mushy mattress. Diane refuses to let me sleep in her bed. I tried it once when she was gone all night. That was a mistake I'll never repeat. She dragged me out by my hair and gave me a backhand slap across the face. I had an ugly bruise for a week.

I never did that again.

I know the boys are with Sandra and they're taken care of. At this point, I'm tired, and I just want to lie down. The idea of her comfy sofa and the warm fireplace sounds better than good. Charlotte must notice my lids droop because she quickly adds, "Is there anything you need before bed?"

"A toothbrush?"

"Yes, absolutely. Second drawer on the left in the bathroom. There should be an unopened one."

"Can I use that blanket to curl up with on the couch?"

"Seriously?" As she stares at me like I've grown two heads, her eyes flash angrily. Oh shit, did I commit a faux pas? I'm not expected to sleep in bed with her and guard her during the night, am I? "You're not sleeping on the couch, Elle." She points upstairs. "My master suite's down here, but upstairs there's a perfectly good guest room. And you already saw the views." She continues, "The bathroom you used last time has a toothbrush, toothpaste, and towels. Everything you need is up there."

"Great, thanks."

"Do you need to charge your phone or have me set an alarm?" She looks at the clock. "What time do you need to get up, and when do we need to leave for class?"

"If you don't mind me taking a shower here, I'll just set my alarm for six forty-five, and if we leave by seven thirty, we should be good."

"Will that give us enough time for breakfast?" She tilts her head. "You have to eat on a more consistent basis, Elle."

It must come out harsher than she intends, and she pats my shoulder gently. "We both need to make sure we are giving our babies the proper nutrients. Breakfast is an important meal."

I shake my head in response. "I know."

Her white bandage starts to turn red as she gestures with her hands. "Charlotte?"

"Yes?"

"You better change that." I point to her wound. "It's bleeding."

Groaning, she cradles her hand. "Good night, Elle."

I trudge up the stairs, pausing to watch as Charlotte double- and triple-checks to make sure the doors and windows are locked. An alarm system I didn't notice before, since it's tucked behind a corner wall, lets out a shrill beep.

Too tired to even bother washing my face, I brush my teeth and snuggle into what appear to be five-hundred-thread-count sheets and a cozy down comforter, waking up too soon from the best sleep of my life.

CHAPTER 28
Charlotte

I knock on Elle's door after she's hit the snooze button a third time.

"Go away," she grumbles. I take it she must not be a morning person.

"Absolutely not," I say in a singsong voice. "It's time to rise and shine."

"I've never understood that expression."

"Is it okay for me to enter the room?"

"I'm not decent!" she yells.

"Elle, I'm giving you ten seconds to open the door," I warn. "Ten, nine, eight, seven, six . . ."

"Okay, okay, come in."

I open the door.

"How did you know?" Elle shoves the pillow off her face.

"That if I didn't come in, you'd go back to sleep? I was young once." I click my tongue at her. "Do you want me to sing to you? My mother used to wake me up by jumping on my bed."

Elle moans, "She did not."

"Yep, but I'm not going to do the same to you. I'll dump a glass of water on you first."

Mumbling, she squeezes the pillowcase over her face. "You wouldn't dare. I've never been a morning person, and, coupled with this insanely comfortable bed and no caffeine, I'm a lazy zombie with an attitude problem."

"Come on, Elle. Breakfast awaits." I toss the pillow aside and hear a grumble rise from her stomach in protest. After I push back the gossamer curtains, the sun shines in. I stare out the window and motion to the lake. "My room has a walk-out patio with the same view." I'm dressed in all-black sweats and a hoodie, my hair in a messy bun. I've removed the bandages from my hands, but you can see the jagged red gash across both of my palms.

"So, you're going to stand here?"

"Until you get up."

"I'm not wearing much."

I cross my arms. "I'll turn my back."

Sighing dramatically, Elle sits up and tosses a flowered throw pillow at me. In the glass, I see what she wore to bed. "Kansas State, eh?" She's wearing a Kansas State shirt with a wildcat on the front, ready to pounce.

"Yeah, thanks, I found it in your drawer."

"Willie the Wildcat." I rearrange the decorative pillow back on the bed. "Best times of my life."

"Is that where you met your husband?"

"Uh-huh," I say, smiling. "So you can see why it holds a special place in my heart."

I notice her phone's blowing up on the nightstand, and I wonder if it's Diane or her ex-boyfriend.

"Hurry," I say to her, "so you have time to eat breakfast before school."

I close the door behind me to give her some privacy. After waiting for the sound of the shower, I reenter, and my hand grips her phone. It's locked, but the message still shows a name and the first part.

Justin: We need to talk.

A second one comes through from him: Need ride to visit dad today?

Dad?

I thought her father was dead.

Does she have a stepfather?

But she said she has no one but Diane . . .

The water shuts off, and quietly I back out of the room, shutting the door gently behind me. Then I busy myself in the kitchen making Elle a sack lunch, my hands trembling.

I decide to cook her some breakfast, and because I'm distracted I first burn a slice of toast. Starting over, I scramble some eggs and replace the blackened toast.

She sniffs the air when she enters the room. "You burn something?"

"Yes, but I'm not making you eat blackened toast. I did a do-over." I point the spatula to the table. "Have a seat—I made breakfast."

She gives me a glowing smile, and I realize that in spite of everything, pregnancy suits her. "Thanks."

I feel bad, noticing she's dressed in her clothes from the night before. "Do you want something else to wear?"

"No, I'm okay." She shrugs. "I only have one class today, and I didn't wear this yesterday to school."

"Do you need a ride home after?"

"Thanks, but I have one." She takes a bite of toast. "Thank you for breakfast." I pour her some orange juice as she swallows another forkful.

"How're you feeling today?" she asks me, her mouth full of eggs.

"I'm better, just shaken up." I give her a wan smile. "I just hope I can hold down food today. My stomach's been a little upset."

"I feel you," she says.

"Think you can be ready in the next ten minutes?"

I've started to crunch a piece of bread, about all I can handle, when a heavy knock interrupts the quiet.

We look at each other.

"Is that Noah?"

"He doesn't usually come in through the front." At first, a glimmer of hope gets me excited. *Did he hop on a plane after what happened last night?*

Last night when my wallet, credit cards, and ID were stolen.

Frowning, I pause as I hear another thud. My address is on my ID.

I read somewhere that most robberies happen in the early morning.

Backing up toward the wall, I begin to be overcome by an evil foreboding. My fingers reach for the cross necklace but only brush against skin.

Is it the man from last night coming to rob my house now? The jewelry and cash and my sanity weren't enough?

I huddle in the corner, my back against the wall.

As I shake my head, my recent conversation with Noah drifts into my thoughts. He had mentioned a car of some type. A luxury one, parked outside the house. What was strange was the grim look on his face when he asked.

Is someone watching the house? Could this all be connected?

"Charlotte?" Stationary, I refuse to move. "Would you like me to answer the door?"

"I don't think we should answer."

Elle slowly makes her way to the front as I warn, "Just don't open the door—the alarm's still on."

"It's the police." She states it matter of factly.

"What?" I'm horrified.

"Come see for yourself."

It feels like it takes me an hour to make my way to the window, but I eventually do and then peer out the curtains over Elle's shoulder. Sure enough, a squad car is parked in my driveway, and two men dressed in suits stand on my porch, looking very formal instead of wearing their usual dark-colored uniforms.

What in the . . .

Both Elle and I seem to respond to the police in an unfavorable manner, as if we're both hiding something. My hands tremble as I reach for the dead bolt, and she takes two steps back, stepping on my toes.

Have they come to arrest me?

The men must notice the movement of the curtains, and the doorbell chimes again, almost as if it's a premonition.

"I have to shut off the alarm."

Elle looks like a ghost, her skin void of any pigment. After deactivating the security system, I'm forced to step around her, because she's frozen in place. "Elle." I touch her elbow. "Are you ready for school?"

She doesn't move a muscle, so I gently move her aside as I cheerfully greet the officers on my porch. "Hello." My hand flies to my clavicle, where I feel the absence of my cross necklace. Every time I encounter the police, it's a fleeting reminder that I'm still in hiding, even in plain sight. I remind myself that they want only to help solve the robbery and aren't here to harm me.

"Hi, ma'am, are you Mrs. Coburn?" The shorter one with the receding hairline speaks first. I nod, my hand tight on the frame of the heavy door.

"Charlotte Coburn?" says the other one, dressed pathetically in a dark-brown suit with black loafers. Everything about him is mismatched. His ears are too big, his nose too narrow. His eyes are small and too close together. His clothing isn't coordinated.

Nodding a second time as confirmation, I never loosen my grip on the wood.

"I'm Detective Williams, and this is Detective Rodgers," the shorter one says. I notice his tie is loosened, and he seems a bit frazzled for a detective.

The other one, Rodgers, is taller, rail thin, and has sandy-blond hair. He looks to be a decade younger than Williams, probably early forties, and he flashes his badge. "May we come in for a minute?"

"Oh, certainly." I manage to open the door wider and motion them inside. "Can I get you anything? Coffee or tea?"

Elle is still standing rigid, her body like a statue of a Greek goddess. "This is Elizabeth," I say to them, as if her name explains everything. They nod to her as she stands there stammering hello.

"Nah, we're good." Rodgers answers for them both as Williams's voice is shut out. I assume he probably did want a cup of joe or a strong drink. He looks worn down. Detectives have to investigate homicides, and with murders dictating their lives and schedules, they have no semblance of normalcy. Whoever heard of a serial killer clocking in for his shift?

Pointing to the sofa, I motion for them to sit.

Elle looks troubled as she shuffles her feet, and I realize she's probably wondering how she's going to get to school.

"Thanks." Williams sinks back on one side, resting heavily against the couch cushions as Rodgers takes the opposite corner. The men are distinctly different. Rodgers perches on the edge of his seat, his long legs dangling out in front of him, his patterned socks sticking out from his too-short pants. Williams settles in, making himself comfortable, acting as if this is his own family room.

"Give me a minute, gentlemen." Turning to Elle, I point to the kitchen. "I made you lunch; it's on the counter. Do buses run at this time, or should I get you a ride?"

"Um." She looks at her phone. "I can still catch one if I hurry."

"Okay." I pat her shoulder. "If for some reason you miss it, don't you dare skip school. Come back, and I'll give you a ride."

Elle glances at the men one more time and then saunters toward the kitchen.

I sink down into the opposite chair, trying to control the tapping of my foot.

After pulling out a notepad and pen, Williams begins. "You were mugged last night?"

"Yes." I clasp my hands in my lap. "But why isn't Officer Mahoney or Sparrow here? They took down all my information after it happened."

"We wanted to talk to you about it, and Mahoney's off; Sparrow's in later." Williams taps the notebook against his knee as Rodgers explains that they are the detectives assigned to the case.

"Mahoney wanted us to check on you," Williams says.

"Check on me?" My hand goes to my naked throat.

Rodgers raises an eyebrow. "He was concerned, to put it mildly."

"Concerned that the perpetrator got away?"

"Yes, and about your safety."

Rodgers adds, "Women like you shouldn't be on that side of town alone."

"Women like me . . ."

Williams interrupts, shooting Rodgers a death stare. "We aren't trying to imply anything, just that it's a dangerous neighborhood, as you unfortunately found out. Seems you're a classy lady, and you live in a more desirable area. Better choices are around here."

I warily eye them.

An uncomfortable silence looms between us. Taking a breath to calm myself, I say, "I know you have good intentions with what you're saying."

They shake their heads in succession.

"What questions did you have?" I keep my voice neutral. "I thought I answered all I could at the station."

"You did . . ." Rodgers smiles at me, his bottom teeth crooked. "But this is serious. Your mug . . . uh . . . situation was the third one that happened this month . . ."

"At that particular grocery store," Williams finishes.

My mouth drops. "And they haven't warned the public?"

"The news has mentioned it, but I'm afraid the store is more conservative, because it leaves a bad taste in people's mouths."

"I don't care. That's not their choice. I would've brought pepper spray or a gun, or something else to protect myself."

"The assailant had a gun, is that correct?"

"Yes," I say.

"A groundskeeper found something early this morning."

"Really?" My ears perk up. "My wedding band?"

Rodgers responds. "Unfortunately, no. None of the jewelry. That rarely gets recovered."

Williams pulls a slim object out of his pocket.

"My phone!" The screen is cracked, and with its spiderweb of slivered glass, the screen is hard to read, but that's fixable.

"We found one other item." I wait for Williams to elaborate. "It's a gun."

"You found the gun?" I say. "Can you test it for fingerprints?"

"We can, but there's one strange thing that's not adding up. It's registered to a Jonathan Randall. Except Jonathan Randall is a convicted felon in prison." He says this like I wouldn't know. I wait for it. "And when we did some searching, we found ties to you."

Without saying a word, I abruptly rise, rushing to the hall bathroom.

CHAPTER 29
Elle

I watch Charlotte run to the bathroom, my body hidden in the corner of the kitchen, trying to stay out of sight and out of mind.

As I gasp, I clasp my hand over my mouth, clearly not doing a good job at muffling the sound.

They found a gun, and it belongs to Jonathan Randall? How could my father's gun be tied to Charlotte's robbery, when he's in prison?

Unless . . . no, he wouldn't have outside interference, especially when he knows I've befriended her. I shake my head. My father has done his share of hurting, but he wouldn't purposefully put me in harm's way.

Or would he?

Was his plan to have someone on the outside scare her so she'd be more inclined to look at me as an asset and a friend?

The sounds of retching are coming from the bathroom. Nauseated, I'm about to join her.

Hurriedly, I take my sack lunch to the living room. "Nice to meet you," I say to both men, my voice too high pitched. They seem startled, like they forgot I was even in the house. Maybe I'm not so bad at eavesdropping, after all.

It was nearly impossible to keep from responding to Justin this morning, especially as I watched his messages come through, but it was necessary. As I'm standing at the bus stop, my fingers start flying across the keyboard to text him, and when he doesn't respond right away, I assume he's most likely already in class.

I decide on a different agenda today: skipping class.

At Sandra's apartment, I thank her for watching the boys, and, crossing my fingers, I ask to borrow her car, with a pinkie promise to fill up the tank. She agrees, as long as I'm back by dark.

Then I ask for one more favor.

I giggle as she calls the high school, pretending to be Diane, and informs them I have a "pressing family emergency" to take care of.

Which I do.

Graduating is important, but this is just my life. No big deal.

Before I leave, I text Justin, telling him to call me later.

I've done this route a hundred times, but never in the driver's seat of a car, except when Diane reluctantly lets me drive on the way home. And never with as much weighing on my mind, and on this conversation.

Instead of dreading this visit like I normally would, I welcome it, because I have so many questions I need answers to, and it's nearly impossible to reach him by phone. I can't just call him collect to request he accept charges, and they require that a prepaid account be set up through a third-party vendor, which doesn't help when I don't have a landline.

I can hardly sit still, because one of the biggest questions on my mind is: How did my father's gun become entangled with Charlotte Coburn?

The scenery rushes past, and I try not to speed. My foot rests heavily on the gas pedal, then relaxes, as I remind myself that this isn't my vehicle and I've already engaged with the police once today. Field after field flies by, the corn and grass and farmhouses tiny dots on the horizon the farther you get out of the city.

My fingers can't decide what to do—they're tapping on the wheel, then pinching my knee, then changing the radio station. I'm lucky I'm not forced to sit still, because then my sore cuticles would be getting the brunt of my nerves.

Around the curve, the looming brick building sticks out like the eyesore it is, out of place with the cows in the pasture and the vast farmland. An ugly building filled with men who have done ugly things.

Today is different, since I don't want to slam on the brakes and escape from the moving vehicle. So I do the opposite: I set the cruise control to avoid rushing toward what I'm apprehensive about.

Impatiently, I go through the usual steps, making sure that when a woman guard uses a metal detector, it's safe for the baby. Thankfully I wore loose-fitting black pants and a long tunic sweater, so I'm able to keep my belly fairly hidden. It's noticeable if you see me on a daily basis, but not if this is your first encounter with me in a while.

After my father is brought into the half-filled room, I notice it's quieter than usual, probably because it's a weekday this time. He pats my hand with his calloused fingers. "How's my Lovebug?" The moniker has never changed, both of us stuck in the time period when he was hauled off to jail.

"I'm okay." I make a sour expression as he leans back in his seat to consider me.

"What's wrong, 'Bug?" His shoulders tense. "What's the problem?"

He doesn't waste any time getting straight to the point. That's what I've always liked—you know where you stand with him, even if it is on shaky ground.

And with it being visiting hours, it's not like we have a lot of time on our side.

"How's it going?"

Burying my face in my hands, I moan, "It's not."

"What's the problem?"

"A few things. For starters, she's pregnant."

"What?"

"You heard me."

"We can use this to our advantage . . ." My father picks at an indentation in the table. "Relationship status?"

"Husband now." I keep my gaze on him as I say the name. "Noah."

His hands clench into fists. "That son of a bitch."

Pushing forward, I ask, "Why didn't you tell me the baby she was pregnant with when you were together wasn't yours, that it was Noah's?"

His face doesn't turn purple like an eggplant as I expect. It fades to white, like a blank sheet of paper. "Because the point was moot. In court, the prosecutor destroyed me with that, used it as my motive for wanting to kill her, because it meant she cheated on me."

"Was it?" I whisper.

"Elizabeth." He looks horrified. "Of course not."

He sits deathly still in his chair, unmoving.

"When you found out she was pregnant, did you suspect she had cheated?" I pry. "Was there any doubt it was yours?"

"No, but our relationship heated up fast and cooled off just as quickly. She got pregnant a couple months after we started dating. I didn't question it, because at the time, I had never heard the name Noah Wilder before."

"How did you find out about him?"

"After I was arrested it came out. I accused her of cheating before this but had no proof." He taps his pack of cigarettes on the table, and I can tell he's dying for a nicotine fix. "I guess a baby is all the proof you need, right?"

"Why didn't I read about this in any newspaper articles?" I'm confused. "I don't remember any article stating the paternity of the baby was Noah's."

"Because it didn't come out until trial." He stares at his hand glumly. "We fought like hell to keep it out, since there was no proof I knew about it prior to the accident."

"There's more." I take a deep breath. I'm seated farther out from the table than usual because of my sprouting stomach, so I lean in to whisper. "Are you having someone on the outside try to scare her?"

"Elizabeth." He stares hard at me. "You can't talk like that in here."

"Are you?" I snap. "She got mugged last night."

Looking dubious, he asks, "Did she get hurt?"

"Someone used a gun. Robbed her at the grocery store."

"They shot her?"

"No, just stole her wallet and jewelry."

"That's it?"

"Was this your idea?"

He says nothing, his fingers still toying with the pack of cigarettes.

"Daddy, they found your gun."

He puts the package down. "What?"

"A gun registered to you. I heard the police say they found it near where she was attacked."

"What the fuck?"

"How did it get there?"

"Not from me."

"And this woman . . ." We don't call her by name, because it's easier to keep her identity ambiguous in case anyone overhears our conversation. "She keeps saying she wants to help me."

"I knew if anyone could get to her, it would be you. You're doing better than expected. She must really trust you."

"Well, not exactly," I explain. "Noah's out of town a lot, and they seem to . . . I don't know, be at odds over it." I scratch my head. "There's all these moving pieces that don't fit. I need you to level with me."

"I have."

"Daddy . . ."

"What, 'Bug?"

"I want to hear the story again."

"We've been over it and over it." He rests his face in his hands. "Jesus, Elizabeth Katrina, you think I like rehashing this every day of my goddamn life?"

"You admit you pushed her?"

"I did." I'm sure he sees the look of distaste on my face, and he hunches his shoulders forward. "But only to get her off of me."

I try to nod empathetically.

"Elizabeth, the entry was small, and she had nowhere to go but down."

"And that's when she fell down the stairs and lost the baby?"

"No." He shakes his head vigorously. "That's where I can't get anyone to believe me—nothing was wrong with her when I left. She grabbed the railing in time to save herself from falling down the stairs."

"Daddy, I'm lost." I search his face, his overgrowth of beard filled with gray. "If she was still conscious and standing when you left, did the miscarriage happen after you left, and she wasn't physically showing symptoms yet?"

"No, I'm telling you, Elizabeth, she was totally normal when I drove off."

"But she had scratches?"

"That she did." He runs a hand through his hair, the cigarette tangled in his fingers. "From self-defense." Silent for a moment, we both know a couple of scratches or bruises are nothing compared with what he's inflicted on other women.

"So you think she threw herself down the stairs?"

"Elizabeth, I don't *think* she threw herself down the stairs—I know she did."

I bite my lip in thought. "Why not just do it then, when you were present?"

"I don't know." He squints his eyes at me in concentration. "I've asked myself that a million times. I can only think maybe it was a rash decision on her part. Nothing told me she didn't want a child throughout the pregnancy."

"But the way you acted made it clear *you* didn't want one?"

This comment seems to catch him off guard. "What do you mean?"

"Beating her." I rub my scar.

He looks like I slapped him.

"Are you worried I might find out something that doesn't add up with what you told me?"

I watch his blue eyes deepen into a slate color as he slams his fist on the table. A guard starts to walk over as his chair scrapes against the tile like nails on a chalkboard.

Motioning to the guard that we're finished, he doesn't even address me, and I watch him walk away without a backward glance.

This has become the story of my life.

CHAPTER 30
Charlotte

They both start to rise when I reenter the living room.

I hold up a hand. "It's okay."

"I hope my ex doesn't have that reaction when she hears my name," Williams banters.

"I think you and my ex took different paths in life." I lower myself back into the chair. "And if by 'ties' you mean he's my ex and in prison, then yes, we are connected that way." Leaning forward, I have to physically restrain my legs to keep them from shaking.

"Are you aware of any connections Mr. Randall might have on the outside?" Williams asks gently. "Any threats he's made?"

"Of course. I'm sure there are plenty, but I don't know who they are." I feel like a fog has warped my mind, the ability to form a logical thought impossible.

I must've tuned the detectives out, because they're staring at me, waiting for a response.

"Excuse me?"

"I asked if you have something for protection. Pepper spray, your own weapon?" Williams says.

"No. I used to have pepper spray, but they confiscated it at the airport. I forgot it was in my purse. And no, I'm not a fan of firearms."

Rodgers is able to lean forward an inch more without falling, which I didn't think was possible. "Can you walk us through the events of last night again?"

Wincing at his request, I trace the cuts on my palm.

"Just one more time. It'll be easy."

"For you," I retort.

Williams eyes me with kindness. "Where did you park?"

"Right by a shopping cart return, southeast corner."

"That's the employee lot, right?"

"I don't know." I shrug. "I'm not familiar with that store. First time there. I only noticed the employee entrance sign because I tried to walk through it first."

"And I bet your last time," Rodgers intones. "Hate to ask, but why stop there? You're clearly a sophisticated woman, and that's a very seedy part of town."

"I know," I sigh. "I wanted pho over there; that strip mall has one of my favorite spots."

"Oh, that Vietnamese place, what's the name?"

"Viet Palace."

"Damn straight." His yellow teeth form a smile, his chew making a distinct pouch underneath his lower lip.

"You went out the front entrance when you left, and . . ."

"And it was semidark, probably closer to ten p.m. The lot was fairly empty, not many vehicles." I twist my hands in my lap, careful to avoid touching the broken skin. "I'll admit, I should've been paying more attention. I only had a couple of plastic bags of groceries, and I was looking down at my phone, texting."

Both sets of eyes are trained on me. "Before I could register what was happening, I was being grabbed from behind, or I should say, the hood of my coat was. At first, I thought someone was tugging on it to get my attention. It took me a second to realize the seriousness of the situation. I was yanked backward and dragged behind a parked vehicle."

"A dark-red truck, is that correct?" Williams asks.

"Yes, maroon colored, midsize, think it was a Dodge."

"Was it their vehicle?"

I muse, "I don't believe so; they never tried to put me in it. I think it was just random. They pulled a gun, I screamed, and it startled them. They ran away after an employee came running to see what the commotion was, into the vacant lot that sits next to the store."

"They didn't do anything else . . . ?" Rodgers stares at my bruised face.

"No, they didn't try to assault me that way."

"You keep saying 'they.' Do you have reason to believe it might've been more than one person?"

"The person was tall, or at least taller than me, but dressed bulky. Presumably it was a man, but I can't say that with one hundred percent certainty. It was one person, but I don't know if someone was waiting for them after."

Williams's pen's poised in the air, his expression unreadable. "Description?"

Frustrated, I say, "I provided this last night to Officer Mahoney and Sparrow." They don't respond, both peering at me. "I could only see their eyes. Green. Caucasian. Everything else was covered, even their hands. Oh, the boots weren't Doc Martens—you know, the ones with the yellow stitching—but more like some type of combat boots."

"Anything stand out about their face?" Williams asks. "Tattoos, moles, or freckles?"

Taking a minute, I consider the question. "Nothing I could see." I can hear the pen moving on the notepad. "Anything else?" I ask.

"Did they use a knife as well? Is that where the cuts on your hands came from?" Rodgers inquires. "Defensive wounds?"

"No, they pushed me to the ground, and there was a broken bottle or something." I finger the red, angry lines across each of my palms.

"And the gun?"

"What about it?"

"Had you ever seen it before?" Williams taps his pad again. "Since it belonged to your ex?"

"No." I gesture with my hands. "But he could've had many weapons I didn't know about. Convicted felons can't own a firearm, is that correct?"

"Yes." Rodgers shakes his foot out. "That's why we want to find out who it's been in possession of."

"These details have been extremely helpful, Mrs. Coburn." Williams closes his notepad with a slap. "We've got one more question before we go, Charlotte, if you don't mind . . ."

My back goes rigid. "Yes?"

"Would you mind telling us why your mother called the nonemergency number for an officer to be dispatched to your house?" Williams frowns. "Is there something we should be aware of?"

I glance down at my hands, bare without the wedding band and my watch. "Nancy called in a welfare check?" I tilt my head, stupefied.

"Yes, just this morning." Rodgers juts his bottom lip out, his uneven teeth prominently displayed.

"That's the other reason we stopped. Might as well kill two birds with one stone," Williams offers. "With your history, we wanted to make sure this incident didn't trigger something that was a cause for concern regarding your health."

Idioms. I despise them. I hate when people spout off figurative instead of literal language. Shuddering at his nonsensical comment, I tug my earlobe in annoyance. "I don't know why she would."

"She expressed concern, since she couldn't get ahold of you."

I hold up my phone. "Well, this was missing."

"Do you need to get checked out?" Williams is nonchalant. "Make sure you don't have any more injuries?"

My mouth puckers, and the tapping of my foot resumes, full speed.

"It's not a bad thing your mother is concerned. She called the police because she was worried about you."

Rodgers adds, sympathetically, "It's further evidence she cares."

Or wasn't getting what she wanted, I demur to myself. But they don't know my mother, so I let the observation slide.

"No, not at all a bad thing." I try not to sound flippant. "Now that I have my phone back, rest assured, I'll reach out to her."

I rise, silently commanding them to follow. "I didn't get much sleep last night, so if you don't mind, I'd like to lie down."

"Of course," Rodgers says, Williams concurring.

Rodgers adds, "We'll communicate to Nancy you're safe, but if you could as well, it'd be much appreciated."

"Please do." My phone buzzes in my hand. "Excuse me, gentlemen; you can see yourselves out. I've got to take this."

I see Noah's face on the screen.

For once, I silence the call, too upset to even chat with him at the present time.

Another call comes through, and this time "No Caller ID" flashes on my screen.

I don't answer strange numbers.

It stops, then flashes again. *Probably Nancy.*

In my mind, I see Jonathan, and this time it's *his* eyes staring at me from behind the ski mask. Warning myself to get a grip, I say out loud, "You're safe. He doesn't know where you live, he's locked up, and he no longer has any hold over you. It's over."

Except it's not over. It'll never be over. Our shared history will always be an internet search away, permanent, like the scar tissue on my abdomen from the emergency surgery I had after I lost the baby.

And because the gun that was originally in my glove box belonged to Jonathan Randall.

I stole it from him when he packed up his shit to leave.

Protection.

It was my protection in case he ever came back. And if it's not in the nightstand . . .

My hand fumbles with the drawer where the green velvet satchel lies so innocently. It is heavy in my hand, which is why I never questioned its contents the first time.

But after untying the cord, I discover it's not the weight of the revolver inside. Instead, another heavy object has replaced it, what to the naked eye is a gun.

Except it's a fake, weighted and designed to be a replica.

It's a decent one, sure. But it's not the gun that's been in my possession since Jonathan moved out a decade ago.

The preposterous nature of this would typically make me laugh. I'd find it comical if it were any other situation and I was holding a toy gun.

But in this case I sink onto the edge of my bed, because it's my safety that's in jeopardy.

My mind drifts to Elle Laughlin.

Elizabeth Laughlin.

Who *is* she?

Ever since she knocked at my door, my life has been fraught with upheaval. My hands tremble as I hold the now-empty cloth sack in my hand. Elle has been a copilot in my vehicle, and she's had access to the gun, and if she took it, it means she had a part in my robbery.

No, Char, you're being crazy. She's a teenager, not a felon.

At least not yet.

But the facts are there, as much as I want to ignore them. Elle is a loner going through a breakup and a pregnancy, and she's in survival mode. I put myself in her shoes. Desperate for cash, maybe she needed to pawn my jewelry.

Unfortunately, this isn't a weird coincidence or something I can write off as ironic. It was a male who assaulted me, but I can't eliminate her as a suspect. She has to have had some type of involvement with it.

Trembling, I ask myself what else besides money she could want from me.

As I bow my head in my lap, my shoulders heave. I knew I never should've answered the door during that storm. I should've listened to my gut when it told me to feign indifference toward a stranger on my porch.

Because who can you trust?

No one.

A loud thud captures my attention through the open door of the master suite.

I pause at the sight of Noah's outline.

He looks unkempt, his tie hanging loose around his neck and his untucked shirt sticking out of his pants. The rolling suitcase and brief-case, an extension of him, are near the hall closet. Wiping a hand over my eyes in disbelief, I quickly smooth a hand over my hair, wishing I had time to brush my teeth and put some makeup on.

"What're you doing here?" I slide the sham gun underneath the comforter so it's out of sight. I want to pinch myself; it's almost too good to be true to see him.

Shaking his head, his jacket hanging limp over his arm, he says, "I can't do this."

My face goes slack. "What do you mean?"

CHAPTER 31
Elle

When I walk in the double doors to school, the final bell's just rung, and, antsy, I wait near Justin's locker until I feel someone clasp their bearlike hands over my eyes.

"Surprise." I can smell the booze, Mountain Dew spiked with cheap vodka, on his breath, his go-to drink, since he can hide it in a twenty-ounce plastic bottle.

"Hi." I shrug his hands off me. "What's up?"

"Where were you last night?"

"What do you mean?"

"I stopped by Diane's. Saw your note and talked to Sandra. Said you left with a police officer." He tugs at my haphazard ponytail. "And you didn't return any of my calls. Did something happen?"

"I didn't know you called. I left you, like, four messages," I say.

"You get arrested? Or did Diane do something crazy?"

"Worse." I punch him in the arm. "You didn't tell me you were going to see Charlotte last night."

"Huh?"

"The plan you said . . ."

"No."

"Don't play dumb with me, Justin."

"I'm not." He says flatly, "I want nothing to do with Charlotte, or you, for that matter."

"Excuse me?"

"It's not my baby," he whispers.

"What do you mean?"

"Rumor has it it's not mine." He slams his locker in my face.

"Who said that?"

"Doesn't matter. What matters is you've been sleeping around."

"Justin." I reach a hand out to touch his shoulder. "You know me. You know I would never do that to you."

"I guess it doesn't matter now."

"What about our baby?"

He shrugs. "Not my problem anymore."

"Justin, you can't mean that."

"Look." He runs a hand through his longish hair. "I gotta get to the skate park. I can't talk about this anymore. I'm too pissed off. I'm gonna go blow off some steam."

Just then, Courtney Kerr walks by, followed by her girl gang, the groupies dumb enough to stay one step behind so they're always in her shadow. I heard it was a mandatory requirement for her clique.

Courtney's stupid pierced nose glints with a diamond stud, probably a cheap knockoff from a store in the mall.

"I hope that doesn't get infected." I squint my eyes at her tiny waist that's not swollen with a baby Justin claims isn't his. "I'd hate to see it spread to your whole face, possibly destroying all your internal organs and killing you."

Ignoring my comment, she pauses to touch Justin's shoulder. "Is everything okay?" Giving me an evil wink, she rubs his bicep as she stares daggers at me.

"It was until you got here," I seethe.

Menacing, she turns her head. "I wouldn't talk to me like that, you dirty slut. Do you even know who the baby daddy is?"

"Courtney . . ." Justin chastises her. "Let's not rub my face in it."

Her posse of girls starts to titter, and I feel my face turn a bright red that spreads all the way down to my toes. Justin says nothing, his face flushed as he stubs his toe awkwardly against his locker.

"You're a real dick," I hiss to Justin. "How could you even think I'd cheat on you?"

Resting his head against his locker, he groans, "What did I do?"

"Nothing. Absolutely nothing. You're an angel."

"Justin needs someone who isn't a fucking psycho." Courtney twirls a piece of blonde hair around her finger. "No one's ever going to want a kid with you. I mean, is it supposed to sleep and bathe in the bathtub of your studio apartment?"

Justin rolls his eyes. "I'll leave you two at it." Picking up his skate-board, he salutes us and stalks off down the hall.

Once again, I'm in the discarded pile.

Hands clenched into fists, I punch his stupid orange locker, launching my left foot into the hard metal. Instead of feeling good, it hurts like hell, and I stumble backward, almost losing my balance.

Courtney and her friends laugh as they sashay back to where they came from. Hell.

My emotions are all over the place, and I start to cry, and without a destination in mind, I drive Sandra's car to Pleasanton Lake, the freedom of having wheels a whole new feeling.

Here I can clear my head and pretend I'm someone I'm not. The sky's cloudy, and the air smells like rain, a promise to unleash another thunderstorm in the near future.

I leave Sandra's car parked close to the lake.

Cursing the heavens, I stamp my feet as I aimlessly walk around the path. Why would Charlotte just heave herself down the stairs *after* my father left? His story just doesn't add up.

That, or every single part of his day was unlucky.

Or karma.

I watch the scattering of ducks as they launch themselves off the rippled water in the pond. Some old men are seated with their insulated beverages and seem curious about my angry scowl as I pass them. After a couple laps, I start to cool off, wondering what else the police had to tell Charlotte about the gun they found.

I go to her house. This time, I have the urge to kick down her mailbox. The squad cars have been replaced with another vehicle in the drive, a newer white sedan parked at an angle.

I was right. He does *drive a BMW,* I think to myself.

A typical suit.

The shades in the house are drawn, as usual, but I'm puzzled about him. Did he come home out of concern? That would be a sweet gesture. I can't imagine the scare of having your pregnant wife mugged while you're away on business.

I wonder what they're doing, wanting a glimpse of this relationship that was doomed at one time. Before I know what I'm doing, I'm standing on the porch, and my hands are shielding my eyes as I unsuccessfully try to peer into the front windows.

It's none of *my* business, but still, it *is* my business.

The choices they both made are the reason I'm stuck living in a shithole while they're cozy in suburbia. And if I'm going to blame Charlotte, some of it spills onto Noah, since he's part of the past.

A shred of light filters through a small splinter in the drapes. A man I assume to be Noah is seated in the chair, facing directly toward me, his shoulders hunched over. He seems sad, the way he holds his head in his hands, and his fingers keep rubbing at his eyes. He twists what looks to be a wedding band on his finger.

Noah seemed happier in the photographs. Now he looks like a wounded animal.

Is he sad because he wasn't here to protect her, or are they fighting because he wasn't here to protect her? I wonder.

I can't imagine travel wouldn't be a strain on a marriage.

Or a past they can't run from.

Charlotte emerges from the master bedroom wearing a slinky pink satin robe. She holds out her hand to show him something. He shakes his head in frustration, putting his hand up as if to shield himself, a sudden dismissal. Visibly hurt, she pauses on the landing, gripping the banister like she's holding on for dear life before she starts to climb the staircase.

Halfway up, Charlotte pauses, the chandelier reflecting off something that catches her eye. She must notice my movement, because at the same time I take a step backward, I hear a scream.

Caught off guard, I lose my balance as my foot catches on a loose board.

"Shit." I land ass first with a thud on the porch as the front door swings open with a bang.

The hunched-over man is now tall, really tall, as he stands over me. I make a move to slide backward, but I don't get far.

"Noah," I say.

His eyes judge my disheveled appearance, my baggy clothing, and my pinched face. As he narrows his eyes, I scoot back against the railing.

Before I know what's happening, I'm being lifted, and I press my eyes together as I wait for the pain.

CHAPTER 32
Charlotte

"Elle!" Surprise registers in my voice as I peer over Noah's shoulder, his arms guiding her to a standing position.

Her eyes are closed tightly, her body rigid, as if she's waiting for him to hit her.

"What are you doing here?"

She slowly opens them, peering at both of us in disbelief. Brushing herself off, she doesn't say a word.

Confused, I say her name again.

Noah glances back and forth between us. "You know her?"

"This is the young woman who does dog walking and house sitting in the neighborhood. She took shelter here during the storm."

"Ah, yes, I remember you told me that."

"Elle, are you okay?" I ask. "Shouldn't you be in school?"

"Yeah, I just wanted to check on you . . ."

"I'm doing pretty good," I say. "All things considered."

"With the cops here earlier . . ."

"Wait," Noah interjects. "The police came by?"

"They returned my phone." I touch his arm gently. "They had some news for me about the investigation." I decide to test Elle. "In fact, they found a gun in the parking lot and said it had female prints on it."

Noah's face goes ashen at the same time Elle sputters, "Are you for real?"

I shake my head. "I didn't believe a woman could be involved, but they seem confident they'll figure it out." I shrug. "Jail time for sure."

"I hope they find him . . . ," she barely whispers. "Or her."

I don't want to further discuss the investigation in front of Elle. Now that I know my gun was stolen, I sense there's something not right about her, and I'll have to bide my time before I spill details she doesn't need to be privy to.

Plus, with a new baby and a robbery, Noah wouldn't be thrilled that I've befriended someone who seems to have a lot of issues. He assumes everyone with a hard childhood has a past like Jonathan Randall's.

And with our past, he would be suspect about her, especially with the half truths and lies. He'd warn me about involving a stranger in our lives.

And I'm no longer trusting of her.

Gazing at my bare skin and barely covered breasts, I wrap my robe tightly around myself, trying to cover up, since we're standing outside. "Do you happen to have any flyers I can give out about your services? One of my colleagues asked about a pet sitter the other day."

"Uh, no." She's caught off guard by this question. "They can find me on the pet-sitting app, though."

Noah steps aside, motioning Elle to enter at the same time I attempt to shut the door. I'm not in the mood for company, my anxiety at an all-time high. Noah and I haven't finished with our earlier discussion.

"Can I call you later? It's not the best time," I explain. "But I'll pick you up at three for your appointment tomorrow after school."

"Okay."

Noah looks between us, his head tilted.

With that, Elle gives us both a once-over before exiting the front porch and disappearing around the corner.

Curious, Noah asks, "What appointment?"

"Doctor."

"Did you adopt a teenager?" He shakes his head. "You are always so giving, Char."

"Not yet. I thought I'd start with having a baby first."

I lean against the now-closed door, shrugging. "What do you mean you can't do this, Noah?" I try to hide my hands behind my back, laying them flat against the door so he doesn't see the way they shake. I feel like I'm standing in front of him a decade ago, the start of the conversation the same as when he told me Lauren and he were going ahead with their wedding.

"I can't sign the papers."

"I thought they were signed?" Closing my eyes, I feel the start of a migraine. "And your project in Tokyo was a done deal."

"I'm not feeling good about it."

"Noah," I say, "I can't do this right now. Last night . . . it brought back so many memories. I can't always focus on you."

He looks like I slapped him. "I know. That's why I came home. I don't want you to worry." His hand grazes my chin. "You focus on your body and taking care of yourself and our baby. Let me worry about the rest."

I soften my tone. "It means a lot that you came back home."

"I'd die if anything happened to you, Char." He licks his lips. "I just don't know what to do about all this upheaval."

I reach out a hand, the trembling lessened. "We'll figure it out." And in unison we say, "We always do." We sink onto the couch, my position always in the middle, as I lean my shoulder against him, shutting out everything but us.

Noah leaves again the next morning, and I'm suddenly uneasy about leaving the house. I walk out the side door to the garage multiple times, turning back around, my chest tightening in response. It's like I'm waiting for a surprise attack.

"Don't stress, Char, it's not good for you or the baby," I repeat over and over as my new mantra. But when I stare at the Jeep, I see a dark figure reflected in the paint, and I'm instantly spooked. Noah left his car, and, putting my dark glasses on to shield my eyes from the world, I retrieve his keys. I surprise Elle when I pick her up at school in it.

"Needed a change?"

"Yes, and my gas light is on." I refuse to admit how the terrifying events of the other night shook me to my core. If she's part of the problem, I don't want her to know how she's affected me. She also seems visibly nervous and quieter than usual, which only adds to the guilt piling up in my mind.

Fidgeting with a bracelet on her arm, she asks, "Are you sure about this?"

"About what?"

"Taking me to the doctor?"

"Of course, Elle. I couldn't get you into my doctor, so I made you an appointment at another highly recommended obstetrician." She gives me a small nod. "It sounds like you're long overdue, and if you're as far along as you think, it's important to both the health of the baby and you."

"Did it hurt when you went?"

"No, you won't feel pain today. They're saving up the good stuff for when you give birth."

She twinges before changing the subject. "Did you get all your cards canceled?"

"Yes."

"Were there any charges on them, like, fraud?"

"Luckily, no. None had been used." I try not to read too much into her questions, trying to chalk them up to small talk. My paranoia isn't going to help either of us right now. I need to focus on Elle and her baby, since I said I would help.

"That's a relief," she says.

I nod, my eyes trained on the road ahead.

When we get to the ob-gyn office, the waiting room has a mixed crowd of the expectant and the "already a parent." You can discern between the two categories, because sheer terror's present on the pregnant moms with distended bellies and no experience, wading into unfamiliar territory. The ones who have been through childbirth are more relaxed but frazzled, their arms laden with coloring books for a toddler or a diaper bag for a baby.

The men with both sets seem overwhelmed, with glazed expressions on their faces, as if they don't know why they are here or how this happened.

I watch as one child attempts to color on the walls, much to the dismay of his father, as the other parents chuckle, relieved for once it's not their kid.

Fidgeting, Elle shifts from foot to foot, which makes me anxious, so I tell her to go ahead and have a seat.

As I check in at the reception desk, I grab the sheaf of papers they give me.

"Three thirty appointment for Charlotte Coburn."

"Insurance and ID."

I bring my hand to my forehead. "Shit." I cover my mouth with my hand. "I mean *crap*."

The receptionist tilts her head. "It's okay, we've all said a word or two."

"I was . . . I have a police report, if you need it, but my wallet was stolen a couple of days ago, including my insurance card and ID."

Flipping my hands over, I show her the jagged cuts.

"Oh my God, what happened?" the receptionist gasps. "I mean, sorry, you probably don't want to rehash it."

"Mugged in a parking lot," I say, "but that's the worst of the injuries, so I'm lucky."

"Is this your first time here?"

"Yes, it's for my daughter, actually." I point to Elle.

"This will be a longer appointment, since we typically do an ultrasound first, followed by the doctor's examination."

"Okay."

"Can you just provide us a credit card, and we'll just charge you the typical copay for your insurance? We can go ahead and work on verifying it."

"Sure, but same boat with my cards. I have cash, if that's all right."

"Yes, no problem. Just bring a printed copy of your insurance next time, if you don't have a replacement card by then."

I bring back the clipboard to Elle.

"That is a shit ton of paperwork," she exclaims as I have a seat next to her. "Is it even more because I don't have insurance?"

I hand her a pen. "I'll fill out the address and take care of the insurance portion. You're going to be Charlotte Coburn, though."

She gives me an odd stare.

"I want to make sure insurance covers it."

"Isn't that, like, fraud?"

"Typically, but I'd like to talk to you after this about something that makes it okay." She gives me a questioning glance, then writes *Charlotte Coburn* on the forms.

I watch her chew the pen lid, likely unsure about her family health history. I almost feel bad. It must be unsettling to not know the most basic information about your past.

"Does it have to be exact?"

"Try to be as accurate as possible."

She slowly writes, her handwriting small and legible. When she's finished, she looks to me for confirmation. "Go ahead and take it back up."

The woman barely glances over the forms before she signals for Elle to have a seat again. Absentmindedly flipping through a magazine, she shoves it back in the stack. "Charlotte?"

"Uh-huh?"

"What's in that room?"

Scrolling through work emails on my phone, made difficult because of the screen, I don't look up, assuming she means the doctor's office. "An exam table and a sink."

"In the room upstairs, the one that's locked?"

"How do you know it's locked?" I keep my eyes trained on the screen.

"Because I mistakenly thought it was the guest bedroom." Elle picks at a hangnail.

"It's nothing, just storage for now." I shrug. "It will eventually be the baby's room."

"Why do you need to lock it?"

"Because I have a ton of storage in there right now. Because of my job, I have to follow FERPA guidelines, which just means I have to keep student records locked for safekeeping."

Elle wrinkles her nose. "What if you accidentally throw away something important that you needed to keep?"

"Then that's an entirely different conversation. I could be subject to scrutiny as a professor." She picks up another magazine and, after opening the cover, slams it shut and tosses it on the end table. "Are you okay?" I ask. "How're you feeling about this appointment?"

"Nervous." She stares out the window, biting her lip. "What if my kid uses crayons on the wall like that one?"

"It'll be fine," I reassure her. "I'll come back with you and provide moral support, if you don't mind."

She considers this a moment, her face scrunched.

"You can kick me out if you feel uncomfortable."

We hear "Charlotte Coburn" being called, and both of us stand. A young woman who introduces herself as Emily, the medical assistant, leads us to a room, first taking Elle's temperature, blood pressure, and weight. Reviewing her medical forms, Emily points to the blank questionnaire regarding family history.

Elle stares at the floor, avoiding Emily's inquisitive gaze.

Sympathetically, I pat Elle's hand. "Unfortunately for our family tree, we've had a lot of gaps and holes in our genealogy. I didn't know my parents, so it makes it hard to fill Charlotte in about her genetics."

A sigh of relief escapes Elle's lips, and I smile kindly at Emily, who shrugs in return. "You aren't the first to be in the dark about your ancestry. Not a problem. We only ask so we can be proactive in case there's something health-wise that could complicate a pregnancy." She moves on to explain how an ultrasound works, then instructs Elle to put a paper gown on, assuring her the procedure is painless.

Elle's flustered, her eyes darting around the room, first to the machine next to the exam table, then to the educational posters on childbirth that line the walls.

I flip open a magazine as Elle disrobes to put on the gown.

She climbs onto the exam table, her legs swinging wildly, her bare feet kicking the metal as she anxiously awaits the arrival of the ultrasound tech. Her body language isn't much different from mine as my feet tap nervously on the tile.

A woman walks in, introducing herself as Jessica. "I'll be conducting your ultrasound today." She thumbs through the papers and peers up at Elle. "We'll check the heart and amniotic sac, look at the fetus, which grows every week. First things first. Usually we're able to do the ultrasound with the wand against your skin without having to insert it vaginally. It won't hurt at all—just the gel we rub on you is a little cold, so be prepared."

Jessica tries to make Elle comfortable as she lies on the table. She talks to her about school and her future plans, and she keeps the conversation light. I listen closely for any other discrepancies.

Jessica asks me a few questions as the "grandma," but I have a hard time concentrating. They don't necessarily tell you up front, but if they can't find a heartbeat with the wand on your abdomen, they try internally, and if nothing but a blank screen shows up, then you're either not as far along as expected, or you might have a blighted ovum, signaling a miscarriage.

My foot taps louder, drawing attention to itself, and Jessica gives me a warm smile, her brown eyes kind.

"You must be excited, Grandma," she says.

Grandma?

The word throws me, since it implies that I've skipped an important step, to be a mother.

I recover, wrapping my hands around my legs, keeping them steady and quiet.

Elle gasps as the cold goo is squirted onto her abdomen, and Jessica moves the wand in a circular motion. "Almost there." Jessica points to the monitor as we both watch, riveted, terrified for different reasons.

We stare mesmerized at the movements on the screen that confirm a baby is indeed in utero. "Congratulations, Mama." Jessica pats Elle on the shoulder.

Elle turns to me, her expression one of awe.

"After the appointment, you'll get a very important souvenir." Jessica grins at Elle, who's still rendered speechless. "Would you like to know the sex of your baby?"

Her blue eyes widen. "You can tell that already?"

"Yes. You're further along than most women that come in here for their initial appointments."

I want to interject and ask to know, but it's for Elle to decide.

"You know what? I don't." She tugs at the gown she's wearing. "I want to be surprised."

Giving me a timid smile, she beams at the screen and then at me. I knew when she saw her baby in the actual flesh that there would be no question as to its importance in her life.

Jessica congratulates us once again before exiting.

A few minutes later, the obstetrician walks in, accompanied by Emily. "Hi, I'm Dr. Cheryl Avanetti." A red-haired woman with cornflower blue eyes peers at us from behind glasses. She has a smattering of freckles, and everything about her is small—from her tiny nose to her thin lips. Her petite frame matches her delicate features. She looks to be in her early forties, her hair pulled back into a chignon, her pale face framed with tiny diamond studs.

"Hi, Charlotte," Dr. Avanetti says. "And you are?"

"Mom." I offer my hand.

Warmly, she shakes mine, then Elle's. "Nice to meet you both."

"You met Emily, my very capable MA." Dr. Avanetti scrubs her hands at the sink, then slips on some latex gloves. "Judging by the ultrasound and what you wrote as the last date of your menstrual cycle, I'd guess you to be around fifteen to sixteen weeks."

The doctor explains today's appointment and the next steps. "I'll do a Pap smear, which is just a physical exam to make sure everything is working properly and intact. Have you had a Pap before?"

"Yes," Elle says.

She peers over her glasses. "Do you have any questions or concerns?"

Elle shakes her head, hands clamped on both sides of the table.

"Is this your first pregnancy? Any miscarriages or abortions?" I tense at the word, the meaning so powerful, yet its weight isn't the same when it's uttered by someone who doesn't know your history.

"Yes, my first one, and no to your other questions."

"Perfect." Dr. Avanetti smiles at her with her small teeth. "Okay, cold hands coming up." Emily hands her a speculum, and as she starts the exam, I skim a magazine.

"When will my next appointment be?" Elle asks.

"Another three to four weeks." Dr. Avanetti looks at a calendar on the wall. "Provided everything is normal on the labs. You'll get your blood drawn after this."

"Today?" Elle's face pales, her mouth aghast.

"Guess we won't have to worry about this one getting tattoos." Dr. Avanetti pats her knee. "Nothing to worry about. Just a routine draw. We do it to check your HCG levels, which are your hormone levels, and to make sure nothing harmful is passed to the fetus."

When she's finished with the exam, Dr. Avanetti signals to Emily.

"Okay, you can get dressed. Make sure you take prenatal vitamins, get lots of sleep, no alcohol, no smoking, stay away from secondhand smoke, no hot tub, minimal caffeine. No raw fish. This packet contains a list of recommendations."

She shakes both of our hands again. "I'll see you in a month. Congrats to you both, Mom and Grandma." My face reddens, and Emily interrupts just then, handing Elle a packet of dos and don'ts, a list of foods to eat and foods to avoid, and, last but not least, the sonogram.

"Okay, Charlotte." Emily helps Elle off the table. "Please get dressed, and I'll meet you in the lab to introduce you to our phlebotomist, who'll draw your blood."

Shakily, Elle puts her clothes on, and I follow her out into the hallway.

"I'll wait here." I motion to a bulletin board with smiling babies and their overjoyed parents. Must be ones Dr. Avanetti delivered.

"I can hold that." Elle nods her thanks as I hold her handouts and the sonogram, tears streaming down my cheeks as I stare at the grainy photo, signaling life.

CHAPTER 33
Elle

I'm more nervous than I thought I'd be, going to the doctor.

First, I've been to the gynecologist only once.

Second, the reality of a baby and the pain I've heard is unbearable is starting to become real, and I am finally starting to grasp the fact that I, Elizabeth Laughlin, am going to become a mother.

If I choose.

A single mother.

A poor mother.

When we get back in Noah's car, I stare out the windshield in silence. This time, instead of nervous anticipation, the silence is one of sheer amazement. Staring at the sonogram, I can't believe I'm growing a little peanut in my belly. It seemed so surreal before today, and now, with the picture, it's confirmation. Real-life confirmation. In some ways, I feel like I won the lottery, but in other ways, the reality of my life choices is overwhelming.

Then I think of Charlotte, and even though she's married and I'm not, she's still somewhat alone, her husband always out of town. She's still able to manage.

She also has money, I remind myself, and a job.

I feel conflicted about what my father told me. Charlotte seems to genuinely love children and was just as excited as I was in the room. Even when her relationship with my father was on the rocks, I can't see her throwing herself down a set of stairs out of anger.

Because not only was she putting the baby at risk, but she also could've died. And my father's temper is a real beast. I've witnessed it many times, firsthand.

Shuddering, I think back to the table incident, when my mother almost died. This led to my parents' contentious divorce afterward, with my father moving in with his brother, Tyler.

My mother took me with her to a small apartment, since Robbie, the former friend of my father's, had grown bored of her now that she wasn't off limits. I was shuffled back and forth between them like a chess piece, a forgotten pawn in a game that all of a sudden no one seemed to care about unless it involved pissing off the other one.

My mother's next relationship was just as volatile, except this time she moved on from weed to harder drugs. She couldn't afford the rent, so she moved in with Roger, a custodial worker with a bad back. Roger was addicted to pain pills and sold anything he could find, and before I knew it, my mother was spending most of her days on the streets trying to score drugs or shooting up in the bathroom. Roger went to prison for drug trafficking and wasn't around to help with the bills, so we moved in with my mother's mom, my grandma.

I would see my father half the time, but he also had a girlfriend. He didn't want me around strange women, or girlfriends, until it was serious, he said.

Living with my grandma, I had the best times of my life.

She made cookies and cooked dinner and taught me to knit. We would snuggle up and watch reruns of all her favorite shows. *I Love Lucy*, *The Dick Van Dyke Show*, *The Mary Tyler Moore Show*.

Her agreement with my mom was that she couldn't use in her house; she had to get clean. She didn't want drugs affecting her life or mine.

But everything crashed after my father went to prison. With no one to help with the bills or me, my mother grew increasingly depressed. She also had her own form of PTSD and blamed herself for not putting my father behind bars earlier, when he'd beaten her up. She blamed herself in a way for the death of the unborn baby. She couldn't rise above her own demons, and she never really had a chance. She was dead within a year of his going to prison.

I snap back to the present, the warmth of the sun hitting my face through the window. All of these emotions rush to the surface, and I'm once again wrenched by my situation and the adults who got me here.

Resting my hands on what is my future, I remind myself I have one goal. I have to prove my father's innocence so we can have a roof over our heads and our family back together again, as fractured as it is.

I tamp down my feelings and thank Charlotte for taking me to the doctor.

"You're welcome." Charlotte turns down the music. "Have you read any books?"

"I'm reading *Animal Farm* in class."

"Personally, I prefer *Down and Out in Paris and London*, but no, I meant on pregnancy."

Feeling stupid, I mumble, "Oh, no. I haven't."

"I've got some stashed on the bookshelf for you to read. It'll make it easier to stomach all the changes and make you feel like you're not a freak for having weird symptoms or ailments. Your hormones are acting up, and you'll wonder about your sanity at times."

"Yeah, my boobs hurt, and I could sleep twenty-five hours in a twenty-four-hour day."

"That's typical. You'll have more energy at some point."

"Have you had any weird cravings?"

"Before, it was more like certain smells associated with foods or beverages got to me. I used to like to drink a cup of coffee in the morning, and the aroma, which I usually love, made me nauseated the entire pregnancy. Even now, I've become accustomed to drinking tea."

"I feel better knowing I'm not alone in this."

"We will grow together, literally."

Pretending I left my backpack at school, I have her drop me off there. I'm not comfortable with her taking me to the apartment, even though she dropped a package off there before. I don't need to see her pity.

It's days like today I wish the apartment complex had an elevator to use after I get off the bus. Drained, I don't remember falling asleep when I get home, but at some point, I must get sick in the middle of the night, because I wake up disoriented.

Twisted like a pretzel on the bathroom floor, a threadbare towel draped around me, the apartment reeking of beans and tar, I sit up to rub the sleep out of my eyes.

I don't hear Diane moving around, but she must've left food on the stove.

My mouth salivates as I check the tarnished pan on the burner.

Jackpot.

She made rice and beans. Shoveling the leftovers in a bowl, I grab a glass of tap water and settle on the couch. The television is now silent, and the grandfather clock in the corner chimes the hour. It's an antique heirloom, or so she claims, and Diane will never get rid of it, even though it takes up most of the corner space in the living room. Plus, it would take burly movers to carry the heavy mahogany down four flights of stairs.

While I wait, I scarf down the food and gulp the water.

Feeling guilty, I tell myself I should've saved some food for the boys for dinner. Who knows if Diane brought any more groceries home.

My phone chirps at me, notifying me of unread messages.

Callie, a girl who pretends to be my friend, has sent multiple texts.

Both are photos, and they take forever to load in this apartment without Wi-Fi.

The pictures Callie sent cause butterflies in my stomach, and not the good kind. These are the anxiety-provoking, unsettling ones that cause agonizing pain. In the clear-as-day pictures, Justin is walking with Courtney, and she's whispering in his ear as he grins.

The next one is of them embracing at his locker.

The next text makes my stomach tumble even farther.

Rumor is Court's preggo and Justin's been sleeping with her for a couple months now. Thought you should know.

Is this some kind of sick joke? I wonder.

Justin is attractive and sensitive, and I used to consider him an all-around nice guy. I never would have believed this message a few months ago, but lately, he's shown another side. Abandoning his pregnant girlfriend and engaging in robbery are not traits that made me fall in love with him.

And why would Callie make something like this up? She has no reason to lie to me. We aren't close, but we are friendly. I refuse to get close to any chicks, their overblown drama and gossip stupid.

Some guy didn't call them when he said he would.

They got in a fight with their mom over their allowance.

Their dad grounded them for sneaking out.

Those aren't real problems, at least not to me.

Angrily swiping out of the picture, I consider my options. *Who do I confront? Justin? Courtney?*

I call him and am sent straight to voice mail.

I try again.

Same thing.

When I forward him the picture, it is returned as undelivered.

WTF?

I shoot him a text.

Same thing.

Checking to see that I still have prepaid minutes, I feel my head pounding like the drumbeat to a marching band. This asshole blocked me; he had to have.

Wailing, I unleash a fury of tears, my body heaving. A slap in the face was him being unsure of having a child with me.

But a gut punch is him not only screwing my archnemesis but also knocking her up.

It can't be true. There has to be some mistake. He couldn't have been careless with both of us.

Sure, Courtney is cute, if you like ditzy blondes with Daddy's money and no personality.

And who doesn't? I roll my eyes.

But she's the one person who has always put you down, I tell myself, *and Justin knows this. He wouldn't. He just wouldn't.*

Or would he?

I reach in the cupboard for some generic Tylenol, a headache hammering like a mallet on my skull. I take the bottle and shove it in my backpack.

Angrily, I stamp down the stairs, the pair of black leggings I'm wearing practically the only item in my closet that fits, thanks to pregnancy. And Justin.

I leave the house and head to my first class of the day, my phone clenched in my fist.

I've never been so intent on getting to school.

When I get there, he's going to pay for this. And so is Courtney.

CHAPTER 34
Charlotte

I stay in bed longer than usual, languidly reading the morning newspaper, something I still like to touch and feel in my hands. Moving to my belly, I tenderly rub my abdomen, the scar not such a big deal now.

A sense of déjà vu comes over me, like I'm reliving this heartbreak.

In a way, I guess I am.

I fold the paper and rest my head against a pillow, thinking back to my relationship with Jonathan Randall. We were opposites, he and I.

I was an early-morning riser, and he was a night owl. I would start the day perched at our kitchen table with a warm cup of coffee, voraciously reading the newspaper. Jonathan hated anything that meant sitting still. He always had to be on his feet, and he liked building things and using his hands. He claimed he was allergic to the monotony of what he called a traditional schedule or corporate America.

When I met him, it was a chance encounter. Like most couples back then, we met serendipitously, though I shudder to use that word now. This was before dating apps caused people to forgo face-to-face interaction for swipes based on appearances.

Jonathan was installing the ventilation and air-conditioning system in the elementary school I worked at, my first position out of college.

I had taken a longer path to finishing my degree than most and had worked in the fifth-grade classroom for the past year.

He was not like the guys I had dated in high school and college. He had lived.

Or, rather, lived in a way that was different from my upbringing.

He was the antithesis of every man I had dated.

And my mother couldn't stand him, so that made him even more attractive to me.

Instead of pretending to be rugged by wearing flannel and the North Face, he actually was. He rode a motorcycle, hunted deer, fished, and loved taking road trips with no planned destination and nothing but nonperishable food and a map, preferring the outdoors to human interaction. He was quiet and reserved most of the time, until he was not.

When his temper flared, it was unrestrained, as I would come to find out.

He was divorced when I met him, five years older than I, already a father to a child, and had an ex-wife who would rarely let him see his daughter, or so he claimed. She still managed to call him repeatedly and hang up, either sobbing or screaming.

As I shut my eyes, the memories come flooding back.

It was a November day, right in the middle of peak holiday season, squished between Halloween and Christmas. The winter was particularly miserable. People from the Midwest comment every year on how bad the last one was, forgetting during the humidity of the summer months what the next season has in store, but this one stands out in my mind.

Maybe because of what happened.

I remember it clearly: the overcast skies and the below-freezing temperatures, my pregnancy magnifying every ailment. Jonathan and I had only lived together for a few months at this point, and I was about five months along. I went from the overbearing nature of my mother to a domineering man. We shared a small rental, a tiny one-bedroom house with a basement.

Hormonal, I was fighting with him more than usual over nothing noteworthy. Who should wash the dishes, what channel to watch on TV, his inability to pick up after himself.

It didn't help that I was torn between two men, him and Noah. Except Noah was married.

On this particular afternoon, a Saturday, a vehicle pulls into the drive, tires squealing. I open our flimsy curtains to watch the icicles bounce from the gutter in protest as a car door is slammed.

The front door seems to rattle off its hinges as Jonathan barrels in.

Surprised, I step away from the window. "You're home earlier than usual. Weather?"

Instead of responding, he yanks me by the elbow toward him. "You wanna tell me something?"

"Huh?"

"I'm not going to repeat myself."

"What're you talking about?"

He grabs my chin roughly, spittle flying. "Are you sure it's even mine?"

"Are you being serious right now? Who am I going to find in this Podunk town we live in besides you?"

"That's not an answer."

"Of course it's yours. Why would you even ask that?" I make the mistake of raising my voice to him. "You never let me go anywhere without you."

"Don't you dare yell at me." Like a snake rising up before striking its target, he exhibits a crazed look in his eyes. Before I can twist out of his grasp, his hand collides with my cheek. "If I hear any more rumors, you'll be black and blue."

"Like last week?" I seethe. "If there's anything wrong with this baby—"

"Now you wanna threaten me?" He grabs a fistful of my hair, my hands protectively shielding my massive belly. "Go get me a beer. Then get the fuck out of my sight."

With a shove, he pushes me into the wall, holding my head right below a portrait of us taken at JCPenney. One happy family.

Vigorously shaking my head in disgust at the memory, I am separated from my past by a loud beep from the nightstand.

Feeling a sense of renewed anger, I rip the newspaper in half. A voice mail pops up as I shred the paper, and in a way, it's mildly therapeutic.

I snatch my phone and hit the voice mail button harder than I intend.

"Hi, Mrs. Cobalt," the unidentified caller says, mispronouncing my last name. "We have Elizabeth in the office at Washington High. It's crucial you return our call immediately. She's been involved in a serious accident."

Accident?

Who leaves a voice mail like that to leave your imagination to run rampant on all the scenarios? Just the mention of that word, *accident*, makes me shudder. My hand flutters to my chest. Willing myself to breathe, counting forward and backward to twenty, I dial the missed call.

A gravelly voice answers on the third ring. "Washington High, Mrs. Irene Marsh speaking."

"Hi, Irene, this is Charlotte Coburn. I just missed a call about Elle."

"Elle?"

Impatiently I draw the syllables out. "Eliz-a-beth. Elle Laughlin."

"Who is this?"

I snap. "You just called and left *me* a message."

"Yes, I did." She ignores my brusque tone. "Elizabeth's being transported to the hospital."

"What? What hospital?" The room starts to become distorted. "Is it the—"

"She's in serious trouble."

"What do you mean?" My voice trembles. "How bad is she hurt? Did she miscarry?"

"What?" It's her turn to be surprised. Marsh pauses. "No . . . Elizabeth's the one who caused injuries to another student."

I'm silent, letting the news sink in.

"I've got another call coming in. Elizabeth's with Principal Mitchum and a police officer at Covenant Hospital. Can you meet her there?"

Throwing some clothes on, I seize my purse off the island. I don't know why I bother, but I shoot off a couple of texts to Elle.

There's no reply.

Sprinting through the automatic doors at the hospital, I notice a uniformed cop talking to a tall, unpleasant-looking man dressed in an ill-fitting suit and tie. My eyes drift past them to the plastic waiting room chairs, where Elle's hunched body is crumpled up.

"Elle." I'm relieved to see her in one piece, seemingly unhurt.

She stares up at me with red, puffy eyes, and the skin around her left lid is black and blue.

"Oh my G-God, Elle," I stammer. "I was so worried about the—"

"And you are?" the tall, balding man interrupts.

I ignore him for a moment, fixated on Elle. "What happened?"

Elle glues her stare back to the floor, her hands limp on her knees. From this angle, she looks noticeably pregnant.

Turning to the man, I repeat the question. "What happened?"

He braces his hands on his hips. "Excuse me, but *who* are you?"

"Elle's—Elizabeth's aunt."

"Where's Diane?"

"I'm Diane's sister." As I thrust my hand at him, he rebuffs my gesture.

"I can't talk to you. You're not the guardian."

"Diane's out of town." I shrug. "I'm the one who's in charge."

He starts to argue, then shuts his mouth. Shaking his head, he mutters, "Then let's go to the vending machines and have a word."

He nods to the policeman to sit next to Elle, then turns briskly on his heel as I struggle to keep up. I follow him like I'm the one in trouble, my head bowed as his steps echo across the hospital-grade tile in front of me.

He makes a left and enters a small break room, where a Coke machine stands next to a couple of tables shoved together.

Pivoting, he introduces himself. "I'm Principal Mitchum. Douglas."

"Charlotte."

Touching his bald spot, he says, "Elizabeth managed to come to class today, which is a source of contention in itself—her absences are a problem, but I'll come back to that in a minute." He jabs a frustrated hand in the air. "She punched a student."

I stay quiet.

"Hard enough that she knocked her out. Currently she's being stitched up; her cheek and lip got the brunt of it."

"What?"

Clearly not used to repeating himself with students, and certainly not adults, he flares his nostrils. He enunciates every syllable.

I fumble for a chair to sit down in. "Who is the student, and what started this?"

He tilts his head, staring hard at the fading marks on my palms. "They got into a full-on brawl. The other girl, Courtney Kerr, got the brunt of it. Elizabeth just has bruising on her face."

"Where were the teachers?"

"It's always the teacher's responsibility to break up misbehaving kids, isn't it?" he snaps.

"That's not what I meant," I sigh. "I just wonder if there's another side, if someone saw the exchange."

"You mean the *fight*."

"What did they have a fight about, I wonder?"

269

"I hoped you might be able to provide some insight." Leaning his head back warily, he comments, "They don't run in the same circles, but Elizabeth, for all her faults, typically isn't a fighter."

"That's good."

Mitchum adds tersely, "I say that because she's not at school enough for us to know what she's capable of." Another jab.

"Well, it's lucky it's just bruising. Elle . . . I mean Elizabeth, is four months pregnant."

"I knew it." His eyes narrow. "Now supposedly Courtney's pregnant."

We stare at each other dumbfounded.

"Shit," he mutters. "I probably shouldn't disclose that. It's an unconfirmed rumor." He frowns. "I used to see Elizabeth with Justin Pence. Lately, I've seen Courtney with him. Know anything about that?"

My face must give away my disgust as I wrinkle my nose.

Rolling his eyes upward, he whistles. "Dammit. We might have our answer right there."

"Um, Elizabeth's ex—how well do you know him?"

"He's a senior." Mitchum fixes an uneasy stare on me. "I know we've called in the past to report indecent behavior by the two of them on school grounds, in addition to truancy."

Vacillating on what to say, I shake my head in consternation.

"Am I free to take her home?"

"You can check with the cop." He steeples his thin fingers. "But Elizabeth's been expelled from school, and I'd retain an attorney if I were you. Courtney's family will most likely press charges."

"And she comes from money," I add.

He narrows his eyes at me. "What's that have to do with anything?"

"Her father is an attorney. I know of him." Numbly, I ask, "What about her schoolwork?"

"Does it matter?" He rises, his hand drifting back to his sparse hair. "She wasn't going to graduate anyway." Then he mutters, "She's just another drain on the system, like her father."

The words sting, and I bite my tongue.

Her father?

What does the principal know about Elle's dead dad? I don't follow Mitchum back into the hall, instead resting my head in my hands to contemplate this.

CHAPTER 35
Elle

The policeman, a burly, annoying guy named Juan, finishes asking me rapid-fire questions, one after the other. He wouldn't be so bad if he didn't grunt after every answer, as if it's confirmation I'm being truthful.

Principal Mitchum ambles down the hall, but Charlotte isn't with him.

Inside I'm panicking. *What if she's so upset she just leaves me here to deal with Courtney's family and the principal?*

Then you'll have to call Diane, I suppose, *who won't answer and won't leave work. She'll tell you to fend for yourself, that it's time to be a big girl.*

I bury my head in my hands.

As he halts in front of me, Mitchum's shiny brown wing tips step into my line of vision.

"Elizabeth." His stern voice commands that I acknowledge him. Tears run down my cheek as I gaze up.

Juan stands and moves to a chair opposite us.

I moan, "Why doesn't anyone believe that Courtney made the first move and I responded—appropriately, if I might add."

He stares at me, unflinching. "Your aunt is going to take you home. You are *not* to return to school property. Do you understand?"

I timidly shake my head.

"Verbal, please."

"Yeah, I mean, yes, sir."

"If you do, it's considered trespassing, and you will be arrested. Mrs. Marsh will mail you a packet with your final grades and discharge papers. I recommend you find a GED program or a way to test out of your senior year. Some of the local community colleges offer classes, if you need them, or there's a couple of alternative high schools. It's almost the summer, so it shouldn't be a problem to start summer school."

I stay silent, afraid my voice will crack if I speak.

"Any questions?"

"You mean, I can't come back *ever*?"

"You're expelled," he adds, "and it's not like you bothered to attend when you had the choice."

"What about Courtney?"

"What about her?"

"Will she be suspended?"

"Elizabeth, when will you learn that every action has a reaction and every choice has a consequence?" He sighs. "We have zero tolerance on fighting, so yes, but her family will claim self-defense and try and fight it."

I whimper, "She started it."

"Stop talking." Wagging a finger at me, disgustedly, he says, "I ask the questions."

I direct my attention to the sound of approaching footsteps. When I look down the hall, I see Charlotte moving at a snail's pace, each step deliberate. When she stops beside Mitchum, it's like I'm staring at a ghost. Her skin ashen, she stands there, stoic.

"Elizabeth?" he snaps.

Unable to meet his eyes, I bite my lip hard enough I taste blood. Instead, I stare directly at Charlotte. Her face contorts into a frown as she considers me.

"You need to go home," Mitchum says, turning to Charlotte. "Now."

Charlotte steps forward, reaching for my arm to help me up. The cops already confiscated my backpack.

"Let's go." Her voice is cold.

Heaving myself out of the chair, I avoid her eyes, a storm brewing behind them—and I'm the sole reason. Holding me by the elbow, she practically drags me along beside her. As soon as we reach the exit, she comes to a standstill.

"What the hell happened?" she spews. "You're endangering your child's life so you can have a silly tiff with another high schooler?"

"It's not a silly tiff, whatever the hell a *tiff* is."

"Why did you attack Courtney?"

Glaring at her in defiance, I lash out. "None of your business."

"I drove you to her house, tried to ingratiate her into an evening with us when she needed a ride. How did it come to this?"

"No, what you did was you *forced* her on me. Someone who I hate."

"That's a strong word, Elizabeth."

"That's why I'm using it, *Charlotte*," I sneer.

She throws her hands up in the air. "Why would violence be the answer? It doesn't solve anything." Walking toward the parking lot, she snaps, "I have a class to instruct. I've got to go."

"What about *your* past?"

She spins arounds fast enough it makes me lightheaded. "What about it?"

"Is there anything you'd do differently," I inquire, "since we're so focused on how I'm a loser?"

"I never said that."

Motioning with air quotes, I ask, "You ever have any 'accidents' or 'lie' about something you did?"

She stares at me blankly.

"Get in trouble at school?"

Charlotte's mouth tightens. "No, I can't say I did."

"Push someone down a flight of stairs," I sneer, "or yourself?"

I instantly regret saying this as the words hang in the balance between us. Charlotte's face drains of color, her lips turning from pale pink to white. "If there's something you're implying, then let's hear it."

"Nothing." I gulp for air. "I read about you is all."

Crossing her arms, she takes a step back. "You read about me?" Her lip trembles. "Wow, you *read* about me." She spits out, "Tell me what you *read*, Elle, since you know everything at seventeen." Her eyes slant into narrow slits. "Is there something you want to tell me about my past I don't know?"

We have a standoff, each glowering at the other. Her hands are holding on to her handbag, while mine are poised on my hips. The one thing we have in common: we are both defiant.

"I just want you to know what's out there. Some of the articles . . ." I pause. "Some mention you threw yourself down a flight of stairs when you were pregnant, causing you to lose your baby." I then whisper, "Is it true?"

"Where would you read that?" Her face is drawn into a grimace. "That's disgusting."

"Just some posts on Reddit." I shrug. "I'm not saying you did . . ."

Big tears start to roll down Charlotte's face. "I'm sorry . . . I can't . . . I can't do this with you."

Fuck. I want to bash myself in the head. I'm taking out all my anger on her and showing my cards at the same time.

I suck at this.

And here I'm supposed to be flattering her and building her trust.

Diffuse the situation, I order myself as I try to control my wobbling knees. I've hit a nerve, and I'm about to lose access to Charlotte permanently. I think of what's at stake and how my father will never speak to me again if I mess this up.

"This is why I stick close to my home and stay away from all of this." Charlotte waves her hand at the surroundings. "Because I can't escape from the court of public opinion."

"I wasn't trying to suggest—"

"Yes, you absolutely were." She strides past me to the car. "Sounds like you have your mind made up about what I am." Spinning around, she says, "You know, you and Courtney have a lot in common. You are both mean girls, Elle. You just try to use your wrong-side-of-the-tracks persona as a reason you get to act the way you do."

"I'm not trying to judge you," I huff. "That's my point. Not everything is always as it seems. I didn't start shit with Courtney, just because that's what she and her friends said. I'm innocent in this. Well, not entirely, because I hit her, but I wasn't the one who started it."

"Normal teenage behavior isn't starting fights at school." Her voice drips acid. "Nor is it stealing someone's personal property." She opens her door with a ferocious intensity. "You are a real piece of work, Elizabeth Laughlin."

Shaking her head, she slams the door in my face.

If I don't jump in the car, I will have lost my chance to make things right with Charlotte, if I even can. If she refuses to speak to me, I'll be at a dead end and I'll never uncover the truth. I have no doubt I will be cut off from her permanently.

When Charlotte is untrusting of you, it's over.

And she doesn't need me. I need her.

"Here goes nothing," I groan. I jog around to the opposite side and hop in.

"No, no you don't." She turns to face me with swollen eyes. "Did you ever think that maybe I have a very good reason for why I carry a gun? And yet, you stole it from me."

"What're you talking about?"

She ignores my question. "Better yet," she seethes, "maybe I was hurt before in the past? Maybe I'm in danger? Maybe a restraining order didn't help, and he put me through a wall?"

I'm chilled to the bone as the pupils of her eyes dilate.

"You know nothing about my life," Charlotte says coldly. "And I know nothing about yours. Minus the fact that since you showed up, drama seems to follow you everywhere."

Ashamed, I stare at my ripped cuticles. "You think I took your gun?"

"Elizabeth, you're smarter than this. Don't play dumb. My gun was in the glove box, and then it disappeared. Now I don't have any protection, and, oddly enough, it was found near the scene of my robbery."

"You can't think I had something to do with it?"

"You're telling me it's a mere coincidence?"

Solemnly, I say, "I swear on my unborn child's life I did not take your gun, Charlotte."

As she presses her eyes shut, I watch a tear slide down her cheek.

"I want to hear your story, Charlotte. Not just what I read. Your ex. What did he do?"

"Wonderful! I'm glad you want to hear it, considering I don't want to talk about it." She wrings her hands in her lap. "Shame on you. You have no right to come into my life and dictate what I tell you or don't. You don't get to try and hurt me because you've read some articles and are now an expert on everything Charlotte." Then, murmuring, "I've got to get to class," she rests a hand on her stomach. "Where can I drop you off?"

"Please don't make me go back to Diane's," I whimper. "I know I messed up today, but the baby—"

"Why not? She's your foster parent and has a right to know about your expulsion."

"She does not."

"You can't run from everything, Elle."

"I'm not running, I'm fleeing," I grumble. "Diane's a drunken, sloppy train wreck."

"Then how is she your foster mom?"

"Because the system doesn't care. No one wants me," I spit out. "The government pays her a monthly stipend to take me off their hands."

Charlotte recoils like I slapped her. "Stop playing the victim, Elle."

I reach for her hand, and it's ice cold. She doesn't even wipe the tears away; she just lets them roll down, the collar of her shirt damp.

"Charlotte, I believe you." I squeeze her limp hand in mine. "I wasn't trying to make an accusation or say I didn't think you were telling the truth."

"It doesn't matter about your opinion." Her voice is harsh. "A court of law did, and it makes no difference if you believe me or not. I was there, and you weren't." Her eyes meet mine, and I see unchecked pain that sears me to the core.

I feel like shit.

Absolute shit.

The reading on my asshole meter keeps rising.

Why did I ever think Charlotte was a bad person?

Because he told you she was, I remind myself. Starting to feel like a puppet on a string, I want to go berserk and yank the cord.

"What possible motivation could I have for wanting to hurt my unborn child, the only innocent person in this?" Snot drips down her nose, and I feel a protective rush as I grab a tissue out of the box balanced on the back window.

"I'm sorry." I chew my lip. "Charlotte, you're the first person I've had to talk to in a long time, and I just want to know about you. I shouldn't have questioned you like that with what I found. It was stupid, but you seem so scared of something and so guarded, and I want to know why."

CHAPTER 36
Charlotte

"I don't know you, Elle." I wipe a tear away. "You were a complete stranger until a couple of months ago."

"Yeah, I know." She slumps down in her seat. "I just wanted to ask you questions about your life, but I went about it all wrong."

I start the car and put it in reverse. "I don't know what's so fascinating about mine, or why you seem to have so many questions."

Elle leans forward, her head in her hands.

"Noah and I, before this happened, wanted to ask a huge favor of you, but I don't think it makes sense anymore . . ."

"What?" she whispers.

I don't answer, my concentration on driving. "Where are we going?" I ask instead. "I'm running late now."

"Can you drop me off at your house?"

"That's not a good idea."

"When can we talk?"

"Elle, we have been."

"No, I've been taking out my anger on you. Directing it at the wrong person. Trying to make you feel shitty."

"At least you admit it. That's a start." I pause. "Tell you what. Noah will be home at nine. Why don't you come over and hear our proposal tonight . . . that is, unless you're grounded for life, and if you were my child, you would be."

Sitting in silence for a minute, Elle stares out the window, lost in thought.

"If you come over tonight, you need to be prepared to honestly answer some questions. Noah isn't going to tolerate any attitude, and neither am I. If you can't be honest with both of us, this isn't going to work, and I won't be able to have you in my life. Noah and I are trying to focus on our baby in the best way possible, and I simply can't let anything jeopardize that."

We sit, with only the radio noise echoing through the cabin.

"What's it going to be, Elle?"

"You." She says softly, "I choose you."

"Good." I nod my head at the progress we are making. "I'll drop you off at the store. I'd like you to pick up some prenatal vitamins for both of us. Here's some cash, and I'll see you tonight."

"Why'd you pick this store?"

"Because it's close to a bus stop, and I'm done grocery shopping for a while." I hand her a crisp one-hundred-dollar bill and warn her, "I want my change tonight. See you later."

CHAPTER 37
Elle

When I get to Charlotte's, I'm more apprehensive than I was during the rainstorm. How long before she finds out who I really am and what I'm really doing here?

And Noah, he probably hates me for involving his wife in all my bullshit. I wonder if he'll see right through me.

Timidly, I knock, shifting from foot to foot while I wait for them to answer.

After a couple beats, it's Charlotte who opens the door, examining the outside world over my shoulder. As I hand her the bag of vitamins and the change and receipt, she invites me in.

"Noah's stuck in New York." She flips the switch on for the fireplace and eases into the middle of the couch. "His plane had mechanical issues, so I told him I would just talk to you."

After leaving my tennis shoes by the front door, I settle on the floor, my back resting against the easy chair.

Charlotte seems worn out, but more than that, depressed, like she has been crying, her cheeks red and splotchy.

"How was class?"

"It was good. Test day, so I administered that." She pulls a throw out of a wicker basket next to the couch. "It's supposed to rain again tonight, and I'm chilly. You want one?"

"No, thank you."

"Did you tell Diane what happened today?"

"Not yet. But I will." Defensive, I add, "She'll get a letter, so it's not like I can hide it."

"What do you think she will say about this?"

I pick at a seam on my leggings.

"Wait, that's a dumb question." Charlotte smacks a hand to her forehead. "You never go to school, and you do what you want."

I start to disagree but close my mouth instead.

"When I asked you earlier about why you punched Courtney, there's obviously a history between you two. I want to know why you are enemies; what prompted this kind of dislike?"

I can't pull my legs all the way up to my chest, so I stretch them out. It feels like I'm being probed by a therapist. "Courtney started making fun of me in middle school about my homelife. Being poor, being in the system. It wasn't just that she would tease me—it was that she made it a point to tell the other kids. She would constantly flaunt what she had in my face, but even more than that, she'd make it a point to rudely point out all I didn't have."

"Okay, so this has been going on for a long time?"

"Yeah."

"Which brings us to today."

"I got upset," I say.

Charlotte raises her brows at me.

"Okay, very upset."

"Punching a girl is your definition of upset?"

I shrug. "She's always had a crush on Justin—my ex. It killed her when he chose me over her, because she's not used to the word *no*. And as you saw when we dropped her off, her *daddy* can buy her everything except a boyfriend."

She nods at me to go on.

"The other day I got a text with some pictures of them hanging out, and I lost it. I heard they were hooking up."

"And you believe it?"

"I have no reason not to."

"You're a smart girl. Do you think he would cheat on you?"

"He dumped me at the end of our senior year. Who knows?" I shrug again. "He has the future on his mind."

"And this has been going on for a while? Him and that girl?"

"No." I shake my head. "I think it's recent."

"Ouch." She winces. "This is awful."

"It gets worse." I pause. "Supposedly she's knocked up."

"Wow. That's fast." Charlotte doesn't look as surprised as I would expect, but then I remember she was living with my father while pregnant with Noah's child.

"Uh-huh." My eyes prick with tears. "So Jerry Springeresque, right?"

Abruptly I rise, the overwhelming urge to go to the bathroom and blow my nose hitting at once. When I reenter the living room, I curl up in the overstuffed chair, tucking my feet underneath me. Charlotte's still seated facing the fireplace, her eyes staring dully into the distance.

"So, back to the incident today." She rotates her head toward me. "Did you just walk up to Courtney and punch her?"

"No."

"Elle . . ."

Annoyed, I sigh. "That's not how it happened. I saw her and her friends walking by after class, and I confronted her. She went to grab for my stomach, and I didn't know what she was going to do. I went into protective-mommy mode."

Charlotte's intense gaze never leaves my face.

I continue. "So I pushed her so she wasn't in my space . . . and she got me near my stomach, and then I hit her—yes, I did."

Cradling my stomach, I look down at my lap.

"What're you thinking about?" she asks gently.

"That I'd never let Courtney Kerr—or anyone for that matter—hurt my baby."

"It's a powerful instinct, a mother's need to protect her nest."

"I'm starting to understand." I give her a small smile. "But I didn't purposely try to go after Courtney. I might be a lot of things, but violent isn't one of them."

Charlotte's quiet for a minute. "I'll talk to Courtney's parents. See if we can sort this out before they press charges."

"What're you going to say?"

"I don't know yet. Let me worry about that."

"What did you and Noah want to talk to me about?"

"Before all this happened, Noah and I had wanted to ask you something." A look of sadness crosses her face. "I just don't know if it's a good idea now."

Hoping it's not illegal, I slowly get up the courage to ask. "What do you mean?"

"I mentioned to Noah that I don't feel safe in the house right now with what happened . . ." Her voice trails off. "It brought back some very dark memories, to say the least, and Noah's potentially got an international trip where he'll be gone for an extended period of time. As you can imagine, it's hard being here all alone."

"Understandable." I look at my hands. "I can't imagine being pregnant and practically alone. Oh wait," I joke, "I can."

She stares at where her wedding band would be. "The only thing is, I don't want you here if you think there is any truth to what you read online about me being guilty." She cringes. "I have to be in the best possible mind-set, and I need positivity right now. I can't get bogged down by the past. I'm tired of it eating me alive."

"I'm really sorry, Charlotte."

We both flinch as we hear the first sign of a storm, a rumble of thunder. Charlotte automatically starts to tremble, and I notice she presses her fingers into her wrist, feeling for her pulse.

"So, back to what Noah and I discussed, we talked about the possibility of you living here while you're pregnant and until you get on your feet afterward."

"Seriously?"

"Where do you sleep at Diane's?"

I toy with my bracelet. "On a mattress or the couch."

"So you don't have your own room?"

"No."

"Would she mind?"

I smirk. "No."

"There are some stipulations to you staying here, Elle."

Sullen, I peer at her.

"We're happy to provide a home for the time being." She rises from the couch. "But you're finishing your GED, you'll have chores, and you'll help with errands. In return, you'll have no financial worries with your pregnancy and can rest assured you'll have healthy meals and a well-stocked pantry."

I raise my brow. "Okay."

"There's another thing. You'll need to write everyone involved today an apology, including the principal and Courtney."

Angrily, I glare at Charlotte. "Are you crazy? I'm not writing the bitch who got knocked up by my boyfriend a sympathy card. Now you're off your rocker."

"Karma will take care of her."

"Does karma do that?" I narrow my eyes at her, but a voice inside warns me to be careful. "Take care of bad people?"

"Of course."

"Not a chance in hell." I pick at my ragged nail bed. "She's the reason I got the nickname I now have."

"What do you mean?"

"My dad died of cirrhosis. I couldn't pronounce it for years. I was seven when he died, and I got it confused with the one that means bad breath."

"Halitosis?"

"Yep." I shake my head. "Everyone told me I was crazy, that no one dies from that. Then they started calling me 'Skunk Breath.'" Rolling my eyes, I add, "That was started in middle school by that bitch."

"Courtney made up the name?"

"Yep," I groan, "and a song. Then she enlisted a bunch of her friends to call me that."

Looking resigned, Charlotte says, "Fine, no apology to Courtney directly, but you will write her family a letter. And the school."

I start to protest, but she ignores my outburst. "Go on up to bed. There's Tylenol in the drawer for what I'm sure is a painful bruise. Get some sleep."

"You like to be in charge, don't you?"

Charlotte refuses to take the bait. "I think you have pushed every button of mine today, so yes."

With no argument left in me after the day from hell, I rub my eyes tiredly, the railing my lifeline for making it to the second floor. When I sink down on the mattress, I don't bother getting undressed. I simply roll over and tug the throw at the end of the bed over me.

I'm starting to drift off when I hear a knock.

CHAPTER 38
Charlotte

I open the door to the guest room, where Elle is half-asleep, her eyes vacant. But when I say "I wanted to give you this" and hand her the sonogram, they instantly light up.

"Oh my God, thank you."

"It got stuck between the console and the seat in the car."

She smiles at the picture, elated.

After a moment, I can see the wheels spinning in her head as her body collapses back against the pillow. Pausing at the door, I say, "You know, Elle, you can have this baby and give it up to a family who can't conceive. Don't feel like you're alone in this. And I'm here for you, if you need to talk."

She nods.

"I'll take you tomorrow to register for an alternative high school."

After shutting the door softly behind me, instead of going back downstairs to the master suite, I decide to head to the last room on the left. With my cross necklace gone, and the small key with it, I had to find my spare.

I unlock the door and slip inside, locking it behind me. The air's stale and musty, and I'm reminded to do a better job of lighting candles or spraying air neutralizers.

But now I have a purpose, and this space won't be vacant for much longer.

This room has always been off limits to anyone else, even Noah.

I finger the thin curtains and stare out at the steady trickle of rain, the manner in which it removes impurities in the air. I push open the windowpane and am hit with a blast of cold, but I don't mind, the cleansing air soon filling the room.

I can't believe our baby would've been almost ten now.

And the one I lost in high school practically an adult.

Sinking down into the rocking chair, I collect my thoughts, staring straight ahead for a split second, letting myself feel something.

Guilt, remorse, apathy.

Quietly singing a lullaby, I rub my belly, feeling satisfied and complete.

Eventually I nod off and fall asleep in the chair, hands glued to my abdomen. It's only when I hear birds chirping and become aware of a stream of sunshine playing tricks on my face that I wake up.

I rub my eyes, my back stiff from the chair, my throat parched.

Hurriedly, I tiptoe out of the room, locking the door behind me as I slip the key into the pocket of my robe.

After falling asleep in my bedroom, I wake up again at a more reasonable hour.

Elle's asleep on the couch when I reenter, so I start breakfast, making pancakes and eggs. She hungrily devours the food before we head to an alternative school I researched in the area. I expect her to argue, but she's quiet on the ride over.

After we explain what happened at her public school and answer an overabundance of questions, she's allowed to enroll in a probationary period, which calls for zero disciplinary action in the first ninety days or automatic dismissal. They have summer school, which will be imperative if Elle wants to stay on track.

"Hopefully I'll be graduated by then," Elle mutters as she walks me back to the Jeep, which I have filled up with gas and made peace with in the interim, no longer seeing Jonathan's hooded figure coming at me.

At least not for the moment.

Smiling sympathetically, I agree. "I hope so too."

Since Elle's allowed to start class that morning, I leave her at the new school, and instead of barricading myself in the home office or a vacant room like I normally would, I plop down at the nearest coffee shop. As I start to answer emails from my students, my mind keeps drifting to Elle. After I sigh louder than I intend, an elderly man considers me with curiosity. My face flushes red, and I smile at him.

Typing notes on next week's lecture, "*Beloved*, by Toni Morrison," I can't wrap my head around the fact that Elle's pregnant as well. Out of nowhere, this teenager shows up on my doorstep, and now I'm caught up in her life, for better or worse.

I want to call Noah and tell him the good news, that Elle's agreed to stay with us, but I get his voice mail. He's most likely working, but I talk myself into believing he's probably with another woman. He'll find one in New York so he can fly to Tokyo while I'm at home nursing our baby.

I kick my foot out angrily and catch my shin on the foot of the table. It doesn't help my plight, and I hiss a cussword at the dark oak.

Focusing back on my laptop, I jab the keyboard with my fingers as I access Noah's email.

This time, Noah's responded to Lauren, his email generic enough, but flirty.

Don't let her get to you, I warn myself. *You're having his baby, not her.*

My temperature rises, and, flushed, I feel perspiration dripping underneath my armpits.

And here I chastised Elle for how she reacted to Courtney, I admonish myself.

Dr. Everett has recommended that when I want to berate Noah for the past, I should do the exact opposite. Shower him with love and affection instead of anger and recrimination.

Taking a deep breath, I write him a sweet email and attach a picture to it.

Then, giving up on work, I browse the internet for a new duvet cover for the comforter in the guest bedroom, baby clothes, and a glider I think would complement the nursery.

I also find a gift for Lauren.

The site asks if I want overnight shipping so it can be delivered tomorrow. Perfect.

After I submit the order, I overhear someone at the table next to me mention the time.

I gasp at my phone.

Muttering another curse word under my breath, I realize I'm late picking up Elle. *If I had my watch, I would've been inclined to look at it,* I think sadly.

After slamming my computer shut, I rush to a nondescript gray building that looks a little too much like a prison from the outside. There's nothing cheery about it, the outside unmarked, the architecture meant to fade into the industrial office park.

Elle is standing outside wearing a yellow parka, her blonde hair billowing behind her in the wind. Another girl stands next to her with a pierced nose, extensive tattoos covering her arms. She's wearing a concert T-shirt, but it's definitely not the Jonas Brothers, I think wryly.

I detest the smell of smoke, but worse, when the girl shifts, so does her face, and I watch as a puff of air is expelled from her lungs and a cloud of smoke dissipates into the air.

When Elle realizes it's me, she quickly says something to the girl, who stubs the cigarette out underneath her worn shoes. After unbuckling my seat belt and throwing the Jeep into park so fast it sputters, I jump out of the car. "What the hell are you doing?"

"I'm eighteen," the girl says, shrugging.

"And she's pregnant," I retort.

"And we're leaving." Elle grabs me by the elbow, her lips pursed in a tight line. "Hi to you too."

"You can't be around smoke."

"Why?" Her blue eyes narrow at me in defiance.

"Do I need to give you a lesson in secondhand smoke and birth defects?"

"It's not going to matter, anyway."

Incensed, I yank out of her grasp. "Great, so that means you can be reckless with your body and the life of your child?"

"As if you haven't been?" Elle shoots back. She clasps a hand over her mouth.

"What the hell are you talking about?"

"Nothing." Elle huffs and shoves past me, sliding into the passenger seat. In order to keep my cool, I have to lean on the hood of the vehicle to collect my thoughts, too angry to face her. Closing my eyes, I count to ten.

Then twenty.

I take a deep breath as I climb behind the steering wheel, and tears spring to my eyes, my focus blurred as I stare at the road.

"I shouldn't have said that," Elle murmurs. "I'm really sorry."

After sitting quietly for a strained interlude, I glare disgustedly at the profile of Elle's face. "No, you shouldn't have."

The tension grows between us as we sit in uncomfortable silence.

"Why did you stay with him?"

"Who?" I'm confused. "Noah?"

"No. Your abusive boyfriend." She shakes her head. "I can't imagine letting anyone hurt me if I didn't have a choice."

"Do you always have a choice, Elle?"

She considers this for a moment.

"Think about Diane," I say. "Do you feel like you have control over the situation?"

"No. I feel helpless."

"Okay, then put yourself in my shoes and walk with me. What if you were in a bad situation, and you didn't feel you had any power to stop it?"

"But I'm not old enough to move out," Elle mumbles. "Adults make the decisions for me."

"That might be true, but sometimes we find ourselves in situations and we forget, or it's constantly told to us, that we don't have a choice." I pause for a break. "Take Justin, for instance. You have no control over how he responds or supports your decision with the baby, do you? Yet you didn't make the baby alone, did you?"

Elle is an intelligent girl, and I can tell she's absorbing my words. She finally mumbles something, but it's barely a whisper, and I have to strain to hear her over the traffic noise. "What did you say?"

"I'm just angry about this whole situation, being pregnant and alone . . ."

"But you're not alone. We just talked about this last night." I bite my lip. "And don't tell me I was reckless, when you weren't there. I've made some dumb mistakes, but I never intended to lose a baby to a staircase."

She shrinks in her seat when I say this.

Good.

With Elle, I can no longer tiptoe around the subject of how I lost the baby or sugarcoat it by calling it an accident. If she wants to keep implying horrible things, then she needs to hear the disgusting truth out loud.

"I think I'm directing all my anger at you instead of at Justin and Courtney."

"Any word from him?"

"He unblocked me, and now he wants to talk, said we need to clear the air, whatever that means. He's all over the place. He'll never get on board with the baby." Her shoulders start to shake. "He wants me to have an abortion."

"You aren't going to, are you?" I don't think it's possible to clamp the steering wheel any tighter than I already am.

"I don't know," she groans, "and now he's got Courtney knocked up. I don't think I could do that. Justin doesn't get his way on this, just because he doesn't want to be a dad or accept responsibility."

"That's a mature stance to take."

After a moment, she adds, "Some people just aren't cut out to be parents."

"I used to say that about my ex." I lick my lips. "That he wasn't cut out for it."

"Did he get offended when you said that?"

"No, not really. He knew it was true."

"Don't people get better at it with time?"

"I suppose some, but not all."

Elle nods her head. "Do you think Noah will be a good dad this time around?"

I study her intently as I repeat her flub out loud.

"'This time around'?" I peer at her with curiosity. "Is there something you know that I don't?" I try to say it lightly, but the inflection is there.

"I just meant . . . hell, I'm tired." She pats her forehead. "I don't know what I'm saying. I just mean—do you think he'll be around, since he travels so much?"

For now, I choose to ignore her paltry answer. "I think he'll be more present after the baby's born. I know he's trying to get this lucrative deal done so he can do precisely that, be there when the baby arrives. I just have to keep that in mind." Then, giving Elle a side glance, I beg, "Can you take a chill pill, please?"

She looks down miserably at her feet. "Yeah."

"I know you are going through a huge transition, but I've got raging hormones as well, and the constant attacks on my character aren't helpful. If you truly feel I'm a horrible person, then tell me. You certainly don't have to feel obligated to stay with us."

"I don't need to think about it," Elle groans. "I know you're only trying to help."

"It would be less of a burden if you stopped trying to shove me on the other side with the other people who've let you down."

"I know." She rakes a hand through her blonde hair.

"Is there anything we need to pick up from your apartment?"

"Um . . . we don't need to go there. I can just bring my stuff over later. I don't have much."

"We might as well go now while we have some free time." I force a smile. "You have to have something."

Evidently resigned to the fact that I'm not taking no for an answer, Elle mutters, "I guess."

"Plus, I need to talk to Diane and clear this with her." I flip the visor down. "Regardless of how she treats you, she's going to wonder if you don't come home and then call the police on us for kidnapping a minor. I want her to know how to reach you, and where."

It's quiet for a minute, and the only noise is Elle's incessant biting habit.

"What's on your mind?"

"I was just thinking about the boys." Elle stares out the window. "I don't want them to feel like they don't have me around anymore."

"You really care about them, don't you?" I touch her arm. "Don't worry; they're welcome to visit."

"Can I just give you Diane's number?" Elle offers. "You can call or text her. You might get a better response with a text. She doesn't answer numbers she doesn't know. She'll assume you're a bill collector or the landlord."

"Will she be home today if we stop over?"

"No, she'll be at work, but if for some reason her car's there, you can talk to her."

Placated, I change the subject. "How was your class today?"

"Annoying."

"Did something happen?"

"No." Elle furrows her brow. "Nothing happened. I just hate school, and they shove everything into a small amount of time. I just feel so far behind." Her jaw tightens. "And these stupid boys just make cracks and mess around. They're so disruptive."

"I'm sorry about the other kids." Wrinkling my nose, I say, "Just think, if yesterday hadn't happened . . ."

"I know. Believe me, I know."

The rest of the drive is shrouded in silence, and both of us seem to be dwelling on our own thoughts pretty hard.

I'm obsessing over Noah and Lauren, so much so that I have to slam on my brakes, almost missing the turn Elle is pointing at.

The streets become avenues and the people more destitute as we head east. This seems to bother Elle, who seems to tense up, lowering herself into the seat, like she's hiding from the outside.

CHAPTER 39
Elle

I've never actually paid attention to the details of the faces on my side of town before, maybe because I'm so focused on my own survival. Before, they were shapeless and nameless, and I was one of them. It's weird as I sit on the passenger side, watching my neighborhood through Charlotte's eyes.

Worn and haggard, we all look equally oppressed.

Charlotte's doing her best to keep her expression neutral, but I notice a grimace at the sight of a homeless woman and a mixed-breed mutt lying on the curb, discarded newspaper shielding her from the world.

Neglected, just like me.

I hear a sharp inhalation.

Pointing to the next traffic signal, I direct her to take a right. Up ahead on the corner, a man peddles Nikes and knockoff Prada bags.

My apartment complex is more like a slum, one gigantic building after another, all a faded mud brown, all with rickety balconies that to the naked eye even *look* unsteady. Broken glass bottles and cigarettes and the occasional empty syringe litter the sidewalks.

"Third one on the left."

She puts on her blinker, waits for a passing cyclist, then pulls into the half-empty lot of the Meadowlark, a highly unoriginal name for this monstrosity. Why management thought they could dull the perception of poverty by calling it a bird's name, I'll never understand.

"You can park in spot seventy-two." I point to Diane's empty parking space. Thank God she's not home. I would never introduce the two of them, but I have to pretend like I'm making an effort.

Diane would spit and chew Charlotte out and probably blow my cover.

"This Diane's spot?"

"Yeah."

"It's okay I park here?"

"Yep."

I watch Charlotte start to tug off her seat belt. "Let me come with you and help you carry your stuff."

"Uh, no, thanks." I quickly unbuckle mine and open the passenger door. "I don't have that much, and we're on the fourth floor."

Shuddering, I cringe, thinking of Charlotte walking through the cement hallways and entering our smoky and dirty apartment. Diane can hardly be bothered to get off the couch to put anything away when she's home. Plus, four people in a two-bedroom makes it seem even more cluttered and unkempt.

Eyeing me warily, Charlotte asks, "Elle, if you have to walk up four flights of stairs, then so can I." Watching as a vagrant tries to scoop a piece of metal out of the dumpster, I challenge her to say something.

Glancing around cautiously, she asks, "Are you sure you're okay?"

"I live here. These are my people."

"Fine, but I don't want you lifting anything heavy."

"I have a roller suitcase." I shrug. "There's a ramp I can take down, so it'll slide easily."

Conceding with a raised eyebrow, she rests her hands on the wheel. "I'm going to give Noah a quick buzz while you're upstairs, but call me if you need help, and I'll come up."

Forcing a smile, I walk across the parking lot until I reach the stairs. There's a ramp around the back of the building, used mainly for deliveries, since this place used to be some type of psych ward or old hospital.

Or maybe that's a rumor an older kid told me when I was younger to scare me. I decide the stairs will be faster going up. But halfway up I'm short of breath, so I grab the rusted railing for support.

When I reach our apartment, I'm annoyed to find the door isn't even locked.

Appalled, I enter to find the kitchen even messier than usual. If Charlotte's talking to Noah, she'll be preoccupied for a while, so I decide to do some light cleaning. I load the dishwasher and start it and then wipe down the kitchen table and chipped counters, and since the space is so tiny, I use a couple paper towels to wipe up the floor. I can't get down on my hands and knees, but I manage to do a quick once-over, since the boys tend to spill juice or drop crumbs when we do have food.

The living room's a disaster, and I can't find the vacuum, so I just carry a garbage bag and empty the ashtray and toss bottles and cans into it. Old newspapers and bills are strewn around the place. I leave the bills but notice a couple unopened envelopes from my previous high school.

An unopened letter postmarked Huberton Correctional Institution is underneath the pile. I don't dare take it with me. Scanning the contents of my father's note, I discern that it's an apology for his tantrum last time I was there. Of course, he doesn't call it that. He calls it a "lapse of judgment." I toss it in the trash with the rest of the mail.

I walk into the boys' room and reach for my hiding place in the back of the closet. It's an old built-in shelf that no one uses. It's not really hidden, but it's not big enough to store anything larger than jewelry or a small weapon, so it feels like a safe to me.

The few items I own are stored here. The bedroom reminds me of the aftermath of a hurricane: toys and puzzle pieces are scattered like garbage and debris, and barely any of the cheap carpeting shows through.

After I step on a Lego, I almost lose my shit. I grip the closet door in pain, then grab my roller suitcase and pack some of my clothes. I've had this suitcase for years, and not because I go on vacation. It was given to me by the foster system as I moved from place to place.

I tear a piece of paper out of my notebook and write Diane a note telling her I'm staying with Justin for the time being. After taping the note to the fridge, I leave the boys a separate one telling them how to get in touch with me. I write down my number, just in case they can't find the original Post-it.

I lock the door when I leave and don't bother looking over my shoulder, the stink in the hall enough to cause me to dry heave. Taking the ramp is easier going down, the wheels on the suitcase still in good shape, sliding smoothly down the concrete slab.

Charlotte must have her Bluetooth speakers on, because her window's cracked an inch or two and I can hear her conversation from the parking lot. I stand behind a blue pickup truck, and her voice sounds impatient.

Agitated, she says, "Then what should we do about her?" And then, "I don't want her at the house." I assume it's Noah on the other end who must be talking, because she tries to interrupt, then goes silent.

My stomach curdles, and it's not from the apartment fumes this time.

Closing my eyes, I sag against the bed of the truck.

My face burns in embarrassment.

I clench my fists. *Nobody ever wants me.*

I trace the scar on my inner wrist and sigh.

Should I head back to the apartment and forget about Charlotte and what my father asked me to do?

She's not the one who was on trial.

He was.

She's not the one that was found guilty.

He was.

My gut tells me to run, but I'm rooted to the spot, contemplating my next move.

I wait until I hear her say bye, and then I swallow hard, getting the courage to put one foot in front of the other.

I'm shifting my balance, deciding what to do, when I feel a tap on my shoulder.

CHAPTER 40
Charlotte

"Why're you just standing here?" My eyes dart back and forth between Elle and my SUV.

"Um, I thought I forgot something."

Tilting my head, I glance at her single suitcase. "How long have you been standing here?"

"Just for a minute." She touches her belly. "I was out of breath and took a pause."

"Crap, I knew the stairs were too much." I rush to grab the suitcase, prying it from her loosened grip. "Come on, let's get you sitting down."

She follows slowly, her footsteps awkward and unsure. After clicking the trunk button, I easily lift the suitcase, which is lighter than I expect, into the back before helping Elle settle into the passenger seat.

Her face looks peaked, and the bruise around her eye's a greenish yellow. "I'll make you some tea when we get back to the house." I gently tug the seat belt over Elle's lap into place, as if she were a helpless child.

"Are you sure you and Noah are both okay with me staying with you?"

"Yes, of course. Why would you say that?"

"Well, earlier, you said you didn't think it was a good idea."

"Elle, I just want you to understand and trust I'm trying to help you. I know that can't come easy for you, to trust people, but trying to hurt those who want to help you is downright mean, not to mention counterproductive. Can't you agree?"

She mutters, "Yeah."

"Then it's settled. We have our agreement, and you'll stay in school and be a support to me. We can have crazy pregnancy cravings and be pregnant ladies together."

"And Noah's cool with it?"

"He's totally fine with it. He's the one who originally suggested it . . ." My jaw clenches. "After the robbery."

She rubs her wrist as if she's in pain.

"Are you okay?" I ask.

I watch her face color, the fair skin turning red. "Yeah."

"Do we need to stop at the mall? How are you on maternity clothes or toiletries?"

"I think I'm good."

"Well, let's at least run to Target—a gal can do a lot of damage there."

"I haven't been there in a long time."

"Let's go, then," I say. "I need some maternity clothes, and I'm sure you do too."

After perusing every aisle, we've filled the cart to the brim with Elle's favorite shampoo and conditioner, her choice of a shower curtain and bathroom decor, maternity clothes, and some notebooks and pens for school. I also buy groceries to stock the fridge so Elle and I can eat at the house more.

"Thank you," Elle says, gesturing to the cart, "for all of this."

"You're welcome." I smile kindly. "I'm glad to help."

As we head back to the house, Elle's phone starts to chime from its position on her lap. After she quickly glances down, her face turns a sickly shade of white.

"Everything okay?" I murmur, peering over at her with concern.

"Uh, yeah." She focuses on what's going on outside, but her fingers go straight to her mouth.

"Is it someone you don't want to talk to?" She doesn't respond, and I assume she's lost in thought or she doesn't want to talk about it.

Finally, she says, "It's Justin."

I quizzically raise an eyebrow. "Is he being awful?"

"He just keeps telling me I'll be a terrible mother and that I shouldn't have the baby." Her blue eyes fill with tears. "And that Courtney is the one meant to have his baby."

"What?" I exclaim. "What a terrible thing to say."

Her small shoulders start to shake.

"You want me to respond to him for you?" My eyes drift over to Elle's phone as I try to unobtrusively scan the message. Muffled sobs drown out whatever she says.

She punches a button on her phone and swipes a hand across the screen. "No. I just deleted it. I'm not going to respond."

"That's good. That's the right thing to do." I stop at the gated entrance and push the button on the visor. "Look at me, Elle."

She keeps her head down as I gently brush a piece of matted hair stuck to her wet chin. "You are going to be an incredible mom. Don't ever sell yourself short. You've been raising your younger siblings like they're your own. The rest I'm going to help you through. The pregnancy will be an adjustment, but with books and advice, you'll be fine. You're not the first to have a baby. It'll be all right." I pause. "And, if you decide to give it up for adoption, then that's a terrific option, but there's no reason to not have this child. Don't let some idiotic boy try and make you question your choice, just because he's a coward."

Elle nods, sniffling. "I know."

Trying to make her smile, I ask, "Do you want me to kick his ass?" I see a small grin appear on her face.

"Seriously, where does he live?" I kid. "We can go and give him a scare."

"That's the thing: his parents kicked him out, so he couch surfs at his brother's." Elle looks embarrassed at this admission. "Such a loser."

"Oh, Elle, he doesn't deserve you. What the hell is it about this kid?" I smile at her. "I will admit he's good looking. It's the green cat eyes, huh?"

She looks spooked when I mention his eye color, her chewed fingernails the focus of her stare.

"Justin used to make me feel loved on a deeper level, past my looks and the things you can't change about yourself." When she says this, it takes me back to my father's funeral and how Noah made me feel complete.

"And now it's like it was all a dream. I never imagined we'd end up like this."

"Do you love him?" I say. "Or did you?"

She touches her wrist, the one with the leather bracelet she always wears. "I thought I did at the beginning, when it was fun and we enjoyed hanging out, but as time passed and shit got real, when life got real, I realized *we* didn't mean as much to him. And *I* didn't mean as much to him."

"Very well put." She starts to sob, and, handing her a tissue, I say, "Here, dry your eyes. You have me and Noah, and he can have Courtney. Sounds like they deserve each other. Now I wish I hadn't given her a ride home that night."

"I still don't understand why you did."

"Because I thought that by doing her a favor, she'd owe you one and she'd remember it the next time she thought about being mean."

"Yeah," she points out, "but *you* did her the solid, not me."

"I understand how she operates now."

"Speaking of that situation," Elle says glumly, "there were a couple letters waiting at the apartment for me from the school."

"What did they say?"

"I haven't opened them. I'm kind of scared to."

"Let's read them together, and we can go from there."

After Elle gets out of the passenger side, we carry in the grocery bags. Elle instructs me to leave her suitcase in the Jeep while she runs to the bathroom. I watch her hightail it to the downstairs half bath. Hearing her vomit, I decide to bring the suitcase upstairs so she doesn't have to mess with it.

I feel sorry for her. A cramped suitcase carries the entirety of her life.

As I roll it into the closet of the guest room, I hesitate. I don't want to intrude, but she did mention mail from the school that needs to be opened immediately. I'm worried we'll forget to talk about it later, and I certainly don't want Elle to face additional punishment because she forgot to show me. For teens, responsibility with mail isn't at the top of the list.

I unzip the front pocket and touch a stack of envelopes. After sliding them out, I see that Elle has two unopened letters from her high school.

I reach my hand down farther into the pocket and feel a lump. When I pull out a plaid coin purse in the bottom, change rattles.

I balk at my snooping, since I've already lambasted Elle for being untruthful, and a wave of fresh guilt washes over me. Even though Elle's a guest, she's still a stranger, and shouldn't I know what baggage she's bringing into my home? The gun is still in question, and I'm not entirely sure Elle is innocent, which is part of why she is here.

Digging in the other front pocket, I hear a rattle, and a box of candy falls out.

My favorite sour candy. I grin. There's nothing like sugary pregnancy cravings. I reach my hand in to help myself to a few pieces, but instead of Sour Patch Kids, something else falls out.

Instead of finding sweets, I finger the plastic of my credit and debit cards. These are the ones that disappeared when I was mugged outside the grocery store.

After walking into the bathroom as my throat threatens to close, I steady myself against the edge of the sink and then catch a glimpse of my reflection in the square mirror. All the color has drained from my face, leaving my skin bilious. In contrast, my neck and chest have transformed into an angry shade of red as a wave of hives flares up on my skin, signaling my distress.

My driver's license is tucked between the cards, my picture from a few years ago smiling back at me. I scan the cards twice, just to make sure it's really my name imprinted on the plastic and I'm not imagining it.

Nauseated, I sink down onto the toilet, clutching the box and my cards in a death grip. *But you can't take them,* I remind myself. *She'll know it's you who took them, and you can't let her know.*

Disgustedly, I tuck the evidence back into the box. Evidence that Elizabeth Laughlin is a conniving thief and confirmation she lied to me about stealing my gun.

You're the one who asked her to move in. I smack my fingers to my head in frustration.

Was this the plan all along? I wonder. *Get me to take pity on her so she could rob me blind?* I know from the sheer size and strength of my assailant it was a man who attacked me.

But Elle was somehow involved, even if she didn't do the dirty work herself.

An ice-cold tremor runs down the length of my neck.

Elle knows Noah is gone, potentially for months.

I shove my fist in my mouth to avoid crying out. I've been so stupid, letting this girl into our lives, trying to help her when all she really wanted was to hurt me. She knows I'm alone most of the time, an easy target.

Standing up, I resolve to tell Noah and warn the police.

I stare in the mirror at my tired eyes.

Being financially unstable can bring out the worst in people, and Elle's situation is a pretty dire one. *What if they try to kidnap my baby?*

Hearing Elle's voice before I see her, I swiftly drop the candy carton in the trash. She comes into focus behind me in the mirror.

Wiping a hand across her mouth, she stands there with a strange look on her face. "What're you doing?"

"I, uh . . . I carried your bags up and then felt nauseous."

"I said I could do it."

"You're pregnant."

"It doesn't mean I'm crippled, and last time I checked, so are you."

Elle peers into the walk-in closet, where her suitcase is lying opened on the floor. "What were you doing in my suitcase?" she asks coolly.

Meeting her gaze in the mirror, I'm physically unable to turn around and face her. It's like I'm avoiding a head-on collision. "I was going to hang your clothes up for you."

"Please don't."

"And I wanted these." I hold up the two envelopes.

"I would've given them to you if you'd asked," Elle sighs, snatching them from my hand. "I wasn't holding them hostage. I told you about it."

"Here's me asking." Without thinking, I add, "I'm more worried about me forgetting a deadline to contest it. I don't want you to get in any more trouble. In fact, I'd still like to see you go back to your old school."

Her mouth drops. "Really, there's a chance?"

I nod convincingly. If Elle thinks I have a plan to get her what she wants, maybe she'll back off, and it'll buy me some time to figure out exactly who's involved in her ploy.

"Okay, fair, I get that, but can we agree that you don't go through my shit?" She nervously thumbs through the front pocket. "I have a right to privacy, remember?"

"You're absolutely right," I interrupt, throwing my hands in the air. "I should've just asked for it. It won't happen again. You have my word." Subdued, I apologize again. "I'm sorry, I'm new to this."

In another circumstance, it would be humorous watching Elle now, frantically patting the pockets of her suitcase, searching through her backpack like a maniac. Giving up on her search, she darts her eyes suspiciously around the bedroom. "I don't mean to be so sensitive. It's your house—you probably worry I'm carrying a knife or a shank, given my background, huh?"

I try to act natural. "No, I trust you." Pasting on a frozen smile an ice queen could appreciate, I shrug. "I hope you trust me too."

"Yeah, I just—I don't have much. I think it's from having nothing of my own." She gives me a menacing stare. "That's why I'm so possessive of what I *do* have. You know, because I've lost so much."

"Possessive?" I tap a finger against my cheek. "Yes, that's a good word to describe it. If you tell me what you're looking for, maybe I can help?"

"I'm craving candy. I thought I had a box in here."

"Oh." I put a hand to my forehead. "I tossed a box I thought was trash. It's in the wastebasket."

Her eyes widen into sapphire saucers. "You found my Sour Patch Kids?"

Elle practically bum-rushes me to the bathroom, uttering a sigh of relief when she sees them resting at the bottom of the trash can, the lid of the carton closed.

Innocently enough, she asks, "Was it empty?"

"I don't know." I give her my most dazzling smile. "I didn't check."

She seems appeased after the sighting of her candy and then asks, "Do you mind if I take a nap?"

"No problem. Can I have the letters back, please?"

She presses the mail in my palm, clearly uninterested in what her former high school has to say about her behavior.

"Have a good nap. I'll make us dinner and tea later when you wake." My voice cracks as my heart explodes like a bomb detonating in my chest cavity.

I shut the door behind me when what I want to do is slam it, lock it, and throw away the key.

Carefully, I tiptoe to my office, locking the door behind me.

I log in to my bank account and confirm that I reported the cards as stolen and that both were canceled, so it's not like Elle or her accomplice can use them. Uneasy, I still send an email to the fraud department, letting them know I've discovered my debit and credit cards and advise that I will provide an update soon.

Once afraid of what would happen to me outside of the locked and bolted doors, I'm now petrified of my own house and what it holds inside. A stranger's sleeping in my home, and I worry I've opened Pandora's box by letting Elle into our lives.

CHAPTER 41
Elle

With a sigh of relief, I exhale into my pillow.

Thank God I didn't pack the other letter, the one from my father.

I knew it. I knew Charlotte would go through my shit. I just didn't think it would be immediately upon entering her house.

First her phone conversation in the Jeep, then this blatant attempt to spy on me.

Noah doesn't want me here now, probably because she told him about the fight at school and he's convinced I'm a bad seed.

Even after shutting my eyes, sleep's impossible.

I try to relax, but my mind wanders back to the day I was informed that my father was found guilty of manslaughter and he was being hauled off to serve his sentence.

Nervous energy courses through my veins, hard to tamp down. Being here in such close quarters with Charlotte is hard, and I feel like a caged animal. At first, I thought staying here would be a good idea, an easier way to get to the truth.

But am I going to be able to help him? I ask myself.

Pacing the carpet in the bedroom, I try to figure out what I need to find out to exonerate my father. If it's possible. If he's being truthful.

If I'm honest, I have to admit that doubt has ensnared me like a noose and is twisting around my neck.

Scared I'll wear out the carpet, I finally go out to the balcony to get some fresh air.

When I come back inside, I decide to fully unpack so Charlotte won't have another reason to search my meager belongings. The closet already has empty hangers and a laundry basket. I stand back when I'm finished, noticing how my clothes take up only about a fifth of the space, and in a walk-in closet, it's depressing to see how little I own.

But material possessions don't matter, I remind myself, and, patting my stomach, I whisper to the baby, "Because you belong to me, and we're in this together, and we're going to save our family."

Restless, I make my way downstairs and almost crash into Charlotte, who's balancing a laundry basket with a blanket draped on top in her arms.

Sometimes Charlotte focuses on me like she knows me or at least remembers me, but she hasn't put two and two together yet.

But she will, and I know I better have answers when she does.

"You're up." She says it as a statement.

I fake a yawn. "Yeah, I couldn't sleep—guess it's just getting used to a new place."

"Well, I'm going to put this down and head to bed. I'm not feeling the best. I think it's just pregnancy exhaustion."

"You want me to start the kettle and make us some tea?" I offer. "I saw noncaffeinated packets in the cupboard."

She rubs her neck like she's holding all her tension there. "No, thank you. I appreciate the offer. If you need anything, knock on the door. If I don't answer, I'll leave my phone plugged in by my bed." She adds, "I think Noah's going to make it back for a few days."

"That's great," I say, nodding. "I'd like to meet him more formally this time."

She seems startled when I say this, but she doesn't say anything else. Instead, she silently turns and heads to her bedroom.

A lock clicks behind her.

Tea sounds good to me, so I start the kettle, then wander into the living room. The television—that'll provide a welcome distraction. Peering at the screen, I flip aimlessly through the channels, at first thinking the chime of the doorbell is part of a movie.

When it's followed by a knock, I freeze.

With its being late afternoon, I'm sure Charlotte isn't expecting guests. She's a private person by her own admission.

Maybe it's Courtney's parents coming to read me the riot act.

Except they don't know I'm staying here. They'd first go to my address on file, which is Diane's, and she wouldn't give me away to them.

She'd support my decision to clock Courtney Kerr. In fact, in spite of everything, she'd be proud I stood up for myself.

Unsure what to do, I glance in the direction of Charlotte's door.

It doesn't move.

Should I go get her?

No, she wanted to rest. And she looked in dire need of a nap.

It could be one of those annoying telemarketers or a door-to-door salesman.

Another loud knock pulls me to my feet.

I gawk through the curtains.

Expecting someone obnoxious, I'm surprised to see it's a dark-haired woman, hair twisted up in a bun, a black Patagonia vest over her checkered blouse, with skinny black jeans hugging her petite frame. She's not very tall, probably five four or so.

She looks harmless. Probably a neighbor who just needs to borrow something. This is the type of neighborhood where you feel comfortable asking your fellow humans for a cup of sugar.

Darting my eyes to Charlotte's door again, I see that it still stands firmly shut.

I shrug, unlocking the dead bolt.

If she's selling makeup or a pyramid scheme, I can send her away with a death stare.

"Hello." I open the heavy wooden door to glare at her through the screen.

"Hi, I'm sorry to bother you." She pats her pockets, embarrassed. "Do you happen to have any doggy-waste bags?"

"We don't have a dog."

"Oh crap." A hand goes to her forehead. "I thought I saw you with one before."

"I dog sit for the neighbors," I say with a smile. "If you're ever interested . . ."

"Yeah, that'd be great." Then she adds, winking, "We can always use a good pet sitter."

We look at each other for a moment as she observes the nasty bruise near my eye. Then her eyes trail down to my burgeoning belly. "Are you . . . are you pregnant?"

"I am. But this didn't happen because I told him I was," I laugh, pointing to my face.

"Phew. I never want to ask someone and be wrong."

She starts to turn and then stops. "How about a plastic bag, then? I hate to leave it in their yard."

"Of course."

"Will your mom or dad mind?"

"No, they'd be happy to get rid of the plastic," I joke, "as long as you promise to recycle."

"Great." She rolls her eyes. "My pup sometimes goes twice, and I don't want to just leave it."

"Yeah, and not in this development." I peer behind her. "Where's your dog at? I'd love to meet him. Or her." There's no four-legged friend in sight. "I love dogs."

"He's with my walking buddy. She's got ahold of him and is standing where he marked his spot so we don't forget." She grins. "He's an Australian shepherd, Ozzie."

Apparently sensing my unease, she adds, "You should come meet him. He's got the most beautiful blue eyes."

"Sure. Let me go grab you that bag. Be right back." I shut the door in her face as I search first in the laundry room, then the kitchen. I find leftover plastic bags in the pantry. Grabbing a couple, I stop in my tracks when I see she's let herself in and is now standing in the foyer.

Stunned, I watch her shifting movements.

Her eyes are glued to the pictures on the wall before she looks at the photograph of Noah and Charlotte in college on the side table. After picking it up, she spits on it, rubs the glass, and puts it back down. I want to confront her, but I'm shocked at this behavior. Does she know Charlotte personally, where she can intrude like this? I'm already on thin ice with her, so I don't want to be rude to a neighbor. But this is batshit crazy.

Leering at the open staircase, the woman cranes her neck.

What a weirdo. Some people have no boundaries. I mean it *is* a gorgeous house, but still, have some manners.

Then I remind myself I showed up the same way.

But I came with a purpose, and I didn't just let myself in.

This woman is just plain annoying.

Blushing, she spots me eyeballing her. "You must not have heard me call out I was coming inside."

"I didn't." I step forward, handing her a couple bags. "Here you go—a couple extra in case Ozzie needs to go more than once."

She holds the bags to her chest. "Thanks. You're a lifesaver. I'd hate to lose my dog-walking privileges in our neighborhood."

"Oh, you're one of us," I say. "The lake attracts so many people, but rarely do I meet actual neighbors."

"Yeah, I know," she agrees, "which is silly, because I live a few streets over. But I didn't want to walk all the way home, since we were right here."

"Not a problem." I usher her to the door, nervous at her uninvited intrusion and weird behavior. "What street are you on?"

Her smile widens, showing small, even white teeth.

Almost too white.

Professionally done, I decide.

She holds it in place but doesn't answer.

"Wait." I snap my fingers, making up two street names on the fly that I'm sure exist somewhere but not here. "Are you on Collins or Wilshire?"

"Collins." Confidence restored, she lets her forced smile drop to a more natural, relaxed state.

"I love that street!" I exclaim. "We looked at a house there first."

"Yeah, it's quaint. We have enough room, so we don't feel like we're on top of the neighbors, if that makes sense."

"Absolutely," I say, smirking, "but they have bigger lots on Wilshire." Considering the street doesn't exist in this subdivision, the yards and setbacks can be as large as you want. I've been walking this neighborhood and know this part of town inside and out, including all the street names.

Yanking the screen door open, I ask, "Mind if I follow you out to meet Ozzie?"

Her eyes retract in her skull as if she thought I'd forget about the fictitious dog. "Oh yeah, sure." She waves up ahead. "He's just around the corner."

Rooted to the spot, she peers behind me one last time, intent on searching for something . . . or someone. Her eyes home back in on the sideboard, to the pictures of Charlotte and Noah. Cheerfully, she points to the frame. "Is that your dad?"

I motion toward the door, hoping she'll take a hint. "Uh, no," I say. "Oh, I'm sorry. Stepdad?"

"Nope." I give her a nasty smile, lowering my voice to a whisper. "My real dad might as well be dead."

She points to the picture. "Is this Charlotte Pritchard, by the way?"

I've never heard this last name before. "Uh, I know her with a different last name. She's married now," I offer. I hesitate about what to tell this strange woman, so I deflect. "Do you know her?"

"Yes, I do," she chuckles. "We go way back, all the way to college."

"You teach with her?"

"Yeah, I didn't realize until I saw the picture that this was her house. Funny coincidence." This woman, as cute and innocent as she seems, is giving me the willies. I've heard that people who work in academics are more introverted, but this woman is the opposite—she's downright intrusive. "Oh, and I found this in the driveway." Obviously aware of the tense look on my face, she rests the object delicately in the palm of my hand. "You must've lost this?"

It's Charlotte's cross necklace, with the small key still attached.

Stumped, I ask, "Where did you get this?"

She points outside to the driveway. "It was just lying on the cement."

Tripping over my words, I say, "Okay, wow, well, thank you." Scared I'm going to tangle it, I set it in a small bowl on a decorative shelf in the living room. *Did the cops mean to return this when they found her phone?*

I've had enough of her wandering fascination with this house. It's now eerie.

Motioning her forward, I have to practically push her out onto the porch to shut the door behind us. I wonder if Charlotte will notice the door isn't locked and shut me out.

Charlotte Pritchard is a name I haven't heard.

I'll have to ask my father about this on our next visit, assuming he shows up for it.

CHAPTER 42
Charlotte

I'm lying down, staring at the ceiling, hugging a pillow to my chest.

I'm starting to feel like a hostage in my own house, and the idea of Elle staying with Noah and me is now starting to seem incomprehensible. *If Elle and her boyfriend were involved in my already-precarious situation*—I start to gag, a hand over my mouth—*what else are they capable of?*

The idea that Elle could concoct a robbery while I'm pregnant and alone, especially given the previous trauma I've been through, is unconscionable. And, after all, I've tried to do what I can to help her thrive and get out of her tenuous situation.

Violently ill, I vomit until I have nothing left inside but acid that burns as if it's corroding my stomach lining. Trying not to get more worked up than I already am, I shut my eyes and turn on a podcast to try to drown out my intrusive thoughts.

The podcast is nothing but filler, and I think back to the disastrous Lauren encounter in college and how, after a few months of hell, I transferred to another university and Noah and I lost touch.

I was living with my mother at the time, a few years after I graduated from college. Jonathan and I had been dating only a few months, and because it was a Friday, I was dreading the weekend and my free time. Jonathan was not turning out to be a sweet, simple man but a tyrant.

When I walk up the sidewalk to the front door of my mother's house, she is already waiting for me. She flings the door open before I can insert my key into the lock.

"Whose car is in the driveway?"

"Noah's here, and he wants to see you."

"N-Noah . . . ," I stammer, my fingers automatically smoothing my hair. "What do you mean, *Noah*?"

"He drove up from Kansas City."

I feel faint.

"Give me a minute to gather my thoughts." We both know this is code for going back out to my car to smoke a cigarette, fix my hair, dab on perfume, and freshen up.

"Okay, hurry." She winks at me.

When I come inside, the two of them are chatting like old friends. Melancholy, I am reminded of our freshman and sophomore years in college. Noah would sometimes come home with me and stay the weekend.

"You couldn't just call?" I joke, his eyes smoldering when he sees me.

Immediately he rises to greet me, kissing my cheek. His hug lasts longer than it should. "God, Charlotte—wow, you look great!" Holding me at arm's length, he grins. "You haven't aged a bit."

"Noah, you act like you haven't seen me in decades. I'm twenty-four." I roll my eyes. "Too young to look old and haggard."

"And she gets her beauty from me," my mother cuts in. "Noah was just telling me he was engaged, but they *broke it off*."

"Is that so?" I unravel my scarf from around my neck. "Who was the unlucky lady? I'd like to send her a congratulations card. She dodged a bullet."

"Isn't that the truth."

"And here you show up on my doorstep after all these years. Must be lonely."

"Well, you're the one who left town and disappeared for the last couple years. After you switched colleges, it wasn't the same."

"I have that impression on people," I say. "Well, thanks for stopping by."

"How about a drink?" Noah suggests. "I'd like to hear what's going on in your world."

"I don't know." I hesitate. Noah is my kryptonite and can hurt me like nobody else. His reappearance on my mother's couch has me flustered.

"He's not engaged anymore," my mother says pointedly. "Charlotte, I was just about ready to make Noah a drink. Would you come help me in the kitchen, please?"

I start to argue, but she grabs me around the wrist and drags me to the kitchen. "Charlotte," she hisses. "What're you doing?"

"How could you invite him in?"

"Because I know how much he means to you."

"I'm dating someone."

"That man-child, Jonathan, is not a boyfriend. He's a drunk." Nailing me to the wall with an icy stare, she huffs, "You stay with him, and you might as well shrivel up in a ball and die . . ."

"Mother . . ."

"No, you listen to me. Your father and I have given you a good life. Jonathan's a loser, going nowhere, and you'll be stuck in this small town, at the hands of him, until he sucks or beats the life out of you."

Defensive, I say, "We're in a good place right now."

"Yeah, today. What about tomorrow? Don't think I don't notice the bruises you try so hard to cover up, young lady. Makeup only goes so far."

"Noah slept with my roommate in college."

"By accident." She shoves a cup in my hand. "You've done worse. Now go take this to him." She feigns a headache and goes to lie down, and Noah and I talk, and we talk.

319

For hours. Until two in the morning.

At first, he doesn't want to tell me who his broken engagement is with, but I blame the alcohol for his lowered inhibitions.

I'm stupefied that not only did he start dating Lauren Sheffield, my old roommate, the following year, but he also got engaged to her right after they graduated.

A knock on my bedroom door sends me crashing back to reality. It takes an interval to place who is trying to get my attention, and why.

Elle.

It's Elle.

"Just a minute!" I holler.

Reluctantly, I unlock the door and peer out at her.

"I'm gonna make a salad. Would you like one?"

Is she going to try to poison me? I think frantically. *Is this the second phase?*

"Uh, no, but thank you. I've got work to do upstairs."

"Okay, I'll make two in case you change your mind later." She gives me a big grin, but instead of returning her smile, I shut the door in her face.

CHAPTER 43
Elle

Charlotte disappears upstairs to work, so I settle myself on the couch. I'm watching the cooking channel, one of those shows that require contestants to use assigned ingredients in each of three courses. Giggling as the amateur chefs are tasked with using pine needles in the dessert category, I am interrupted by a shrill noise.

At first, I think it's the doorbell, but it starts and stops intermittently, and I realize it must be Charlotte's cell phone. Without being able to see her, I hear her voice rising an octave, but I can't tell if it's from anger or surprise.

It becomes more high pitched, and I gaze up at the second floor in concern, where she's either disappeared into her office or the other bedroom. I'm about to go up and check on her when I hear a slam from above. A moment later, her footsteps clatter as they move impatiently across the landing. Rotating my head, I see Charlotte flying down the stairs, careful to avoid the slippery rug at the bottom.

"Shit, shit, *shit*." The cussword sounds weird coming from her mouth.

I mute the volume on the television. "What's wrong?"

"The meeting I'm supposed to lead is on my calendar for tomorrow but is actually tonight." Shrugging into a camel-colored trench coat, she points to the kitchen, her earlier attitude replaced with a cheerful smile. "Thanks for making dinner. Mind if I take the salad with me?"

Hastily she halts at the door, her eyes darting to the upstairs before focusing on me. "Are you okay here by yourself?" She asks it as a question, but fear is written on her face.

"Sure," I say, nodding my head. "I'm just going to watch TV and do some homework."

Dashing to grab her purse and heels, she wags her finger at me. "Don't answer the door for any strangers."

After she exits into the garage, I hear the engine rev up, then her tires squealing out of the driveway. I don't know her policy on eating in the living room, so I decide to eat my salad in the kitchen. I slide into the corner of the built-in table, a cozy nook in her kitchen, and, sipping a glass of water, I speculate about the dark-haired woman who showed up.

Should I mention to Charlotte that she stopped by? But I don't even have a name to give her.

I go back and forth, wondering if she's a potential threat or harmless.

Something doesn't jibe, and the necklace she brought back isn't sitting well with me. The person who grabbed Charlotte took her wallet and necklace and could easily find her address now. If Justin or my father had anything to do with it, neither has admitted their involvement, which means . . .

What if her intention was to case the place and come back with more people tonight?

And you just let the woman right in, I chide myself.

She was acting suspicious and asking way too many questions. It was like she was memorizing the floor plan and deciding what to steal.

I shudder. *What if she comes back tonight and I'm alone?*

Anxiously, I stand, then rinse my dishes and load them in the stainless steel dishwasher.

I knew Charlotte would never look in a decorative vase, but she would snoop through my room. Figuring it would be safer in the living room, I retrieve the cross necklace. I watched Charlotte remove the key from the chain and use it to access the basement on the night of the tornado.

Fingering the metal key, I realize I'm either living in a house with a cold-blooded killer or I'm ruining Charlotte's life because I've interrupted any peace she was working toward.

Charlotte has never left me in the house alone, and who knows when I'll get another chance. I scan the high, vaulted ceilings, checking for cameras or a telltale sign she's watching. For someone as paranoid as she is, I would suspect nothing less. She'd be the kind to have some high-tech spy shit. I don't spot lenses or blinking lights.

Making sure the house is locked up in case the woman decides to show up again, I take a deep breath. Do I want to take the chance of getting caught? This might throw Charlotte over the edge and put me into dangerous territory if my father is telling the truth about what she's capable of.

But a small flutter in my belly propels me forward. "I have to do this for you," I say.

Making up my mind, I tiptoe to the basement door, unnecessarily, since I'm all alone in the house, but it seems fitting for this expedition.

As I peer down into the darkness, I find myself overcome by a sense of dread. I tell myself that if Charlotte has nothing to hide, then I won't find anything suspect. After all, I'm the one who has to prove my father's innocence, his guilt already decided.

But if he's not guilty, then why hasn't he proven it? I ask myself.

He's just making more empty promises—his typical MO. He's had ten *years, Elle.*

Shoving my mistrust to the back of my mind, I flip on the light switch.

Carefully, I descend the steps, the rough-hewn wood uneven, like no one's ever intended to come down here. The basement's a far cry from the rest of the house. Upstairs is warm and inviting, decorative and cozy.

There's plenty of space, but it's all unfinished—one big, gigantic room. The air's damp and the lighting dim, and it's as if I'm headed to a somber burial no one wants to attend. By the time I reach the bottom stair, the air's cooler but musty.

The rest of the house is organized, but down here it's in disarray except for the labeled boxes. They're scattered all over, the contents labeled by black Sharpie markers. Some are marked *Easter* and *Thanksgiving*. One box says *Mom*, another *Dad*.

They're taped shut, and nothing seems curious or out of the ordinary.

None are labeled with my father's name or anything that piques my interest. Noah's name appears on quite a few totes, and clothing sticks up through the flaps of one box.

"They need a trip to the Salvation Army," I murmur.

One overflowing plastic container is filled with pictures, and photographs spill out when I open the lid. I settle back on my heels, scouring through picture after picture.

Inside the container is a large shoebox with a duct tape label that has *Jonathan* scribbled on it. Sucking in air, I'm apprehensive to even open the lid. Some pictures were taken when Charlotte was pregnant, and I get weepy as I watch her glowing smile or her hand resting peacefully on her belly.

A couple pictures are with my father right behind her. In some he grins, and in others he seems aloof. But what rocks me most is what I find in a manila folder.

They say a picture is worth a thousand words.

These ones say a million.

In photograph after photograph, Charlotte's battered body is on display, close-up and personal, bruised and welted. You can tell she took most of the photos, because they are the type they used to take with the old Polaroid cameras, the ones where the prints would spit directly out and develop in your hand immediately. Dates are listed in the blank spaces underneath the pictures, no words needed to caption them, the violence enough.

There are a couple of her beaten face, and my mouth goes dry, as if a wad of cotton was shoved into it. Some were even taken when she was pregnant. You can tell when her bulging stomach is present in the photos, which also showcase bruised thighs and even deep bite marks.

Covering my face with my hands, I don't know what's worse—that my father is a domestic abuser or that he was found guilty and I'm trying to absolve him of that.

Angrily, I slam the lid back down as if it could keep the memories in the past and away from me.

I turn to Charlotte's old yearbooks, perusing something out of a happier time. Her college acceptance letter and some blue ribbons for track from high school. She excelled at the hundred-meter dash. I am astonished at her mile time, which puts mine to shame.

After closing the plastic top, I don't see anything else but old books. Then, searching the opposite corner of the basement, I find what looks like a ghost town: large objects covered with faded, mildewy-smelling sheets.

Curious, I peek underneath one of the smaller items.

Holding my breath, I realize it's a crib. The wood must have gotten wet at some point, because it's rotted and peeling. There are boxes of baby clothes, rattles, and old bottles, some missing their tops.

Feeling ill, I finger the rungs of wood, heartsick for Charlotte. How horrible to lose your child to a flight of stairs and a fist. I wasn't even planning to have a child, but to think of the emotions, raw and tragic, I feel my eyes begin to water.

Not to mention, how I've treated her and the things I've said . . .

No wonder no one comes down here. I guess in a way, it's a disturbing shrine to her past. Growing emotional, I wipe a tear hanging in limbo at the corner of my eyelid.

When I rise to stand, I use a piece of furniture to guide myself up, my body heavy and weighted. Making sure everything is left as it was before, I don't dare take the shoebox with me, but I do pocket a few photos I want my father to see.

I walk along the length of the basement and reach the stairs. The handrail's like a crutch, and I use it to maneuver the steps in the murky lighting. Because of the darkness, I don't notice the splintered wood until my loose-hanging sweater catches on the middle part and it's too late. It violently yanks me around, and, losing my balance, I'm headed down the stairs.

Gasping, I claw for something, anything, to take ahold of.

I manage to clamp onto a secured piece of railing still attached to the wall, and I hold on for dear life. My sweater's in tattered ruins, but I'm more concerned about the baby.

The pounding in my chest feels like a marathon is taking place in my heart as it thuds to the beat of its own skittish track. Then, silently mouthing a prayer, I calm my scattered nerves as I ascend to the top, pausing to grasp the door handle when I get there.

These stairs could definitely be the cause of many miscarriages, I think grimly.

Staring back down at the darkness, I ignore the collapsed wooden piece that hangs at a slant from the wall. Pissed at myself, I chide my behavior. *How can you be a mother when you can't even protect yourself?*

In protest, I slam the basement door as hard as I can. With a sigh, I rest my head against the wood paneling, my hands on my abdomen. When I bring my fingers up to lock the door, a red stain appears, and, fearful, I glance down, expecting to see my stomach covered in blood.

"No, no, no," I whisper, feeling faint.

Apprehensive, I reach down to my belly, my horrified eyes frozen on my midsection. It's then that I notice the deep cut on my hand. I start to scream until I realize a loose nail must've caught the skin and punctured it. Patting down my body to search for more injuries, I notice a couple scrapes on my elbow and right arm, but besides that, I'll be all right.

The baby will be all right.

I say another silent prayer.

What am I going to tell Charlotte I was doing in her basement? There's no way she won't notice the broken railing; it's going to have to be replaced.

But maybe she won't notice . . .

It's not like she goes down there.

Would Noah mind if I reached out and told him about the railing? Would he send someone to fix it and keep it a secret from Charlotte, or would he assume I was being sneaky by going into the basement?

Pushing away from the door, I instruct myself to get a bandage and some ointment. I don't see a first aid kit in the hall bath, so I decide to check her master one.

It's locked, and the key doesn't even fit into her door handle.

Curious, I wonder if it works on the upstairs room.

Charlotte said it would be the baby's room, but I've never met anyone who locked up their own bedrooms in the name of storage.

But what do I know?

I live in the projects, and nothing is worth stealing, so that might be why I can't relate. I assumed she was suspicious about me, and for good reason, I remind myself. I don't have an impeccable record, and she has no reason to trust me. I'm a bona fide stranger.

Forgetting the bandage for the moment, I try the lock. It opens, and I'm not in a storage room but a nursery.

This room definitely belongs to a baby. A new baby. A future baby.

Floored, I stare at the wallpaper, gold-and-cream foil that perfectly coordinates with the matching curtains framing the window. The crib and changing table are white wood with antique brass accents. All of it looks pristine, except for the wooden rocking chair and matching ottoman in the corner, likely family heirlooms. The pattern on the footstool's been upholstered to match the fabric of the changing table. It's designed with robin's-egg blue doves.

I open the mirrored closet doors and see that already the shelves are lined with baby clothes. All organized by color, they're in every imaginable shade from white to burgundy red to navy. The child has a larger wardrobe in its first closet than I've had my entire life.

The built-in shelving is stocked with bottles and pacifiers, blocks, and nursing gear.

But why is it locked? I wonder.

I cross the plush carpeting to stare out the window. And that's when I notice long metal bars shielded by the curtains covering the glass. They ruin the views of the lake. Is Charlotte worried her baby could fall out the window? They *are* long and narrow, I suppose.

A twin-size mattress is placed against one wall, and I wonder if this is for her or Noah to sleep on when the baby comes.

I'm about to head back downstairs when I hear a loud ring vibrating from inside the house.

I wonder if Charlotte forgot to take her phone with her.

My heart thuds in my chest as I pause, my hand on the wrought iron staircase, craning my neck to see if it's coming from her office.

It doesn't sound like her iPhone, though.

As I walk down toward the kitchen, the sound intensifies.

I hear the noise before I locate the receiver.

When her cell phone was stolen, she talked on the stationary one, but I didn't pay attention to the location. It's in the pantry, and by the time I find it under some recipe books, it's rung seven times and then quit again. I pick it up, just in case, but the person on the other end has hung up, and I'm left with the annoying dial tone in my ear.

Placing the receiver back on the hook, I notice the voice mail light is blinking, indicating a message. It's probably just a student, but it can't hurt to listen.

Holding my breath, I play the message.

And then replay it.

"Charlotte, it's your mother. Your psychiatrist called and said you've missed a couple of appointments, so I wanted to check on you. I think you forget that I'm still listed as an emergency contact on your forms. The police confirmed you were okay, but I'm deathly worried about you."

CHAPTER 44
Charlotte

"Charlotte, so glad you could join us," one of the other writing professors says as I hurry into the conference room, a veiled hint of annoyance in her voice.

"Sorry I'm a couple of minutes late," I apologize. "I should've planned better for traffic."

"Yes, well, we just wanted to make sure you had your agenda planned out," Dean Walters chimes in. "Go on up and get started when you're ready. I've already made the announcements, and I'm bribing everyone with food."

"Absolutely." I remove my trench coat and set my laptop on the podium at the front of the room. After pulling out a thumb drive with my presentation, I cue up the projection screen. Watching twenty or so of my peers stop their conversations as I clear my throat, I give them a shaky smile as they eyeball me in earnest.

I know I'm an anomaly. Not one to seamlessly fit into the world of academia, I'm not part of their cliques, instead preferring my own company. It's not necessarily made me unpopular, but I'm not well known either.

I introduce myself and then touch upon goals for the next month and strategies for helping struggling students. I discuss the books and assignments I've chosen this semester for my classes and the reasons behind them. This meeting is designed to empower the staff, provide alternative ideas, and create an environment of team building that will encompass our entire English department.

After I'm finished with my slides, the room erupts in applause, and I give my colleagues a warm smile, wringing my hands in front of me. My nerves are racked by a combination of standing in front of a roomful of people and the fact I had to leave a potentially dangerous girl in my house.

"Charlotte," says Dean Walters, striding from the side of the room where she was perched against the doorframe. "That was fantastic. You really have a knack for mentoring."

"Thank you, Dean Walters." I grin at the tall, mousy brunette. Dr. Walters is a fascinating woman, whip smart and brilliant yet incredibly awkward.

"You know, I'd really like you to consider helming our Readers Are Leaders mentorship program. Can you spare a few minutes after the meeting?"

I nod my head and take a seat, frowning at the clock. Every minute that ticks by gives Elle another opportunity to ransack my house. Everything is locked up tight, I remind myself. She has access only to the common areas and her bedroom.

She can't hurt you, she can't hurt you. I keep repeating the mantra in my head as I watch my next colleague present on changes to the literary division.

After the final speaker has finished, Dean Walters, true to her word, finds me in the hallway. "How about we speak in my office?"

"Certainly," I say, following her to the large corner office at the other end of the building. It's decorated in rich mahogany and heavy fabrics, the bulky, wine-colored drapes exuding a rich and bold exuberance, the patterns emblazoned with gold stitching and copper leaves.

Her desk is double the size of the one I have in my study, and I assume it took more than a few men to deliver it to its resting spot.

Dean Walters sinks into a lavish leather chair with a high back that seems comfortable, from the way she sighs as she settles into it. It looks the opposite of the chairs seated in front of her desk, and I suppose that's purposeful, meant to keep visitors from wasting her time and to keep meetings or uncomfortable conversations to a minimum.

Dean Walters starts with small talk as an attempt to make me comfortable. "Are you still enjoying the online presence?"

"Yes, I am."

I've taught at the college for the last three years, but this is one of the first times I've ever spoken one on one with the dean in her office. We are well past the formalities of my addressing her as Dr. Walters, but I still try to be professional with my colleagues. "I'm enjoying the three classes I'm teaching, Rosemary Marshall's been a great assistant, and I feel like my students are progressing in their coursework."

"That's fantastic," she says. "That's exactly what we hope for, now that we've awarded you a permanent teaching spot."

"What?" I ask, sure I've heard wrong. "Are you offering me a tenured position?"

"Yes, I am."

"That's fantastic. I'm . . . practically speechless."

Dean Walters leans forward conspiratorially. "I'd really like you to consider overseeing this mentorship project I mentioned earlier. It would involve your mentoring a cohort of students. Would that work with your schedule?"

"How many additional hours are needed per week?"

"Of course—that's a legitimate question. The class is three hours a week, and you'd be responsible for working with a group of students to advise and hone their writing skills and potential."

Trying not to tap my kitten heel against the desk, I respond, "I'm assuming some grading and additional work from home would be necessary?"

She nods. "Yes, this class is a pass-or-fail grade, though. It's for students selected from a panel of their peers and instructors. They don't receive the typical A-to-F measurable grade."

"I'd like that, but first I'd like to offer a precursor, since I know we can discuss sensitive matters."

"I'm all ears."

Giving her a coy smile as I stare at the family photograph on her desk, I say, "My only concern is that next semester I might be a little busier than usual."

"Is that so?" she asks, not unkindly. "Well, I won't pry, but I hope it's good news for you."

"Yes, it is." Unable to contain my emotions, I gush, "I'm pregnant."

"This is fantastic news! Well, I don't like to be presumptuous, but I thought I noticed a little baby belly." She raps her knuckle on the desk. "You've wanted this for a long time, haven't you?"

"Yes, w-we have," I stammer. "It's been a long road."

Recognition appears on her face as she lowers her voice. "Before we had the twins, I had a miscarriage. It's . . . God, it's the worst, so I completely understand why you would want to wait to announce that."

We talk for a few more minutes, and my palms start to sweat. I can barely focus on what she is saying, my mind drifting to Elle and what trouble she's getting herself into.

Dean Walters starts to flesh out the type of class she envisions as being successful. My phone keeps buzzing, and I wonder if it's Noah calling me.

Would it be rude to glance in my tote?

Biting my lip, I murmur a response to her next question, pressing my hand on the zipper as I reach down into my purse. The phone reverberates again, followed by a beep, signaling I've received a voice mail. Eager to be on my way, I twist in my seat.

Dean Walters slides a pair of spectacles on. "Let me check Dr. Adler's calendar and arrange a more formal meeting to discuss the details. He's been involved in this since the beginning, and I know he mentioned your name as a candidate. He'll be thrilled you've accepted, and he'll want to collaborate on the class material."

The antique clock on the wall chimes the hour.

I manage to glance down at my cell, and my mouth tightens in disbelief.

What in the hell is she *doing calling me on my personal cell? I just changed it again. She was right when she said she always manages to get it. She's as ruthless as a telemarketer.*

I squint at my screen, my stomach starting to squeeze as if it might burst, and an uneasy feeling shoots through me like a lightning bolt, immediately ruining my mood.

"Charlotte," she inquires, "is everything okay?"

"Oh yes, sorry." I smile at her. "I've got a meeting with Dr. Rhodes in five minutes."

Dean Walters taps her finger against the computer screen. "Does next Friday work for you to meet with Dr. Adler and me . . . say . . . ten o'clock. My office?"

"Let me confirm. I'll check my schedule and let you know by this evening."

"No problem." She rises to stand, giving me a wink. "And congratulations on your two excellent pieces of news."

We shake hands before I wobble out the door, trying not to lose my balance in my small but uncomfortable heels as I rush down the hall. My Jeep's parked on the other side of the building, and I have to remind myself that tripping and falling is not allowable at this point in time.

I want to catch Dr. Rhodes in the biochemistry department before he leaves for the night.

I'm in luck.

He's in his midsixties but dresses twenty years younger and has the air of someone with superior intelligence. His glasses aren't typical bifocals but stylish lenses that only add to his persona.

"I'm glad I caught you," I say, knocking on his office door. He's seated at his desk, browsing something on his computer, his glasses resting between his forefingers. "I'm Charlotte Coburn in English literature."

"Hello there." He moves his glasses back on his face and swings his chair around to greet me.

"I read in the paper about your expertise in poisonous and toxic chemicals. You helped with a case a couple of years ago where a man was trying to kill his wife with rat poison."

"Ah, yes, a side gig to teaching." He groans. "Catching unhappy spouses in the act of ridding the world of their partners with murder instead of divorce."

"Would you mind taking a look at this?" I hand him the plastic container with the salad Elle prepared for me. "This is a sensitive topic, so if we can keep this private."

"Of course." He nods as my lower lip trembles.

"I tried to help a—let's call her a displaced youth—and I'm concerned she might be trying to harm me."

Other people might consider this ludicrous, but not him. He's seen it all.

He waits for me to continue. "I'm starting to suspect she was involved in my recent assault, and I'm pregnant, and I think she wants to harm . . . my baby."

He takes this as seriously as I hoped he would. "Have you contacted the police?"

"They are involved in the assault case, yes." I touch his arm. "And this will only help my case."

"No problem." Dr. Rhodes stops me before I shut his door. "And Charlotte?"

"Yes?"

"Please be careful." He hands me his card. "My cell is on here if you need anything. No off hours. Please call with any updates or concerns, and I'll be in touch on this."

I rush to my Jeep. Now it's time to deal with Nancy.

I call Elle repeatedly, but she doesn't answer.

A bead of perspiration trickles down my back as I drive home.

What could Elle possibly be doing right now?

CHAPTER 45
Elle

My jaw drops. I thought her mother was dead. I hit the redial, and before I can say a word, Charlotte's mother interrupts me. "Well, hello, it's about time you answered your phone."

"Um . . ."

There is so much I want to ask, but I feel like I'm talking to a ghost, because her mother's dead, at least according to Charlotte.

"You know, I only told the authorities about the letter because I want you to heal."

My hands clamp down, gripping the arms of the chair, as the room starts to spin like I have vertigo. As I'm trying to figure out how to introduce myself, I realize that the sound of an engine has creeped closer and into the driveway, and now I hear the motor raising the garage door.

Then, Charlotte frantically skids to a halt in the kitchen, her heels leaving a black mark on her concrete floor. Her eyes are wild as she stares at the phone in my hand.

"It's your mother," I say calmly, handing her the phone. I retreat to the other side of the kitchen. She lets out such a deep breath that I don't know how she held it in all this time.

I can almost smell the fear as she rests the phone on her shoulder.

"Hi, Nancy. I got your message." And then a pause. "Yes, that one too."

Her mother is having a one-sided conversation with herself as we regard each other from opposite sides of the island.

"No, everything is fine." I can tell Charlotte wants to be anywhere but talking on the phone to her mother. "I have a class to instruct." Without saying goodbye, she hangs up, her hands fumbling with the receiver.

Before she can turn around to chastise me for answering the phone, I say, "I thought your mother was dead."

I can hear the lump as she swallows. "It's not that simple."

"I think it is. You're either alive," I say, raising an eyebrow, "or you're dead."

"We have a complicated history."

"Most people do with their parents."

"I don't think you've been truthful about your family either." Charlotte comes closer, leaning her elbows on the island. "Is there something you want to share with me?"

In life, there are occasions that make you feel breathless, and this is one of those times, but out of fright. I'm waiting her out. I want her to tell me what she knows.

My eyes drift to the butcher block behind her. If Charlotte knows my true identity, I should plan on protecting myself. There's no way she would knowingly allow Jonathan Randall's daughter in her house.

I move my fingers slightly beneath the edge of the counter so she doesn't see them tremble. "I lied to you."

"I know this."

To try to buy time, I respond with, "And you lied to me."

"Correct."

"My mother died of a drug overdose. Not a car accident." I wonder if this piece of information is enough or if she's waiting for more.

338

I give her time to answer. Her face completely neutral, she says, "Okay."

I'm wringing my hands as she keeps looking at me. I notice the gash on my hand is starting to show red through my sweater, so I shove the fabric into my palm as a makeshift gauze pad.

I wait until she turns her back to grab something from a drawer before I rinse my palm in cold water. On alert, I watch to see what she's pulling out. It's the two envelopes from my high school. I ignore them as she sets them on the island.

"And what about your mother?" I ask. "Did she try and cut your ex loose from prison?"

"What do you know about that?"

"Just a guess from something she said."

"Anything else she tell you?"

"No." I shrug. "Unfortunately, you walked in before I could get her to share embarrassing details from your childhood."

She lets out peals of laughter. "Fair enough."

"Why is she dead to you?"

"It's thirty-five years in the making." Charlotte tilts her head down, ashamedly. "I blame her, okay?"

"For?"

"It's complicated and won't make sense to you."

I snort. "Try me."

"She reached out to my ex. Wants me to forgive him for what he did." She moves around the kitchen as if she can't be still. "If it were just me, then maybe, but a baby was involved."

"And you don't agree with her for wanting to forgive him?"

"He had a daughter, and she said I should consider this." I can feel heat on my face, and I'm relieved Charlotte is messing around in the refrigerator. "That he's paid his dues to society."

With a hardened stare, she says, "I can't forgive him. And if I ever see his daughter, I'll tell her the same thing. He deserves to rot in hell.

And for any demon seed he had, she's probably just as broken and worthless as him."

It takes every fiber of my being not to burst into tears.

I want to change the subject more than anything.

"How was your meeting?" I bite my lip, hoping she doesn't notice my woeful face.

"It was good." Charlotte forces a smile. "I can't believe I put it on the wrong date. My brain is so fuzzy right now."

"Pregnancy brain," I giggle.

I ask her if she had a chance to eat the salad I made.

"It was delicious, thank you." She gives me an inquisitive stare. "What have you been doing since I left? I tried to call your cell."

"I fell asleep watching a movie."

"The point of you having a cell phone is so you answer." Charlotte frowns. "What if it was an emergency?"

"I'm sorry." I point at my belly. "You are forgetful, and I'm tired."

She nods, but there's a pinched expression on her face.

"I guess my mom was more persistent in calling."

"I guess so." I shrug.

It's Charlotte's turn to change the topic, our conversation about her mom finished. She points to the envelopes marked *TIME SENSITIVE* in massive red block letters.

"I haven't even opened them," I say.

"I know. I wasn't going to open your mail, but they're important for us to stay on top of." She unseals the ivory jacket of the heavier one. "Would you like me to open it?"

"Yes, please."

Charlotte reads the first one out loud. It's an outline of the due process for disciplinary action at my school. An appeals procedure is outlined for me to pursue if I wish to attend a meeting with school administrators and the school board.

I fidget with my hair. "This is scary stuff."

"It sure is," Charlotte agrees, "but it's important we talk to them. Let me look at my calendar, and we can schedule a meeting."

She hands me the second letter. "You open this one."

It's not as thick, and inside are my transcripts and final report card. Mostly Cs and Ds.

The only A I received is in my art history class.

"I want you to consider enrolling in some college classes after your GED."

Thrusting my chin out defiantly, I say, "I haven't decided if I want to go to college. I'm going to have to get a real job, and my grades suck. Not to mention, I'll have a baby."

"I know you can do better than these grades. Why do you hate school so much?" She murmurs, "Are kids mean to you because you're pregnant?"

"No." I scrunch my face. "No one noticed until recently."

"Then why do you hate it so much?"

"I just . . . I just don't see the point."

"In having an education?"

I shrug.

"You will see the point one day," she groans. "And I don't mean to seem old when I say that—*maybe* wise, but not old. Knowledge is invaluable. I can tell you're a smart girl, Elle."

"Really?" I sneer. "The dumb girl from the wrong side of the tracks that got knocked up in high school and ruined her life?"

"You don't really feel that way, do you?"

I glance at my disgusting fingernails.

"Just because you're pregnant doesn't mean you ruined your life." She gives me a halfhearted smile. "You have all the time in the world to accomplish what you need to."

I don't mention that I haven't had time to focus on school because I've been helping my imprisoned father—the one she put behind bars—with his plea of innocence.

Agitated, I swipe a strand of hair behind my ear. "How do you know?"

"Because you sell yourself short," Charlotte says. "And you don't consistently attend. You're bored, and no one pushes you to do better."

I start to make a snide comment but stop short.

Charlotte points upstairs. "I'm going to go upstairs and grab some stationery for those apology letters."

"I'll just watch some TV." I grab the remote and reach for one of the faux-fur blankets in the wicker basket next to the couch. Pulling it over my lap, I hide my injured hand as I watch Charlotte head to the staircase. When she returns, it's with what looks to be expensive stationery, by the elaborate design and heavy paper stock. These are generic greeting cards with no specific announcement shouted from the front. Inside there is a blank space to write a personalized note.

I hold up the ornate stationery. "Thanks for the cards."

"No problem. I'll drive you to class in the morning. Leave me the letters, and I'll drop them off at your high school."

"I can't be there, can I?"

"No, not on school premises."

"Okay, I'll seal them in an envelope." I give her a tight smile. "Do you think we can convince them to let me back in if we provide your mother's snickerdoodle cookie recipe?"

"Potentially," Charlotte says with a laugh. "But I wouldn't want them to get the magical powers my mother promised she put in the batter."

"If it makes Courtney Kerr a less evil version of herself, then I'm all for it."

"Speaking of, make sure you write Courtney's family one." Charlotte raises a hand to cut off the expected interruption. "I know she did something horrible. And she's a bully and a wretched, awful person. But step back. Maybe your ex promised her that his relationship with you was over, and she didn't know you were pregnant. Now her life is affected just the same."

"It's hard to feel bad for someone who has the perfect life."

"And look how she turned out." Charlotte muses, "Maybe Courtney is awful and didn't care either way about your feelings or your relationship. And clearly Justin didn't either."

"You sound like you have personal experience with this."

"I do." I start to ask a question, but she cuts me off.

"Fine, I'll do it."

"You don't have a choice." She hands me a fancy ballpoint pen to write with. Her phone beeps while I'm beginning the first note, and I watch as her eyes narrow at the screen. Without glancing up she says, "Don't stay up too late, young lady. You've got school and a baby to think about."

I take it as my cue to go do a load of laundry. The blood is going to stain my sweater if I don't get it in the washing machine soon.

As I retreat to my room, I glance at the basement door to confirm it's closed and padlocked, fearful that Charlotte will find out I've been down there.

CHAPTER 46
Charlotte

When I arrive at Elle's old high school, I stay in the Jeep a second, contemplating how I want the conversation to go—the best potential outcome and the worst.

Mrs. Marsh is seated in her usual position at the worn desk, hair wrapped in a stern bun, glasses dangling from a chain around her neck.

"Hello, I'm Elizabeth Laughlin's aunt, Charlotte Coburn."

"I remember you." She sniffs, "You look a lot more pregnant than the last time I saw you."

"And I feel a lot more pregnant."

"They come when they're ready, that's for sure." Marsh lifts her glasses up on her nose. "If you want to see Principal Mitchum, you'll need an appointment."

"Elizabeth speaks so highly of you, and I know she'd want you to know this." I lower my voice like I'm sharing an important secret. "There have been some changes with her living situation, and I'd like to fill Principal Mitchum in. Elizabeth is no longer living with Diane, but with Justin. It's very important he know because of the prior incident."

"Why didn't Diane come down?" she harrumphs.

"When does Diane ever come to the school?" I respond sharply. Tongue-tied, she can't argue with this, so she immediately buzzes the principal.

Mrs. Marsh's definition of buzzing is actually shrieking across the ten feet to his office, where the door's half-closed.

"Elizabeth Laughlin's aunt is here!" she hollers, tapping her nails across an ancient keyboard. An audible grunt from the office is followed by the creak of leather.

Marsh doesn't offer me a seat in the lobby, so I continue to stand, moving to a bulletin board across the room with monthly accolades and the yearly fund-raising goal to build a new arboretum. They should probably invest in a new computer for Marsh, I suppose.

Behind me I hear, "So we meet again." Principal Mitchum's voice causes me to unmistakably flinch, and I swivel, pasting on my best smile.

"Charlotte." I offer up my hand, wondering if this time he will take it. After he shakes it, I wish he hadn't, his handshake damp and limp—the worst kind, in my opinion.

"This way," he says, motioning as if I'd get lost crossing the room. We head into his sparse office, with its drab colors and brown everything—chairs, carpet, and desk. All worn and old. The only expensive piece of equipment in his office is his seminew desktop computer. Instead of pictures, his only personal effect is a leather swivel chair that looks like it's followed him through the years by the amount of stuffing it's missing.

Maybe they can add upgraded furniture to the list of needed expenditures. I shudder to think of what the actual classrooms look like.

Per the usual in academic offices, the straight-backed chair in front of his desk looks the opposite of comfortable, and Mitchum waves me into it.

Without wasting a breath on formalities and reminding me of the hospital police officer, he gets straight to business.

"I know we met at the hospital under not-so-pleasant circumstances." He steeples his fingers as he did in the hospital, but this time I notice he's unmarried. "Now that some time has passed, what can I do for you?"

Watching his eyes twitch, I see his demeanor as that of a man who's supposed to be in charge but is constantly harassed by stay-at-home moms who think they know better than he does. I have to keep this in the forefront of my mind to get what I need.

"First, I'm sorry I didn't make an appointment, and I mean no disrespect, but I'd like to get your opinion and provide an update on Elizabeth, even though she's somewhat out of your hair."

I see a light flicker in his eyes.

Men love sharing their opinion and, better yet, when you ask them for theirs.

"Charlotte, let me be frank. First off, I'm unclear why her foster mom isn't here."

"Good question, and a valid one." I take a deep breath. "Diane is a single mom to three foster kids, two of whom need constant care and attention, plus she works. I'm the closest to her, in both proximity and confidence. Part of the reason I'm here is because Elizabeth turns eighteen in a couple of months, and she's living with her on-again, off-again boyfriend, Justin Pence. The relationship concerns me, and I'm also here because of the incident between Courtney Kerr and Elizabeth, which involved him indirectly."

I have his undivided attention, so I continue. "I'm concerned about Elizabeth and her mental health. She just had a miscarriage, and I know you and I can see how this is probably—dare I say it—a relief, considering the age and turmoil of everyone involved, but it's still upsetting. It's a delicate subject, and I know this isn't your responsibility, but I want you to be aware of my concerns, since you see both Courtney and Justin."

A sigh of relief escapes his lips, a glimmer of compassion in his eyes.

I continue. "I want to be able to offer Elizabeth comfort as my niece, but with me being"—I motion to my stomach—"also pregnant, I'm not the one she wants to hear from right now."

He nods.

It might be a bit of a stretch, but I add, "In positive news, I've spoken to the Kerr family, and they are not pressing charges."

"That's a relief for you."

"And for you. I'm assuming the school district will be relieved, since I know that, internally, that must be a cause for concern."

His flush spreads into his collared shirt. Loosening his tie, he says nothing.

"Elizabeth wanted me to bring this to you." He glares at the top of my head when I reach into my purse, grabbing the envelope.

"Here." I slide it across the desk. "She wanted me to give this to you." He grabs the letter between the tips of his forefingers as if it's dangerous, and I quip, "It's not going to bite you."

"Look, I know she's had a hard upbringing."

"I couldn't agree more. It's so hard to grow up like she has. That's what I wanted your expert opinion on. Is there anything you'd suggest we do to help with her emotional state?" I lick my lips, leaning forward. "With the scars I've noticed, and I don't want to assume, but it looks like she's been cutting herself."

I sniff, and he hands me a tissue. "And her father . . ." Mitchum takes the bait as I let my voice drift off.

"The one and only Jonathan Randall." He taps his fingers on the desk. "The fact Jonathan's in prison has got to be tough on the girl. Being shuffled around, one parent behind bars, the other dead of a drug overdose."

The name.

What's in a name?

Everything.

The last time I heard it spoken like this, with such derision, a verdict was being read to remove him from society. I feel like I'm sinking into the floor, my legs jiggling like Jell-O.

As I hear his name said out loud, the room closes in on me just like the memories. I picture Jonathan's face, then Noah's, as if the two of them are a mash-up.

After Noah and I reconnected that night at my mother's, we both went back to our lives, but there was a darkness I couldn't shake. We started communicating, and my heart, as much as I pretended it was mine, still belonged to him.

Then one weekend, Jonathan was out of town at a jobsite, and Noah came to visit. Neither of them knew about the other, for obvious reasons. We went out and I felt like myself again: young and free, albeit somewhat intoxicated. Noah and I had sex a few times that weekend, and when he left, I was inconsolable. Time was irrelevant, because I couldn't picture a life without him. It was reminiscent of a high school crush, and nothing else mattered but the two of us.

When Jonathan returned, it wasn't the same, and he could feel the distance.

At first, he smothers me with affection, but it doesn't last. It's a short while before he puts me in the hospital with a broken toe and needing stitches in my kneecap. Of course, I tell the doctor it's from tripping over a children's desk at school, but we both know the truth.

When a pregnancy test confirms what I suspect, I know it isn't Jonathan's, because his touch makes me cringe. We also haven't slept together unprotected for a long time.

Terrified I'm about to lose the only man I've ever loved, I'm more fearful of Jonathan's reaction. He will make it a point to destroy not only me but also Noah and the baby.

I make the choice to lie to him.

I justify it by telling myself I'll wait until there's a good time to tell Jonathan the truth.

But with an abuser, there's never a good time.

And then it is too late.

"Charlotte?" Mitchum interrupts my thoughts as I stare silently at his navy paisley tie. "I'm certain he'll get out soon, and it's unlikely to be very positive for Elizabeth." Looking dismal, he puts his head down. "I'm not surprised she got pregnant in high school. The whole situation is sad, and I must say I hope you or Diane can persuade her to seek therapy at some point."

"We aren't going to appeal her expulsion, and I wanted to sincerely apologize for her actions." Reaching in my purse, I pull out a second envelope. "If you could pass this one along to Courtney's family, it'd be appreciated."

Mitchum gives me the most genuine smile he can muster. "Good luck, Mrs. Coburn. I'll keep an eye on Justin and Courtney on this end."

I shakily rise, forced to grip the desk to steady myself. "Thank you for your time, Principal Mitchum."

As we exit his office, I ask Marsh one last question.

"Can you please point me in the direction of the bathroom? This baby is pressing hard on my bladder."

She hands me a hall pass, which I loop around my neck, but instead of going to the ladies' room, I head for Justin's locker, where I followed Elle last time I was here. I drop an envelope through the narrow slats and head back out to the Jeep.

Even though it's sunny and in the midfifties, I tremble as I walk back to my vehicle. Blasting warm air, I sink into the leather, resting my head in thought.

The Jonathan Randall is Elle's father.

Torn, I chew the inside of my cheek.

With another stop to make, I'm relieved to see that Elle sent a text saying she's busy doing homework in the computer lab at school.

In no rush to pick her up, I drive to the other side of town, trying my best to ignore the overflowing trash cans, the graffiti, and the abundance of people trekking back and forth on the side of the street, hustling for money or drugs. After double-checking the locks, I turn the music up, choosing Beethoven's Symphony no. 9 for this jaunt.

With shallow breathing, I gently rub my belly, reminding myself everything is going to be just fine.

Elle Laughlin isn't trying to hurt you.

Or ruin your life.

Elizabeth Randall is.

Her coming into your life, I tell myself, smirking, *is not just a coincidence after all.*

Pulling into the Meadowlark, I hit a pothole harder than I intend, the pavement dented and uneven. Noticing Diane's parking spot is empty, I assume she's at work.

Or maybe not. That's one thing I believe Elizabeth on—that Diane's a degenerate, a waste of life.

Elle keeps her house keys in a tiny pouch inside her backpack, and I took the liberty of making a copy. I'm aware the apartment's on the fourth floor, and since it has no elevator, I have to miserably drag myself up the stairs.

The doors are not all marked, and some have faded paint where their numbers used to be. Scanning my choices, I knock on what I assume to be the correct one.

Giving it a minute, in case someone answers, I peer around the concrete hallway. Raised voices echo from one apartment, loud television noises from another, and, pinching my nose, I gag at the putrid odor of garbage.

After fumbling for the keys, I slide the second one into the lock, and I careen into Elle's world the same way she upended mine. I'm not surprised at the apartment, or appalled. It's exactly what I envisioned, from how Elle alluded to it.

Small, cramped, dirty, and messy.

The smell of smoke permeates the air, along with a rotten stench.

I peek into the sink and see it's overflowing with dirty dishes. Unwashed silverware and chunks of food have backed up the garbage disposal. Waving my hand in the air as if this will magically erase the smell, I then glance around the kitchen; the table is overflowing with toy cars and mail.

Flipping through the pile, I discern that most are addressed to Diane. A lot of the envelopes are stamped in red with *Final Notice*. They are mainly bills and mailers, so I can't believe my luck when I come across a yellow manila envelope addressed to Elizabeth Randall, compliments of the Huberton Correctional Institution.

It's already been opened. "Diane, you nosy little spy," I murmur.

Thinking back to over a decade ago, I recall glimpsing Elizabeth in the back of a blue station wagon as she and her mother drove away. It broke my heart at the time, her sad face pressed against the back window. She was little, just a young girl. But I'd never considered she would come back into the picture. *My picture.*

This gives me all the proof I need that Elle and her father are planning something against me. She did take the gun, and it's somewhat fitting it was used on me, considering it belonged to her father.

But why now, a decade later?

She needs the money.

Or maybe revenge.

Or a bit of both.

When Jonathan pled guilty to driving under the influence and all the charges that stemmed from that, he lost his firearm privileges, but he never disclosed he had any weapons. When I found the gun, I hid it, because if anyone needed protection, it was me from him, not the other way around. I've kept it with me all these years, just in case I ever need to protect myself.

I wonder if Jonathan convinced her to use Justin to mug me, or if someone on the outside he knows from prison or his past did his dirty work.

After walking into the bedrooms, I start with what must be Diane's, the bed unmade and the air stale like cigarettes and body odor. I hold my breath as I check to see if Elle has any belongings in here.

Empty liquor bottles are discarded underneath the bed, along with empty cigarette cartons. Various ashtrays line the windowsill, as if they are collectibles, and the side table is covered with spare change and candy wrappers. The closet doesn't have an actual door, an old sheet hung to separate it from the bedroom. I find nothing but clothes, the dirty mixed in with the clean, piles of them, and plenty of shoes, yet most are missing their match.

The cluttered bathroom is between the two bedrooms, and the other bedroom is mainly taken up by a bunk bed. It's messy, but this one clearly belongs to the boys. It's filled with toys, Legos, and cardboard boxes colored with magic markers and cut into the shapes of swords and shields.

The dresser's filled with boys' clothes, and if not for the letter addressed to Elizabeth, it would be like she has never existed in this apartment. After stepping into the closet, this one with a broken door, I find more kids' stuff and a couple of items that must belong to Elle. A scarf, a windbreaker, and a high school sweatshirt.

Feeling around in the back, I hit my knuckle on something rough: a cutout in the wall, a built-in shelf covered by a hand towel. Reaching my hand forward, I manage to grab a clump of papers, and, unable to see what they say in the dark, I step out.

"What do we have here?" I murmur.

All are envelopes addressed to Elizabeth Laughlin from Huberton Correctional Institution, inmate 107650. I whistle, shoving them in my tote. A chronicle of their communication.

About to step back into the living room, I'm interrupted by a loud scream.

"Who the hell are you?"

I reach my hand into my bag, a can of pepper spray now handy, as my eyes dart to the window for an escape route that doesn't exist.

A woman with glasses and disheveled hair stumbles into view, clearly intoxicated. Her voice slurs. "What the hell are you doing in my house, lady?"

She has a bottle in her hand, and my jaw drops in horror as it dawns on me that she might throw it in my direction. Moving my tote bag to cover my abdomen, I use it like a shield.

"I asked a question." The woman twists her face into a snarl, her wrinkles intensified by her furrowed brow. She's probably midfifties, but time hasn't been kind.

Putting my hands in the air, I murmur, "I don't mean any harm."

She mutters, "You one of those damn social workers trying to take my check away?"

I don't respond, and she turns back around to head into the kitchen. I wipe a bead of sweat off my brow.

Meeting her in the other room, I watch as she manages to pour some of the bottle into a plastic cup and spill the rest. "Just because she doesn't stay here every night don't mean she don't live here."

"No, not at all." I keep the bag protectively guarding my midsection. "You must be Diane."

"Of course I'm Diane. You're in my damn apartment."

"I'm from school, a friend of Elizabeth's."

"She doesn't have friends, just that idiot boyfriend."

"We can certainly agree on that." I give her an even smile. "She sent me here, actually. My name is Mrs. Marsh. I'm a teacher at her school."

"Huh?" Diane glares at me. "She wouldn't let nobody in my home."

I hold the key up as proof. "I have her key. She just wanted her mail."

Annoyed, "You must be the one who parked in my spot."

"Yeah, sorry about that," I apologize. "I only came up for a minute."

"No problem. The tow truck's on its way."

"Crap," I murmur. "Really?"

Diane nods, an evil gleam in her eye. "No one's supposed to park in my spot.

"Why wouldn't she get her own damn mail? Not like anyone sends anything, except her father."

"What's your take on him?"

"My take on him?" She sneers, "He's a typical loser."

"He being released soon?"

Diane leans heavily on the kitchen table. "Not unless Elizabeth can help it. He has her so twisted up about it."

"What do you mean?"

"He always trying to convince her he's innocent."

"What do you think?"

"He got his judge and his jury. He where he supposed to be. She won't buy it, though." Diane then grumbles, "And he talks her ear off when she visits him."

I'm asking too many questions, but this old bat won't remember in a few hours. "How often is that?"

"At least every month—due to go tomorrow." She fumbles underneath the coupon ads for a cigarette lighter. "Now, what did you say your name is?"

"I'm her teacher."

Skeptically, she raises her heavily penciled-in eyebrows. "Since when do teachers make house calls?"

"When their foster parents don't take care of them." With that, I turn on my heel, locking the door behind me. I wish like hell I could throw away the key to this apartment permanently.

In a way, I feel sorry for Elizabeth Randall. A product of her environment and the system, she's the one who is suffering. What kid doesn't want to believe their parent is innocent and was wrongly accused? Don't most convicted felons try to convince everyone around them they didn't commit the crime? That doesn't mean Elizabeth is wrong for trying, or a bad person. She's just a misguided teenager in crisis.

I shoot her a text that I'm running late as I speed across town.

I'm torn between helping her and kicking her out.

I'm at odds—at two ends of the spectrum—over what to do. I don't want to rationalize her intentions, but I also don't want to prematurely judge the situation. Noah and I have a new baby to consider, and this doesn't help her case. I have to get to the bottom of what she wants with me. This wasn't a chance meeting on her part.

If it's her father's innocence, I'm afraid I can't help.

The question remains: Can I give Elizabeth what she wants?

I make sure the letters are securely hidden in my tote; I predict they will be sordid reading later on tonight.

Remaining calm, though my foot taps restlessly on the brake, I attempt my best poker face when I pick her up.

"Are you okay?" She notices my flushed face right away. "You look awful."

"I feel like crap."

"Can I do anything?"

"I just need to lie down."

"Anything exciting happen today?"

I want to mention that I acquired some interesting facts, but instead I stare straight ahead. "Not really, just a lot of driving and meetings."

"If it's easier, I can always take the bus. Not a big deal."

"I'd prefer you didn't." My tone is harsher than I intend. "Being pregnant, you have to think of someone else besides yourself."

Reprimanded, Elle leans back in her seat, closing her eyes.

We ride in silence, my driving faster and less focused than usual, my eyes darting around the road as I switch lanes and zigzag in and out of traffic.

Elizabeth breaks the silence. "Are you sure you're fine?"

"Yeah, why?"

"You seem, I don't know, like you're off. Are you having really bad pregnancy symptoms?"

"No, not at all."

"Is Noah okay?" she pries. "How's his trip?"

"Yeah, he's great." My voice doesn't match the forced smile on my face.

"You seem tense."

Squinting at the road, I shrug. "I'm just . . . I just have a lot going on."

"I know. I'm just one more worry. I know, Charlotte, I'm sorry." She leans over to pat my arm as I curl my fingers on the steering wheel. "Tomorrow I'm going to stay and work in the computer lab after class."

"Oh, really, what for?"

"We're doing a project for Western civilization, but it's a group one."

"How're the lab partners?"

"They're okay. I just hope they pull their weight."

"I have a meeting tomorrow at the college," I mention. "Just let me know when you're finished."

"Of course."

With that, we drive home, my knuckles white from clenching my fists.

I want nothing more than to take Elle back to where she came from, so I can disappear, away from Jonathan, my mother, and Lauren.

Away from the past that keeps catching up with me no matter how hard I try to outrun it.

CHAPTER 47
Elle

Charlotte hurriedly locks herself in her bedroom when we get back to the house.

I decide to take a walk around the lake, wanting to clear my head and think about everything that I want to talk to my father about tomorrow, when I see him.

With the strange woman who came over and the robbery, I don't want to leave the front door unlocked. I hesitate, then decide not to bolt the french doors in the kitchen. Charlotte has a privacy fence that wraps around her backyard with a gate that goes through the wooded area, toward the lake. I doubt anyone will be climbing her fence to enter her house while I'm on my short walk.

As I watch a group of twentysomethings jog, I think about what my life will look like in a decade. If I'll still be in the same poverty-stricken situation, or if I'll be able to rise above it for the sake of my child.

I've watched people grow, but can they change?

Well, certain people can change. I bite my tongue. Even in my mere seventeen years on earth, I've noticed that adults tend to reflect on shit and make amends as the years go by. But I also realize that money is the root of evil and a motivation to act accordingly.

I know Diane's sister called her after fifteen years of silence to apologize for telling their family Diane was a lesbian. She's not, but after that, the fact that her mother was a devout Baptist led to her being cut out of the will, so she didn't get any inheritance. It caused a lot of tension with her siblings, and she spiraled even further down, drinking and gambling incessantly.

I consider my own predicament.

It's been ten years, and I'm *still* searching for my own truth.

And as much as I want to believe my own father, it's hard, because Charlotte's the definition of kind. As hard as I try, I can't imagine her in the horrific role he's put her in. She has her quirks, but I imagine I would also be overly paranoid if I had been heaved down the stairs like a piece of garbage.

Case in point: when I come back to the house, the french doors are locked, and Charlotte is nowhere in sight.

Flustered, I have to jog all the way around the block, since there's nowhere to enter the front yard from the back. Breathing heavily by the time I reach Charlotte's porch, I ring the doorbell multiple times before she answers.

She peers at me through the screen door, and her voice quivers. "Why wasn't the back door locked?"

Putting my hands out in an apologetic gesture, I explain, "I just wanted to go for a quick walk."

"Did I miss a step?" Then she snaps, "That's not what I asked."

"I couldn't lock it. I don't have a key."

"It doesn't matter. You don't *ever* leave this door unlocked when you leave, do you understand?"

"I'm sorry, Charlotte. I wasn't trying to cause trouble."

"Doesn't matter."

She still hasn't moved to allow me to enter the house. "Can I please get a copy of a key or a garage door opener in case the door is ever locked?"

"No." Tremoring, she clutches the door handle. "And why didn't you tell me a woman stopped by the house the other day, Elizabeth?"

I stammer, wanting to ask her how she knows.

It must've been the outside cameras. She must've gone back and watched a clip. And Charlotte doesn't call me by my real first name usually, so it throws me. It's said in the same tone my parents used to use with me when they were upset. That parental tone that means you're in deep shit.

"I didn't know it was a big deal."

Charlotte looks at me in disbelief, rubbing her eyes.

"She wanted to know if I could dog sit." I rush on with my story. "She heard about me from the neighbors." I don't add that she snooped in the house. I don't want to scare Charlotte any more than she is right now.

"How did she get my address?" Her hand reaches for her throat. "Can we not have random people show up here, please?"

"It wasn't a client," I say. "She didn't find me on the app."

"Once again, it doesn't matter, Elizabeth. You're not grasping the seriousness of the situation. Let me be clear. I don't like visitors, and I certainly don't like strangers. I was just mugged at a grocery store. Can you not understand how harrowing that was for me?"

She pauses. "Unless," she says, "*unless* it was someone I know. The cops seem to think it might be an acquaintance." I stand there, my forehead drenched in sweat. "You wouldn't know anything about it, would you?"

"I don't," I plead. "Can I please come in the house and get some water?"

"What did she look like?" Charlotte moves away from the door to the window, finally allowing me to enter the house.

I'm floored. *Wouldn't she know—that is, if she actually had a working camera out here?*

359

"Brown hair, slim, looked like a typical soccer mom, wearing a vest and jeans. Said she's a neighbor," I say, as if to imply she's harmless. I don't dare say she used a different last name for Charlotte and that she mentioned they knew each other.

Pointedly, she responds, "You said you were a neighbor, too, when you showed up." Charlotte then looks to the frame on the side table, turned ever so slightly, opposite from the way it had been. "Did you move this?"

"She just commented on your pictures from the foyer."

"She was in the house?" Her voice is wooden. "You let her in?"

"Only in the entry."

Charlotte chains the dead bolt. "Unbelievable. Do that again, and you can go back to Diane's."

The comment stings.

Charlotte tilts her head. "Lauren, hmm . . ." Standing guard at the window, she murmurs, "Maybe I should call the police."

"Are you sure?"

I watch as she goes from visibly anxious to outraged, her hands tugging at the ropes on the drapes.

Yanking on them hard, she pulls the curtains, and they're too thick to rip, but Charlotte becomes entangled in the hem of one. As she starts to trip, she doesn't let go of the tapestry, and I'm able to reach her before she falls.

Holding her elbow, I lead her to the couch.

She sinks into the middle and buries her head in her hands.

Scared of her reaction but aware I'm to blame, I rest on the edge of the couch next to her. As I hand her a throw from the basket, I can't ignore the physical pain on her face.

I could never imagine a world where I'd reach for Charlotte's hand, but I do.

When she looks at me, it's with a glazed expression, like she's staring straight through me.

CHAPTER 48
Charlotte

Closely staring at Elizabeth, I repeat the name Lauren.

Elizabeth looks terrified at my outburst, her hand trembling over my frozen one.

I ask her to describe the woman to me again.

"Did you see what she drove?"

"I didn't see her get into a car. She disappeared around a corner." Trying to be helpful, Elizabeth adds, "A black car did drive by me on my walk around the block . . ."

My face must go white as a sheet, and I jerk my hand away.

"Who is Lauren?"

Holding up a hand, I interrupt. "Let me think." A moment later, I whisper, "I think it's Lauren."

Elizabeth scrunches her face. "Who?"

I don't answer.

"Why are you scared of Lauren?" she asks, louder this time, tugging on my hand.

Contemplating how to answer, I scream internally, *Lauren is a threat to everything Noah and I have built!*

But Elizabeth is young, and even though she's going through her own pain of a breakup and might understand more than most at her age, there is still a divide in our years and what compiles over time with someone you love.

I ponder what to tell Elle and how much she needs to be privy to, in case Lauren becomes a threat to her and the safety of either of our babies.

Moving from the chair to settle on the floor, Elizabeth asks, "Should I be worried about Lauren?"

Leaning back against the sofa, I mold my body to the shape of the couch. I wrap the blanket tighter around my shoulders, as if it could fend off the ghosts of my past.

Elizabeth doesn't take her eyes off me, the blue only intensifying in her irises.

Picking at the edge of the blanket, I say, "Possibly."

I wrinkle my nose, shoulders hunching over the pillow.

"Do you teach together at the college?"

"No. We were roommates in college."

Her eyes widen. "Oh, she's the one in the old pictures I found." She stares at me guiltily. "I saw an old picture of the three of you in the office."

Now is not the time to ask her where she found a group picture. I thought I burned them all, but maybe Noah had one in his stuff.

"Are you not friends anymore?"

"No, not quite." I shake my head. "We don't pretend to get along. Lauren's . . . she's mentally disturbed. She's not supposed to be out . . ."

"Out from what?"

"The hospital."

She looks at me, waiting for me to spill, tapping her feet on the area rug. "Is she dangerous?"

I decide I owe her an explanation.

My voice monotone, I say, "I met Lauren sophomore year of college. We were assigned to be roommates in our dorm." Pursing my lips, I add, "We were really close at first and spent our free time together.

Our lives became so entwined we did everything together—rushed for the same sororities, hung out with the same groups of friends, and even shared our clothes. She was like a sister."

I pause. "Except it felt wrong, like she was slowly morphing into me. I didn't realize the extent our lives were overlapping until I started noticing that clothes she borrowed would mysteriously disappear, holes would appear when I put something on, resulting in some embarrassing walks of shame—I think that's what it's called these days . . ."

My eyes look down to the sound of thumping, and, sheepish, I realize it's my twitching feet. "Then I noticed my favorite locket, the locket my father gave me before he died, was missing. She tried to convince me I must've left it back home when I went to visit. It went from bad to worse when she copied one of my term papers, and I was almost kicked out of college. They accused me of plagiarism, because she handed hers in first. The professor—"

Elizabeth interrupts, "How could you live with her after that?"

"She always had a story ready. Her grandma died, and she thought she was going to flunk out. But yes, it doesn't explain why almost ruining my academics was okay, or why she lied to the college. Luckily, I was able to show them my notes and the research printouts, since this was done in a school library."

"Please tell me she got in trouble? Or expelled."

"She was able to appeal, and she wrote a letter of apology to me."

"They accepted that?"

"The dean involved me at the end. Because of the tremendous impact her grandma's death had had on her and her stellar grades, her punishment was helping the professor for a hundred fifty hours and submitting her *own* paper." I smirk and add, "Plus, her family made a very generous contribution to the university."

Elizabeth mutters, "How could you live with her after she betrayed your trust like that?"

"I couldn't, so I transferred," I confide. "That's not even the worst part. I thought it was odd my old friends wouldn't return my phone calls. She told everyone I was suicidal and that she felt threatened by me because I'd been acting crazy. She was worried for her safety after I supposedly set her bed on fire . . ." Then I finish, "With her in it."

I pause. "She tried to reconnect with me a few years ago, and I thought she had changed. She knew Noah back from our college days as well, and I tried to bury the past." Taking a big breath, I clench the pillow to my chest like it's a life jacket. "I walked in . . ." I have to spit out the words. "To her in my bed with Noah last year."

Her mouth drops open. "What did they do when you walked in?"

"Stopped." I wrinkle my nose in disgust.

"What did you do?"

I feel rancid, like I've swallowed poison, repeating Lauren's offenses. "But I'll never forget the expression on her face . . . she just looked me straight in the eye when she left, like she was trying to get caught on purpose. It was pure evil."

"Please tell me you beat the shit out of both of them?"

"Elizabeth, you can't always fight your way through life with fists . . ." I can't help but give her a small smile. "But believe me, I wanted to, as I'm sure you can imagine. I had a broken heart. Not unlike you right now."

"She came after your husband?" Elle's mouth sags in disgust. "But it obviously didn't work, so what does she want with you now?"

I focus on my belly. "She can't have kids . . . and . . ." Then I stutter, "I-I hope that's not what she's coming after." I pause. "Elizabeth . . ." Then, giving her an unflinching stare, I say, "I think she wants my husband and our child."

Her jaw drops in horror.

She sits there in stunned silence as I close my eyes to consider my options. I don't know whom to trust, and I'm confiding in a girl who could be just as dangerous as Lauren.

"Everything okay, Charlotte? Earth to Charlotte." She snaps her fingers when I don't respond. "Earth to Charlotte," she repeats.

I hate when people snap their fingers at me. It didn't use to bother me, until Jonathan started doing it to get my attention, and then I responded like Pavlov's dog. It became the forewarning noise I'd hear before he took a fist to my face or pummeled my body. He was smarter than the average abuser, which made him that much more dangerous. Most of my bruises were in places that weren't noticeable to the naked eye unless I was undressed.

Elizabeth does this as if my reluctance will be fixed by a dose of reality in the form of her cracking her claws at me.

I shoot up like a rocket, and when I swivel around to face her, I see it.

Her fingers are the same—narrow—and they're angled precisely where his would be.

And those eyes.

They have the same matching ones, she and Jonathan.

And when both are distrustful, a hardness appears in their usually soft blue eyes, which turn steely.

I noticed the mannerisms before, but now I have the full picture, the history.

I recoil as if she has slapped me.

If I make eye contact with her now, the recognition will be frozen on my face for her to see.

And what then?

I step back far enough to clear the large area rug.

"I'm going to lie down." I nod my head, avoiding Elizabeth, whose eyes are drilled into the back of my neck.

I need to figure out what I'm going to do with both Lauren and Elizabeth. One thing's for sure: I'm in a quandary, because I'm afraid to be alone with Elizabeth, scared I won't be able to hide my contempt for her.

You have to pretend like everything's normal, I caution myself, *at least until Noah is home and can help remove her from the house. He's going to be disappointed our plan to have Elizabeth in our lives didn't work out.*

I'll pretend like everything's normal and engage in our usual chatter. Except there's a nauseated feeling in my stomach. It might be morning sickness, but I lean more toward fear.

CHAPTER 49
Elle

I'm worried about Charlotte, who doesn't reappear all afternoon or evening.

The next morning, I'm contemplating how to get to the prison, about to text Sandra to borrow her car.

Charlotte's in the kitchen, preparing breakfast and humming, acting as if yesterday didn't happen, but I can tell by her pretend smile that doesn't reach the corner of her lips, making it lopsided, that she's still reeling.

"Hey, I was thinking, would you mind just taking Noah's car today? I've got to get to the college, and you might as well use his vehicle while it's sitting here."

"Are you sure?" I narrow my eyes. "I'm not the most advanced driver, as you know."

"You have to practice, Elle, or you'll never learn to drive."

"Okay, fine, as long as you're okay with it."

"How about this? Just make sure you're home by dark. Is that fair?"

The prison drive will put more miles on his car than a trip to school, so I ask Charlotte if she minds if I run some errands.

"No problem." She seems relieved to have me out of her hair today.

"Aren't you going to grab your backpack?" Charlotte asks after handing me the keys.

"Oh yeah, duh." I hit myself in the forehead. "I'm a bit slow today."

"You have a five-month checkup with the obstetrician this week. Don't forget," she reminds me as I secure my backpack in my hand. "I might text you later to grab some groceries."

"Okay." I'm sure my face is beet red, and I hurriedly exit, afraid she'll ask more questions on what I'm doing today. I don't dare use Noah's navigation system to guide me to the prison. *You know it by heart anyway,* I tell myself.

I hope my father's in a good mood today and that all will be forgiven with our last visit. Even with his letter, I never know how the inside of his mind operates on a day-to-day basis—if he sits and stews on our time together or if he's able to move forward. It seems like so much of our time is focused on the past that we can never move on.

When he trudges out from behind the solid wall that separates us, I give him a small smile. He doesn't seem distressed, his eyes not as focused on his steps as they usually are. If he was upset last time, he's really going to be pissed when he sees what I brought.

He folds me in his arms. "I'm sorry about last time."

"You should be," I whisper in his ear before we pull apart and sit. He places his package of cigarettes on the table.

"Lovebug, it's hard living in that time period." He shakes his head. "And never leaving it behind or being able to grow from my mistakes."

"Like these?" I set a couple of the photos down I took from Charlotte's house as evidence. "What are these photos?"

He looks horrified. "Where did you get these?"

"Where do you think?"

"Not my finest moment." He scratches at his beard. "Why did you bring these here?"

"It doesn't help your case."

"I know."

"We have to talk about that night," I say. "I don't care if you don't want to. If you want my help, I have to have all the facts." I pause. "Obviously, Daddy, if there's something you're not telling me," I say, looking him straight in the eye, "then you're not only putting me in danger; you're also putting your *grandchild* in danger."

There. I did it.

I dropped my own atomic bomb.

"What?" He grins, standing up to half hug me before the guard issues a warning. "Are you kidding me?" Instead of the anger I assume, or have come to expect, I see euphoria. "Guess I can't smoke these, huh?" His teeth are tar stained from tobacco use. "Gives me a reason to quit."

He then asks, "How far are you along?"

"About four months."

"Does she know?"

"She's been taking me to the doctor."

His jaw's set in a hard line. "I'm not okay with this."

"Okay with what?"

"That you're around a dangerous woman when she could hurt both of you."

"Says the man in prison." Then I haughtily respond, "If you were around, I wouldn't be in either situation."

A wistful sigh exits his mouth, and he seems unsure how to proceed. "Want anything from the vending machine? I could sure use a Pepsi." I take the hint. Inmates are not allowed to exchange money or use the vending machine in here. It's for guests only, and we have to purchase the items for them if they want something.

"I brought cash."

"Good. I'll take a pop and some pretzels."

I nod and then feel his gaze on my back as I walk to the machine.

I punch buttons to receive the only family meal we'll have had together in over a decade. Nothing like an overprocessed and junk food–laden lunch. When I sit back down, I slide him his drink and the bag of minipretzels.

The fact that *this* is our life, that *he* made this our life, causes me to lash out. I know I'm acting spitefully, but I'm angry. "I just don't see it."

"See what?"

"This side of her. A conniving side of her that would make her lie and accuse you of something so terrible. She's so kind . . ."

I listen as the guard gives us a five-minute warning over the loudspeaker.

He rests his elbows on the table, looking me dead in the eye. "The night it happened, I was leaving her, had packed up my shit, my truck was full. She called me to come back, said I had left a couple more boxes. I didn't think anything of it, just trying to be done with it all."

"But why did you finally break up?"

"She wanted to. Now it makes sense—she was pregnant with Noah's child. Probably thought he would help raise it."

I can't help but add, "Not to mention, she wouldn't fear for her life."

We sit in silence, the reality of our conversation and what he wants me to provide hanging weighted in unspoken words.

"Did you know about any other miscarriages she had?"

"News to me." Then he changes the subject. "That boyfriend of yours helping out at all?"

"No," I mutter. "He's out of the picture."

"Seriously? What happened? I thought you were going to get a place together?"

I deliver a stinging blow. "We were no more going to live together than you and me." I slide my chair back, just in case this last insult sets him off. "He got another girl pregnant."

Looking dumbfounded, he doesn't know what to say. That makes two of us.

I take a sip of water and ask, "Have you ever heard her mention a Laura or a Lauren?"

"In what way?"

"A woman showed up at her door, acting strange. She said it was her old roommate, who went off the deep end and was trying to steal Noah."

"Roommate from when?"

"College."

"She never mentioned anyone. I thought she lived in an off-campus apartment, but she did go to two different universities, I think." He pauses. "But the woman Noah was engaged to back then was named Lauren."

"Wait, he was engaged to her?"

"Yes. I don't know what happened after, obviously nothing, but yeah."

He takes a long swig of his Pepsi. "She never talked about any friends or people from her past. I didn't think she had any friends." He tilts his head. "You know, it was weird, it was like she was completely alone, by all accounts. No one really seemed to know her. No one except me. And look how that turned out . . ."

"But why would she want to hurt you?" I squeeze the edge of the table with my hands. "In this permanent way?"

He runs his hands through his salt-and-pepper hair. "We've been through this, Elizabeth." He adds, "Because I could feel she was cheating on me, and she knew I knew it." He stares me down. "And you just told me your boyfriend knocked up another girl. Doesn't feel good, does it?"

My eyes start to tear up, and he softens his voice. "You know it ruins your self-esteem and makes you question a lot of things, especially your relationship. And if you're supposed to have a child together, well, I'm sure you can imagine what that did to me."

"But it also makes you the main suspect . . ."

"True. Which is why I've needed your help."

"If she's lying, then how will I ever know?"

"Because I didn't push her down the stairs." There's such a look of anguish in his eyes. "There has to be something in her past that can help. Or maybe you can get her to confess she lied or embellished the story . . ." I see a tear in the corner of his eye. He adds, "I wish like hell I hadn't come back to her place that night."

"Why would that have made a difference?"

"Because she set me up. She thought Noah would come in and save the day, protect her from me, except it didn't turn out that way." He slides a cigarette behind his ear. "He always was a little pussy from the city."

"You didn't know him, did you?"

"Nope. Never met him. Never spoke to him. Still haven't. Charlotte's relationship with him came out at trial. Or at least the details."

"And Charlotte said what, exactly, happened that night?"

"She told the police I started breaking shit when she asked me to move out, which I did, but some of it was just junk I wasn't taking with. I didn't know she had made a call to the police, claiming domestic assault, while I was still packing. They came and spoke to us, and I told them I'd get the hell out as fast as possible. And I did—I took off like a bat out of hell from that devil woman."

"And then what?"

"I get a call from Charlotte about an hour later telling me she needs me back at the house, that I've got a few items left. I'd already had a couple beers—okay, yeah, I was pretty unsteady—but she started to get hysterical. I remember Katrina pregnant, and I didn't want the wrath. So I drove back over. It was just supposed to be a pit stop on the way to the bar."

"She was inside waiting for you?"

"Yep. I honked because I didn't want to go back inside. She comes flying out of the house, tells me she can't lift the boxes, and, even though I said, 'Tough shit, not my kid,' I gave in. Another thing used against me at trial that I brought up, since it wasn't my kid—I didn't care what happened to her or it."

"Was anyone there?"

"No. There were no other cars in the driveway, and I didn't see anyone." Gesturing in the air, he then explains the layout of the house. "When you walk in the side door, which was the door we always used, there's a small entryway, but you only have two choices. You either go straight down the basement stairs or up three small steps to your left, and you're in the kitchen and the rest of the house."

"And you followed her into the house?"

"Yeah. I stood at the entry, and a small box with some magazines is just sittin' on the step to the left. I made a snit about it not being important enough to drag my ass all over town for, and then boom! Before I knew what was coming at me, I was being attacked. Claws and fists, she came at me."

"Charlotte did?"

"Yes. And the next day I was arrested."

What if Charlotte's really not lying? I rest my chin in my hands. *What if this horrible tragedy happened through no fault of her own, and I'm dredging it up and making her relive it moment by moment?*

The thought of that gives me pause.

His blue eyes meet my pensive gaze, as if he knows what I'm thinking.

"Watch out, Elizabeth," he whispers. "That Jekyll and Hyde personality of hers can't hide forever."

When I stand to leave, tears shine as he gives me the allowable goodbye hug. Giving my forehead a kiss, he squeezes my shoulders. "Love you, 'Bug." He steps away, his eyes watery with tears. "Talk soon, okay?"

I don't respond, and as I exit the prison, I think about my father's disposition, so similar to mine.

But he's never changed his story, not once, I fiercely remind myself.

Even so, there's a nagging feeling rearing its ugly head in the back of my mind. The shreds of doubt keep building up.

CHAPTER 50
Charlotte

When I pull in the circular driveway, I notice what I didn't in the dark. A weathervane in the shape of a dove is perched on the red shingles.

A replica of the one at George Washington's Mount Vernon and a tribute to peace, I think, *which is why I'm here.* After I press the doorbell, which is hooked up to a camera system, Courtney's high-pitched voice comes through the speakers. "My dad's not here."

"I came to talk to you."

"I don't think that's a good idea."

"Then can I speak to your mother?"

"She's, uh, out somewhere."

"When will she be back?"

"Does it matter?" Courtney's sigh crackles through the speaker box.

"This isn't about what happened at school. I need your help. You're the only one who can help me. It's about Elizabeth's mental state. I'm worried."

"I'm not prepared for visitors . . ."

There's a lull, and I wait, my foot tapping, this time in anticipation, not from nerves.

The door opens, and Courtney appears.

A different version than before.

Her face is pale, with no contrast in color this time between her blonde hair and tan skin.

The green eyes, the same as her father's, are dull.

When she brushes a strand of tangled hair off her face, I notice her cheek, the line of stitches that cover the taut skin. My eyes move to her lips, where small spots of darkness indicate the lacerations.

She says, "You need my help?"

"I do. I'm concerned about Elizabeth."

"But why me?" She raises a hand to her face. "Clearly, we're not friends."

"Because if Elizabeth harms . . ." Abruptly I stop talking, my eyes veering off in both directions. "Can I talk to you about it in private? Is anyone around?"

Courtney shifts nervously on her feet. "Just our landscaper. He's out back priming some bushes."

"You mean pruning?"

As she rolls her eyes upward, I see a glimmer of the real Courtney. "Yeah, that word." Not one to miss out on juicy gossip or be left out of a secret, she has a twinkle in her eyes. "How is she acting different than her usual crazy self? You know what she did to me is going to take *forever* to heal."

"That's what I wanted to talk to you about. I think we can help each other." I purr, "I'd owe you a huge favor."

And Courtney, for all her faults, understands how the game is played.

She ushers me in without another word.

As she leads me down an insanely long foyer, we pass multiple rooms. For all the wealth this family has, the house is decorated as if it's a model home but no one lives here. There is not one personal effect in sight. Not one family photo, not one picture of Courtney, not one inspirational quote.

The house is bleak, a reflection of Courtney Kerr's homelife. From the outside looking in, she's untouchable, fashionable, and wealthy.

But on the inside, she's an emotional mess, unable to stabilize because she has no stability in her homelife. No one takes an interest in her feelings or emotional stability, and at this age, that's crucial.

I feel sorry for her, not because she's some sad little rich girl but because I could see her survival mode come into play the instant she wickedly called out to Elle at the diner.

Both girls are so immersed in their own sturdy grit that they don't realize how similar they are.

We walk into what must be some kind of teen recreation or game room. Posters cover the walls, or at least the empty spaces where the flat-screen televisions don't hang. A built-in shelf with every video game system you can imagine is along one wall.

Courtney points to the well-stocked bar. "Help yourself."

"I'm good."

Unused to guests, I presume, she takes a seat without offering me one.

I settle on what looks like a big beanbag chair, overstuffed and unbelievably comfy, and with my burgeoning belly, I'm glad I don't have to lower myself very far into it.

"Are you starting to get uncomfortable?" she asks.

Confused at what she's inferring, I shrug.

"I remember when my mom was pregnant with my brother. She could hardly move by the time she hit six months. She was huge—gained, like, forty pounds."

"Wow, yeah, the scale keeps going up. I tell myself it's water weight."

I can't determine her brother's age range by the type of posters and games. I'd predict he's close to her age, by the parental guidance rating, but it's unclear.

"How old is your brother?"

"Seven."

"And did your mom have an easy pregnancy?"

"She died."

Hesitating, I shift in my seat. "A long time ago?"

"During childbirth." She must get my incredulous expression a lot. "Brain aneurysm."

"Then your mom isn't here to talk to, even if I wanted to," I say gently.

"Oh, I have a stepmom. She's barely thirty, and she's usually gone, sleeping around on my father, who is equally as terrible. But," she says, raising an eyebrow, "he did buy me a new monogrammed LV bag, since I've been home from school and have had his 'affairs' invade my personal space. And his wife—she suggested plastic surgery if my face doesn't heal properly."

Her eyes fill up with tears, and she must assume the victim card will work like magic on me. Because it always does.

"Then you'll understand my confusion on why you stole my watch."

"Huh?" Her crocodile tears dry up immediately. "What're you talking about?" She starts to rise. "I think you should leave."

"Sit," I command, the edge in my voice enough to make her sink back down into her seat.

"I did not steal anything from you, regardless of what that little bitch said."

"For the record, Elizabeth has never said a word."

"Then what are you—"

Interrupting, I wave my hand in the air, bored of this exchange. "Courtney, if you're going to rob someone, you shouldn't post pictures on social media wearing said items." Then, unclear whether she understands what I've said, I rephrase. "I saw your Instagram account."

She manages to stutter, "B-but we're not friends on there."

"But you *are* with Justin. And from his account, I saw a picture you posted a week ago, wearing a very expensive watch—*my* Tiffany watch."

Snidely, "Try and prove—"

"The watch is at least twenty years old."

"Yeah, and it's from my daddy." Courtney licks her lips. "He can testify to that."

"He won't attest to anything, Courtney, because it's engraved. I know it was dark that night, but if you paid the slightest attention, underneath the watch head, there's a very sweet message."

"I know. It says, 'The time I've had with you, my sweet daughter, is priceless.'"

"It's from my mother."

"I thought it was from your husband."

"Doesn't matter who it came from." My face burns as she catches me in a lie. "You and I both know that's my watch." Courtney doesn't need to know about my tenuous relationship with my mother.

After yanking my phone out of my purse, I wait for it to unlock via facial recognition and then scroll through my photos.

Courtney whispers, "What're you doing?"

I don't bother telling her I'm going to record our conversation. Instead, I say, "I was going to show you the pictures of the watch, *my* watch." I meet her eyes, which are now filling with what I conclude are actually real tears. "I'm sure I can dig up some old photographs of me unwrapping it. And don't bother deleting your Instagram or the post," I say with a shrug. "I've already taken screenshots and sent them to the police."

Courtney's facade is starting to crack, and she looks like a scared little girl right now, albeit a rich one.

"Right now, I need your help. You're intelligent, more so than you ever let on, and I'm just going to say it. You're the only one who has the power to help."

Tilting her chin, she's clearly thrown.

"Justin gave you up."

"What do you mean?"

"He laid out the whole story."

She plays dumb. "What story?"

"That the robbery was your idea."

The astonishment on her face is real; she's not acting in a drama right now.

She swallows, and her skin starts to become mottled.

"Good to see you finally getting your color back." With her right where I want her, I continue, "Justin told me you suggested robbing me with my own gun. You saw my watch that night at the diner, commented on it, and told him you wanted it. Then he, you, and Elle came up with the plan together to mug me. And shortly after, you three had a falling out because you were sleeping with him behind Elle's back."

"I did no such thing." Wringing her hands in her lap, she protests, "I need a stiff drink. Want one?"

"Oh yeah, duh."

She rises, realizing her dumb question when she glances at my protruding belly. "Can I move to the bar without you freaking out on me?"

"At your own risk," I say.

Courtney pours a vodka sour. "Aren't you supposed to stop me? You could totally go to jail for supplying to minors."

"Except it's not my home, I'm not your parent, and I didn't provide or purchase the alcohol." I shrug. "So in this case, no." Steering Courtney back to the topic at hand, I ask, "Is there anything you want to tell me?"

"I don't know, Charlotte." She takes a long sip. "Besides the fact that you have it all wrong."

"Pregnant women shouldn't drink."

She gives me a snide look. "Obviously."

"So that was a lie?"

"I prefer rumor."

"Then give me your side of the story."

"I'll just talk to my daddy."

"I don't think you understand the seriousness of this, Courtney." I give her a somber look. "Justin's prepared to meet with the detectives handling the case this afternoon. They've suggested jail time, even with you all being minors. You said your birthday's in the summer, right?"

"So?"

"Because they want to try you as adults, so the punishment is stricter. Make an example out of you because of who your dad is."

Her eyes betray her fear. "So why come to me, then?"

"Because I don't think you're stupid, and I think Elizabeth and Justin assume you're dumb enough to take the fall for them." I shrug sadly. "I think you got duped into doing something you didn't want to."

Her shoulders heave as she touches her swollen face. "Any jury would take pity on me right now. Elizabeth beat me up."

"Yeah, but they won't see you in the flesh like this." I hoist myself out of the chair. "I have to go. I have a meeting with them first."

"Wait." Courtney gives me a pitiful glance. "That's not exactly what happened." She takes a deep breath. "I didn't have anything to do with a robbery or a mugging or hurting you. Leave me out of that. The only thing I'm guilty of is borrowing your gun." Then she adds, "And giving it to Justin."

"You mean stealing," I correct her. "And you also stole my watch."

She cries, "I did not steal your watch!"

"So back to my gun—"

"It was in the glove box the night you got pulled over."

I didn't believe Elizabeth when she said she hadn't taken it, but maybe she is more trustworthy than I thought.

"Why did you take it?"

"My stepmom has men in and out of here all the time, and sometimes . . ." Her busted lip quivers. "I've had one try and come into my bedroom in the middle of the night."

Before I can say anything, she holds up a hand. "Nothing happened, and they could've been drunk or lost, but it scared the shit out of me. I had our repair guy install a lock on my door, but Daddy freaked out and thought it was because I was trying to hide drugs or boys. It's extra protection. I never want to use it, but if I have it," she says, jutting her chin out defiantly, "it will definitely make them think twice."

"Okay," I say, "but where'd you get the metal replica of a gun?"

"When you were talking in Daddy's office, it was on his shelf. I just grabbed it and switched them out. He gets gag gifts all the time from clients and friends." Eyeing me with interest, she asks, "Where did you get the gun?"

"Doesn't matter," I say. "From an old friend."

I mull over what she just told me, but something isn't adding up. "Your father is a criminal defense attorney, and he doesn't have a weapon in case a demented person comes after him for payback or an intruder breaks in?"

"We have a top-of-the-line security system, and yeah, he has guns, but they're locked up. His office is always locked if he isn't in it, and they're locked in another cabinet so my brother can't play with them."

Makes sense to me.

"Let me recap—you admit you took the gun from the glove box, but you did not discuss robbing me with Elizabeth and Justin, and you did not have a part in planning it?"

She shakes her head. "But Justin saw the gun and asked to borrow it."

"Out loud. I can't hear you." Or more precisely, the microphone recording this on my phone needs to hear verbal confirmation.

"Charlotte, I like you—you gave me a ride home, and you seem, or seemed, sweet. I did not talk to anyone about trying to rob you. Yes, I took your gun."

"Something doesn't add up."

"What?"

"My watch. I was wearing it the night I was mugged. If you weren't involved, how did you get it?"

"I didn't steal your watch, Charlotte, I swear."

"Then how did you get it?"

"I told you."

Something doesn't add up, but enough of the story does. At least for now.

"Will you show me out, please?"

"Of course. I wouldn't let you wander around alone." She rewards me with a smug look. "You could steal something."

"Speaking of, can you first reunite me with my watch? You can read the inscription from my mother to me." I follow her down the hallway. "Plus, I'm tired of using my phone as my timepiece."

Grunting, she hollers up the stairs. "Dana!"

"I thought only the landscaper was here?"

"Dana!" she screams again, louder.

A tall, willowy woman with buttery blonde hair and brown eyes appears at the top of the stairs. An even taller, dark-haired man emerges behind her like a mirage, his washboard abs defined in his tight-fitting T-shirt.

"Can you grab my Tiffany watch off my dresser? The yellow and gold black-band one?"

"Yes, sweetie." The woman waves at me. "Hi, I'm Dana, Courtney's stepmom."

Courtney turns to me with her poker face. "You really think I'd let you into my house without an adult present?"

"You're good," I say.

"Dana and I have a very specific agreement that she does what *I* want, when *I* want it." Courtney gives me an evil wink. "This way, she can still do *who* she wants."

Watch in hand, Courtney examines the inscription one more time, shrugging at the initials on it. "Whatever, here you go."

"And Courtney, a word of advice." I lower my voice as she shows me to the door. "If you want people to actually think you're pregnant, I'd cut back on the liquor."

Giving a gleeful laugh, Courtney pats me on the shoulder. "Oh, you really believed that? Nah, my friends and I started that rumor. I couldn't get Justin's attention, so we made a couple pics look like the real thing, and bam, it spreads like wildfire."

"Did you sleep with him, or was that a ruse?"

"What does a Rubik's Cube have to do with . . . never mind." She rolls her eyes. "No, Justin didn't touch me. It was just a joke, so tell Elizabeth not to worry—I'm dating an older guy. She can have him."

Wanting to strangle her, I understand now what a devil in disguise looks like. I'm not going to lie; I'm enjoying watching her squirm over my Tiffany watch. I know she didn't steal my watch; she *borrowed* it. I purposefully left it in her daddy's office the night I dropped her off, after she acted like such a brat to Elizabeth, before I knew she was *Jonathan Randall's* daughter. Regardless of this, Courtney Kerr is like Lauren Wilder, a man-stealing wench.

I assumed correctly it would end up in Courtney's well-manicured hands. He'd maybe ask his wife, who wouldn't recognize it as her own, but Courtney would. She played right into my trap. I just wanted to give a mean girl a dose of her own medicine. With a final gleeful laugh, I slide my shades on and give a backward wave to the Kerr residence as I drive off.

CHAPTER 51
Elle

When I reenter the land of the living, or at least the concrete parking lot in the middle of hell, a woman is resting her back against the trunk of Noah's car, arms crossed.

Unnerved, I am reminded of the day Diane stood waiting, a cigarette dangling from her mouth.

As I get closer, I halt in my tracks.

It's the same woman who came to the house.

Lauren.

The unhinged one.

This time she's wearing an oversize jacket, sunglasses, and jeans, her brown hair covered by the hood.

Prepared to turn and run for the guard station, I hear her call my name. "Elizabeth Randall, Jonathan Randall's daughter?"

I swivel my head. "How did you find me?"

"Because I followed you from Charlotte's. Does she know you took the car? Something tells me if she did, she wouldn't like where you went."

"You fucking psycho." I reach for my phone, but it's not allowed inside—it's in the console of the vehicle the crazy woman is perched against.

"Do you realize you're driving my husband's BMW?"

"What? That's impossible . . ." I glare at her. "You're crazy. Why can't you leave Charlotte and Noah alone?"

"Charlotte isn't who she says she is."

"Yeah, I know, she's a little off sometimes, but she's not a bad person." My hands clutch at my belly in fear. "Do I need to call the police?"

"I know you don't trust me, and you have no reason to. But you're visiting your father, who has a history with Charlotte. And with Noah. And with me."

"What do you mean? How is my father tied to you?"

"Look in the glove box."

"Huh?"

I start to spin on my heel, desperately wanting the police to escort me to my vehicle. What if Lauren tries to kidnap me and steal my child? Charlotte told me she couldn't have children, and it was making her dangerous and capable of violent tendencies.

"Give me the keys."

"No way."

"Then look inside."

"What are you talking about?" I scream. "I don't want to turn my back to you. I don't trust you. You're a husband stealer and probably a baby snatcher."

"I'll take a step back."

"Oh, like that makes me feel safe." I roll my eyes. "Like you can't attack me."

She shows me her hands. "My purse isn't on me; neither is my phone. This is the car I followed you in." She points to a white Mazda. "Tell you what. I'll get inside my car. You do the same. Everything you need to see is in the glove box, and if you trust me after, I'll be waiting right here."

"Where is it?" I ask.

"Where's what?"

Triumphant, "Your wedding ring? Charlotte wears one, or at least she did until it was stolen."

"She lost my ring?" Lauren gasps. "I knew I shouldn't have given it back to Noah."

"Oh sure," I snort, "how convenient."

Except she looks genuinely upset.

What a good actress, I huff. *She lost out on her calling in Hollywood.*

At an impasse, I shove my hands in my pockets as Lauren disappears inside her car.

Frantically, I run and unlock the BMW at the same time, then slam the locks in case she tries to jump in. After pressing the engine button to start, I'm about to say screw it and drive off when I make eye contact with her through the tinted glass.

Her sunglasses are off, and I watch tears stream down her face.

Fine. I'll do what she told me to do. I reach forward, but the glove box is locked. What is it with these rich people acting like they run around with drugs and guns and have something to hide?

Duh, I remind myself, *they do.*

I lower the passenger window, motioning for her to do the same. "It's locked." Bet she didn't expect this response.

"I know." She tosses me a key through the open window.

Frantically opening the glove box, I first notice a plastic gym membership card and a work badge of some sort with Noah's picture.

My mouth drops in confusion. No wonder I couldn't find anything on a "Noah Coburn." Underneath are the registration and insurance cards, and the name matches the one on the badge.

All three say Noah Wilder.

An entirely different address from the one in the Pleasanton subdivision is listed on the registration and insurance papers. The car model is accurate, but the other driver is listed as Lauren Wilder.

Noah Coburn doesn't exist.

I figured that, with his career, he didn't use social media, but I've been told LinkedIn is utilized by business professionals, and he never came up in a search.

I had presumed Charlotte's married name was Coburn, since it changed in the decade since she was with my father. I'd imagined they'd have the same last name.

Rolling down the window again, I can only think to say, "Wilder?"

"Care to get in my car with me now," Lauren asks, "just so we can make sure our conversation isn't being overheard?"

Swallowing hard, I power the window back up and step out before reluctantly climbing into Lauren's vehicle.

Lauren speaks before I even can. "The car is ours, mine and Noah's. We're technically still married, which is why I'm still on the registration and insurance."

"I don't understand . . . is this like a polygamy thing?"

She gives a bitter laugh. "It sounds like it, but it's not. Charlotte and Noah are not married and never have been."

"You didn't cheat with him?"

She shakes her head.

Baffled, all I can do is murmur, "But I've seen Noah; his car sits at their house. They're married." I shake my head incredulously. It doesn't add up.

"And you might've seen a black Mercedes sedan. That's the private investigator Charlotte's mother hired."

"Nancy?"

"Yes. Charlotte and her mother have a strained relationship, to say the least." She furrows a brow. "She reached out to Noah recently, since they go way back, and let it slip she was worried Charlotte was losing touch with reality."

"Did she know Noah and her were in a fake marriage?"

"Nancy's the one who contacted him to ask if we had split." Lauren tugs on her lip with a finger. "It's complicated, so I'll spare you the details. Noah and I are—or, I should say, we are *in the process of*—getting a divorce, so we tried a separation first." She hands me a thick envelope. "Here are our divorce papers. I've signed them, and they're ready to go. Except we decided to call it off."

Sure enough, a dissolution of marriage for Lauren and Noah Wilder.

No children. No child support payments. And their separation date is listed as a few months ago.

Lauren starts to explain. "We all went to college together. Noah and Charlotte were friends before I came into the picture. They were good friends, the best of friends. It was a strictly platonic relationship, but when Noah met me, sparks flew. Charlotte and I were rooming together at the time, and she was unhappy . . ." She cringes. "To say the least."

As Lauren starts to recount her story, I shudder in fear. The story is the exact same one Charlotte told me, but backward. According to Lauren, Charlotte tried everything she could to ruin Lauren's life after she started dating Noah.

"She even stole my term paper." Lauren shakes her head. "But after she set my bed on fire, I realized how dangerous she was. The university agreed to expel her, but instead of calling it that, she transferred out to avoid scrutiny. Her father had been the mayor of the town she grew up in, and her mother gave a generous donation on his behalf so no one would ever know the reason."

"And Noah stayed friends with her?"

"No. They lost touch for a few years. He didn't think she was crazy, and in his mind, he felt sorry for her. She lost her father suddenly, and then we started dating, and in a way, she lost her best friend, so he didn't see it the same way I did."

"Even after your bed was lit on fire?"

"He believed it was an accident. She said she knocked a candle over."

"On your bed?"

Her eyes roll. "Exactly. But she said she had been sitting on mine, since hers was filled with clothes she hadn't put away yet, and accidentally she knocked the candle off the ledge."

"So how did he come back into her life?" I still can't wrap my head around the fact that Noah is a pretend husband. At least to Charlotte.

"Charlotte's mother reached out to Noah a couple years after she left school. He and I had gotten engaged after college, and then I broke it off around this time. They had a one-night stand, and she got pregnant. I had a lot of wedding jitters, which is why I called off the wedding the first time, so we eloped. It was right after we got married that he found out she was pregnant."

"So this is the second time that Charlotte is pregnant with his baby?"

Her face becomes wan. "That's what I wanted to talk to you about."

CHAPTER 52
Charlotte

In a better mood now that I got the gun situation cleared up and Courtney put in her place, I drive home feeling a smidgen better. Having dealt with one teenager successfully, I've had a boost of confidence that I can handle Elizabeth just as flawlessly.

Contemplating what to do with her now, I plan on asking Noah, who might have his own ideas on how he wants to proceed.

Without delay, when the garage door lifts, I notice something's off.

I put the Jeep in park and sit for a moment, surveying the garage. It's like when you're accustomed to seeing the same oil stain on the concrete or a mop and pail in a perpetual spot, and then it disappears.

My mind takes a second to play catch-up.

A couple of Noah's boxes are missing.

That's it. I slam my palm on the wheel, accidentally honking the horn.

Would Lauren have . . . no, it's impossible. Absolutely not. She couldn't get into the garage.

I exit the Jeep, reaching down into my handbag for my pepper spray and then holding it just in case. I open the door handle slowly into the house, making sure to step over the loose piece of tile in the mudroom that always creaks.

I'm greeted with silence.

It's deafening at first, since in my head, I can hear the screams and accusations flying.

I heave a deep sigh of relief. This poor baby has been subjected to enough anxiety and terror for a lifetime. Nothing looks out of place, the house is quiet, and cautiously I take a few more steps forward.

Hollering into the two-story entry, I don't hear anything but my voice echo back.

As I scan the room, I take note of the fluffed pillows and the folded blankets. The living room looks model perfect, nothing out of place.

I wonder how much time I'll have until Elizabeth comes home. When I put the tracker on Noah's car so I could record his movements and make sure he wasn't visiting Lauren, I had no idea how handy it would be for Elizabeth. For as cunning as she's been, it was quite the misstep when she took the Beemer this morning to the penitentiary. There are no errands that are 180 miles round trip.

I hope she at least gassed it up.

After logging in to check her location, I can see she's getting closer.

I text Noah about his missing boxes and settle into the middle of the couch. My mind drifts to his whereabouts and what he's doing.

When I check his account, it flashes *Invalid password.*

Must be a mistake.

I type it and hit enter again.

Password incorrect.

I clench my fists. *What in the . . .*

Did he change his password? Or worse yet, did he figure out I can access his email?

My hands start to tremble, and I scream at the perfectly organized, uncluttered house that I'm living in with a stranger. Uncontrollable anger follows, and I brush my hand under the decorative pillows, knocking them off the couch. I pick one up and start bashing it against the couch cushions, as if I'm having a pillow fight with myself.

The pictures on the sideboard are out of sync with my current life, reminiscent of a past gone by, one that no longer exists.

Everything on it must go.

A wave of fury sweeps my arm across everything in its path—every knickknack and every frame is lifted off the surface, landing with a loud crash on the hardwood.

Glass sits in tiny flecks on the floor, along with wooden splinters.

About to head into the kitchen for a dustpan, I notice sunlight glinting off something shiny in a shallow vase on a lower shelf.

At first, I assume it's a piece of broken glass that took cover from my wrath in the container, but when I reach into it, I drag out a thin gold chain.

Confounded, I stare at it as if it's an illusion.

Sinking down into the middle part of the couch, I thread it through my fingers, the small cross a tiny nub in my palm. My hands are shaking, to the point I can't get the clasp secure around my neck, so I set it down on the side table.

I tell myself to relax as my mind deviates into treacherous territory. It splits off into ruminating thoughts on my necklace, the robbery, Elizabeth, Lauren, and why Noah hasn't responded to any of my text messages yet.

The sound of the television doesn't comfort me tonight; instead, it's mindless chatter. I'm unable to commit to a television show or channel, my fingers clicking through the nightly lineup at a frenzied pace.

I sigh, staring at the mess I need to clean up.

Nancy always told me that if you're restless, start in on your chores, and you'll know then if you actually have housework to do or if you're avoiding a problem. It's probably why we always had a clean house.

I've wheeled the vacuum out, focused on the small bits of glass I don't want to cut my foot on later, when I hear my name.

"Charlotte?" I blow a chunk of loose hair off my face and look up in recognition.

Elizabeth is standing there, her hand wrapped around the car keys, her backpack on her shoulder.

"What happened?" She gazes at the now-empty sideboard.

"The photos?" I tuck a strand of hair behind my ear. "I'm having that cool framing store on Meeker Street do a collage for me of coordinating frames. I want to hang them on the wall and put some new knickknacks on the table."

"You had to break everything to start over?"

"Something like that," I mutter.

"Is everything all right?" she asks. "I mean, with you and Noah?"

Elizabeth can't easily kneel down beside me on the floor, so she does a half crouch next to me. I realize her intent stare isn't on the floor. It's on my left ring finger, where I'm now wearing a three-karat sparkler.

"Where did you get this?"

I glance up at her—and it's not icy, but it's not kind, more of a deer-in-the-headlights expression. "What do you mean?"

"The ring."

"It's my wedding ring from Noah. Luckily I wasn't wearing it when I was robbed."

Elizabeth sighs. "I know you and Noah aren't married."

"What do you mean?"

"I looked it up." She shrugs. "You were married, but not to Noah."

"We live together, so I didn't think I had to be specific."

"Charlotte, I don't care that you aren't married. Why did you lie?"

"Because it's coming," I say haughtily. "And I hate being pregnant and unwed. It might seem old fashioned to you, but I don't care."

"You weren't married to your ex when you were pregnant."

"That was different." I'm done discussing the topic of both men. "Oh, I had a very enlightening conversation with Courtney today. She's not pregnant, did not sleep with Justin, and is *very* sorry for spreading false rumors." I don't feel the need to mention that Courtney stole my gun and gave it to Justin to borrow, this generation's word for steal.

Elizabeth's jaw hits the floor. "How did this come about?"

"It doesn't matter." I give her a mischievous smile. "It's taken care of." I add, "I know what it's like to have a girl come into your life and take everything away from you, because her name is Lauren." I mutter under my breath, "I want the same thing you want, Elizabeth." I study her face. "Justice."

She seems taken aback by this. "I'd love to hear what she said." Her nose wrinkles. "And how many times she mentioned Daddy's money."

"It was like talking to a psychotic wall of gibberish." I tug on my ear. "Painful, to say the least."

"Speaking of school, were you able to drop off the letters?" she asks hopefully.

"Yes. I dropped them off with Mrs. Marsh."

"Did you see anyone or speak to the principal?"

"I didn't. I told them we plan on appealing, but that's the extent of it."

"Oh." Her face fell. "I see."

"Don't worry, we will go see the principal together and make a case. It's best to let this die down in the meantime. I spoke with Courtney's father when I was there, and he said he would think about the best way to move forward." I pat her hand. "It will all work out." Then, giving her a knowing smile, I say, "We just have to stick together."

I make excuses to leave the room. Now that I know that Elizabeth Randall, née Laughlin, is machinating to amass a whole lifetime of hurt to stab me with, it's time I put my own plan into action.

CHAPTER 53
Elle

I hear Charlotte moving around upstairs, and, unable to sleep, I peer down the hall.

A sense of unrest is pitted in my stomach, and, real or imagined, I can't seem to lessen the tension.

A sliver of light casts a soft glow underneath the door.

She must be working, because she's been locked in there for hours.

My drive home was fraught with worry and resolve. I told Lauren before we left the prison parking lot that I would stay somewhere else tonight. She kept hounding me that Charlotte was teetering on the brink of insanity. I saved her in my phone under an alias, and I agreed to text her in the morning.

Except my text messages came back undeliverable.

And as I drove, I kept reflecting on snippets of our talk.

There's no room for debate on whether Lauren and Noah are married, especially now that I've seen proof that she and Noah are getting divorced.

Maybe Charlotte is really ashamed that she's still in second place to Lauren after all these years. She could be nasty to her, but it doesn't make her guilty of throwing herself down the stairs or wanting to get revenge now on Lauren.

What if it's Lauren who has another motive?

What if she's jealous because she can't have children and is upset that Noah and Charlotte reconnected so quickly and are expecting a baby? What if she has her own reasons for wanting to hurt Charlotte? I can't imagine that splitting up with a husband of ten-plus years would be easy, coupled with the fact the ink hadn't dried on the papers before he'd moved on to her old nemesis to have a child with her.

Maybe it's put Lauren over the edge.

Either way, I need to take myself out of the war zone I'm in between these two women. Charlotte, guilty or not, is no longer my target. After seeing my father today, I can no longer believe in his innocence. As hard as this is to admit to myself, I'm going to side with Nancy, Charlotte's mother, and go the route of forgiveness. If she can forgive my father after years of watching him violently beat her daughter, then I can forgive Charlotte for the choices she made under duress. I might be out on my ass in a couple months, but it's time to come clean to Charlotte that I mean her no harm but that I'm Jonathan's daughter.

And in a public place with no sharp utensils.

Resting my head in my hands, I hate that I'm so . . . conflicted. I want to hate Charlotte. But there's something raw about her and authentic and peaceful.

A trill interrupts the quiet as Charlotte's phone rings. I hear her say, "We need to talk about Lauren."

Followed by, "I mean it, Noah, this is serious."

Without warning, the office door barrels open, and I quickly nudge my bedroom door shut. Her footsteps are brisk on the staircase as she scurries downstairs for some reason. Maybe she doesn't want to risk my overhearing their private phone conversation?

A door closes with a thud downstairs, and without thinking, I'm standing in her office, the full moon creating an eerie path across the beige carpet as it beckons me to the window seat.

It's dark now, and whether she turned the light off on accident or purpose, I don't know.

Her computer screen is still on the home page and hasn't locked.

I take a deep breath. It's now or never.

A couple tabs are open at the top of the screen. One is geared toward educational literacy in the college classroom, and another is a forum for community college professors. The third is for an email account, but it asks me to enter a password.

At an impasse, I tap my fingers shakily on the keyboard. I'm up against a timer, except I don't know the duration of the countdown.

Search history, check her history! my brain screams.

When I click on the list of web pages, it goes from screaming to an all-out, full-throttle roar. Charlotte's history is a combination of articles on how to kidnap pregnant women and how to cut a fetus out of the female body, stories about women who have kidnapped pregnant women and cut the babies from the womb, and other grotesque articles on how to remove a fetus from the mother. Some are for when the mother is alive, some when she is dead.

Horrified, I encounter one link that is a forum for people with suggestions on how to lure pregnant women, like by joining Facebook groups for expectant mothers or by offering them donations. One suggests giving them free breast milk as a scheme.

I rapidly scan her desktop files and click through some Word documents. There are plenty of essays and an old syllabus she wrote for one of her classes. As I'm about to search through other files on her computer, I notice one entitled *Justin*. Shakily, I start reading a letter to Justin, *my* Justin, except it's written as if I'm the author.

Tears scald my eyes as Charlotte writes that I no longer wish to be in contact with him and blame him for his part in Charlotte's robbery, and the last part causes my hand to stroke my stomach out of fear.

Charlotte writes that I decided an abortion would be the right decision and that she took me to have the procedure. She threatens to issue a restraining order if he tries to contact me.

My heart drops in my chest with a final thud as I read the last part. She writes, *I know I thought I could set my father free, but I can't. I've visited him more in the last few months to try and prove he wasn't the monster I thought he was, but he is. He confessed to me he was his usual alcoholic self that night and doesn't remember pushing Charlotte down the stairs but was blackout drunk. I'm starting to see a therapist to talk about how I feel so I can move forward.*

Charlotte even threw in some details that she never would have known about the prison had it not been for . . .

Letters from my father.

I'm puzzled. I didn't bring any of those with me for fear she would read them. How would she have access to them? I kept them hidden in the closet at Diane's.

She went to the apartment.

No way. Diane would never talk to her. Diane doesn't even know I kept the letters.

How did Charlotte get in? Did she sweet talk the boys and search the place?

With a sinking feeling, I hastily stand, sure I'm going to be sick.

Did Charlotte already give Justin this letter?

She went to the school and dropped off handwritten notes you wrote, expressing your apologies, I remind myself.

Would she know who Justin was?

Come on, Elle, don't be an idiot. She can search him on social media as quickly as you can, and he's super active on there.

Or she could've just asked for him at the school, or waited.

I think I hear a slight creak on the staircase.

Holding my breath, I quietly shut the laptop screen so the light disappears. I set it back on the windowsill and slowly move toward the other wall.

There's a small rustle, and before I know it, a flash of light is bathing the room in a soft glow as Charlotte flicks on the switch.

We both jump, neither anticipating the other one. I don't know who's more afraid right now of the person standing in front of them, she or I.

Moving her hand to her rib cage, she squeals, "Way to take fifteen years off my life!"

I force myself to meet her eyes. "Same." Under my breath, I whisper, "But you already did."

"What're you doing in here?" She's wearing a long nightgown and robe, this one more demure than others I've seen in the past.

"I was looking for . . . I wanted some more stationery," I say lamely.

"For what?"

"To write the boys a note." I feel a sharp pain, and I tense up for a moment.

"Did the baby just kick?" Charlotte asks, eyeing my abdomen. I don't want to say yes, don't want her to touch me, the horrific topics and articles she has been reading enough to make me vomit.

I have to stay calm. I can't give Charlotte any indication I know what a freak she is. I need to go back to the bedroom, lock the door, and call 911. Immediately.

"Yes."

"Can I feel?"

"Of course," I say, her hand moving toward my belly as she keenly watches me.

Wistful, she says, "I can't wait until I feel our baby move."

"Be careful what you wish for." My face burns, and I add, "This baby might grow up to play soccer, judging by the strong legs."

"Did I ever show you the nursery?"

"No, you didn't. I was going to ask what you had in mind for colors." I fake a yawn. "Do you mind showing me in the morning? I'm tired."

"Is it from all that driving?" She tilts her head. "I bet you're exhausted from being in the car for so long."

"Well, I did make a lot of stops today," I say. "Not to mention, the project we were assigned has a lot of research to it."

"Oh, it'll be quick." She gives me a warm smile. "Just a quick peek, and then we can both go to bed."

I've assumed Charlotte has a backup key, and I watch as she unlocks the door, my toes digging into the carpet as if they could permanently attach to the fibers instead of following her in.

"Is there a reason you lock the door?" I blurt out.

"I'm terrified someone will steal my baby." She shrugs. "Or take it away from me."

When she ushers me in, she points longingly to the crib. "Do you like?"

"I do." I gush over the colors and exclaim over the rocking chair and the matching ottoman.

"It was my father's rocking chair," she says proudly.

"It must be hard to imagine him not being alive to meet your baby."

"And it's even harder with Nancy and our strained relationship." She rests her fingertips on the crib. "But I'm sure one day we'll fix it."

"You will," I say. "This is such a gorgeous nursery, Charlotte. You put interior decorators to shame."

"You think?" She beams. "I hope so." I avoid asking about the bars on the window, sure it fits into the baby-snatcher theory.

I start to make my case about going to bed when Charlotte interrupts me. "Was your day really that draining, or was it more mental than physical?"

"School is more mental, I'd say."

"Funny you say that, since you didn't go to class today." She raises her hand, exposing a small object. "Do you know what this is?"

Shaking my head, I see a tiny black box, but I don't know what it does.

"Take a stab."

"A type of recording device?"

"You're right, it's a recording of some sort." Rubbing her fingers over the smooth surface, she says, "This is what I like to call my insurance. It provides me a snapshot of the most intimate details of the people in my life."

Shit, she's been videotaping me this whole time with secret cameras? I've heard about those being mounted in the faces of teddy bears, nanny cams of some sort, to watch babysitters or catch cheating husbands. I thoroughly searched my bedroom and bathroom, along with other parts of the house. I wasn't able to locate any.

"You film people?"

"Movements, actually. This is a GPS tracker. Do you know what that is, *Elizabeth Randall?*"

My body stiffens when she uses my full name, complete with my father's last name. "It tracks locations."

"Yes, very good." She holds it up again, examining it. "So today, when you told me you had class, you actually went to the penitentiary to visit your father, the infamous baby killer Jonathan Randall." As I start to interrupt, she holds up a hand. "Let me finish. There'll be time later for you to explain what the fuck you're doing in my house."

Frozen, I rest my hands on my belly, the baby giving a larger kick than normal, which I take as an ominous warning.

"First, you shouldn't have put that many miles on our car without asking. I didn't give you permission to use Noah's BMW for that purpose. Secondly, this little gadget was able to give me constant updates and even warned me when you were speeding. I must say, I'm impressed—there were times you drove slower than the speed limit. Did you know that can be just as dangerous?"

"Don't you mean Noah and Lauren's BMW?"

Her mouth tightens. "What did you say?"

"You heard me. This pseudomarriage you have isn't working out so well, is it?"

"What are you talking about?" Her face drains of color. "Have you been talking to Lauren?"

"Does it matter?" I sigh. "You both deserve each other."

I try to maneuver around her, but she blocks the doorway. Arms crossed, she curls the corner of her lips into a snarl. "Why?"

Trembling, I look her straight in the eye. "Why what?"

"Why did you have to upset the harmonious path we were both on, Elizabeth?" A hand reaches down to my burgeoning belly. "I'd moved on from my past, and I must say, I've kept to myself for a long, long time. Why did you have to come and upset the life I've built?"

"Because you ruined the one I didn't get a chance to build with my father."

"I did not." She throws her hands up in the air. "Look, your father can spew out all the bullshit lies he wants to, it's his specialty, but he's in prison for what he did to me, is he not?"

"He is."

"So, what's the problem?" she groans. "Why did you come here looking for trouble?"

"I didn't." I gulp. "It wasn't intentional."

She takes a step forward and yanks hard on a piece of my hair. "Let's try this again. You did or did not come to my house intentionally, knowing who I was?"

"I did."

"Okay, we're clear on that. You sought me out for what reason?"

"To meet you."

Her fingers move to my neck, and she squeezes. "You wanted to mess up my life and make me pay for your father's mistakes?"

"No, I just wanted to know why."

"Why what?" Charlotte lets out a shrill squeak. "Why he's rotting in jail and I'm here?" She snickers. "Because he's guilty, Elizabeth. Don't you understand, little girl?" She scrunches her nose. "Nothing you do can change what he did. Or save my baby. And now, I have more of a claim to the one you're carrying. An eye for an eye, shall we say?"

"Please," I beg her, "please don't do this. Charlotte, I'm not trying to hurt you."

"And to think I brought a surprise for you." Out of the front pocket of her robe, she hands me an envelope. "This is for you." I expect it to be a copy of the letter she wrote on my behalf to Justin. Instead, it's a letter stating I've formally been withdrawn from the alternative high school I just started attending.

Complete with Diane's signature.

"I recently spoke to Diane, and with a generous donation, she's agreed to let you part company with her, under the table, of course, until you turn eighteen in a few months. I needed her signature on a few forms, and I thought you'd be much happier this way."

"Not going to school?"

"I thought you'd be grateful." She feigns hurt. "You should be thrilled. You hated going."

"I . . . I don't know what to say."

Charlotte claps her hands together. "The next few months you'll be on house arrest." She caresses my cheek. "I have a feeling it'll be more bed rest." She points to the twin mattress still in its plastic wrap. "This will be your new quarters."

"Wh-what . . . ?" I stammer. "Why?"

"I want to make sure nothing happens to the baby."

I shouldn't even ask, but it slips out before I can stop it. "But what about after the baby comes? What do you intend to do with me then?"

"Don't worry, I don't plan on hurting you, sweetie." She tucks a lock of my hair behind my ear, sending a shiver down my spine. "You'll be promoted to the role of nanny."

She's opening her mouth to speak when we're interrupted by a door slamming and a male voice in the foyer yelling out, "Charlotte!"

"Be right down!" she hollers, kicking the door of the nursery shut behind us. "Don't bother screaming for Noah. This was his idea. He suggested you as the solution to our problem," Charlotte warns. "But if I shared with him that you were Jonathan's child, he'd kill you right now with his bare hands. He'd never want a baby from a Randall."

She guides me to the corner where the twin mattress is laid against the wall. There're a couple of boxes and a roll of packing tape, items she's ostensibly planning to return to the store.

The evil side, the Hyde side, is on full display as Charlotte grabs me roughly by the nape of the neck. "Or," she says with a shrug, "go ahead and press your luck. Being locked in here is much better than being dead, but I'm not the betting kind."

It's pointless, the start of my scream drowned out by the sticky mat of the tape clamped down on my mouth. When I reach my hands up to touch the adhesive painfully affixed to my lips, she slaps a pair of cuffs around my wrists so they are tethered in front of me.

"Shh . . ." She gives my cheek a sharp slap. "We don't want to make Noah regret coming home tonight."

With a soft smile, she gently guides me down onto the rough plastic of the bed. "It's been a very interesting evening. Get some sleep, Elizabeth Randall."

CHAPTER 54
Charlotte

"Surprise!" Noah calls from the bottom of the stairs, except there's no glee in his tone. The opposite, in fact. His eyes dart around the dark living room, and for once, no suitcase rests at his heel. His gaze is narrowed at the wall frames and his constant presence in them.

"Noah." My mouth drops to the floor. "What're you doing here?"

"You're not happy to see me?" He cackles. "That makes two of us."

"It's not that. I didn't expect you home. You scared me." I reach behind to make sure the door is securely locked, with Elizabeth behind it. "And you shouldn't come over unannounced in the middle of the night like this."

"Is someone here?" Noah looks at me suspiciously. "I thought I heard you talking to someone." His stance seems guarded, hands on his hips, his expression unreadable.

"Just myself," I say. "Who else would it be?"

"Whoever you've been seeing. That ring on your finger is blinding me from down here." He curses. "Dammit, I knew I wasn't the only one."

Before I can respond with the truth, he briskly climbs the stairs and roughly grabs my hand. His mouth plummets to the floor. "Wait, what are you doing wearing Lauren's engagement ring?" He glances down at the large oval diamond on my finger. "I had that sealed tightly in a box."

"It got stuck," I pout.

"Where is her diamond wedding band?" His lips tug into a frown. "I hope that's not part of your jewelry collection now."

"I only meant to try it on," I offer quietly.

He sidesteps around me in the hallway and walks toward the office.

"Why do you have it?" I say, following on his heel. "I thought it was over."

"She packed up a bunch of stuff for safekeeping. Guess she didn't plan on wearing them anymore. What does it matter?" He then says pointedly, "I didn't know I had to worry about someone snooping through my personal belongings."

Baffled, I wrap my robe tighter around my expansive waist.

"Where's your laptop? I need to show you something."

"It's in the office," I murmur, trailing him. "Let me grab it, and we can take it downstairs. I can make you some coffee or tea, if you want. Or a nightcap."

"No." He strides across the room and picks it up. "There's no time."

"No time?"

My hands shake as he seats himself on the edge of the desk, as if he's a professor about to deliver some bad news to the class.

"Have a seat." He motions toward the window seat. "This won't take long." I perch on the window ledge, nervous that somehow Elizabeth will remove the tape and start screaming bloody murder. I'm trying to save her child, not endanger it.

With the icy tension between us, every sound is magnified. When I hear a small thump against the shared wall, I instantly freeze.

Noah also notices it. "Are you sure no one is here?" He stands up and taps on the wall where the noise came from.

"Anyone in there?" he hollers.

Closing my eyes, I reach for my necklace, rubbing the cross in prayer. *Please don't answer, Elizabeth, please don't,* I silently plead.

"No one is here." I point at my attire. "Would I wear this ratty old thing?"

"You are, for me," he reproaches. Thrusting the laptop at me, he says, "What's your password?"

Impatient, I pluck it out of his grasp. "I'll enter it." I click out of the open tabs before handing it back to him. He moves from his stance on the desk to sit directly next to me, our thighs touching. For some reason, in this moment, the intimacy I crave with him troubles me.

I watch as he logs in to his email, where a new folder has appeared, one with my name on it. Apprehensive, I twist my fingers in my lap as I glance at the large quantity of emails stored here.

"A lot, huh?" He points to the massive list, with my email address present on every line. "Why do you keep harassing her?" He runs a hand through his hair. "Why can't you leave her alone?"

"I don't know what you're talking about." I shrug. "How do I know it's not spam?"

"Lauren told me about the gift you sent to the house," he grunts. "The jumbo box of pregnancy tests with a note that said, 'Keep trying, don't give up.'"

I hunch over in silence, staring at the ring on my finger that's not meant for me. That belongs to *her.*

"And now you're going to apologize."

Dubious, I ask, "You want me to write her an email?"

"Yes." He grabs my shoulder. "Don't worry. I'll tell you what to say."

"I think I'm capable of writing an apology note."

"No." He glares at me. "Verbatim, word for word, you will write what I say. Log in to your email."

I ignore his command. "Did you move the boxes in the garage?"

"I've been slowly moving things out, yes."

"Where are you taking them?" Trying to keep from becoming hysterical, I intone, "Back to Lauren's?"

"This obsession with Lauren has never been useful, Charlotte." His hazel eyes flash with green sparks, and his tone drips acid. "Never. Not everything is tied to Lauren and me. We are getting divorced. Finished. She isn't your competition. Or your worst enemy."

He leans closer, never removing his steely gaze from my face. "You are."

"Are you moving out?"

"I never moved in."

"I thought you wanted to store your stuff here while you figured it out?"

"I did, and I have."

I whisper, "What do you mean?"

His jaw is set as he contemplates me. "It's over between us, Charlotte."

Woeful, I reach for his arm. "We're not doing this old song and dance again, are we?"

"Charlotte, cut the shit." Noah shakes out of my grip. "It's time we both come clean."

I slam my hands on my thighs. "Why are you being so hateful?"

"I'm not," he sighs. "But there isn't a baby."

Pointing at himself and then back to me, he says, "*We* are not having a baby together."

Angrily, I motion at my midsection. "How do you explain this, then?"

"You cheated, or actually"—he rubs a hand through his hair—"it's not cheating, because we're not even together. I assumed it was someone else's, which is why I've been so distant lately."

I feel like I've been slapped, or worse, punched. "I would never cheat on you."

"Then explain to me how this immaculate conception happened?"

"I don't understand." I'm sure a look of confusion crosses my face. "From having sex."

"Charlotte, I had a vasectomy."

Speechless, I watch as the world blurs in front of me, and I feel like I'm going to be sick. I prop myself against the window, my shoulders sagging. "They aren't always foolproof."

"We've only had sex, what, a few times? And only once was unprotected."

"I got pregnant before," I say defiantly.

"Charlotte, listen to me." It's like I'm coming toward a head-on collision, and I'm the one who's going to be severely hurt and receive the brunt of the damage. "I had a vasectomy after you got pregnant the first time."

"But you want kids . . ."

"No, I don't." He grimaces. "And I certainly don't want them with you."

I stand up, stunned, as he cuts me to the quick with the daggers in his eyes, even from his seated position below me.

"Come on, Charlotte, I'm not in the mood for your mindless entertainment. It's late, and I have to get going."

"How could you lead me on again?" Then I murmur, more to myself than to him, "How could I let you lead me on again?"

"Don't you get it? I wasn't trying to, Char. You offered me a place to stay when I was in town . . ." He adds, "Then, when I said Lauren and I were separating, you begged me to use your garage for storage. Except you just kept moving my stuff into the house."

I interject, "And you had it all worked out, didn't you? A free place to stay, a warm body to sleep with—"

"That's not fair. I told you we shouldn't sleep together. Especially with the past breathing fire down our necks. I was concerned with how vulnerable you might still be, and I told you so."

"You're the one who keeps toying with my emotions, Noah!" I screech.

"Charlotte, you are one of the most vindictive and spiteful people I know." He jabs a finger in my face. "I remember college, and all the shit you pulled. And even now, you're no better."

"Why did you come back, then?" I demand, stepping back until I hit the edge of the desk.

"I was lonely the first time." He rubs his chin. "It's not even a good answer, but I was. And this time, I had something to tell you. I thought you deserved the truth."

He points to the laptop. "Check your email." I'm about to argue when he nods at me. "If you want the truth, you'll have to."

I sink down into the desk chair, afraid to breathe as I enter my password and my in-box fills the screen.

Except there is nothing new from last time I checked.

"Nothing's here." I thrust the laptop at him.

He takes it out of my hands and says, "I know." Putting his hand on his heart, he speaks. "My truth is right here."

We consider each other for a moment. I want to slap him, run my nails down his perfect nose, but I don't. I wait.

"When you got pregnant the first time, I freaked out. I went from a broken engagement to eloping, and you call me out of the blue and drop this bomb on me. I told you I didn't want you to have it, that I didn't want a child. You blatantly disregarded everything I said like it was just *your* life that would change." He runs a frustrated hand through his hair. "I even sent you money to go to the clinic."

It feels as if lava is coursing through my veins, as if every square inch of me is on fire.

"Then I thought: Okay, she wants a kid, hopefully she'll raise it with Jonathan, and he'll play the daddy role, and we'll all move on with our lives. But you couldn't, could you? You had to call and tell me he's abusive and lay all this shit on me." He takes a breath. "I was barely twenty-five. How could you think I'd want my kid raised in that environment?"

"I thought we would raise *our* child," I say bluntly. "Together."

He stares at me in awe. "Oh yeah, sure, like that was in the cards."

"It was never about the child, was it?" I shout. "It was always about your own selfish needs."

Noah screams, "I didn't and don't want children, which I expressly communicated to you!"

I glare at him. "I thought Lauren wanted kids."

"She did." He rubs a hand over his tired eyes. "I never told her about my vasectomy. She thought the infertility was her fault, but it wasn't. I made the choice to have one on my own. I just blamed her for it."

"Is that why she left you?" I snap. "She finally found out?"

"No." Noah stares at me and says point blank, "You need to forgive him."

"Who, Jonathan?" I yelp. "Don't you dare start on me with the forgiveness shit." I flail my arms at him, and he responds by standing up and over me, the anger on his face raw, much like I imagine mine is. He grabs my arms and holds them tight to my sides in a viselike grip.

"It wasn't him that pushed you that night."

I can't move, both because my arms are forced into my sides but also because I'm rooted to the spot.

Laconically, Noah admits, "It was me, that night. Not Jonathan."

And now I'm going to suffocate. I sit absolutely still, the fight sucked out of my lifeless body.

"What're you talking about?" I feel like a deranged person whose cage has just been rattled. "I never saw you that night."

Resignedly, he says, "I know. That's why I'm standing here now."

I tilt my head in horror as he continues. "Jonathan left the first time, and you were hysterical. You came outside wailing at him, the cops came, and then you called him to come back."

"But I felt him grab me . . ."

"No, you *thought* he came back inside and shoved you. And it makes sense: he had just slammed the door and left." Noah shoves his knuckles in his mouth. "But I did. You were bent over and messing with something in the entryway, and I don't know what came over me, it just . . . I didn't even go there with that intention, but when I saw him, and then you, and . . . I just, I pushed you."

The ragged breaths I take sound like gasping wheezes.

I manage to spit out, "But why?"

"Lauren and I were married. I knew it would destroy her and us if she found out I slept with you. That would be the end of us. And I'd be tied to you and a baby, and Jonathan was a ticking time bomb . . . it wasn't long before something bad was going to happen. I almost saw it as doing you and the baby a favor."

"Were you trying to kill me?"

He hangs his head.

I wait for him to deny it, but he doesn't.

The face that I used to consider handsome now looks ugly to me, the monster in him finally appearing in the flesh. Selfish and self-serving, egotistical and now maniacal. The future I built a house of cards on has just folded in on itself like a cheap bridge table.

"I don't know what my mind-set was at that point. I just wanted out of the whole situation and out of your life."

"You have to, you have to tell someone." I beg, "You have to tell the truth."

"No. I can't. I'll never admit to this again. I just thought you should know." He rubs a hand over his face, as if to diminish me. "Don't you get it, Charlotte? We can never be together. Our entire friendship has been filled with lies and half truths and reads like a soap opera. I just want a sense of normalcy back." He pauses. "But I have to know: Whose pregnancy test and sonogram did you send me?"

"It doesn't matter. Just a friend." I shake my head, and I don't know what I'm denying, but it's all I can do, the only movement I can make, as I sit in shock. The trauma of his admission, the guilt, now overcomes me.

Jonathan Randall isn't the monster I thought he was.

And his only daughter is locked up in the next room over because of me.

Worse yet, I convinced her Noah was in on this, and now we're both stuck in our own prisons.

CHAPTER 55
Elle

As I'm sitting on the uncomfortable mattress, my back against the wall, I'm tempted to throw myself against the bright, soothingly painted walls of hell and cause a commotion, one Noah and Charlotte can't ignore.

But something holds me back.

A gut instinct, my intuition, maybe?

Charlotte said Noah wanted a baby, but not that he knew I was Jonathan Randall's daughter.

But there's something else.

Maybe it was how cold and uncaring his voice sounded when he entered the house, or the surrender, as if he had nothing left to give, so he would lay it all out.

But what, I wonder, does Noah have to tell Charlotte that she doesn't already know?

With my ear to the wall and my body as slack as one can be when their hands are bound by harsh metal, I listen to the inflection of their voices, both hurt and angry.

Carefully, I peel at the tape on my mouth, giving out a little yelp when I finagle the last piece off my lips. The admission that Noah makes is earth shattering, and I start to perspire, beads of sweat pooling in the crease underneath my tender breasts.

When I asked my father if anyone else was at the house that evening, my next guess for revenge would've been Lauren. In terms of a motive, if I had just married someone and found out they knocked up a chick during a one-night stand during a relationship break—and not only another woman, but also one I despised—then that would give me plenty of ammunition to hurt her.

Plus, Lauren supposedly couldn't have children.

Not even my father mentioned her as a possibility.

But in Noah's case, my father probably thought he didn't have the balls. He was right that there was no reason to look at Noah. A perfect record, good looks, steady income, and by all accounts, a kindhearted and decent person.

But then you have the evil undercurrent that was running beneath the surface, hidden to everyone above.

My father was the perfect fall guy.

In a sense, Noah's plan was ingenious.

My father had a prior record, a history of abuse that could be confirmed with pictures and medical records, and a drinking problem.

Last known person to see the victim.

There would be no other suspects.

Even the cops were involved that night in the dispute as my father packed up to go.

And worse yet, who's to say he wouldn't have eventually put a fist through another wall or hurt Charlotte or Noah when he eventually found out the child wasn't his?

But it wasn't him. It wasn't my father, Jonathan Randall.

I can picture that night as Noah sat in the dark, staring at his wedding band, a newly minted husband with a wife at home and a pregnant girlfriend inside.

He was confused, frantic, irrational.

But most of all, he was terrified he would lose the future he had begun and be tied to a past he didn't want.

He took a gamble.

My father left, and Noah had to decide. Now or never. All he had to do was throw a hand over her eyes and shove. By the time she realized what was happening, she'd be at the bottom of the stairs, either dead or gravely injured.

I'm tempted to give a brief round of applause to Noah Wilder.

He's brilliant and unremorseful, watching someone else spend a decade in prison for his crime while he climbed the corporate ladder.

And poor Lauren, to be led to think she couldn't have kids because Noah got snipped without telling her. And Charlotte, who has driven herself to insanity for someone she wants so badly, someone who is like a drug she can't quit.

I'm starting to get angry at everyone involved, pitying my father as he swore his innocence up and down while we ignored his cries. We hung him based solely on his past before he even went to jail.

As I gnaw on the inside of my cheek, the temptation to shout and kick and hit every fucking thing in the room becomes paralyzing. It isn't until I realize that the room next to me is no longer filled with Charlotte's wails and Noah's apathetic rebuttals, but quiet, that I get scared about what's coming next.

CHAPTER 56
Charlotte

The overwhelming urge to hit him overpowers me.

His choices, his lies—they affected my life, the trajectory of it, and the course of his daughter's, not to mention those of everyone else involved.

There's nowhere to go; the chair is pressed against the wood as it rubs into my skin.

"Get away from me."

He takes a small step back.

"Farther."

Rolling his eyes upward, he says, "You aren't in charge, Charlotte," but still takes another step backward. If he doesn't move, I am prepared to pummel him in the face, my anger boiling at the surface, ready to explode if it gets just one degree hotter.

"I can't have children because of you." I bury my head in my hands, and that fateful day I heard the news flashes back. The conversation with the fertility specialist still plays in my head, as if she's sitting across from me right now, discussing my broken female organs.

"I know when you had that tragic fall, they were concerned about saving not just the baby's life, but your own. What happened to you is . . .

unfathomable. No other words for it. Let me remind you, Charlotte, you are courageous and strong and put your abuser away. I admire you."

And with that, my future was sealed as a barren woman. And so was Jonathan's.

"So now for this email." Noah's shrill voice interrupts my thoughts, but I don't bother looking up at him, preferring to stare at my lap. "I'll dictate it as you type it."

"You still want me to apologize to your wife over email?"

"Yes."

"You're crazy."

"No, you are. And you have gone crazy." He chuckles. "Truly, it can only be viewed as that."

I lock hateful eyes with him, the green faded back to hazel. He adds, "You know what? You're right. You can't be trusted to properly convey what I want it to say. I'll take care of it." He raises an eyebrow at me as he types. "You're apologizing to Lauren for how you have treated her over the years, specifically the unintended and spiteful pregnancy. That you lied to me about being on the pill, and you slept with me to try and get back at her. When you found out we got married, in anger, you threw yourself down the stairs for attention, thinking I would leave her then."

"But that's not true . . ."

"Then you're going to tell her that you can't live with the lies, that the guilt is too much. What you put Jonathan through, and me, and her." He gives me a sad glance as his fingers fly over the keyboard. "And the baby. Killing your child because you were unbalanced . . . that's the tragedy. And as we approach the decade mark, it's too much for you to live with."

He continues. "And as for your current pregnancy, you've been faking it. All a hoax." He hits enter and with a devious wink shuts the laptop.

Noah reaches for my swollen belly. "You think I couldn't tell you were wearing a fake pregnancy bump?"

I blush as he commands me to stand up. He lifts the maternity shirt I'm wearing to reveal the bodysuit underneath, the silicone bump realistic until you uncover it.

Touching it, he murmurs, "Wow, that really is misleading, but well played." He whistles. "I bet you'll be relieved to stop wearing it."

"Yes," is all I can muster.

"I must tell you: I'm relieved you're not pregnant. I wouldn't want to be responsible for the death of another unborn child." He snorts, pulling a small orange bottle out of his pocket. "I'm going to give you two of these to take."

"What for?" I glimpse at the label. "What're they?"

"Headache medicine."

"Bullshit."

"You're right. They are a little stronger than the average pill." He shakes a couple into his palm. "Fentanyl. It's an opiate for all the pain you're in."

"Are you serious?"

"Do I not look serious enough?" He brushes a sweaty piece of hair off my temple. "You wrote your suicide note, are you not ready?" Reaching forward, he pushes his finger down my throat, causing me to gag. "You'll swallow both of these, understand?"

My eyes water as I choke. "Don't worry, Char, it'll be a quick and painless death." He clasps my chin in his hand. "You always wanted us to be together. I'll be right here with you in your final breaths."

"Elizabeth!" I scream at the top of my lungs. "Elizabeth, help. Please help me!" My slaps at his hands are useless as he slides the lethal dose into my mouth, my only defense biting down on his finger, which only angers and impels him to shove them deeper down my windpipe.

CHAPTER 57
Elle

Terrified at the coldness of Noah's hardened voice, I imagine it slitting Charlotte into pieces, sliver by sliver, like a knife. Until he jabs it straight into her heart.

Charlotte's moaning something, but it's muffled, and I strain to hear through the wall.

I gasp as it turns into a shriek.

My name.

She keeps repeating it over and over, begging me to come save her. I move my hands to cover my face in fear. Noah didn't know I was here until now. If he's going to commit one murder, actually two now, a third is a nonissue. And, thanks to Charlotte, who just sealed my fate, he's going to kill me and the baby next.

In fact, it'll be perfect. Another perfect crime for Noah Wilder.

With her dead and desperate for a baby, he could claim she killed me in a rage after discovering my true identity and then committed suicide.

And now that she needs saving, she's dragging me into the fire. As if I can help her from this room with bars on the window and a lock on the door.

But I don't care about her. Or Noah.

I care about the baby who's just landed a kick in the middle of my abdomen. It's that baby's life that matters, the sonogram safely tucked in my notebook. I can't be the next victim of either of these two lunatics.

Trying to make an escape to the outside is useless, the bars too close together to even get a wrist out, let alone my entire body. I crawl on my hands and knees on the carpet over to the closet. I have to search for something to use as a weapon of self-defense.

It will be only a matter of time before Noah finds the key on Charlotte and appears in the doorway. I have to be ready to face him and defend myself. Being pregnant, I can't move and bend like I normally do. My movements are wobbly and unsteady instead of agile, which greatly affects my ability to fight off Noah.

As I awkwardly try to shift my weight to search through the closet, my hands tire because of the cold metal around my wrists. Unfortunately, the endless rainbow of baby clothes and bottles is not helpful to my situation.

I pause for a second.

Last time I was sneaking around the house, I was interrupted by the phone when I was in here. I ran downstairs without taking the key with me.

The other key is my way out.

But did Charlotte find it and take it with her?

Clawing at the carpet with my fingers, I push and pull the thick fibers apart, my wrists aching, to search for the tiny but important piece of metal, my concentration shot as Charlotte lets out a painful sob.

My head swivels as I hear my name again, this time out of the mouth of Noah.

Frantic, I paw through the strands, and my fingernail makes contact with something sharp that stabs the skin underneath.

It's not the key but a nail.

I push up off my knees, my heavy body hard to lift without the full mobility of my hands. Scanning the room, I see nothing but furniture to use to protect myself. The ottoman is now my only weapon—it's that or breaking a piece of wood from the crib, nearly impossible with my limited capabilities.

Startled, I hear a loud crash from the other room.

Then my eyes widen as I watch the door handle start to move, slowly turning as someone tugs on it from the other side.

You're safe, I tell myself. *It's still locked, and Charlotte has the key.*

Except I hear a clink followed by a snap, signaling the lock's removal.

Charlotte's scream interrupts the silence as Noah yells in return. She must be fighting him, because I hear a thump and then signs of a struggle. Both pant and grunt like boxers in a ring, neither ready to stay down and admit defeat.

I don't know what's worse: knowing violence is mere feet away and not being able to see it, or knowing it's about to intrude upon your space and there's nothing you can do to stop it. Either way, it's bad.

I'm in shock, riveted to the carpet, my head sweeping left to right and back again as I wait for my turn. This goes on for what seems like minutes but is probably a matter of seconds. The howling increases in noise but the voices die down, as if there's nothing left to say between the two of them, their secrets out in the open.

Suddenly, a loud stamp pierces the silence, then complete and utter silence.

My ear pressed against the door, I hesitate, afraid to enter the outside realm yet scared to stay on the inside. Stay in prison or face Noah and Charlotte.

As I'm about to chance it, I hear the lock click again and watch in dread as the handle twists open, my body still resting against the door. Expecting Noah, I back up a few steps, holding my belly as if I can protect the baby from the sight of him.

Instead of Noah, it's Charlotte, or the ghost of her. Her fingernails are tinged blue, and her pupils are nothing but tiny dots. Her breathing is shallow, and it seems to take all her oxygen to whisper, "Run, go get help."

Trembling, she reaches a hand around my ankle and moans "I'm sorry" before her eyes roll back in her head and a gurgle escapes her discolored lips.

I'm fixed to the spot, my body convulsing at the sight of Charlotte's lifeless body, the nude bodysuit showing beneath the ripped nightgown, her robe nowhere in sight.

I strain to hear footsteps as I peek behind her, the whereabouts of Noah unknown. I'm afraid he's ready to pounce as soon as I exit the room.

A shot of adrenaline rushes through my overstimulated body, and I sprint into my bedroom, frantically locking the door behind me. I might have energy, but it's not the good kind. My brain fog is heavy, to the point where processing information is impossible. I whisper to myself what I need to do. "Find your phone, call 911."

I search the room, unclear where I left it, my eyes darting to the bed and dresser, before the realization dawns on me. *My cell's on the nightstand.*

She disconnected it. *Will it even work?*

Numb, I stab at the numbers on the screen, the cuffs delaying my bumbling movements as I dial 911. A woman answers on the first ring. "What is your emergency?"

The words tumble out as I tell the dispatcher what happened. It's hard for her to understand what I'm saying as I stammer through answers to questions about Noah and what happened to Charlotte. I didn't see any blood or stab wounds, nor did I hear a gunshot. I just know she's unmoving.

After I confirm that an ambulance and the police are on their way, I have a decision to make: run outside or stay locked in my bedroom.

Am I able to jump from the balcony?

I peer outside through the curtains, and though it's hard to see much of anything in the dark, the drop would be far too steep to manage in my normal state and impossible while pregnant.

"Ma'am, are you still there?" the dispatcher chirps from the speaker.

"Yes," I whisper, "I'm going to go outside." I don't hear what she says next, muting the phone in case Noah hears the sound.

I slowly unlock the door, certain he will launch himself on me with a surprise attack.

It's eerily quiet now that Charlotte's no longer making noise, her body sprawled to the left of me, soundless as she sleeps.

Or at least that's what I tell myself. She's just having a peaceful rest. Maybe he drugged her with sleeping pills. I can't grasp death yet, because I have to focus on my own survival.

Because usually Noah enters from the garage, the front door is still shut, and I nervously edge toward the staircase, jumping at the hum of the radiator from the basement. As I tiptoe down the stairs, I notice the basement door is slightly ajar, the padlock still hanging from the handle.

I rush past it to the kitchen, the butcher block full of knives on the countertop. I grab the biggest blade. My hands haven't stopped shaking since they were cuffed together.

As I start to pass the basement door, I notice a flash of color coming up the stairs.

Startled, I turn to slam the door shut and snap the lock back into place.

I'm not strong enough.

Noah's on the other side, pushing with all his weight against my lesser force. It's hard to get a grip on anything, and my phone drops in the process, shattering when it hits the ground.

In that split second when my attention diverts to my broken screen, he's able to shove the door open as I crash backward into the wall directly in front of him.

We stare at each other.

With menacing eyes, he reaches for my throat and wraps a rope he must've found in the basement around my neck like a noose. He starts to tug it closed as I choke.

You have to fight! I scream internally. *Fight or you'll never get a chance. You'll lose consciousness.*

I thrust the knife forward as hard as I can, and the shiny blade disappears into his stomach. His eyes register shock as his hands drop from my neck to feel where the redness has appeared. I pull back and launch it again into his skin, pushing with all my strength as he takes a step backward. Then I repeat the motion, aiming for another spot that isn't bleeding through his shirt.

He staggers backward through the open basement door, loses his balance, and falls backward down the staircase. His hands reach out to grasp for something to save him, the railing, but it's broken. And right now, I can't focus on the fact that I was going to ask him to replace it.

He lets out a bloodcurdling scream, but I ignore it by slamming the door shut. I padlock it and move toward the dead bolt, my hands covered in bright red that I can't imagine is blood.

I awkwardly reach for my phone, a tough feat as it slithers out of my grip, the sturdy voice of the 911 operator long gone. My movements are clumsy as I hurry to unlock the dead bolt, the phone in my outstretched fingers.

Taking one last backward glance, I glimpse Charlotte's body through the wide-open slats of the railing, her arm sprawled out as if she's reaching for someone to save her. The only one she ever wanted was a snake pretending to be Prince Charming.

The door swings open in my face. Relieved, I assume it's the paramedics or police.

It's neither.

A dark-haired woman gapes at me.

"Oh, Lauren, oh my God, thank God you're here."

425

She starts to say something but stops as she takes in my disheveled appearance. Her eyes narrow at the sight of the dark red soaking into my clothes.

"What happened?" She takes a hurried step forward when she sees the blood. "The baby, she tried to get the baby, didn't she?"

"Noah," I heave. "He lost it." I motion behind me. "And so did she."

"What're you doing here?" Her face is stony. "I thought you were staying somewhere else tonight?"

"It doesn't matter." I try to step around Lauren, but she blocks my exit. "What're you doing here?"

"Noah sent me a weird message and asked me to meet him here." She reaches out to touch my wrists. "Then I got a weird email. It read like a suicide note, but it was from Charlotte, and I never know what's going through her head. She sends me lots of distraught emails." She shudders as I shake my head. "I was worried about you both."

"Lauren, you don't want to go inside," I say. "He's dead."

She acts like she doesn't hear me. Instead, she steps around me to enter the foyer. "I was worried. Every time I called your phone, it kept going straight to voice mail."

"Charlotte had it disconnected," I say. "I realized after I got home it wasn't working, that texts weren't going through." I add frantically, "Lauren, you don't want to go up there."

She ignores me and starts to head toward the staircase, peering upstairs. Her face crumples as she stares at Charlotte's body above us. "What is going on? Did she . . . did she kill Noah?"

"I did," I barely whisper.

Shock registers on her face as she catches hold of the railing. "What?"

"He tried to kill me." I add, "After he killed Charlotte."

"No, why would he hurt you?" She looks stunned, her clutch tightening on the banister to hold herself up.

426

"Did you know Noah pushed Charlotte down the stairs so she lost their baby?"

"No." She juts her chin out defiantly. "He wouldn't do that."

"Noah, not Jonathan, should be in prison."

The two of us stand and face each other, our eyes locked in an ugly showdown, and I finally win out, if you can call it that, as her shoulders start to shake. Her tiny frame hunches over as tears fill her eyes. She lets out a guttural sound, like a wounded animal would.

"Where is he?"

"In the basement." I hold my trembling hands up. "But it's locked."

Lauren walks slowly to the basement door, as if she's walking to her own funeral. "Where's the key?"

"I don't have it." I turn on my heel, feeling an urgency to be away from all three of them, unable to trust that anyone in that house doesn't have blood on their hands in some shape or form.

I walk as fast as I can all the way to the end of the drive as sirens blare in the distance. Unable to hold myself up anymore, I keel over, vomiting on the pristine yard that looks like it's straight out of an advertisement in *House & Garden* magazine.

Lauren comes out and sits on the steps, her head in her hands. We don't speak, both keeping our distance.

When the cops show up, I recognize Officer Sparrow.

"I guess bad things do happen in the suburbs, huh?" He greets me with a tip of his hat. "That or it follows you wherever you go."

All I can do is stare at him solemnly and point in the direction of the house.

EPILOGUE
Elle

Four months later

I'm sitting in the living room of my apartment, or I should say *our* apartment, my father's and mine, when a knock on the door startles me as I'm putting the finishing touches on my writing assignment for class. I'm trying to get it all out of the way before the baby comes.

I stayed at the alternative school—the schedule was easier to work around—and I'm trying to make up for lost time this summer. My father promised to send me to community college to start with, and I have a newfound appreciation for education now that it doesn't seem like an unattainable goal.

"You stay put." He motions for me to stay seated. I couldn't get up if I wanted to without help, my belly swollen to the size of a watermelon.

I hear a voice I know all too well, and I don't know whether to feel relieved or agitated. They have never met, and it's odd having it be right now, after what happened.

"You have a visitor," my father says as the guest enters our small but tidy living room.

I nod as Justin steps toward me, his tentative steps a far cry from his usual self-confident gait. The skateboard is nowhere in sight.

"Are you good?" My father raises a brow at me, his overprotective instincts kicking in when it comes to me and the opposite sex.

"Yes." He ushers Justin forward, and with one fleeting glance over his shoulder, he gives us space to be alone. I haven't seen Justin since that time in the hospital, a vague memory. After the police and paramedics came to Charlotte's, I passed out from shock. He came by with flowers, but I was out of it.

After that, the weeks passed in a whirlwind. My father was released from prison after Lauren found evidence incriminating Noah.

Noah had practiced writing the suicide note for Charlotte on his own paper before deciding to email it. Probably because they didn't have the same handwriting, and it would be easy to trace back to him. Unbeknownst to Noah, Charlotte also had her laptop recording their conversation that fateful night, and his admissions were no longer his dirty secret.

It was hard for Lauren to reconcile the fact that Noah had lied to her about the reason for their inability to conceive and that he had been the one to push Charlotte down the stairs. Not to mention killing her.

The irony is not lost on me that Noah died of a broken neck from a fall down the basement stairs, exactly how Charlotte lost their child and almost her life.

Justin tried to contact me, but I had nothing to say. Our problems and relationship seemed so minimal compared with the big picture of reuniting with my father and giving birth to a child.

"Mind if I sit?" Justin points to the opposite side of the couch.

"Be my guest."

"I owe you a lot, but I could only give you a little." He shifts his body so he's facing me. "And I'm sorry. I understand why you haven't returned any of my calls. I deserve all of the anger you have for me. And you're right and wrong on certain things, so I'm going to clear the air with us, once and for all, before our baby girl comes."

"Wait, how did you know it was a girl?"

Sheepish, he grins. "You think your father can keep his mouth shut?"

"It would do him a world of good if he did," I mumble.

"Elizabeth, you have to know. Nothing happened with Courtney. I didn't cheat with Courtney, and I never touched her. I swear on our little girl's life: that was a vicious rumor. There was . . . nothing. Not one ounce of truth to that. She never thought she was pregnant or nothing."

He takes a deep breath. "And I'm sorry I let her convince me you were cheating on me. I feel so dumb."

"Thank you for that," I say softly.

"And about the mugging. Courtney did give me the gun. That's why we were texting in the first place. I did it. I tried to hold Charlotte up in the grocery store parking lot. Courtney wasn't supposed to give me a real gun; she said it was fake. It was just supposed to be a scare tactic. I put Charlotte's cards and ID in your stuff because I thought no one would ever find it."

"But why?"

"I didn't have the money to even help with an . . ." He can't say the word out loud now that the baby is a real thing between us, my belly ready to burst with new life. "I'm sorry, I thought it could be a new start for us. Away from Diane, away from Charlotte. I didn't trust her. If she was everything we thought she was, stealing from her was a better deal than you being kicked out of Diane's at some point."

I nod. It's not a good reason, but I can understand his train of thought.

"It was stupid, and I never meant to scare her or hurt her." He whispers, "We just needed money."

Curious, I ask, "How did you find Charlotte, if she wasn't at the college?"

"I followed her from her house." He leans his elbows on his knees, a lock of hair falling over his eye. "She was headed in your direction, and when she made a detour, it seemed like the right place to mug her."

"Well, you succeeded in that."

"It's terrible, all of this." He brushes a hand through his hair. It feels weird to discuss Charlotte now that she's dead. Noah gave her a lethal dose of an already-potent opiate. The paramedics tried to reverse the effects of the fentanyl with naloxone, or Narcan, but it was too late.

I shudder as Justin continues. "And I can't stand the thought of you raising the baby alone."

"Don't worry. I'm not." I grin. "Grandpa Randall is going to help."

My father hollers from the other room, "Geez, can you stop calling me Grandpa? You're aging me."

"That's not what I meant about you being a single mom."

"I know, Justin." I sigh heavily. "But I'm just getting to know my father for the first time in my life. There's no way I could move halfway across the country from him when I'm finally getting to know him."

"I understand." His eyes are a deep shade of green, part of the reason I fell in love with him—how I could get lost in them. If it was ever that, which I'm not sure it was. After a few months apart and all the twists and turns, our time together as a couple seems like nothing more than a dream.

"I'm here." Justin rises to stand. "Just know that."

"I do." I don't get up to walk him to the door, but I hear the finality of the thud as it closes behind him.

When I manage to stand, my father is in the back bedroom putting the last details on the crib he built.

"It's beautiful." I cradle my belly. "I love it."

He beams, and we stare at the furnished nursery as the sunlight streams in through the window, a sweet gesture that is simple but would have seemed surreal a few months ago.

All of a sudden, it happens.

I feel liquid between my legs.

"It's time," I say.

"For dinner?" He shrugs. "Okay, I can make us something to eat. What would you like?"

"No, I mean, it's *time*." I point to my abdomen. "The baby."

He starts to freak out, running around the apartment like a madman, grabbing items and putting them back, as I calmly grab my overnight bag, which is already packed.

"Are you ready?" I whisper to him as he pats his pockets in confusion, then swivels around to grab his car keys off the counter.

"No." A bead of sweat appears on his brow. "But the baby is, and that's all that matters."

The next couple hours are like a fog—the ride to the hospital, the epidural, and, finally, the worst part, labor. And then, on her terms, stubborn like her mom and her grandmother, she appears.

All pink skin and a tuft of blonde hair.

When they bring my father back into the room, I start to sob as he leans over the bed, wiping away my tears. "Lovebug, I caught a peek, and she's beautiful." He whispers, "You had the most perfect little girl: six pounds, eight ounces."

In this moment, I feel deep sorrow, an intense sadness as my mind drifts to Charlotte. In place of happiness, I have a hollow spot where I feel compassion for her. She lived the last ten years believing in the innocence of a man who didn't deserve it and being angry at my father. Her chances of having children of her own were ruined, and she could never come to terms with that. Or with Lauren. Both in love with the same man.

Such a waste of life.

And time.

And for what, in the name of love, or lust, or jealousy?

My father squeezes my small hand in his large one, as if he knows what I'm thinking about. "Everything is going to be fine."

A nurse returns to the room, holding a small bundle in her arms. She places her in my arms, stepping back with a beaming smile.

I look down and my heart melts. Nothing else in the world matters in this moment.

Just her.

She's perfect, and her tiny fingers and toes seem miniature in my arms.

I count all ten of both, just to check.

My father stands next to me, his breath on my shoulder, as I hand over the small bundle of joy so he can hold his granddaughter. Her eyes are the perfect shade of blue, matching my father's and mine.

Tears flow freely down my cheeks, but this time, they aren't born out of anger or hurt. This time, they symbolize redemption and forgiveness.

As I watch my father gently touch her cheek, her name emerges.

Katrina, after my mother. And Dove, to symbolize peace.

Katrina Dove Laughlin.

It has a nice ring to it.

ABOUT THE AUTHOR

Photo © 2018 Diana May

Marin Montgomery grew up in the Midwest but traded cornfields for the desert, and she now calls Arizona home. Originally slated to go to fashion school on the West Coast, Montgomery has always been passionate about writing short stories and poems. After finishing her MBA, she decided to write her first novel at the encouragement of her childhood best friend. When she's not thinking up her next psychological twist, she can be found playing a mean game of Scrabble, binge-watching a variety of television shows, and hanging with her goldendoodle, Dashiell.